Praise for *Glow* by Jessica Maria Tuccelli

An Okra Pick of the SIBA Booksellers

"Fans of *The Help*, this one's for you: A tale of ghosts, slavery, racism, and redemption wrapped up in an epic testament to the power of maternal love."
—*Ladies' Home Journal*

"With *Glow*, Jessica Maria Tuccelli has brought our Southern past to visceral and gorgeous life. Prepare to be drenched in the fierce humanity of her characters, bewitched by the powerful music of their voices, and seared by the beauty and tragedy of their stories." —Hillary Jordan, author of *When She Woke* and *Mudbound*

"*Glow* is a beautifully wrought debut novel about magic, nature, history, and the undying bonds of mother love. Jessica Maria Tuccelli is a remarkable new writer to watch." —Amy Greene, author of *Bloodroot*

"An intricate and fascinating story spanning several generations. Every page seems to introduce a new twist to draw the reader in and keep the pages turning."
—Kathy Habel, *The Free Lance-Star* (Fredericksburg)

"A wonderful debut novel . . . by turns engrossing and appalling, fascinating and horrifying." —Karen Virag, *Edmonton Journal*

"Full of historical detail and tinged with mysticism . . . Tuccelli's novel brims with the love and fierce loyalty that bind [its] disparate generations together."
—Deborah Donovan, *Booklist*

"In Tuccelli's sweeping debut, mothers and daughters are fiercely tethered over six generations and beyond death. . . . [The] elaborately woven plot serves the story well, peppering the novel with moments of lingering beauty and shocking violence."
—*Publishers Weekly*

"Linguistically complex, vivid, and inventive. I can't think of another book even remotely like it, with the possible exception of Eudora Welty's *The Robber Bridegroom*. Jessica Maria Tuccelli takes enormous risks in her book, which pay off in subtle and interesting rewards. We'll be hearing a lot more about this writer."
—Mark Childress, author of *Georgia Bottoms* and *Crazy in Alabama*

"The collage of voices that comprise Jessica Maria Tuccelli's lovely *Glow* speak to us less of our national differences than of the great interweaving that is a constant in the American experience. Written with perfect pitch and impressive confidence, *Glow* is a debut novel of great craft, uncommonly sure storytelling, and elegant narrative vision." —Dave King, author of *The Ha-Ha*

"Ms. Tuccelli has rendered a novel of such precise honesty that it casts its own bright incandescence upon its readers. The language is varied and musical throughout, and the characters as recognizable as one's family. I will care about these people for years to come." —Mark Spragg, author of *An Unfinished Life* and *Bone Fire*

"As a nation we are haunted by certain histories, our past forever weighed down. Many manage to live without being much troubled by a nation's sorry mistakes, but here is a novel about individuals profoundly, perilously affected by antebellum America, and how those lives reach forward, abide, as 'haints,' as miracles." —Michelle Latiolais, author of *Widow* and *A Proper Knowledge*

"In this powerful novel, Tuccelli masterfully handles the revolving first person, rendering each character distinct, individual, and, always, believable. Race and history are never easy to write about, but she does it beautifully, making us care about these people and their own personal stories. This is a debut novel, but it reads like the work of a seasoned writer. I was enormously impressed. *Glow* belongs on the A list." —Steve Yarbrough, author of *The End of California* and *Safe from the Neighbors*

"Peopled by a chorus of voices as varied as they are remarkably rendered, *Glow* is unflinching in its portrait of slavery, violence, and prejudice. . . . A genuine page-turner that is also lyrically fearless, structurally challenging, and beautifully composed." —Scott Cheshire, *Tottenville Review*

"The book flows along with toughness and tenderness, people in love with the land and willing to suffer and sacrifice personal desires to survive. . . . The overlying tapestry is a harsh, beautiful, and realistic portrayal of a significant portion of American history. Remarkable!" —Viviane Crystal, *Historical Novels Review* (UK)

"What shines through so many of the family stories over the many generations is the sense of compassion, hope, love, and the ties that bind the families together. . . . Recommend this one to teens who enjoy Southern historical fiction, family sagas, and spunky heroines." — Jane Ritter, *School Library Journal*

"A beautiful debut novel that far exceeded my already high expectations. Lyrical, enlightening, and wonderfully good for the soul." —Emily Gatlin, Reed's Gumtree Bookstore, Tupelo, Mississippi

"Tuccelli beautifully brings to life the pioneering people of the North Georgia mountains. Full of folklore, forbidden loves, and the strength of the human spirit." —Emily Gibbs, Murder on the Beach, Delray Beach, Florida

PENGUIN BOOKS

GLOW

Jessica Maria Tuccelli lives in New York City. *Glow* is her first novel.

GLOW

Jessica Maria Tuccelli

PENGUIN BOOKS

PENGUIN BOOKS
Published by the Penguin Group
Penguin Group (USA) Inc., 375 Hudson Street, New York, New York 10014, U.S.A. • Penguin Group
(Canada), 90 Eglinton Avenue East, Suite 700, Toronto, Ontario, Canada M4P 2Y3 (a division of Pear-
son Penguin Canada Inc.) • Penguin Books Ltd, 80 Strand, London WC2R 0RL, England • Penguin
Ireland, 25 St. Stephen's Green, Dublin 2, Ireland (a division of Penguin Books Ltd) • Penguin Group
(Australia), 707 Collins Street, Melbourne, Victoria 3008, Australia (a division of Pearson Australia
Group Pty Ltd) • Penguin Books India Pvt Ltd, 11 Community Centre, Panchsheel Park, New Delhi—
110 017, India • Penguin Group (NZ), 67 Apollo Drive, Rosedale, Auckland 0632, New Zealand (a
division of Pearson New Zealand Ltd) • Penguin Books (South Africa), Rosebank Office Park, 181 Jan
Smuts Avenue, Parktown North 2193, South Africa • Penguin China, B7 Jiaming Center, 27 East Third
Ring Road North, Chaoyang District, Beijing 100020, China

Penguin Books Ltd, Registered Offices: 80 Strand, London WC2R 0RL, England

First published in the United States of America by Viking Penguin,
a member of Penguin Group (USA) Inc. 2012
Published in Penguin Books 2013

10 9 8 7 6 5 4 3 2

Publisher's Note
This is a work of fiction. Names, characters, places, and incidents either are the product of the author's
imagination or are used fictitiously, and any resemblance to actual persons, living or dead, business
establishments, events, or locales is entirely coincidental.

THE LIBRARY OF CONGRESS HAS CATALOGED THE HARDCOVER EDITION AS FOLLOWS:
Tuccelli, Jessica Maria.
Glow : a novel / Jessica Maria Tuccelli.
p.   cm.
ISBN 978-0-670-02331-8 (hc.)
ISBN 978-0-14-312292-0 (pbk.)
1. Mothers and daughters—Fiction.   2. Mountain life—Georgia—Fiction.   I. Title.
PS3620.U27G58 2012
813'.6—dc23
2011037553

Printed in the United States of America
Set in Fournier MT Std
Designed by Daniel Lagin

For Joel

GLOW

Family Tree of
SOLOMON B. BOUNDS *Pioneer*

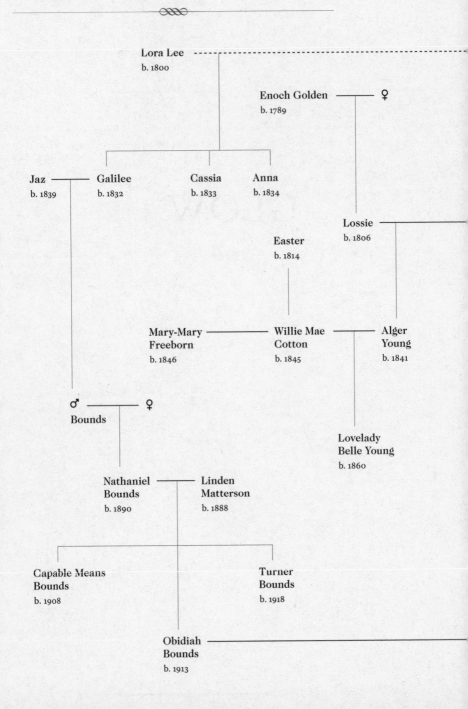

Lora Lee
b. 1800

Enoch Golden
b. 1789

♀

Jaz
b. 1839

Galilee
b. 1832

Cassia
b. 1833

Anna
b. 1834

Lossie
b. 1806

Easter
b. 1814

**Mary-Mary
Freeborn**
b. 1846

**Willie Mae
Cotton**
b. 1845

**Alger
Young**
b. 1841

♂ — ♀
Bounds

**Lovelady
Belle Young**
b. 1860

**Nathaniel
Bounds**
b. 1890

**Linden
Matterson**
b. 1888

**Capable Means
Bounds**
b. 1908

**Turner
Bounds**
b. 1918

**Obidiah
Bounds**
b. 1913

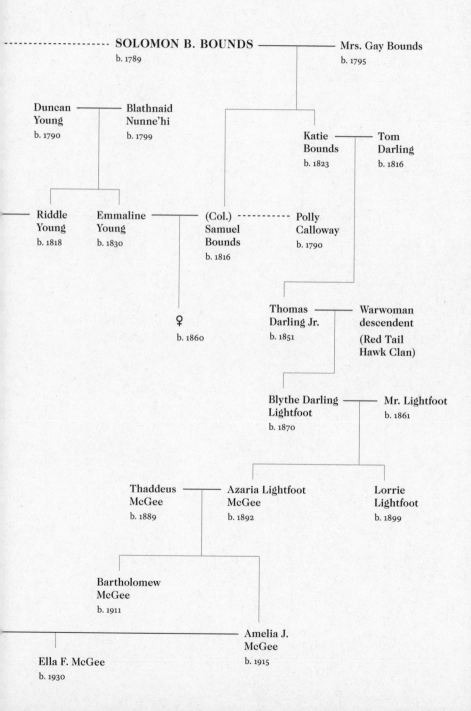

HOPEWELL COUNTY

County Seat: Persimmon

Area: 327.1 square miles

Incorporated communities: Persimmon, The Fertile Valley, War-woman Hollow.

History: Once inhabited by the *Muscogee Confederacy*, later by the *Cherokee*, and first settled by *Ulster Scots* circa 1786. Officially formed in 1819 when the *men of the Cherokee Nation* signed the *Treaty of Arundale*, ceding their lands in the *Anighilahi mountain range* of northeastern Georgia. Among the earliest settlers: the *McGee, Matterson, Moore, Blood, Fairstone,* and *Crisp* families.

Reputed to be one of four Georgia counties failing to ordain secession from the United States prior to the Civil War (see: the Recent Unpleasantness), though scant evidence exists to substantiate the claim. Nevertheless, the county fielded two regiments for the Confederate cause.

Its first turnpike, known then as the Public Road and now as Unicoi Route 101, was a conduit of slave transport from neighboring states, at times illegally, as the acts and resolutions of the Georgia legislature (see: Property Laws—Slaves) governing the slave trade were in constant flux.

Development in the area continues to be hampered by its rugged topography, rendering the land relatively untouched by industry since its inception.

Points of Interest: The *Cuchulannahannachee River* flows through the foothills of this rather exceptional mountain range and is home to over one hundred fish species. The county's most scenic landmarks include *Blood Bald*, Hopewell's highest peak (4,706 feet), War-woman Mountain, and the Fertile Valley westward. The *Takatoka Forest*, dominated by oak, hickory, buckeye, chinquapin, sassafras, and pine, as well as flowering varieties of magnolia, spreads across most of this lush region and is home to an abundance of native orchids and wildlife. Thickly forested ridges, hidden coves, thundering waterfalls, and gentle runoffs mark the terrain. Hopewell, Georgia's rainiest county, has an average rainfall of seventy-two inches.

People: Not to be mistaken for Southerners, and if so, will politely inform the visitor of his error. Influenced by the richness of their remote terrain, as well as the confluence of cultures preceding them, they are Anighilahian, self-sufficient, inventive, proud, and rightly so.

No matter what trouble he stirs up, what law he breaks, Obidiah Bounds will always be her cool sip of hyssop nectar on a sunny day. Mia knew Obidiah was hers the first time she laid eyes on him. She had to be about three, which would have made him five. You could call it puppy love, a crush, good old infatuation, but the feeling has never died. He didn't start out dark and broody, prone to gloominess on the clearest of blue-sky days. He was shy as a youth, that's true, but he was not angry—not at that age. That's the thing about knowing someone your entire life. You have a common history; it binds, provides a depth that new friendships, new loves, can never create. It lets two folks be in the room together without having to explain their silences. Or their passions.

Barely a week ago, the police hauled him off. His draft number called, he boldly, purposely, refused to enlist. For what job? Mess man? Slop man? Cook? He could shoot a pea off a squirrel's head. He had a law degree. He wasn't going to fight for freedom in another country when he didn't have it at home.

It's not that simple, she had said.

No, it's not, he'd agreed.

And now she was alone with their child.

Nothing was as she had hoped or planned.

It was 1941. October 28. Three days before the largest picket Washington, D.C., would ever see.

The sound of shattering glass shocked them from their sleep. Ella's back pressed into her chest, and Brando sat up and barked.

"Stay here," Mia whispered to the child. She crept down the hallway to the front room, where chilly air was roughing its way through a jagged hole in the window.

"I told you to stay in the bedroom."

"But—"

"No buts. I don't want you to cut your feet."

She heard the shuffle of Ella's compromise. The child didn't go back, but she didn't walk out any farther than the hallway.

Mia bit down on her bottom lip, the pain steadying her as she untied the note attached to the rock. She shivered as she read it, but not from the cold. It was typed on her very own Remie Scout, the telltale sign the *k* that always stuck, leaving not only the embossed sans serif but also a faint *k* ghost of itself.

The next one won't be a rock.

As she unrolled the paper further, the hair on her arms shot up. Not only had someone sat in her chair, at her desk, in her house—that someone had typed up a list of names and places, an onslaught of personal details, an itinerary of sorts. *Her* itinerary. From the NAACP office to the name of the grocery where she food shopped and, worse, the address of Ella's elementary school, the time she dropped her off and picked her up, how her daughter preferred a waffle cone to a cup with her butterscotch praline.

You can't hide.

Frantic, alone, she acted instinctively. Get Ella out, keep her safe.

She opened the icebox and packed a paper sack, tossing in whatever she could wrap quickly. They dressed and ran to the bus depot. She would bring Ella back home. Buddy was right, she told herself—Ella was better off inside that homespun chrysalis.

"Only one seat left," said the dispatcher.

"Please check again."

"Lady."

"She can sit on my lap," she said.

"She's too big for that. Do you want the ticket or not?"

"When's the next one out?"

"Tomorrow morning."

Her heart went flying.

"I'll take it."

It was a matter of seconds—from the moment the driver pulled the door shut until the bus yawned out of the depot, with Ella watching her out the window the whole time—before Mia's heart broke all over again and she started second-guessing herself.

She had been fifteen when she gave birth, eighteen when she left Hopewell, and back then she hadn't figured she could protect anyone from anything, much less her baby daughter. Throughout those three years, she had felt her angst fade away only when the human tumult of day died into the wildlife quiet of night, Ella asleep in the cradle next to her bed, Momma and Poppa snoring below on the second floor. Protection. What mind could she have had of it? That had been Momma's domain; Momma was the fiercest momma bird she had ever known.

Ella still thought of Mia as a sister, Obidiah as a friend, but Mia knew the child knew the truth.

After the bus rounded the corner, she sat on a wobbly plastic chair across from the dispatcher's booth. From within his cage of metal and glass he cast her a look of disdain, his lips pressed in a line of uninhibited disgust. She looked away, refusing his judgment. Moments later, she heard the dull tock of his heels as he locked up. Soon, he too was lost to the night.

She pulled the note from her pocketbook and read it again. She knew who it had to be. No signature required. For the past month she had canvassed every day, even rousing the support of a few merchants along the U Street corridor, where most regard her as an outsider, not Negro, vaguely white, what are you? Some kind of pinto, powwow, featherhead, Injun?

She couldn't let it go, the note, the yellow-dog anonymity of its threat, the invasion of her house, and she headed back, uncertain of what, or whom, she would find there. Leery of the men she passed along the sidewalk, her hands bunched into the pockets of Obidiah's woolen overcoat, and she felt the cold bite of the change he'd left behind. She pressed her fingers into those coins, warming them as if touching his chest, the inside of his arm, the back of his neck. His scent permeated the collar, and the coat's bulk safely hid the curves of her body. Any one of those men with their faces hidden in the shadows—and they were all men at that hour—might be the owner of Top Pantry, her neighborhood's only supermarket.

She spent all night in the front room bundled in the overcoat, using the cold to keep her awake, her eyes married to the scene outside the hole in the pane, a saturation of desolate: the moon-drenched tiles of the Victorian row houses, the blurred halo of the streetlamp, the slow roll of tires along the wet asphalt, an ambulance siren. Let them come, she thought. Let the owner, the manager, the bag boys, the stockroom clerks, let them all come for me. She silently put them on notice: With her only treasure in the world on her way back home, she didn't feel vulnerable anymore.

She didn't notify the so-called authorities. She knew what they would say. That she had brought it on herself. That rabble-rousers like her got what they deserved. That she was lucky someone hadn't already bombed her house.

With the first spark of daylight she began making calls, informing her colleagues of the threat and working out the final details of the picket. She rang Buddy, let him know to pick Ella up in town, and then dialed Mr. Wilkins. Ella would transfer to the local in front of his house later that day, and he would keep her company. Mr. Wilkins didn't answer, but she wasn't too worried. Not yet.

When the phone rang that evening, she rushed to answer it. She knew it would be Buddy. She had told him to call her as soon as Ella arrived.

"I swan, Mia, if you weren't my own sister I'd wring your neck." His voice was far away, tinny, the line crackling in sync with a storm brooding on his end. "Ella ain't here. The local broke down. I'm going out to Wilkins's."

Oh God.

The scent of lingering paint caught her off guard as she hung up, and her eyes smarted with the recollection of the previous night, just hours before the breaking glass had awoken them. Ella's homework finished, the dishes washed; the child was helping her with posters for the picket, stenciling each letter with a frown of diligence, the pencil tip held tightly in her hand: *Don't buy where you can't work.*

What does it mean, Ella had asked, sprawled across the carpet in the front room with an arm draped over Brando's back, each keeping the other warm.

It means we don't shop at Top Pantry because . . . Mia's voice had drifted off as she set two stoneware bowls of water on the dining table next to the tempura pigments and the paintbrushes. In the water's surface her face jiggled to a standstill, a little thinner than usual, a little sadder around the eyes. White folks opened their big white store in our brown neighborhood and won't hire any brown people to work there? Did the child need to have a name for it yet?

. . . because the folks who own it won't let anyone who doesn't look like them work there, she'd said finally.

Ella pondered this for a while. What do they look like?

Mia had tried again, treading gingerly, not wanting to spoil the beauty of her daughter, not wanting to seed ugliness in her head.

They won't let folks with brown faces work there. Only pink faces like them. White folks, she conceded.

Not even you?

Especially not me.

Why not?

Because some folks don't know any better; they weren't taught to do the right thing.

Therefore all things whatsoever ye would that men should do to you, do ye even so to them: for this is the law and the prophets. Matthew. Chapter seven verse twelve, Ella said with beaming confidence.

She had nearly choked on her cigarette. The message was right, it resonated with her more than the child could understand, but it sure as heck unnerved her that Ella could quote Bible; but then, that was one of the blessings of being reared in Hopewell County—having the guidance of the good Lord Jesus and His disciples, even if you were better off making decisions for yourself.

Her head still humming with the memory, she stepped into the water closet, ran the tap, splashed her face. Pushing a strand of hair behind her ear, she thought to redo her braid but her hands were trembling too much. Ella would be on Mr. Wilkins's porch, Buddy would bring her home, make her some hot cocoa, and everything would be fine. Her breathing slowed. And then she started. Someone was padding down the hallway to the front of the house.

She bolted out, rage-filled and derelict, with, of all things, a plunger in her hand—and then she froze. In the reflection above the cardboard patch in the window stood someone she knew well. Not the owner of Top Pantry but a young girl with blue ribbons in her hair. An old friend from her childhood. Lovelady. Mia blinked again and squinted into the dark but saw no one. She held her breath, but all she heard was the sound of her own hurtling heartbeat.

A play of light?

Exhaustion teasing her mind?

As she resumed her vigil in the front room, willing the telephone to ring, her ear hungry for her child's voice, she continued to feel Lovelady's presence. Not the physical sensations she had once felt, the frenzy of bubbles in her toes or the dodgy run of chills down her back, but something more visceral and foreboding. It left her unnerved. They had not parted on good terms, to say the least. Yet she would admit it to no one but herself, Lovelady had been with her all these years; she was certain of it. Obviously not in the flesh, not even in the spirit, but in the way your hand feels after the one you love has let it drop. She sometimes reflected on or imagined what had become of her friend, but she did not linger on the fantasies. She hoped Lovelady had found peace. And though she would not credit Lovelady for the life she now led—the demons she chose to fight were of her own selection—she most certainly believed her friend watched over her, and she was grateful, despite the summer of 1924, the summer they had met, the summer that had tossed her life on its head, a summer she thought back on rarely if she could help it. But it was there. She could testify: It is possible to not think about something and be acutely conscious of it at the same time. The memories were not faint impressions. They were quite alive.

Another glance at the telephone and then one at her wrist, where the band of Ella's watch fit her on the furthest notch, the tightness a comfort. There was just enough time to get to the depot and catch the next bus.

She decided quickly but without the panic this time.

Obidiah would take care of himself. She could count on him for that. And the picket would go on without her.

But she must hold her daughter again.

From INSTRUCTIONS TO ENUMERATORS
U.S. CENSUS, 1940 QUESTIONNAIRE

Personal Description

453. *Column 10. Color or Race.*—Write "W" for white; "Neg" for Negro; "In" for Indian; "Chi" for Chinese; "Jp" for Japanese; "Fil" for Filipino; "Hin" for Hindu; and "Kor" for Korean. For a person of any other race, write the race in full.

454. *Mexicans.*—Mexicans are to be regarded as white unless definitely of Indian or other nonwhite race.

455. *Negroes.*—A person of mixed white and Negro blood should be returned as Negro, no matter how small the percentage of Negro blood. Both black and mulatto persons are to be returned as Negroes, without distinction. A person of mixed Indian and Negro blood should be returned as a Negro, unless the Indian blood very definitely predominates and he is universally accepted in the community as an Indian.

456. *Indians.*—A person of mixed white and Indian blood should be returned as an Indian, if enrolled on an Indian Agency or Reservation roll; or if not so enrolled, if the proportion of Indian blood is one-fourth or more, or if the person is regarded as an Indian in the community where he lives. (See par. 455 for mixed Indian and Negro.)

457. *Mixed Races.*—Any mixture of white and nonwhite should be reported according to the nonwhite parent. Mixtures of nonwhite races should be reported according to the race of the father, except that Negro-Indian should be reported as Negro.

E. F. McGEE

My God, my God, why hast thou
    forsaken me?
Why art thou so far from helping me,
    and from the words of my roaring?

—Psalm 22:1

The bus left us here. Me and Brando. My dog. I showed the bus driver my ticket and he said, Okay, missy, but you got to make the transfer to the local at Dry Creek on route one-oh-one near Ol' Wilkins's farmhouse. We been in that bus a long time. Not sure how long though 'cause I left my watch on the nightstand. The sun, she wasn't awake yet when my sister Mia put us in the bus in her rush rush rush, and now the sky is real pretty like a painting that can't stand still—it keeps changing. Red and smoky with hot orange yellow lava liquid outlines, kind of like God drew a picture of a sunset and an invisible hand is coloring in. Makes me sleepy watching it. The driver said the local would pick us up at half past four. Must be at least five o'clock by now.

Brando's hungry. So am I. We already ate the cornflakes and the slice of hallelujah pie. The pie was crumbly and dry, not like Momma's at all, but Momma never had to skimp on milk and Mia doesn't have a cow. She lives in D.C. and must take a streetcar to a small shop far away even though there is a large shop right around the corner. Sometimes the small shop runs out of milk. A cow is much better.

I slip my hand into the paper sack Mia packed and pull out my favorite. A hard-boiled egg. Brando's eyes follow my fingers as I crack the shell.

I cannot resist.

I give him the yolk and all the bright white, the entire thing.

My behind is cold. This here bench is made of something shiny and cold. My hands are cold too. No gloves. Mia makes me wear my gloves clipped to my coat, you know, like little kids wear? But I am eleven now, so when Mia disappeared from the bus window I took them clips off my gloves. Now the clips are in my pockets and my gloves are on the bus.

I flip the earflaps of my squirrel hat down and tuck my fingers into my coat cuffs. I think of buttered toast and hot chocolate and other such warm thoughts. I tap my feet as if I am hoofing a musical number on the silver screen. I am sitting way up in the balcony where a person can sit if they are lucky like me. Last week Mia said there is no time for motion pictures, no time for fantasy. We have a war going on overseas! We have a war going on at home! Mia is twentysomething and my brother Buddy is twentysomething plus four.

When I nestle my chin into my muffler, my spectacles slide down my nose and turn foggy from my breath. My spectacles are spectacular, says Buddy. The air smells like autumn but feels more like winter snapping at my face. *Winter* is a wonderful word. *W* is my favorite letter. When I give Brando a kiss, it is the shape my lips take. Wish my name was Wanda. Or Wilma. Or W.E.B. But no. It is Ella. Ella Frances McGee.

"Maybe the local ain't coming, huh, boy? Maybe it missed us?"

Brando wags his tail. Tilts his head as if he is thinking.

Folks say he is as big as a horse, but this is not true at all. He does have big paws. And knobby knuckles. And thick nails that click across the floor. And when we sleep he circles one, two, three, and plops his big brown body down next to me in a tight ball, and when I awake he is sprawled across the bed and I am hanging to the floor. Nothing like a horse at all.

We watch Mr. Moon rising high in an eerie sky and the trees turning black and spindly. Ol' Wilkins's farmhouse across the way looks like a dead man staring. Funny how some places get unfriendly in the dark.

If I squint real tight, I can see the flick-flicker of my town in the valley below. Buddy is waiting for me, Mia said. If I reach my hand out, I can cover up the whole town. This means it is far away.

I wish Mia hadn't made me hurry. Go go go, lock this, close that, don't step on the glass, don't look back. Run—

I hug Brando tight and he licks my face.

Buddy gets up early 'cause he has a farm and grows corn and cows. He will be hot under the collar he had to wait up for us. In Hopewell you can hear crickets chirping at night, not cranky ol' streetcars that clank and clatter, and Buddy's wife Cal will fluff my pillow just how I like it, and folks will say, How you all? when they greet us on the street and Jack-a-dandy it sure do feel like rain, if they have a crick in their neck, and if someone passes away they will say, Right sorry for your loss, which is what folks said to me after God called Momma and she went to Him on May twenty-seven, nineteen forty-one, almost five whole months ago.

When they lowered Momma down, a terrible sound came out of my mouth. I could not make it stop. Then folks brought ham with red-eye gravy and trays of biscuits. I would not eat. No! No! No! Under the stairs I went. I would not come out or say hello to the guests squished into Momma's love seat with plates on their knees, shaking their heads, pointing their forks at me.

I have a secret. I saw when Momma died.

It was a Tuesday night long after my bedtime. A storm was churning up the sky. When the wind whipped it made our floorboards moan like a man in pain. I pulled the covers over my head and snuggled closer to Brando. I could hear the radio crack-crackling in the living room and then Momma clicking FDR shut and shambling into the kitchen. After Poppa died Momma spent late nights playing solitaire and talking to him. Momma would tell him all he was missing. Only this time she sounded different. She wasn't speaking her usual mur-murmuring. I heard her laughing and talking quickly as if we had real live company. And then she went quiet again.

I snuck downstairs and pushed in the door a sliver. There was Momma at the table. Her face in the window over the sink. She was crying and smiling at the same time. Then I saw all this light fill the room. Lots and lots of bright speckles. So many speckles that I saw more speckle than the room itself, like cloudy trails of fireworks after the color fades.

I was not afraid. I felt funny fizzles of joy.

And then the lights all floated together and wrapped around Momma and I could not stop watching, and even though I wanted to call to her, no sound came out of my mouth. Brando was barking but it was muffled and far away. My ears filled with the roar of water. Then the light, it pulsed as if it was breathing. My knees buckled and I slumped to the floor.

I woke to Brando's soggy breath, his wet nose snuffling my face. I was lying half inside half outside the kitchen door. I heard a bird singing. It was morning. I looked up. Momma was slumped over the table. I stood up. Momma was passed away.

I talk to Momma sometimes. Like now.

I say, "Momma, what should I do?"

I wait, listening to the silence in my head. Then I hear her. "Go up to Mr. Wilkins's front door, Ella," her voice says, "and see if he is home. Ask him if you may use his telephone to ring Buddy. Everyone must be sick with worry about you by now."

"But he is a hunched old goat," I say. "And he smells like glue."

"Now, sweetie, you know better than to be unkind."

"I know, Momma, I know," I say.

We cross the road. I do not want to go, but there is nothing around here but corn, not another homeplace in sight.

I eyeball the front porch. It sags. The banister is broken. There is no welcome mat. We amble up anyway. I knock real soft. Then bold and loud. And then I jiggle the door handle. No luck. The door is locked. And then I cup my hands over my eyes and push my nose against the window. The curtains are too thick to see a thing. So we trot around back and I rap on the door. There is a round hole in the door where the knob should be.

"Anybody home?" I say, and bang bang bang.

That old man is either sleeping like the dead or has got up and moved away.

I look for Buddy in his pickup. Or Cal riding her motorbike with the red sidecar. I watch my breath make clouds. And then I decide. We must walk to the valley below.

Above, the sky is filled with bright pinpricks where the heavens show through. I like to think they are God's windows and the twinkling is angels covered in glossy feathers walking by and looking in. The dying cornstalks whisper as we pass. They wave their arms in the wind as if they are inviting us in, but I do not know what they say or if they are friend or foe, so I do not answer them.

My suitcase sure weighs something heavy. I have all my most important books. *Alice's Adventures in Wonderland* was Momma's when she was a girl. It still smells of lavender. I also have the Good Book. It says, "This Holy Bible is present to Thaddeus McGee" inside the front flap. I took it from Poppa's casket even though it was not mine to take, Poppa on a cooling board, Poppa in a pine box, and I opened it up and gave him a kiss, and he looked just like he did in life only more tucked in, and I missed him so I took his Bible from his hands, they were crisscrossed neat. Now that Bible is mine.

If I could fold the road up like an accordion we would leap from peak to peak and be with Buddy and Cal toasting marshmallows by the fireplace and laughing it up by now.

I can finally read the big white letters painted on the side of a barn in the valley below. It says HOPEWELL COUNTY, all lit up by beams, same as when you hold a candle under your chin at Halloween. I lived there all my life until Momma died. Then I went to live with Mia in D.C.

Home is much better.

A car whooshes by. Up and over the hill, it is gone. And then. It rises and creeps back down.

It is not Buddy in his pickup or Cal on her motorbike with the red sidecar.

It is bruised and beaten up. I do not like it.

It waits.

And now it rolls alongside. It grinds up the gravel as it prowls. Brando bristles. His tail is low. His ears are back. I double his leash around my wrist and stare straight ahead as we walkwalkwalk.

The window cranks down. There are two strangers inside.

"Need a ride?" says the man on my side. His voice sloshes slow and deep like a record at the wrong speed. I look at him right in the eye. He pushes back his hunting cap and rubs his hand over his head and scratches at bald patches and sucks the wet from his teeth. A spray of juice lands at my feet. "Cat got your tongue, girlie?" he says. His lips are smiling but his eyes are not.

The man at the steering wheel leans over. His neck is long. His head is floppy. His eyes are two burned holes in a face of whitewhitewhite. He smirks. "Lose your tribe?" he asks.

Clouds rustle across the moon and the stars twinkle brighter. I walk faster wishing we were homehomehomehomehomehomehomehomehomehome—

"Don't run away. We ain't gonna hurt you," the man with the burned eyes says.

I say, "No, thank you."

They laugh. The man with the smile opens his door.

Brando's tail shoots up and his ears stand tall. He growls. I shout, "Come on, boy!" and we run down the road. "This way, this way, Brando," and we head for the cornfields. And then my head cracks back. I gag. I grab my neck. The one with the smile is yanking my muffler. He reels me in. I drop my suitcase. I kick. I claw. He wraps his arm around my chest. Rot and slop leak onto my cheek.

The driver gets out of the car. He rattles the trunk handle.

And Brando barks. It echoes in the empty all around. He jumps on the smiling man, and my arm jerks up and down. The leash holds us together. And then he sinks his teeth into the smiling man, into his forearm. The man hollers and cusses. He lets me go, and I trip and fall. My chin smacks the ground and my heart flaps out of my mouth, and I scream as the man bats and belts my dog, but Brando will not stop. His lips flutter back and he snarls. I try to stand, but then I hear a loud pop like Buddy's rifle makes. Brando bolts. The leash wrenches my arm and I feel a sharp pain. My body is heavy. I slump back down. I cannot hear a sound as I drown.

I look down and see myself bent like a rag doll staring up. Next to me, Brando is pacing. He howls like a hundred dogs. Another pop. Brando totters. We are crumpled on the side of the road.

I look up and see a curling cloud, a misty twin, staring down. I blink and she fades away.

The two men are muttering. "Get the goddamn pry bar, Simon," one says. "You get it," says the other. The men kick the car and then they punch each other.

I can shift my head and see Brando on his side. There is light shining out of each of his eyes. This means he is still alive.

His eyes follow my arm. I touch his fur. It is wet. My throat hurts and my belly aches. I whisper, "I'm here, I am right here, boy. Hold on tight. Don't let go."

And I pray to Momma. I say, "Momma, please, please come for us. Please come for us. Please send the speckles now."

But there is no answer.

And now I hear the thunder. I smell the rain. And then, down the road, I see two lights. They begin to grow. The men see them too. They shout at each other. And then they scramble into their car.

"Go," I whisper. "Go."

The engine rumbles. Gravel spews. I roll over. I must protect my dog. My arm lags behind, and I hear a cry. It is my own.

The men speed away.

But we are not alone. The lights are growing closer, bright as shooting stars.

"Here, here," I whisper. I stretch my good arm long.

But the lights swish right by.

Drops of rain start to patter onto the road. I must curl up with Brando to keep us warm. I kiss his long snout.

And then he closes his eyes.

My eyes are heavy too. I try to keep them open. But they are tired. They want to close. So I let them.

AMELIA J. McGEE

W hen I was a child, Momma informed me that there were no such things as ghosts. I was crushed and confused because my best friend and confidant, Lovelady Belle Young, was in fact a ghost. When I begged Lovelady to come home to prove Momma wrong, she flat out refused, saying she wasn't in the business of convincing folks of her existence and that naysayers were just plain old scared of haints and besides, didn't my Momma and Poppa believe in God and Satan, and surely they had never seen them in person.

Much as I hated to admit it, Lovelady had a point.

My brother Buddy, four years my senior and therefore wiser, according to him, suggested I keep my bond with Lovelady to myself lest I remain forever friendless in the corporeal world, or worse, burn in the raging fires of eternal damnation with Beelzebub himself.

And so Lovelady remained my secret.

I discovered her in the Takatoka Forest, which poured down War-woman Mountain into what my family called our backyard. I wasn't supposed to be in those woods. Momma had forbidden it, saying my curiosity was stronger than my common sense. Buddy had warned me about the wild boars. He said they feasted on folk like me: nimble-legged nine-year-olds with smart mouths. He said beware of old women, those shrunken apples who lived in the hills; they could steal your soul with death dust. Even worse was Giasticutus, a giant catawampus who smothered children with his wings before swallowing them whole. But Buddy said a lot of things. He was free to roam as he pleased.

I had no such freedom, but my imagination never abandoned me. I was *Mia the Swashbuckler*. Armed with neither side sword nor buckler, I surged across our land, valiantly defending insects from death: When a ground mason stung and buried a cricket, I dug up its prey and slipped the anesthetized victim into my pocket for later examination and joyful liberation.

Momma, why do spiders have eight eyes and *we* only got two? Why didn't God give birds eyes on the *front* of their heads? How does a flower get its color? Why is it *called* a flower? I would ask.

And Momma would reply, Because our Lord provided.

But if the weather was fine and she had enough time, she would clap a palm to her forehead and say, Mia, *why* do you ask why so much? and off we would go, up a craggy hill to the home of Old Maid Hailey, a retired librarian from Milledgeville who had forfeited the luxury of a front parlor displaying staid family portraits and meaningless glass dainties for a room bursting with the sacred scent of old leather, beeswax, and balsam. I loved to tick my fingers across her complete set of *Ranger Riddick's Wildlife of the World* and down stacks of *Grier's Almanac* and *National Geographic*, never able to decide which title to pick. Whenever Old Maid Hailey allowed me the privilege of borrowing as many as I could carry in my hemp sack, I was overjoyed as well as honored. She had once been my teacher, her front parlor my school, and I her favorite pupil, which I attributed to my studious and exuberant nature. With Buddy as my only competition, the contest had not been hard, and though I looked up to my brother, it had been satisfying to best Buddy in something.

My hemp sack swelling with the promise of answers, I would jabber with excitement as we descended the hill until Momma decreed my blessed silence. Upon our return to our homeplace, she would loose me once more to rove and chatter within the limits of our backyard.

Despite Momma's fastidious nature, her call for harmony, and her distaste for clutter and mess, she allowed the flora and fauna to multiply and divide unchecked on the land behind our home. It was there, amid the untamed growth, that I read my borrowed tomes aloud to my only company that summer I was nine: the aged oaks, the majestic hickories, the fading chestnuts, and our recently departed Granny Blythe.

Granny Blythe was our maternal grandmother and burying her in the backyard our way, as she had died in Hopewell County, where there were white cemeteries for white folks, colored cemeteries for colored folks, but nowhere to bury an Indian.

According to Granny, long before white folks ever set foot in the Taka-toka Forest, her Cherokee ancestors had used lady's slipper, the most magi-cal of flowers, to help them find their spirit guide, and in that very forest could be my guardian angel, a personalized best friend sent by Nature. Unfortunately, Granny passed away before it occurred to me to inquire how to invoke it, and in the weeks following her death, I would lie beside her in the thick bluegrass under the shade of the old pine tree, scouring *The Young Reader's Encyclopedia from Aardvark to Zythum* for astounding facts of nature, hoping to divine some instruction. A sand-colored fieldstone marked her grave, her name excised with a metal awl in the best scratch Poppa could summon: Here Lies Blythe D. Lightfoot, May 2, 1924.

She'd been gone from us just a month when something caught my eye as I headed toward her grave. Maybe it was the rose-colored sunset filtering through the clouds, but it was the richest pink I had ever seen, and it was growing out of the foot of the pine tree.

A pink-mustachioed lady's slipper.

I honored the flower the best I knew, clearing the ground of offending weeds, whispering for it to grow, grow. I prayed to the Lord as well, though my prayers thus far had gone unanswered.

The next day, a Sunday, the Lord—or Nature—made an exception.

After services, Buddy took off in directions unknown, a recent occupa-tion, while I was left to entertain myself once more within the confines of Momma's wild garden.

I discarded my worship frock for a sensible and loose-hanging blue ensemble with a dropped waist and thankfully plain, and skipped to the bank of a narrow branch behind our home. There I espied, to my delight, a tiger-striped swallowtail butterfly zipping about the rhododendrons. Its enormous wings fanned open and closed as it landed on a blossom and fed on the nectar. When it took off, I charged after it with the passion of a plun-dering pirate, hoisting a sprig of orange milkweed high above my head like a saber. "Aaaargh," I shouted as it flew over the springhouse. I lit after it, leaping over the branch and running up the slope, tramping through patches of butterweed and sliding up the yolk yellow mess. I crawled through the log fence, tripped and recovered, then knuckled my way up as the black and yellow creature soared into the Takatoka. Never before had I defied Momma's restrictions, but with abandon now I scuffled after it, plunging through a thicket of mountain laurel.

The swallowtail escaped my clutches anyway, winking in the sunlight and vanishing above the dogwoods and pines. As blood trickled down from a cut on my knee, I flopped down on a rotting log, spit in my palm, and wiped my leg clean.

Through the cream-cupped fringe of laurel, I could still see the back of our house, the paint-chipped shutters, the sloping porch, the board and batten covered in ivy alive with twittering swallows.

But here I was in the presence of towering trees, well beyond the boundary of our homeplace. Here I was.

I will never forget the bubbly feeling that rose from my toes to my neck. A lone woodpecker, its pointed crest a fiery coronet, tapped its beak against a pine tree, and it reverberated a soulful knocking sound unlike anything I'd ever heard in the sweep of our backyard. I danced a silent jig and rubbed my hands together. Turning toward the rise and shielding my eyes from the sun, I saw a small pile of stones that I now know to have been a cairn marking an old Indian trail up the mountain.

The higher I climbed, the cooler and darker the forest became. It was a restful dark, not a frightening one, created by a canopy of old growth. Giant long-legged daddies with rosy, oblong bodies scurried as I slipped by, and bronze-capped snails left glossy trails up stout trunks of tulip poplar. Moss too climbed up its bark. Stacks of mushrooms billowed out of woody crevices: teacup pink, mottled umber, jelly brown, their shapes shifting from cupcake to saucer flat. Glistening stems of ghost pipe poked out of the layers, life sprouting everywhere from death. It was glorious.

The buckeyes had already begun to turn yellow and red, and when a branch of water blocked my path, I used a fallen limb to steady myself, stepping from slippery stone to stone, the stream churning around my ankles. I continued up the mountain, pushing through a bower of pink to the sight of more water tripping down rock steps. The cascade gurgled like a newborn baby while damselflies hovered above and blue skinks slithered under prism-flecked stones. How could Momma want to keep me from all this?

When I came upon a clearing of ferns, I knew I had found a fine place to stop. On the far side was a pile of mossy boulders shaped like a grand throne and agreeably vacant. Just then, as I leaped over a shallow riffle to the tune of knightly trumpets, I heard a snap of branches. I stood still and listened. I took another step forward. So did something else. I waited and then walked three paces before I heard it again. Could it be a deer? Oh, how delightful that would be! But it was too heavy to be a deer. Giasticutus? An old hag? No! A wild boar! It had to be. Jumping Jehoshaphat! I clutched my buckeye branch and crouched ready for battle, bared my teeth, and with a mean slice to air, growled.

There came a girl's giggle, high and light.

"Who's there?" I demanded.

"Who's there?" her voice rang, as if from all around.

"I asked you first," I said.

"I asked you first," she echoed.

"You most certainly did not! Don't you got no respectability? Creeping up on a person. Stop sassing me and show yourself."

"You show first."

"I'm right here in plain sight."

Her laughter swelled around me, and it was as sweet and colorful as a handful of jellybeans. With each pop of mirth, I craved even more. And then she fell quiet.

Beside my throne, a honeysuckle thicket shook. "What's your name?" I asked the bush politely.

"Follow," the voice said, so close it grazed my ear.

I reeled about, but no one was there.

Not ready to admit defeat, I scaled the pile of boulders and settled into the warmth of its stored sunlight, hoping my aloofness might draw her out. I lay back, cupping my hands behind my head, my ears keyed to her movement. I tussled with patience, a fine Anighilahian custom that I deemed necessary as a woolen sweater on a summer day. Tugging on a strand of honeysuckle, I pinched a blossom between my thumb and forefinger and slid the petal skirt up from its base. Drops of nectar pooled at the flower's base. I touched the tip of my tongue to the bead. "Tastes like honey. Yum. You try." I offered the vine to my unseen friend.

A hand emerged, but quicker than a drop of water on a frypan it withdrew into the thicket.

"Amelia J. McGee!"

Buddy was charging up the trail, flush pink in his cheeks from the effort. We looked only vaguely related, sunshine and tempest, as folks were prone to saying. In short, my brother had inherited our father's Scotch-Irish coloring and caramel brown mop, whereas I had not. With my black hair and eyebrows to match, I clearly had a good dose of Momma's side of the family.

"Who in tarnation are you talkin' to?" he asked from the edge of the clearing.

"Nobody," I said with a shrug of nonchalance. Whoever she was, I wanted her for myself.

"What are you doin' up here? You know you ain't allowed."

"Reckon I got tired of the strictures set upon me by my brethren," I muttered, doing my best to sound both wise and biblical like our Preacher Reverend. I didn't take kindly to Buddy eldering me.

"Listen, Miss Fancy Pants, you're gonna be in a heap of trouble if you don't get home."

"I'm leaving now," I said loudly, hoping my hidden companion might hear me.

Buddy looked at me as if I'd lost my sense. "I ain't deaf," he said.

Along with the perils of wild boars and catawampuses, Buddy had long ago instilled within me another frightening notion: He bade me never look over my shoulder to the place I had just left. If I did, my toes would turn to salt. He called it Lot's Rot. But as we headed down the trail, the hair on the back of my neck suddenly shot up. I had the distinct sensation we were being watched.

I dared to look back.

There she stood, barefoot in the mist, maybe twelve or thirteen years old, a Negro girl in an old-fashioned white petticoat hemmed below her knees. Her hair hung in long braids, each one anchored by a blue ribbon.

I gaped as she withdrew a broken honeysuckle vine from behind her back. She waved it like a wand and smiled smugly. As she plucked a flower and tongued its nectar, she began walking backward into the blue mist, fading like an aging ambrotype: first her feet, then her legs, until all I saw was her smile. I gasped and slammed into my brother, who had made an untimely stop. Rebounding off his back, I fell onto my hind end. "What'dya go do that for?" I cranked.

"Dunno," he said softly, rubbing the back of his neck. "I got goose-flesh."

As I brushed myself off, I glanced out of the corner of my eye to where the girl had stood. There was nothing to see except the green beam of glow flies.

Dusk had shrouded the woods by the time we reached the foot of the forest, and our home's oil lamps seemed to dim and brighten as we sped by the darkened laurel. The world of night was all about dun and glow. Crickets and tree frogs trilled along with the perky hoots of a great horned owl. I sought its eyes high in the tulip trees and was rewarded by a double reflection of a waning moon. We slid down the butterweed hill and skipped over the branch, landing easily in the twilight cover of our backyard.

Buddy and I groaned. Both our parents were home.

We watched their silhouettes playing against the drawn kitchen shades, Momma pacing with ferocity, her arms flailing through the air, reminding me unpleasantly of a catawampus, while Poppa stood swaybacked, his hands on his hips, rooted to the floor. "Where is she?" my mother exclaimed.

"Bud?" I whispered, wiping a beaded mustache of mist from my upper lip.

He sighed and scrunched his mouth to the left side of his face and sucked on the inside of his cheek, then drove his hands into his pockets and shifted his weight. He appeared deep in thought.

"Bud!"

"Hush now, I'm conspirin'."

I followed his gaze to the corner of the back porch, to his bedroom window on the second floor. Our house was a simple one, built by my father's forebears, a two-room home grown to five. A living room and kitchen composed the first floor, two bedrooms the second, and my room the third, the sleeping loft.

Buddy scratched his chin. "I'm thinking we get you atop the roof yonder, and you climb into my room and skinny on up to yours. We fake you been there the whole time."

He quickly fleshed out a plan: I would scale the ancient oak that grew closest to our house, then inch my way along a limb toward the porch roof, cat-step across the eaves, and slip into Buddy's room. Meanwhile, Buddy would create a diversion. He would run through the chicken coop and set our hens into a dervish.

I was dubious, but he shooed me onward anyway.

With my fingers meshed into the vines hanging from the boughs, I hoisted myself up but slid back down just as fast, my hip pocket ripping audibly. I surveyed Buddy for encouragement. "Hold still," he whispered and ran to the trunk, bending down on one knee. "Get on my shoulders," he ordered.

As soon as he telescoped to full height, I stood. Locking my fingers together, I slung my body over the lowest tree limb and inchwormed to the roof, just as we'd planned. Below, the hens' squawking signaled Buddy's infiltration of the coop.

The sash was surprisingly light to lift, and so I did, spilling myself onto the hard nature of the heart-pine floor. I nosed the sill and squinted into the night for any sign of my brother, but all I saw was Poppa striding into the woods, his Winchester slung across his back, raised lantern in hand.

I whispered a hoarse "Bud?" out the window.

"I'm right here," he said, poking his head into his bedroom before bounding up the stairs to mine. When I didn't follow him, he came back down. "What's wrong?" he asked.

"But look a' me," I said and sniffled, fighting to catch my breath. "I'm grimier than dirt, and I've done near ruined my dress." Tears spurted and my despair doubled. I was mortified to be blubbering in front of my brother.

"I swan! Now's no time to be crying."

While Buddy ran off to fetch water, I toiled to my third-floor garret alone. It had a pitched ceiling that capped a space just tall enough for my father to stoop at its center and just wide enough for a twin bed, a wardrobe, and a bookcase filled with my cache from Old Maid Hailey's parlor. Double-paned windows hung on opposite walls, allowing sunlight to illuminate my haven all day. Now my only light was the moon.

A few minutes later, Buddy appeared with a sorghum bucket, water sloshing over the rim as he set it down.

"Criminy, Bud, you're being awful nice," I said.

"Just watchin' out for you, don't make no big deal," he said, and handed me a washrag.

"Turn around."

Buddy rolled his eyeballs. "Both our hides in peril, and you want to be a belle about it," he said, turning his back.

I shimmied out of my play dress, torn and stained with flecks of bark, dropped my drawers and my slip, and with a kick stowed all offenders under my bed.

"How'd you know where to find me?" I asked, sponging the dried blood off my shin.

"Twarn't nothin'. I been tracking in the woods."

"Tracking?"

"Yeah."

Before I could point out he hadn't been carrying a rifle or wearing his customary squirrel hat, he opened the wardrobe and handed a frock back to me—the same frock I'd been so quick to abandon that very morning.

"Here, put this on," he said.

"My Sunday best?" I refused to take hold of the ornate yellow horror. It was a short-sleeved silk and organdy number that Momma had copied from a *Modern Priscilla* magazine and spent months saving to buy the fabric for and that I despised, from the strangling neck to the hideous paneled skirt with its belt of fake flowers.

"There ain't nothin' else in here," he said, clattering through the empty hangers.

I huffed as I slipped it over my head, overlooking certain necessities such as unbuttoning the collar and drying off my body, resulting in an unfortunate condition: The garment refused to slide into place, and in my alarm I stuck my head into an armhole and my arm out the neck. I snarled as I struggled to free myself.

"S'matter?" Buddy asked.

"I'm stuck."

"I swan." Buddy tugged at my attire, pulling this way and that. "Someone must have left you at our door one night."

I would have kicked him, except for our mother calling our names from the second-floor landing.

We sucked in a collective breath as she mounted the steps.

"Yes, ma'am." Buddy answered in an even voice.

"Aw, now you done did it," I snapped from inside my frock, maneuvering like a fish caught in a net.

"Amelia and Bartholomew McGee!"

Buttons sprang off, hitting the floor and rolling down the slope before settling with a conspicuous ring in a darkened corner as I finally popped my head out of the neck hole.

Momma pressed her hand to her mouth. Her chest rose and fell quickly, from the climb up the steps, I hoped, but I knew better. She said nothing more, and it was awful. A knot formed in my throat and I ran to her, wrapping my arms around her hips. I pushed my nose into the soft folds of her apron and inhaled her lavender scent.

"I'm sorry," I said.

Momma smoothed my hair and pried me loose. She held my shoulders squarely. "Do you know how worried I've been about you?"

I kept my gaze at Momma's waist and scratched a mosquito bite on the back of my leg with the aid of my big toe.

"Nome," I mumbled.

"I just sent your father to the Mattersons' to ask if he could use their tin lizzie to look for you. Never in your blessed life have you done such a thing."

I hung my head. Mr. Sterling Matterson was the richest man we knew, and he fancied himself a *pomologist*. Limbertwig, Russet, Red June, and Yates grew high on the north-facing slope of Strummers Knob, the Matterson homeplace. He owned not only a tractor *and* a pickup truck but also a much-ballyhooed black-chassised Model T Ford with real electric headlights, brass radiator, horn, artillery wheels, and whitewall tires, which he labored to keep clean, a challenge for any man given that each and every one of our seasons included heavy rain. To this point, he drove his pet motorcar only on special occasions, including but not limited to: the birth of Jesus, the death of Jesus, the resurrection of Jesus, Confederate Memorial Day, and Robert E. Lee's birthday. With only a few vigorous turns of its hand crank, it became a speedy demon, as fast as a quarter horse. Momma didn't like to ask for favors of anyone, especially a Matterson, most especially when that favor involved his sacred automobile, and on that count I had to agree.

She raised my chin with a crooked finger. "You know better than to disappear without informing me of your whereabouts. What were you thinking?"

I was stumped for an answer, but Momma didn't wait. "Where were you?" she demanded.

It sailed out of me as if it were God's honest truth, as if I had been spinning yarns my entire life. I was no liar, and yet I told my parent that I had wandered over to Croaker's Bog, which was a mile away and well past my perimeter of play, where I had encountered an enormous bullfrog of such astonishing proportions and beauty that I could not help but chase it. As I described its olive green snout, handsome bulbous eyes, and wide yellow lips, I watched my mother's face for signs of fib detection and, finding none, continued: I tripped and fell into the bog, where the depth of my wrongdoing became apparent.

Buddy's eyes had grown so wide I thought Momma would immediately suspect the enormity of my invention, but she instead appeared to be weighing its veracity, her head tilting from one side to the other as if she were a balancing scale. She said she was disappointed in me, that it ought never happen again, though she did seem impressed by my dubious resourcefulness, and overall relieved by my return. There was an uncomfortable spinning in my stomach, and I was unable to discern nausea from glee.

She and Buddy dispersed, and I peeled out of my Sunday frock and climbed into my nightgown before joining them in the kitchen to await Poppa's return. Though I could smell the scent of supper warming in the oven—onions melted in raw cream butter, slices of cornbread, fried fatback, sweet and sour beans, baked apples glazed with brown sugar—not a single one of my taste buds responded.

An epoch later, we heard the double bang of the screen door and Poppa's brogans sweeping across the floorboards, pausing, most likely, for him to hang his straw hat on the rack and wipe his feet on the floor mat. He turned from the hall into the kitchen and ducked under the entryway. When he saw me, his stricken look dissolved into relief. He hooked the lantern on a brass bracket and unloaded the rifle, and then sat at the head of the table as Momma retold my tale.

I listened with both fascination and guilt.

My father was my hero. I was convinced he was the strongest man in all of Hopewell County. He had a booming laugh that reverberated in a torso as large as a fifteen-gallon barrel bilge. His legs were stalwart and long, and with shoulders broad enough to carry at least two children on his back, he often did. But his most outstanding feature was his beard. When I was six years old, he had shorn it and emerged from the washbowl to chase me around the living room with his chin in the lead. He had meant to amuse but instead had terrified me, and he had since then remained true to his promise never to shave his beard again. Over my short life span his whiskers had already turned like an autumn leaf from an orange blaze to a mellow russet. Poppa was the kind of man who would never deceive his loved ones.

As he took in Momma's words, he sighed and bowed his head, his thick eyebrows sloping down in a mournful manner, his eyes, which were wide set and expressive, dimming, and the thrill of my fib began to dull. Remorse curled up inside my chest.

When Momma finished, Buddy was dismissed, and I was remanded to the living room to await my parents' decision.

I'd survived the sum of my nine years without receiving a tanning, and I remained optimistic. There were my "contentious" and "pugnacious" tendencies, according to my new schoolteacher, but thus far my parents had been lenient or perhaps my transgressions venial, and my punishments restricted to additional chores, occasional lectures, and remedial deprivations, not afflictions from the strap. Suspended from a lone nail on the root cellar doorjamb, it was a black leather shoulder belt with a brass buckle and batwing called the Tanner, originally used by Jonas McGee, my paternal great-granddaddy, in the War of Northern Aggression.

Restless, I fiddled with the antimacassars draped over the winged chair's arms. I counted the bouquets of cornflowers in each line of the wallpaper. Toward the ceiling, in the corner, the paper had begun to curl. I was almost relieved when I heard my mother's call from the kitchen.

The verdict was set against me. I was too stunned to argue.

I followed Poppa down into the damp cellar, which smelled like an open grave. When he reached the bottom, he paused on the last step. "Sure hate to do this, Maggie Mae," he said softly, invoking my nickname, his alone to call me.

I thought about running away, but there was nowhere to go. That would come much later.

Poppa lit the lantern and dragged a chair over the dirt-packed floor. The old bones of the chair cracked under his weight as he sat. He patted his thigh and I leaned into him. With his arms wrapped around me, he breathed in my hair. We sat like this for some time until the floorboards squeaked overhead, followed by a soft dust shower. Poppa's eyes darted up. "Best get on with it," he said.

As he doubled the belt back, I wrapped my hands around the chair and stared into the shadows. Though I knew they were there, I did not see the bushels of potatoes or crates filled with yellow onions or the heavy drapes covering the shelves of brined pickles and jams. I saw nothing. And when nothing was too much, I closed my eyes and ran after the girl with the blue-ribboned braids. I thought she was mine to follow.

The truth, I now know, is the other way around.

E. F. McGEE

Be not forgetful to entertain strangers: for thereby some have entertained angels unawares.

—Hebrews 13:2

T hen a voice sings over me. A mourning dove's woebegone, all is gone all is gone.

"Willie Mae! She's awaking," chirps the hazy songbird.

"You just sit tight with the child and keep her warm. I be out soon," another calls from afar.

The bird swoops down. I press back. I tremble. Her eyes—they move into mine and then again blink-blink. I see myself in them, scratches and scrapes up and down my face, my nose, my chin, and my cheekbones. My shoulder is wrapped in strips of white. It aches.

I remember.

Get the goddamn pry bar.

You get it.

A thought rises like ash and smoke. "Brando," my voice croaks. It leaps off my lips and tumbles and trips, it searches, snout to ground, sniffing hard-packed dirt and orange clay, pinesap, lightning, and rain rain rain, and climbs into beams and rafters. It does not find him.

I sob.

"Now now, don't you fret," sings the songbird. "This Brando, he a big brown hound?"

I nod.

"In the bedchamber being doctored by one set of talented hands, of that you can have confidence."

"Please, ma'am, I want to see him." I wear a flannel nightshirt made for someone full-sized. I wipe my nose on the cuff.

"You best stay put on the sofa and do as Willie Mae says, else you get us both in trouble." She plucks a pair of spectacles from her waist pocket. "These yours?"

I nod.

She hooks them over my ears, and I gaze into her face and realize. Of course this bird is no bird at all but an old lady in a gray blue dress down to the floor. Her face is sprinkled with nutmeg and shaped like a heart. Red seed beads and gray feathers dangle from each ear. When she tips her head, it rattles.

She blinks. "How you feeling?"

"Woozy," I say.

She drifts to a lamp of painted glass and turns the flame up a notion. It darts like a dragonfly, and I follow it up up up over jars of dead miller moths. And then the lady blinks and nods and makes a friendly smile and heads to a fire strumming side to side in a stone hearth tall enough for me to stand inside. Above the hearth is a painting of a man with a kind face. Blue and green bottles twinkle across the long mantel.

This whole place looks homemade.

Over a bubbling pot the lady stirs and seasons and pours and talks to herself.

"Sup this," she says. "You'll feel better." She blows and holds a pink teacup to my lips.

I shake my head and try not to grimace. I do not like the smell one bit.

She frowns and slurps in a sip. "Tastes like it should," she says and smacks her lips. "You certain?" She blinks an eager blink. "I'll tell you my top secret ingredient. Bee syrup. Takes away the bitter and leaves the sweet."

She holds the cup out again.

I shake my head again.

"Maybe later," she says. And I am glad when she swoops over to a table and sets the teacup on a saucer. She talks all the way. "I knew I saw something on the side of the road, so I told Willie Mae to back up. Thought it might be a hurt possum or rabbit. Couldn't hardly see in all that weather.

Turned out to be your little powder blue valise. How do you like that? Lucky thing too. That's when we saw you and your friend lying there." She perches on the sofa and clucks. "Lord have mercy, someone done hurt you." Her eyebrows are two wispy slopes. "My name's Mary-Mary. Mary-Mary Freeborn," she says. "What's your name? Who you belong to? Why you on that road alone?" She offers her hand and I shake it. It is warm and small boned.

I say, "I'm Ella McGee. I have a squirrel hat and a coat and a muffler and some very important books."

Before Mary-Mary can say one more thing, a voice comes from behind a door on the faraway wall. "I hear you yammering in there. Leave the child lone already, she ain't ready for all your nosy questions and worrification." A silvery glow spills from under the door. It opens.

"That's Willie Mae Cotton," Mary-Mary church whispers. "She's bossy, but she's alright."

"I'm older than you, but I ain't hard of hearing," Willie Mae says and strides toward me. "Evening, child." Her eyes are brown with petals of glitter. Long gray braids weave around her head like a crown. She looks like a queen. "Pleased to see you awake. You been out for a couple hours." She slips a tin from her jacket. "Marigold and comfrey," she says, "aids the healing." She dabs my chin. And then purses her lips and sniffs. She spots the teacup.

"The girl was feeling unsteady. I thought it might do her good," says Mary-Mary.

And Willie Mae says, "Don't imagine she could get past the funk long enough to know it."

"It works."

Willie Mae flips the tea into the fireplace. The flames hiss. "Hog-smelly-horse-reek."

"Now, now," says Mary-Mary.

And then the two ladies squabble.

"Ma'ams," I say. Thunder rumbles and the ladies shout louder. I gather all my strength. I say with all my might, "Is Brando going to be okay?"

Their shoulders fall away from their ears and their mouths stop making angry shapes.

"He's mending well, child," Willie Mae says, shaking her head. "My apologies."

"Just a love spat. Like an old married couple is all," chimes Mary-Mary.

"Your dog has a strong spirit. He devoted too. Watching the door knowing you on the other side, a faithful soul. I believe he gon make it, I do. Took some fancy stitching—had to use my best worm silk—but sewing never been a challenge to me, so don't you fret. I flushed out his wounds fore any infection dug in and made a heal-up poultice to staunch the bleeding. It was effusive, child, I can't deny, but I been treating him with easing powders and feeding him crop milk, and he's coming along. He's a good patient, let me do as I need," says Willie Mae with a satisfied grunt. She raises an eyebrow. "How would you like to see your friend?"

I nod.

She scoops me off the sofa. I hook my good arm around her neck. She smells like the sidewalk after a thunderstorm, like rain and concrete. When I stand, she says, "Keep that shoulder steady as you walk. Don't need you double-hurting it."

On a bed so high it has a set of steps, Brando twitches and snores. His thigh is wrapped in a bandage. Two dots seep through like a pair of red eyes.

I am a butterfly.

I hover.

I kiss his nose.

I am happy and do not understand why I cry.

Willie Mae rests a hand on my good shoulder. Her touch is calm. And then I notice for the first time. The silvery shimmer around her head.

"You get some sleep," she says.

When she leaves, the shimmer leaves with her.

I stroke Brando's muzzle. So velvety.

And then I lie down. I hold Brando's paw and listen to the rain tap tap tap on the roof. And then I start to wonder. I wonder where we are. I wonder about the two strange ladies who are nice even though they are very old. I wonder how we will get home to Buddy and Cal.

And then I start to worry.

I worry Mia will be mad at me and Buddy will be beside himself, how could you put her on a bus by herself you know better you only think of yourself you don't know what it's like for me how could I know you only show up when somebody's dead that's just mean, and Cal will tell Buddy to quiet down, and baby Thad will suck his thumb and cry.

Only one ticket only one ticket only one ticket left.

The driver didn't want to take Brando. NO DOGS ALLOWED, he said.

Mia opened her pocketbook and took out all her money, and the driver said, Let's go, missy, you and your dog, I don't want a fuss.

Don't be afraid, said Mia. Everything is all right. She said it so many times I knew it was not the truth.

Then Mia clipped my gloves onto my coat and she buttoned it all the way up, and she wrapped my muffler around my neck so it would not get cold and pushed my hair out of my eyes and under my squirrel hat, and she handed me my blue suitcase with all my most important books, and she gave Brando the bag with our snacks. I started to cry so I wrapped my arms around her neck and she squeezed me.

She said, I love you E. F. McGee. I love you to the moon and back.

I close my eyes.

I am a feather in the wind.

I will never fall.

I dream of Mia. And Buddy and Cal. Everybody is looking for me but we are nowhere to be found.

When I wake my tongue is spongy. This means I have been asleep for quite some time.

And then I hear a thumpthumpthump. Brando's tail! He lifts his head and slobbers my face. He is sprawled across the bed.

"Did I ask you for a grooming?" I ask with a joyful cry.

We ease ourselves down. Brando walks with a limp, but his step is lively. And then we walk to the doorway. We stand in the wedge of light that cuts into the bedroom. I see Willie Mae squatting on a stool in front of the hearth. She spoons batter into a pan with a sizz-sizzle. And then Mary-Mary hovers over her shoulder and leans in and pecks her on the cheek. And Willie Mae grunts. Then Mary-Mary grins and gives her another smooch. Willie Mae swats her away with a dish towel.

Mary-Mary twitters. "Now, now," she says.

I push the door open. It squeaks.

"Morning, child," Willie Mae says.

On the table is a plate stacked with pancakes. My mouth waters. I pull up a seat.

"Hold up," says Willie Mae with a laugh, "and you wait for a fork and knife."

I say grace as the rain claps against the windowpane, and Mary-Mary puts a bowl on the floor for Brando.

"Tasty," I say in between bites. Then Willie Mae sets the pink teacup in front of me, and I drop my fork with a clatter. She chuckles. "Ain't no hoodoo-wrong-brew, just regular drinking tea." Mary-Mary smacks another pancake onto my plate and wrinkles her nose at Willie Mae.

Me and Brando finish eating at the same time. His bowl wobbles across the floor as he licks it clean. I would like to do the same, but it is important to have good manners when you are a guest, so I wipe my mouth and fold my hands in my lap and say, "I'm ready to go."

"Oh, child," says Willie Mae. "We high up in a mountain. Ain't safe to trable when it's steady raining like this. Not safe at all. And you and your friend still got some healing to do fore we make any moves. Soon as this storm stops, I get you where you belong. You got my word."

My throat starts to hurt and my belly twists inside. "I have to ring my brother. His name is Buddy McGee. He lives in the Fertile Valley."

"We don't have a telephone," says Mary-Mary.

"But Buddy is expecting me. And Mia will be upset."

"I'm sorry, child, I truly am," says Willie Mae.

I am not listening. My mouth is bab-babbling and I cannot make it stop and there are tears on my face and Brando barks and Willie Mae gets up quick and her chair falls over with a bang and Mary-Mary flut-flutters over to me and Willie Mae puts her hand on the back of my neck and it is cool and my neck is hot and it feels good, and we rockrockrock.

AMELIA J. McGEE

Though Momma never denied her origins, she never spoke of them, and our homeplace bore no thread of them beyond an embroidered silken sampler, which hung, paradoxically, over the head of my bed, charting her family tree and ending with me. Reared on a reservation near the North Carolina border, Momma had run off as a teenager to marry Thaddeus McGee, a fiddle-playing Goliath of Scotch-Irish stock, and from their happy union had come Buddy and me. Unfortunately for Momma, her status as a runaway didn't stop Granny from tracking her down and bivouacking in her living room on enough occasions to make Momma wish she'd run further away.

Granny Blythe was a delectable oddity, and Buddy and I both feared and adored her. She snored. She smoked. She smelled of talcum and rabbit tobacco. She was missing upper teeth and wore a bridge that soaked overnight in a glass of water. I'd once fished it out only to be caught midheist by the owner. Granny didn't hold grudges, though, as I was a mischief maker of small proportion when compared to the grand pooh-bah herself: Precisely when she knew Momma was looking, she would offer me a pull from her pipe. Her face, already crazed into more hairline crackles than a stoneware pot, would transform from frightful to delightful as Momma gasped in horror.

Before her final convalescence with us, Granny visited only twice a year. When she did, she brought the musicality of a language never spoken in our home. She spoke in quick-witted aphorisms, her English inflected with pops and chops. She spoke of her ancestors and—much to Momma's mortification—*to* them, *in* public, and not in the muted tone my mother enjoined.

Tamping lemon yellow tobacco into the spool-shaped bowl of her cob pipe, Granny Blythe would regale us with her ancestors' life before the *Treaty of Arundale*, before surveyors arrived with their perambulators and measuring tapes, laying out and numbering lots, including the three-hundred-odd to be raffled off in Georgia's third and largest Indian land lottery that would, in 1819, become our own Hopewell County.

The treaty was a thing of legend, living on by word of mouth. With regard to its exact stipulations, folks never quite agreed. Its physical record most likely exists somewhere in the annals of D.C., stashed away in a file box in some forgotten corridor with the other so-called accords and agreements between the government and the Cherokee Nation. When pressed, Granny offered this much. Her forebears were presented with a dubious choice: If they wished to remain on this side of the Mississippi, they were to forfeit title to their land, land they had inhabited for over a thousand years. Ten million acres, to be exact. If so surrendered, the government would, in exchange, whittle out reserves for each chief and his community to till and cultivate and to rear cabins on.

As Granny put it, Georgia State wanted Cherokee land and Georgia State would have it. Better off prying a grouse from the mouth of a coyote.

Those who chose to remain rebuilt their lives on the acreage allotted them, which just so happened to include tracts vested in trust for them by the president of the United States for Moravian missionary schools for the children of the Nation. Granny said if you'd looked *that* gift horse in the mouth, you'd have found nothing but tooth rot. The white settlers were afraid of mixing their children with Granny's people, who were called heathens, savages, unlettered, and unchristian. She said the missionary school was the settlers' idea of training Cherokee young folks to be more like the whites, no offense to Poppa intended, of course, and even then a Cherokee still wasn't allowed to set foot in a white man's place of learning. And don't think *that* tradition has faded away, she'd say; just take a look at Buddy and me. At first, I was puzzled. I'd considered it our privilege to be home taught by Old Maid Hailey. At least that was the impression our parents had left me.

That arrangement changed when I was eight, in any event, with the arrival of one Miss Ida Crump, part educator, part ogre, a Northern import who seemed to take it upon herself to personally enroll me in third grade, Buddy in seventh, at the Persimmon Gap School. Though no fuss was made the day we walked up the steps and into the whitewashed schoolhouse in the county seat, which was just fine by me, I was dismayed by the decision to force us from Old Maid Hailey's nest, on which I had not been consulted. I had not felt disenfranchised by my former educational plan, other than a wish to fraternize with someone besides my brother, and I neither adjusted well nor knew the reason for being replanted. Whenever I inquired, Momma called it fortuitous but was otherwise vague, Poppa deferred to Momma, and Buddy said I was too young to understand. The whole thing struck me as unfair, but then, Granny always said finding justice was as tough as putting socks on a rooster.

Apparently, the land lottery Granny had spoken of was such a matter of civic pride as to be featured in the very first chapter of *Our History, Sketches of Hopewell County*, our third-grade reader: It told how the lots of Cherokee land were awarded in a game of chance played at the steps of the governor's office. With each turn of a corner-chipped page, a new character was revealed, rendered in gracious charcoal lines and fading watercolor reproductions: the prospective buyer who, for the price of eighteen dollars, jots his name on a paper slip and drops it into a large wooden drum; the proud war veteran; the broad-shouldered family man; the handsome bachelor; the veiled widow; the owl-glassed spinster; the forlorn orphan; and the peg-legged invalid. Next came the stately official, sporting a high-crowned hat, placing large black-numbered tickets, each corresponding to a land lot, into a second drum. Standing to his side, a golden-haired lad with rosy cheeks—the stately official's assistant, who spins the drums' wheels, an exaggerated look of excitement in his round eyes. Then the stately official drawing a name from one drum and a land-lot ticket from the other, repeating the process until the drum containing the tickets for the land lots runs out. And in this way, the lucky winners were awarded Cherokee homeland.

When I showed Granny the elaborate drawings and told her I thought they were nifty, she pounded her walking stick into the floorboards and frightened me with the story of *Nunna daul Tsuny*, when the remaining Cherokees in Georgia and neighboring North Carolina and Tennessee were torn root and branch from their towns on the reserved lands and force-marched to settlements west of the Mississippi, where they would join the remainder of the Cherokee Nation, as well as the Creek, Seminole, Choctaw, and Chickasaw Nations. These, like the Cherokee, had once occupied all the Deep South and were now corralled into an area the size of a horse stall. Parcels were squared off and platted, and ten more counties were fabricated, raffled off in what would be Georgia's ninth and final land lottery. There was no more land left to take. Within earshot of Momma, Granny let us know exactly what she thought of our state-funded indoctrination.

In spite of its troubling veracity, or more likely because of it, I didn't like that story and I didn't wish to ever hear it again, and I was not afraid to tell Granny; she never seemed to mind what Momma called my "sass." She looked at me with a knowing eye, as if she detected something in me that I did not, and it was something good, something meaty. Her tone calmed as she sipped a hot infusion of ginger root to aid her digestion and broke into the stories I preferred, of Cherokee renegades and runaway slaves and freedmen, survivors cloistered in the specter-filled mountain gaps.

On the subject of slavery itself, not only did she speak of it, she did so without censor. The ancient Cherokee had owned Africans just as the white had, and so too they had loved and wed the Highlander, the Huguenot, the Dutch, and the Negro. Granny's own mother had married a white man, the notorious Thomas Darling, Jr. She had mellowed and mannered his lost and angry soul and given him back his heart, Granny said, and he had lived his remaining years on the reservation, reformed and content, a member of the tribe. He had passed away when my mother and her brother Lorrie were only tykes.

Nothing is what is seems, Granny said, not at first sight.

It was not very long after Buddy and I made the switch from Old Maid Hailey's parlor to the Persimmon Gap School that Granny's pluck began to fade. Despite Momma's predilection for a quiet life, she invited her to live with us in Warwoman Hollow, in the McGee household, our homeplace. To my mother's surprise—or to her chagrin, depending on the storyteller— Granny accepted.

And so it happened that in spite of Momma's attempt to raise me as common as she could, Granny reared me her *tsi'kilili'*, her chickadee, in the time she had left. What does anything matter, she would say, tapping my chest and my temple, as long as you are Cherokee in your heart?

She no longer told the stories of the hardships of her peopl
shared with me their myths and their beliefs. Granny was a descen
the last living war woman of the Red Tail Hawk clan, and I took this to mean
that I too was of the Red Tail Hawk clan, which pleased me, though as a
young child I didn't really understand why. I wish I'd paid better attention.
I didn't yet think of time as finite. I didn't fully appreciate the stories she told
me until I became adult, and by then I had to make do with snippets pasted
together, a film projected on the back of my mind.

Seven months after she moved in with us, Granny died.

As it did every May, the air outside smelled of wood chips, grass clippings, coffee grinds, shredded newspapers, and manure, which is to say
familiar and complete. The hay season had started, and soon the new corn
would be planted. We did not stop our pendulum clock, nor did we shroud
a single mirror with a black cloth, as Momma put no weight in such supersti-
tions. Buddy was sent to toll the chapel bell fifty-four times, one for each of
Granny's years, while I soft-pedaled in the foyer a few feet outside the living
room, where Granny lay in state. Inside, the haze of camphor stuck to the
back of my throat.

I'd never seen anyone dead before, but there she was, laid out on a cooling board, her body draped in a clean white bedsheet. Momma had always
said I favored Granny when it came to appearances, her once-black hair, her
high cheekbones, the way her face changed into something soft and favorable when she smiled. The Granny on the cooling board didn't resemble
anyone I knew. Her cheeks sagged back into folds at her ears and her pupils
were fogged and gray. Her mouth was open, her lips stretched into a grimace. Momma massaged Granny's jaw and her eyelids dropped, for which
I was grateful, but she still seemed anything but peaceful. And it was made
even worse, seemed altogether wrong, when Momma placed a nickel over
each of Granny's eye sockets. The coins made her look like a full-sized
Orphan Annie with vacant dots for eyes, and I imagined her snapping her
lids open and flipping the nickels in the air, a trick I knew she would have
appreciated. As for Momma, her expressions sped by—determined, stoic,
concerned, but never bereft—as she snipped a long white strip from the
bedsheet with her silver sewing shears. Running the cloth under Granny's

chin, she tied a knot over her stark part, and with a click of molars, Granny's lips closed.

Without looking up, Momma said, "Hand me Granny's gown."

Under my mother's soft-spoken guidance, we dressed Granny in her clan color, purple. She was a tiny person; old age had made her brittle and thin, but her limbs were heavy to lift, which I found peculiar. Now that her spirit had left, I'd thought she would feel light. Then I realized it was the spirit that carries the weight of the body and not the other way around.

When Mr. Wilkins left with Granny in his corpse wagon, the broad bed rattling, the iron wheels clattering, the horses' hooves clopping their way out of our front yard, Buddy and Poppa each took one of my hands, and all of us but Momma sobbed.

Back then Mr. Wilkins was a newcomer and therefore an outsider. Down in Persimmon, he ran Wilkins Funeral Parlor, whose glass front advertised to Hopewell County citizens a new method of embalming called formaldehyde, which Buddy said could light your nose hairs on fire as well as preserve a body for eternity. As if thinking this herself, Momma took off after the wagon, her voice breaking as she demanded Granny back. Mr. Wilkins and his mortuary were newfangled and she wasn't ready to be modernized, she said, but we all knew Momma simply wasn't ready to let her mother go.

We moved Granny to the cooling board once more, keeping her in the shade of the back porch, while Poppa built a plain poplar box, wide at the shoulder, narrow at the feet. Buddy and Mr. Wilkins cleared the ground in the backyard near the old pine tree and dug. *The Lord is my shepherd, I shall not want*, Momma read, her voice wavering and quickly giving out. Poppa eased the Bible from her and sounded the words, stumbling on *righteousness* but getting to the end with strength.

Before we closed her coffin, Momma tucked Granny's cob pipe into one hand and gave me her tobacco pouch to put under the other. Though she would never admit it, I suspect Momma's trust that Nature would tend best to Granny's remains was how her own Cherokee heart lived on, just as she trusted that Nature knew best what to grow in her wild garden, Granny's final resting place. I rubbed my thumb into the worn spot on the pouch's flap, pushing the pouch open. Momma had filled it with fresh tobacco, and my throat tightened. I still loved Granny. It flowed out of my chest. With Granny gone, where would my love go?

After my escape into the Takatoka that June, I continued to mind my grandmother's grave and my pink-mustachioed lady's slipper faithfully, but I did not dare wander from our homeplace or seek my spirit guide again. Instead, I stayed within my mother's sight and her boundaries.

My adherence to Momma's rules seemed to soften her some, and by mid-July, she entrusted me a new duty: the honor of conveying a basket of eggs to the Bounds homeplace, unaccompanied. My tanning still a sore memory, I vowed to return directly.

The Boundses' parcel fit squarely along Blood Mountain Road in the Fertile Valley, every inch of it arable, and it was their own, as they were neither sharecroppers nor tenants, nor had they ever been. We traded our eggs to Missus Linden M. Bounds for her pickled peaches, which were sweeter than the suck of sugar and more sour than lemon pucker. Her peach tree grew in spite of our wet climate and was the only one known to grow for miles. It had been our habit, Momma's and mine, to make the journey together to the Land of Galilee, as the Bounds homeplace was called. No one ever liked to say why it bore this name.

Swing handled and ribbed, my egg basket was one of many that adorned our kitchen. Momma worked the white oak herself, pounding, soaking, and seasoning the splits, and after a basket set, she would affix a wheat penny to the inside to authenticate the year. This was a new one, and the year 1924 shone up at me as Momma set the eggs inside.

I had more than one reason to hum a cheerful tune as I walked down our dirt causeway to the gravel of Warwoman Road, then on to Blood Mountain Road. There was more than the warmth of early afternoon on my face and the squish of clay, which had turned a darker shade of orange from a recent rain: Even then I fancied Linden and Nathaniel Bounds's middle son. Of course, Obidiah didn't know I liked him, or if he did, he had not let on. To me it was obvious, despite my attempts to hide it. I hoped he would be out in the cow pasture.

To my left, the Takatoka hemmed the road, and to my right, double log rails zigzagged in a pleasing fashion along open fields where crab apple trees were already dropping their yellow green fruits and snapdragons clustered in pink. When I came to the giant chinquapin oak marking the halfway point to the Land of Galilee, I scooted past. By far the spookiest of all the trees I'd ever known, it loomed at least fifty feet tall, with scores of deformed limbs clutching at the sky, its sawtoothed leaves beckoning like disembodied hands. It stood alone in the meadow, as if it had frightened away all the other trees.

I scuttled along a bend in the road until I was well out of its reach, only to see my archnemesis, Biggie Matterson, with his cronies in the distance. On the very last day of third grade, Biggie had called Momma a "nigger-loving Injun," and I had clobbered him, knocking out a tooth. Miss Ida Crump, who had no appreciation of family honor, had chastised *me*, saying physical blows never resolved differences and to stop picking on Biggie already. I had balked. He was three years older, a whole two heads taller, and enjoyed his vittles, which is to say he was huge. To make matters worse, Miss Crump had accused me of fibbing when I told her Biggie had started it. She raised an index finger and issued a mysterious declaration: Don't give me reason to believe I've made a mistake, she said. And off to the corner I was sent to ponder whether I truly valued my education while Biggie looked on with bloated vainglory.

Now he was leaning against the fence, idling in the shade of an umbrella magnolia tree, his fat hands plunged into the side pockets of his knickerbockers and his feet splayed out in front of him. His unfortunate features clustered at the center of his face: an almost lipless mouth, a turned-up nose, and porcine eyes. I would have found him grotesque if I weren't partial to ungulates. Simon and Luther Blood, twin brothers constantly in the custody of the truant officer, flanked him, an army of two in matching indigo overalls. Simon was the soft and downy-looking one with the long, loose neck of a goose. His skin was uncommonly pale and he easily sunburned, an inconvenient trait for a farm boy. Luther, on the other hand, wore a healthy tan, but his hardiness was defeated by an unfortunate habit of twirling his hair until it fell out. The schoolchildren funned him in the only way they could: ruthlessly. Perhaps because of this, he had taken to chomping on wads of gum, as if to relieve his nerves, which left him smelling permanently tutti-frutti. He was a champion drooler, meaning he could develop a spit bud between his lips and patiently gather enough phlegm and saliva until it had enough weight to drop in a long, unbroken line to his feet. This seemed to bring him respect among the boys.

What I couldn't account for was the presence of Old Maid Hailey's grandson George in their company. He was a quiet boy with mummified eyes, the oldest of the lot at thirteen. During Buddy's and my tenure in Old Maid Hailey's front parlor, George Hailey had never bothered me a stitch. He would keep to himself, first dusting the books, as was his assignment, eventually sitting off in the corner, listening, but never joining in our lesson regardless of how much Old Maid Hailey pressed. She would seem dismayed by his refusal to participate, her jowls sagging a bit lower, and then her eyes would brighten, as if she refused to give up hope. George became a fixture in the room that I no longer noticed, no more than the marble bust of Robert E. Lee staring blindly from the top of the bookcases or the grim gargoyles at the bottom. Now this silent figure was flaying bark off the magnolia tree with a stag-handle hunting knife. Strips of bark corkscrewed at his feet. I crossed to the wooded side of the road.

"Hey, hey, nigger girl. Nigga, nigga, sorry nigga," sang Biggie. A hint of a wheeze underscored his taunt, the unfortunate result of a "respiratory condition," which our town doctor had diagnosed as *asthma*, and which Biggie liked to brag about the way his daddy bragged he was a *pomologist*.

"I ain't a nigger," I shot back.

The Blood brothers snickered in unison and spilled lazily off the rail. They aligned themselves across the road with Biggie in the middle, leaving no space between them for me to pass. George kept at his scraping and stabbing.

"Whatcha got in the basket?" Biggie crooned.

Simon and Luther held their hands over their mouths in a fit of sniggers.

"Cooter off, Biggie," I said. "And get outta my way."

He drawled, "What a purty dress. You almost look like a girl."

I was fuming and even a little afraid. I'd always encountered Biggie solo, never with his gang. Determined not to let him see either, I ignored him and headed to the field side of Luther Blood. He scuttled over, blocking me. I rolled my eyeballs and scowled at him, but I could feel my pulse beating in my throat. Clutching my basket, I slid over to the center of the road.

Biggie and Simon closed the gap between them. A horsefly buzzed around my head.

"Just let'er go," said a quiet voice.

It was George. He wiped his knife blade on his trouser leg and fastened his mummy eyes on Biggie. I didn't know what the two had between them, but after a silent standoff, Biggie loafed off to the side, kicking a nickel-sized stone into the brush. As he slugged his way back to the fence, he tripped over a tree root and stumbled.

The Blood brothers tittered.

Biggie sneered at them and they instantly sobered. Turning his attention back to me, he raised his arms as if holding a rifle and drew a bead on me and fired. I thought better of saying any more and hurried off.

I didn't get very far before something as sharp as bird shot struck my back. A small rock flew overhead, then another. One clipped the nape of my neck, and I winced. I felt a drip and wiped it off, my hand coming back with blood. Next came the pummel of feet. The four boys were running after me. Or maybe it was three with George paces back, chasing after them. I couldn't tell. The glance over my shoulder was too quick. An alarm went off in my legs, and I became a steam locomotive hammering into the clay, only to watch in dread as the checkered cloth slid off and the eggs jostled in their nest. Two tumbled over the basket's rim and plummeted to the ground, leaving a pair of clotted eyes staring back. The next one wobbled on the brink before it teetered out. The fourth egg I caught, but it broke, its cracked seams bleeding orange yellow into my hand. I flicked it off and hugged the basket in front of me, protecting my remaining parcel. And then a slamming pain in the middle of my back took my breath. I toppled over, diving face first, and my basket flew through the air, flipping end over end.

Biggie had kneed me, and he was squatting on my back.

"Half-breed." His mouth was low and warm in my ear.

I thrashed and twisted, worming around to face him.

"Get off me," I sputtered and swung my fists.

The Blood brothers each caught a wrist. They grabbed hold of my arms and pinned them back.

Biggie pushed up my dress.

"What do we have here?" he said softly.

I felt him pulling on my drawers.

"Where do you keep it?" he hissed.

I froze. I stared overhead and into the clouds. A lone indigo bunting, a bursting shock of blue, perched high in the magnolia tree broke from its sweet song into a sharp spit call. Both Biggie and I looked up. The bunting seemed to be staring right at us, and its call grew louder, as if fireworks were exploding from its mouth.

That's when I broke from my stare and kneed Biggie Matterson where it counted.

Biggie screamed and moaned, cringing and clutching himself. He fell off me, and the Blood brothers, not knowing what to do, I suppose, let go of my wrists.

The woods were a snarled tangle of limbs, but I refused to let them hamper my flight. I flew over the rippling roots, not looking back, even once. I told myself Biggie and the others wouldn't follow me—they were terrors, nothing more, and I wiped my cheeks dry with the back of my hand.

Where I was climbing I didn't care. The forest was muggy, the air almost too solid to breathe, but the thought of home filled me with dread. I'd lost my straw hat. I had no basket and no eggs, no pickled peaches, and I was covered in a putty of mud, blood, and plain old sweat. And then, as if conjured by desire, there it was: high-tinkling laughter like delicate chimes playing in the wind. Above a cascade of boulders I spied her: a wisp of a girl in a white petticoat with blue-ribboned hair.

She whispered, "Higher. Higher!" All my faith was in her voice.

I scrambled up a steep slope, chasing her laughter. No-see-ums buzzed volumes in my ears and I swatted off the bloodsuckers as I wove through tulip trees and red maples, fueled by an odd sense of freedom mixed with shame. When I reached the top of a rise, I stopped. I listened for her but heard only the roaring of water. Pushing through a patch of purple hydrangea, I found myself on the rim of a long gorge.

The gap had to be at least a quarter mile wide, split by two thunderous cataracts plummeting hundreds of feet into a river, which I guessed from its ruddy color was the Cuchulannahannachee. Even from where I stood on the rim, I could feel a shellac of water dampening my face. Wet things, pockets of shocking color and rot, spilled down the steep cliff and into the ravine. I looked across the gap to a wave of mountains, the tops darkened by the roving shadows of clouds. I'd never seen Hopewell County from above. I thought how grand it must be to be a bird, to see your home below, and then to fly far beyond it.

Suddenly, the hairs on the back of my neck rose, and I whipped around just in time to see something shuttering through the trees. I dove back into the hydrangea only to find a fox, sick with mange, skulking across the leaf litter. It looked miserable. It glanced at me with woeful pink eyes before staggering away. Disappointed, I returned to the rim. I was glad to be free of the boys, but Biggie had triumphed over me again, and now this, a hidden someone playing tricks on me. I hollered all my anger into the gap. The sound echoed back a few seconds later, as if there were another me, equally angry, somewhere in a distant cove. Feeling somewhat better, I yelled again, this time greeting myself, "Hallllllloooooooooo!"

"Hello," came a voice behind me.

I whirled back toward it. There she stood, the girl with the blue-ribboned braids.

"Sweet mother Mary," I breathed out. "I'd thought you wasn't real." I reached out to touch her.

She hopped back.

I clamped my hands behind me as a sign of self-restraint. "You a wood nymph?" I inquired politely.

She giggled.

"A fairy?"

"No," she intoned, as if the answer were obvious.

"A ghost?" I braced for more laughter.

A dimple appeared in each cheek. "As sure as eve glom to daylight-dawn."

"Well, I'll be dogged."

She skipped along the rim for several yards before crossing back. "Come," she said, and then she disappeared into the brush. "Call yourself and follow me."

"Call myself?"

She popped her head back out, turned to the purple hydrangeas, and said with authority, "Lovelady Belle Young, take thee with you."

"That don't make a speck of sense."

"Call yourself, lest the spirits claim your soul."

"What spirits?" I asked, uneasy.

"All around you," she said.

"Right now?"

"You woke them from their slumber when you ran over their resting place."

"I didn't see no one."

"They saw you!" She darted back into the woods.

I felt silly and spooked all at once. "Let's go, Mia McGee," I said and bolted after her.

She was agile as a fawn, speeding swiftly between trees and leaping down paths of rocks that were uneven and tricky. When we came to a clearing of mountain laurel, each bush studded with cheerful pink and white star-shaped flowers, she stopped. It didn't look like a particularly portentous, or even special, spot worthy of a ghostly meeting. When I walked up to her, Lovelady leaned in and kissed me on the lips, a quick smack. I covered my mouth, shocked. She giggled and slapped her thighs and began to turn in place, and I felt a strong urge to join her, as if she were the sun and I her only planet. We spun until we could spin no more, and we collapsed together onto the forest floor. The earth twirled beneath me, like I was riding a giant pinwheel, but I knew that unlike Lovelady, it was only an illusion. My new acquaintance filled me with good-natured affection and levity, and I lapped it up.

She lazed onto her back and folded her arms behind her head. I stretched out next to her, taking quick peeks, trying my best not to let her catch me staring. Her eyes were brown with spidery strings of gold. Dark hair grew under her arms and long strands down her legs. When a breeze blew, goose pimples rose on her skin, which was the same amber color as apple-blossom honey.

"Do all ghosts look like you?" I asked.

"What do you mean?"

"So real."

She brushed an acorn cap from her forearm and laughed appreciatively. "I don't know. I've never met another."

I sat up. "What about those ghosts back yonder? The ones I trampled."

Her expression darkened. "*They* are not ghosts," she said curtly. "They are spirits. Ne'er-do-wells. Evildoers. Malcontents."

I'd always thought haints were haints and had no knowledge of haintly hierarchy, but clearly I was with an authority. I fiddled with a tulip poplar leaf, folding its three lobes over and skewering it with the stem, a makeshift teacup. "Why're they buried up here?"

"So no one would find them."

"Criminy," I said. And then it came to me: a thought so wonderful and wrong I could barely keep from spitting it out. I imagined the spirits of the purple hydrangea reaching into Biggie's chest and ripping out his soul. I saw a spirit's hand and it was long and sinewy—the skin dried, age spotted, and gray, its fingernails black, filled with the dirt from climbing out of its grave—and now I could see Biggie's soul in its hand and a big hole in his chest next to his heart. He was gasping for breath, he couldn't breathe, his face was turning red. At the time, it seemed fair reparation.

"A penny for your thoughts," Lovelady said.

I shook my head. "Ain't nothing."

"That so."

"Honest." I gave her such a winsome smile my teeth hurt.

She closed her eyes as if about to take a nap.

"I got into a fight," I said in concession.

"I know," she said, opening them again. "I saw."

This wasn't the response I had expected. I shrank inside my skin, embarrassed to have a witness to my attack.

"He is an evil boy," she said.

"A no-good porker," I said, but my face still smarted with my shame.

"He deserves to suffer."

My mouth dropped. "Do you read minds?"

She wagged her head.

"Then how'd you know what I was thinking?"

"It's only natural," she said, sitting up.

"What is?"

"Revenge."

My ghost was wise.

"So how do we do it?" I asked, no less casual than if I had been requesting a recipe for cake.

"Are we friends?" she asked.

I spit in my hand and offered it to her.

She cringed.

"It ain't unsanitary."

Lovelady seemed uncertain but spit a glob into her hand and held it out.

"Friends," I said, taking it.

"Friends," she said.

We both looked at our palms, me to see if anything otherworldly had happened to it, which it hadn't, and Lovelady to assess how she might dry hers off. With a hint of disgust on her face, she rubbed her hands together.

"You must wait for the right moment," she said at last.

"And?"

"And then you strike."

"With what? My fist?" I had hoped for something more practical, perhaps boils or a plague, a bolt of lightning, something tangible she could whip up. "That it?" I said.

She laughed. "Don't be dismayed. You will know what to do when the time is right, and you will have the strength to carry out your task. I vow his ending will be awful and you will be the cause of it."

"His ending?"

"Don't you wish to see him dead?"

"I reckon," I said, filled with sudden doubts. I was fairly certain God wouldn't appreciate my snuffing out one of his creatures, even if that creature was horrible.

"You mustn't waver when the time comes," said Lovelady.

"Can't you just haunt him a little? Show up in his house at night and threaten him instead?"

"No," she said.

"Why not?"

Lovelady's eyes grew shrewd. "He is your destiny. *You* must vanquish him. He will torment you forever if you don't stop him."

"I'll get him, I will," I said with conviction.

Lovelady laughed again but a second later turned solemn. "Good."

We walked along a branch that widened over broad slabs of stone and over a cataract, filling a pool below. I clung to the bank as Lovelady stepped into the pool, the water breaking around her legs. She held her arms out, testing the water's force. Then she leaned back and floated, seemingly peaceful, only to stand with a sudden sharp intake and eye the shore with fear. Just as swiftly, the mood passed, and she sank to her shoulders and summoned me with her hand.

"I'm fine right here," I said, waving back.

I hated swimming. Due to my less-than-formidable size, I often required the rescue of my brother, which was humiliating, and so I had vowed to stick to knee-deep bodies of water.

"Don't you know how to swim?" she asked.

"Course I do."

I took a few brave steps into the pool. The water was cold but gradually warmed, though each time I swam near her, Lovelady paddled farther away.

"We're too far," I protested, my body shuttling to and fro.

"Just a little more."

When I reached the middle of the pool, she held out her hands. "Now hold your breath," she said.

I had no reason not to trust her. Not yet.

I gulped a big breath of air and we descended.

The water was green tinged but otherwise clear. Below us, trout zipped over rocks and driftwood, leaving sand clouds in their wakes, but when I reached down to settle my foot, I found the bottom was farther away than I had thought. Perception was deceptive beneath the surface, I realized. Lovelady's petticoat floated over her head, and she looked truly like a ghost now: The specters of her eyes, empty and void, were visible through the white cloth and her mouth open, as if in a scream. The effect was unsettling, and I let go of her hands and paddled back to the top, where I called out her name between gasps, half expecting her to have disappeared, or to appear suddenly on the bank. A moment later, she popped up right next to me with a large grin. "Isn't that better?" she said as we swam ashore. "You're all clean now."

"I s'pose," I said, still catching my breath.

She peeled off her petticoat and flipped it over the laurel, then with a pleasure-filled sigh sat down on a bed of violets and moss in nothing but her pantalets, cupping her hands behind her head. Lovelady was heading toward womanhood, while I was still flat as the proverbial board, and though I hoped to stay that way—breasts had always seemed such an inconvenience—I was bowled over by her brazenness, and I let it inspire me. Beneath a high drape of blueberry thickets I removed my own dress and hustled back into the open in my slip, where I sat, clasping my arms around my legs.

"You cold?" she asked.

I grasped my knees tighter. "Nawp," I said, feeling my ears redden.

She sidled closer. "You're not accustomed to having the sun's rays on your skin?"

I scuttled away. "I reckon I ain't used to sitting outside barenakkered."

"We came into the world this way, and there's nothing wrong with it."

That sure wasn't what I was raised to believe. After my run-in with Biggie, I wasn't so certain my nudity, or any of my parts for that matter, were something to be proud of at all.

I felt lonely in the silence. "What do you do when it snows?" I asked.

"I sleep."

"Like a bear?"

She thought for a moment. "Something like that."

"And when you're hungry, what do you eat?"

"I don't get hungry."

"Never?"

"Never," she said.

"Thirsty?"

"No."

"Do you miss it?"

"No," she said. "I do not crave food or drink."

"What do you crave?" I said, trying on her word.

She said with a smile, "You."

I smiled back. I liked being liked.

"You always been a ghost?"

"No. I used to be a living girl like you."

"After I die, I'm going to heaven." I gazed up at the sky. "At least I hope I am."

She smiled to herself as if she knew a better answer.

"When you go to heaven, you get to be with all your loved ones again," I explained.

"What if you could be with them, but first, you could come back and be whatever you wish?"

"When Christ died, he came back as himself," I reasoned.

"But what would you be?"

"I could be anything in the whole world?"

"Yes."

"Animal, vegetable, mineral, or you mean a person?"

"Any of them."

I tensed. "You ain't going to turn me into it all of a sudden?"

She shook her head solemnly.

"Well. I reckon I'd be . . . a river. I'd be the Cuchulannahannachee." I took a sudden liking to this idea and began to gush. "It's a real looker, you know, but it can be fierce too. I could see all of Hopewell County at the same time, and I'd travel to Savannah, and then into the ocean." It almost felt too good, thinking about life beyond Hopewell. Even so, I couldn't help but equivocate. "But still, I'd want to end up with my kin, 'cause I'd miss 'em too much, so I wouldn't want to be the river forever."

"Even if being the river brought you everlasting happiness?"

"I'd be everlasting happy in heaven with my family. Don't you want to go to heaven?"

"I've been," she said, matter-of-fact.

"You been to heaven? No!"

Lovelady nodded gravely.

I was flabbergasted. "Did you meet God?"

"No."

"Why didn't you stay?"

"I couldn't."

"You was just visiting?"

"I was looking for someone."

"Who?"

She faltered. "My mama."

"She wasn't there?"

"I didn't find her."

"Ohhhh," I said, the other possibility gripping me. "Maybe she's—?" I pointed down and cringed at the thought of showers of brimstone.

"She would not be down there," Lovelady said with a scowl.

"Well, if you don't mind me asking, where is she?"

"I don't know. I haven't searched in the longest of times."

"Maybe she ain't dead." I picked a violet and twirled it between my fingers. Lovelady's face drained.

"Ain't you ever thought of that? We got old pictures from when people dressed like you. So she might be really old, but she could still be living," I concluded. "You from around here?"

She brightened. "I'll show you."

We tossed our half-dry clothes over our heads and ran a good mile down to where the Cuchulannahannachee narrowed, where the remains of a dilapidated truss bridge spanned the distance.

"There," she said and pointed up.

On the far side of the gap the light was so clear that I imagined I could see every leaf down to the vein, rather than the vague waves of green covering the peak of Blood Mountain. My eyes found it, the suggestion of a footpath, a narrow dirt brown lane that turned like a milk snake in a series of switchbacks leading to a bump, a house or an old-timer's cabin, covered by an overgrowth of ivy. They still existed around the county in various states of decay; our earliest settlers, intrepid mountaineers, had built them. They were living monuments of sorts. I squinted and imagined the puzzle pieces: the corner of a window, the jutting edge of an oak-shingled roof, a sunken porch, and the top of a crumbling chimney.

"Sure ain't no one living there now," I said.

"No, there isn't," she agreed.

An idea jolted me. "If you want, I could help you find her."

"How shall you do that?"

"Well, what was her name?"

She ran her hand over her mouth. When she finally spoke, it was in a voice so soft I could barely hear it. "I am Lovelady Belle Young. Born of the Fertile Valley. But my mother's name I do not recall."

I couldn't think of anything sadder, and for once in my life I thought better of asking why.

Without speaking, we took off again, zooming down the mountain, and I knew instinctively that she was guiding me back home. When we arrived at the top of the butterweed hill, it was late in the afternoon. The day had already begun to cool off, and the air had the taste of a sweet apple. I leaned in and gave Lovelady a quick kiss. We both put our hands to our mouths and giggled.

"How will I find you again?" I whispered.

"I'll always be with you," she said. "We're linked."

My lips still tingled with Lovelady's kiss as I headed to the back porch, but my hand dropped to my side when Momma came bursting out through the screen door. The late sun surrounded her with an aura of keen-edged light as she stormed toward me, and I couldn't help but take a few steps back. At first furious and then horrified, my mother ushered me into the kitchen, where she washed my scrapes and treated them with a tincture of iodine, blowing gently on every sting.

In between winces and sighs, I told my mother that Biggie had knocked the egg basket out of my hands and I had run off and hidden in a cornfield until I thought it was safe to come out. I was too ashamed to tell Momma the truth about Biggie's attack, and I certainly wasn't going to mention Lovelady.

When she swept her fingers through my hair, I flinched.

"How did this happen?" she asked, inspecting the welt at the nape of my neck.

"I dunno."

"You don't know."

"I fell."

"Backward?"

"Nome. Not exactly."

Momma waited for a better answer.

"A rock, maybe?" I offered her a wan smile.

"And how might a rock have done this?"

"I reckon it got thrown?"

"I see."

"Momma, please."

She looked at me with exasperation. "Please what?"

"Please nothing, ma'am," I said wearily.

To my relief, Momma allowed the subject of the stone thrower to drop. She rested her hand against my cheek. I leaned into her calloused palm, but that was more than my mother could tolerate. After fitting me in a fresh nightgown, Momma directed me to the living room, where I sank into the feather sofa and drank a cup of warm milk.

Hours later, I woke with a start. Buddy was rocking my shoulder.

"How're you feeling?" he asked. "I hear you're raising Jove again."

"Nawp, just got in a scrap with Biggie," I said, craning my neck toward the kitchen, where Momma was orchestrating supper and Poppa sat at the large oak table. The light from the kitchen fell across the hallway and into the living room, which was otherwise dark.

I had slept the rest of the afternoon and awakened to a starless night.

"I'm gonna take care of him for you," Buddy said.

"Don't start nothing. I can take care of myself."

Buddy frowned, which I interpreted to mean he didn't agree.

"Hey, Bud," I said, pulling on a loose cushion thread. "What's a half-breed?"

"Where'd you hear that?"

"Biggie."

Buddy shook his head. "You gotta stay away from him."

"Ain't like I go looking for him."

He hunched his shoulders and let them drop. "It's what folks call people like you and me."

"Why?"

"On account of Momma being Indian."

"But why?"

"'Cause they think who they are, Mia, that's why," he said. "You just gotta trust me. When Biggie comes looking for trouble, you walk away and come and find me. You're too little. You ain't got no advantages when you're small and contrary."

"I ain't puny," I said hotly. "And I ain't contrary."

"You know what I mean."

"Anyone ever call you that?" I asked.

Buddy was quiet. "Folks talk," he finally said. "It's what they do. 'Kay?"

"I reckon," I said, not meaning it, but when Buddy didn't want to give on a subject, I usually had no choice but to let it go. I slid off the sofa, and we headed toward one of the best smells in the world: the sumptuous aroma of pork frying. The kitchen itself was my favorite room in our house, with its stone hearth and carved mantel. A row of bas-relief woodworked hearts, one for each year of our parents' marriage, festooned its length, a handmade gift from our father to our mother on their fourteenth anniversary. On the adjacent wall, Momma's handiwork complemented our father's with feminine curtains of yellow gingham that draped either side of a double window, and a matching skirt that hung from the fireclay sink below the window's panes of wavy glass. From that gingham hideout—during a game of hide-and-seek with Buddy in which I was certain I had been forgotten—I'd once seen Momma slap our father and weep, saying, I would not betray you, Thaddeus McGee. I didn't marry you but for love, and if that love stands in question, I've nothing more to say. Poppa gathered her into him and held her, his body near bent in two as he rested his head upon hers, and answered, I know, Azaria darlin', I know. I'd druther die than see you hurting. Forgive me. The meaning of their exchange had thrilled and perplexed me whenever I thought on it, but one thing was certain: Poppa cherished my mother's passion, whether it was for what she adored—her children, baking, cleanliness—or what she hated, be it mean-mindedness, gossiping, eavesdropping, or lack of charity. He took pride in her quick and merciful breaking of a chicken's neck. And he would sigh with contentment when the same fingers kneaded his sore and aching shoulders. In short, he loved all her sides. Together in this beloved room, my parents were like the rag rug that covered the kitchen floor, concentric ovals of string-bean green and tomato red, the two colors distinct yet interwoven.

The smell of boiled linseed oil, which Momma rubbed into Poppa's chair to keep the bark soft, was still fresh as I leaned into the crook of my father's arm, where it mingled with his sweat and cherry twist tobacco.

"How's my Maggie Mae?" he asked.

He clasped his long arm around my waist, pulling me into him. His expression grew soft and concerned, and I brightened like a plant under the care of a gentle gardener. I told him I was right good, still hiding in half-truth, and nestled my head under his chin, the bristles of his beard a comforting scrub.

A clamor of footsteps up the front porch interrupted the flow of kitchen patter, and Buddy leaped up to answer the door, returning with Capable Means.

Capable, the eldest of the three Bounds brothers, rarely smiled, and he didn't now as he stood under the kitchen threshold, the scent of recently snuffed coal oil lingering in the air. I guessed he had left his barn lantern on the porch. On a night as starless and vacant as this, a guiding light would have been vital, especially since the main thoroughfares were too hazardous for a Bounds to travel, thanks to a few folks who believed in enforcing old codes of jurisdiction confining Negroes to roads designated for their use.

Blood Mountain Road wasn't a segregated road, nor was Warwoman Road, but in the cloak of night, the rules could easily change as certain citizens took it upon themselves to act as self-appointed keepers of obsolete law.

When I didn't return from the Land of Galilee, Buddy had enlisted the Boundses' eldest to help scour the roads for me. But now Capable looked less than pleased to be inside our home. Always polite, he removed his hat, a gray teardrop fedora, and tucked it under his arm.

"This yours, sir?" he asked my father, presenting a basket, *my* basket that Momma had given to me that morning. In it was a nest fashioned out of a red bandanna upon which sat a single brown egg, unbroken.

I slid out from my father's hold. "Look, Momma," I cried.

"Well, Lord have mercy, where did you find that?" she asked from her station at the stove, where she was melting pork cracklings in a cast-iron pan for the cowpeas and rice. On the back burner, poke stalks sizzled in grease.

"On your porch, ma'am, right by the door."

I approached Capable. He stared down at me from what seemed a great distance and handed me the basket. Although the room was filled with the clatter of cooking and conversation, the air around Capable hung like a bell jar of silence.

"Thank you," I said in a voice that felt too loud.

"You're welcome," he said with a curt nod.

Poppa jutted his chin in my direction. "That one's a precious package. Thank you for your help today."

"Anytime," said Capable.

"Tell your mother that I'm looking forward to tasting her peaches," Momma added. "I'll drop by tomorrow with the eggs."

"Here, ma'am," came Obidiah's voice. My pulse galloped at the sound of it. He stepped out from behind his brother, holding a blue quart-sized mason jar filled with Momma's coveted treat. Loose limbed and lean, with ears that stuck out a considerable, though not unattractive, distance from his head, he was dressed as usual in denim overalls and a collared shirt open at the neck, sleeves turned back at the elbows, showing off forearms that were the most marvelous forearms in the world: taut and muscular, the outside a dark chocolate brown and the inside a light toffee with a series of pronounced veins. They were hardworking arms, and I wondered what it would be like to touch them.

Instead I said, "Howdy!" and waved impulsively, curtsying like a fool.

Mortified, I tried to cover by picking an imagined thing off the floor as if it were my original intention, but the smirk on Buddy's face made it clear I'd only worsened my predicament.

Too much of a gentleman to laugh, Obidiah stifled a smile at my awkward traipsing. "Glad you're okay," he said.

When I returned from following our guests to the front door, I saw Momma had set the basket on the counter. I cupped the lone egg in its red nest. As I did, a piece of coarse stationery, folded into fours, fell from the bandanna and dropped to the floor. It was a note, written in a painstaking penmanship, the creases worn soft as if it had been folded and refolded several times. It read:

Dear Mia,

> *Here is your egg. I didn't see no others.*
> *Maybe you shouldn't be friends with no niggers no more.*

> *(Signed) George*

After supper, I dug under my bed for the cardboard bandbox containing my tooth collection and Other Treasures of Merit. I was the proud owner and sometime curator of a beaver tusk, a rabbit incisor, a deer molar still connected to a small piece of bone, and my prized and most recent installment, Granny's bridge, which she had promised to me knowing my passion for teeth, saying, When I'm done using them, they belong to you, though at the time I hadn't grasped the full meaning of what she meant. There was also a water-damaged envelope I had found near our spring the previous summer, which I had been unable to pry open, addressed in brown ink so washed away that I could decipher only the words *General Assembly* and *December 1860*. That, along with a postal card filched from under Buddy's mattress of a bawdy-looking girl posed in a flimsy bathing suit, had composed the archival portion of my collection theretofore.

I plopped onto my bed with my bandbox and George's note, unfolding it once more. Plagued by a sense I should hold on to it as some sort of evidence—though I didn't know of what—I brought it to my nose, expecting a fishy boylike scent, but it smelled surprisingly pleasant, like a saddle blanket after a long day—warm, damp, wild, and gamy. I reread its warning. Why, that George Hailey. Who was he to dispense advice about friendship? He was the worst-off fellow there ever was, cavorting with the likes of Biggie Matterson and the Bloods, rotten boys who would, in my opinion, never amount to anything good. I almost felt sorry for him. It was no secret that George wasn't really Old Maid Hailey's grandson, though she certainly treated him like one. Despite the fact that George did not seem to need or return it, her love was unflappable. But that was the wonder of Old Maid Hailey.

During our tutelage under her roof, she never spoke to Buddy and me as if we were children; she respected our point of view. She wore long, glass-beaded necklaces, which I imagined to be emeralds, diamonds, rubies, and pearls, the bounty trove from a distant land, as I knew Old Maid Hailey herself to be. She came from the old Georgia capital of Milledgeville, she was candid with her past, and I enjoyed each morsel of memory she shared with Buddy and me no matter how many times she retold the same story.

Old Maid Hailey's Christian name was Dorothea, and she wasn't truly a spinster. As a young woman of fourteen, she had been a budding flutist from a family of means, only to leave her parents' opulent home to marry a local gentleman thirteen years her senior, a definitive son of the South who had graduated from West Point.

She lost him in the War Between the States—lost, that is, in the literal sense of the word, for he never returned and no record of his death was restored to her. But she would not be defeated. Forced to fend for herself, she worked as a library assistant, and by 1877 she'd become a Dewey decimal expert known for her keen memory, nowadays called a photographic memory. It wasn't until 1915, when a compassionate stranger sent Mrs. Hailey his coat and his makeshift hospital records, that she discovered her beloved had most likely died imprisoned in Elmira, New York, at Camp Rathbun, the result of starvation, dysentery, smallpox, or typhoid—the stranger's letter was vague on this matter. It was his coat that was at the foundation of her heartache. Captain August Hailey had possessed the foresight to pin a small square of paper to the inside lining. It bore his name, his address, and a brief epistle to his wife revealing a prescience of death, as well as the depth of his love. In exchange for his English verge pocket watch, her wedding gift to him, he had traded a fellow soldier for the deed to a plot of land in our mountains. He had been told it was a plot of verdant soil where fruit trees abounded. He feared, he explained, that his valuables would be stolen before his body lay cold upon the battlefield; he had been witness to such theft in Fredericksburg. He hoped the pilfering living, in their haste, would overlook the note. He wished to provide Dorothea with refuge, should she choose; he knew her affinity for the outdoors. When she turned his missive over, she found the deed itself upon the reverse. Rather than die upon the field, the captain and his manservant, according to the letter, had been captured in Chickamauga by the army of the North and transported to Yankee territory, where Captain Hailey lingered on the brink of consciousness before being sent to a sure death in the barracks of Camp Rathbun. His valuables, listed as one manservant and one coat, were not transferred with him. His servant, being man of color, had been shipped directly to prison, and Captain Hailey's coat had been waylaid in storage for nearly a half century until the compassionate stranger, a hospital orderly, came upon it during the building's expansion. This Good Samaritan did not include his name or address; he wrote that what he was doing was hardly in keeping with the hospital's policy and, with all due respect, he wished to remain anonymous.

Shortly after receiving the letter from the stranger, Mrs. Hailey saved George, then a four-year-old with a penchant for running away, from an orphan asylum. Together they set out for her deeded land. Like the old capital city of Milledgeville, once devastated and now reborn, Dorothea Hailey, no spring chicken, chose a second life, taking with her a stray and as many cherished tomes as she could ship to her patch of land in Hopewell County.

When she arrived, she found the tract was neither rich nor verdant but five acres of hardscrabble, and still she was pleased to have it as her own. She grew a kitchen garden and not much else, and her only livestock was a goat that she kept more as a pet and an old nag that pulled her wagon—not that it mattered, as she preferred to walk. Of course, by the time we knew her, Old Maid Hailey was more than old aged.

I thought it the most romantic story I had ever heard, though I was puzzled how she could cherish both a man who penned a noble note and a boy who wrote such a lowly one. That night, as I tucked my bandbox of mysterious treasures back under my bed—the note included in it—I hoped that Obidiah Bounds would one day love me as Captain Hailey had loved his Dorothea. I didn't yet understand the pain of her loss as tragic.

E. F. McGEE

But the dove found no rest for the sole of her foot, and she returned unto him into the ark, for the waters were on the face of the whole earth.

—Genesis 8:9

Outside there is no light. Not of the moon. Not of the stars. The day is done, and still there is the rain.

"You got to nose them to find them," says Willie Mae.

"I know," says Mary-Mary.

"They smell like swamp lily but they ain't."

"Know that too."

"Don't let their perfume make you linger."

"I *know* what I'm doing," says Mary-Mary. "Stop hanging over me like I was born yesterday, which I sure wasn't. And neither were you, so let me go before both our bones dry up."

Willie Mae holds out a lantern. "Here, take this."

"I don't need it," Mary-Mary says from under the brim of a leather hat with a dangly strap. She lifts a coat and flaps into the arms.

"Fine. Then I ain't gon worry about you."

"Now, now," says Mary-Mary. "I'll be careful anyway."

And then she is gone. Off to collect hard-to-find herbs that are good for old folks and their aches, says Willie Mae.

I shift and settle into the sofa. Brando leans into me. Rests his chin in my lap.

"Why you lifting your arm up and down like you a water pump?" says Willie Mae to me.

I tell her I am testing it. Barely a whole day and already my shoulder is mending.

"Leave it be. No need fussing with something fine healing," she says and brushes my hair out of my eyes.

Brando licks his wounds and scratches them with his teeth.

"We'll have none of that, either," says Willie Mae with a tap to his forehead. "Them stitches got to stay put." The knuckles of her hands are round as tree knobs. Brando looks up at her and then at me, and then grumps before resting his chin back in my lap.

Then Willie Mae feeds the fire and the cabin comes alive with quivering light. Along the walls of logs and clay, ladies shimmy, soup cans jiggle, and men in pointy shoes kick up and down.

"Cutouts from a weekly," she says. "Keeps the house warm."

There are words I can read: *Slave. Bill. Black. Codes.* And words I cannot: "E-man-ci-pa-tion," Willie Mae sounds out for me. "It's a weighty word, signifying many things and nothing at all, and all at once like a poem or a broken promise." She sits in a swivel chair by the hearth and closes her eyes and hums a tune that wobbles in the back of her throat. I watch her feel her song. Her face is old and young at the same time. It must have a hundred lines, but the lines are so fine they are barely there. And her skin, it is worn, but it is not tattered. It is full and plump. And on each side of her mouth, there is a crease where her smile slips into when it is not on her lips.

"You are the prettiest lady I have ever seen," I say.

She hoots. "Don't go talking foolish. Your momma must be a pretty woman."

And I say, "Momma was plain, like me."

"Don't see what's plain about you, child." Her smile climbs out. "Eyes like a doe, you got. Watchful."

"Momma's eyes and mine were not the same," I say. Momma had eyes that flit flit flit when she told a lie, like morning clouds floating by. I'd say, Momma, why are your eyes black and Poppa's eyes are blue and mine are brown? And Momma would say, God got creative when I was born, God got creative.

"Has your mother gone to Jesus?" says Willie Mae with a frown.

I nod and stroke Brando's ears.

"I'm sorry, child. I didn't realize you missing a mother. Very sorry indeed."

"It's okay, she's right here with us."

"Come again?" Her voice is sharp.

I speak slowly. "Momma says you are pretty, but I should mind my manners and not embarrass people. She says she is grateful to you for nursing me and Brando."

"You can tell her she's mighty welcome, from one mother to another," says Willie Mae. She looks around the room. "Anyone else here I should know about?"

"No, ma'am."

Willie Mae rolls to the mantel. "So she stuck or she heaben bound?"

I do not know what she means.

"If she stuck, she roaming the land she once lived, troubling folks with her unfinished business, agitating and tribulating and causing all-around grief." She stretches a hand toward the bottles. "Stuck haints," she warns, "are a troublesome lot. You got to catch them to get rid of them." Willie Mae lowers her voice. "They attracted to lighted places and partial to blue and green glass. You stick a dead tree branch inside, oak, tulip poplar, sassafras, don't matter. You shine a light on it, and wooo! That haint will trap itself inside." The chair squawks as Willie Mae stands.

"Momma's more like an angel watching over me," I say.

Willie Mae wraps her hand around a bottle.

"She talks inside my head."

"Inside your head," says Willie Mae.

I nod.

"She don't visit you?"

I shake my head.

"Try to trick you into dirty-doing something you don't want?"

I shake my head again.

"Show up in your dreams?"

I nod.

Willie Mae's eyes grow wide. "What does she do in them?"

"She hangs laundry. Says she misses me."

Willie Mae chuckles and slides the bottle back onto the mantel.

"Sometimes dreams are more truthful than life, child, but she don't sound like no troublemaker to me. Didn't mean no offense. If there's one thing that gets me in a snit, it's bad-apple haints."

"Can we catch her anyway?"

"Why do you want to do that, child? Your mother ain't no jar fly."

And I stare at my hands.

Willie Mae says, "It's hard missing someone you love. But no, child, it's best not to intrude on her journey. She sound like she on the right path, and I don't believe in getting in the way."

AMELIA J. McGEE

―⊷⊶―

In Hopewell County everybody knew everybody else's family lore, and if you opened the closet and allowed the bones to settle, it was clear we all were linked: by a shared history or by shared blood, whether we admitted to it or not, whether we denied it or not, whether we liked it or not. For example, Mister Nathaniel Bounds's wife was a Matterson by birth, meaning her kin had been slaves of Biggie's kin, a fact reasonably traced by way of surname. Linden Matterson Bounds hailed from Washaway, the only colored cove in the county, as no white person then or now would sell or rent property to Negroes anywhere else in Hopewell.

Once when I was still a tyke and Buddy a youngster of not more than eight, he'd said the folks there lived liked pigs. Momma had stood up from the table, furious. She said that the Negro folks in Washaway were no dirtier than the white folks here, and Buddy had no business speaking of a people living in a place he'd never been, especially when the one person he did know from there, meaning Linden Bounds, was not only our friend but the purveyor of the finest peaches in the county. We all knew Momma had a sore spot on the subject, seeing how she'd been the first of her line to live off the reservation. Granny Blythe had told Momma to take it down an octave, that everything was jim-dandy, and Momma caught her breath and asked if anyone would like some pie.

Our true local history came in morsels like that, some savory, some not.

Of course, our most famous story, that of Solomon B. Bounds of the North Carolina Boundses, wasn't found in any history book—at least none I'd ever seen in Miss Ida Crump's classroom or even Old Maid Hailey's parlor. It was more of something handed down, like an unwanted heirloom with which no one in Hopewell was able to part. Solomon B. Bounds—pioneer, preacher, tobacco farmer, renowned for his generosity and held in high esteem despite any "rumored dalliances" or "dips into forbidden wells"—had been our county's largest landowner, and it was Solomon's son and lone heir, Colonel Samuel Bounds, who had notoriously bequeathed three of his former slave women the entirety of his estate, making *them* the largest landowners in 1869.

There were some who said that the colonel must have lost his mind—only a crazed man would leave his property to Negroes—or that the three women had coerced him into writing them into the will as he withered from a wasting disease to death, the three attending his sickbed. Whatever his motive, no one really knew the truth. Stories were handed down generation to generation, and each family had its own version. Of course, there were those who thought the whole thing bunk, who denied Hopewell County ever had slaves, who said that Mister Bounds had a tenuous connection to the property at best. Not our family. There had been a lawsuit, as notorious as the inheritance. While Colonel Samuel Bounds had no children, his sister Katie, who had predeceased him, had borne one: Thomas Darling, Jr., scion of Collins County, also known as Granny Blythe's daddy. All I had to do was look over my bed at the embroidered family tree to imagine what must have gotten Thomas fired up: He believed he was the only descendant of Solomon B. Bounds's line. He was also "100% white through and through" and destitute, according to his grievance, and the idea of three "high yellows of dubious origin" was enough, or so he thought, to contest the will and prevent the deed from changing hands.

He was wrong.

Despite the long and now infamous trial, wherein white farmers whose land abutted the property in question stated in open court that Colonel Samuel Bounds, may he rest in peace, had no right to leave his estate, some of the best land in the valley, to those three mulatto women—that it would harm the value of all the land surrounding it—the judge, who some said had been a longtime friend of the colonel (others said that he owed the colonel money), did not overturn the will. It was upheld and the sisters won sole and incontrovertible ownership of the land. Two sold off their shares and moved to New York City. But the third stayed. She persevered. Her name was Galilee, and she had been Mister Bounds's grandmother. Obidiah is her great-grandson.

Mister Bounds and his family lived upon the very tract where, according to legend, the pioneer Solomon B. Bounds had raised his original grand homeplace painted the cream yellow of flue-cured tobacco leaves, before the Yankees burned the manse down with all its trappings. Occupying the lot now were Mister Bounds's present clapboard cottage, the apple grove, fruits and vegetables of every nature, the famed peach tree, and the pastures where Mister Bounds grazed his cattle. His was the only farm outside Washaway owned by a colored man.

As for Momma, she bore no grudge against Nathaniel Bounds or his family, as she considered it ancient water under the local bridge.

Yet given George's note and the cut on the back of my neck from the rocks Biggie and his cronies had thrown, it suddenly wasn't difficult for me to imagine a thirsty wolf sipping at that river, quenching a thirst so bad it didn't care if the water had been poisoned.

The day after my scrap with Biggie Matterson would be a momentous one, and in a way I never could have predicted.

That morning after breakfast, I was offered a trip into town with my father in place of my usual chores—a gesture of concern and a means of distraction, no doubt, that my parents felt was in order.

The fog was already burning off the mountains, but I lingered in the kitchen long enough to win a drawn-out slurp of my mother's coffee—a rare treat for me, though Momma drank coffee all year round regardless of the summer heat, and this July was no different. When she shooed me back upstairs to dress in the blouse and smock she had laid out for me, I took off with the speed of a wildcat, keen to start the day's journey.

Once properly attired, I tugged on my work boots, grouching to myself as I yanked at the laces. They were Buddy's hand-me-downs, and I hated wearing them. In my entire life I had never had a pair that fit properly, always a mile too long or narrow. These old boaters were both, and they bit my heels and pinched my feet with a fury. I wobbled down the stairs, a midget in clown shoes.

Stumbling my way past the kitchen, I couldn't help but overhear my parents' hushed tones, and so I loitered in the hallway.

"I don't care *what* kind of head he has on his shoulders," Momma was saying. "He's sweet on that girl—Caledonia. I caught him making eyes at her at the picnic last Sunday, and I know that moony look. You wore it yourself not so many years ago."

Buddy making eyes at a girl? Since when? And why Caledonia Moore? Not only was she three years older than he was, she was a tart. According to Momma, that is. Caledonia wore bright red lipstick and lacquer to match her red locks, and didn't care one whit what any of us thought, not even her parents. She wore her hair to her shoulders with long bangs because, she said, foreheads were unfashionable. Her only saving grace, in my opinion, was that she rode a bicycle, which Momma considered yet another demerit against Caledonia's ladyhood. And when I thought about Buddy, his wandering off without explanation . . . Why, that Caledonia! No wonder he hadn't squealed on me that day he found me in the Takatoka. He had his own secret to cover. And yet he'd had the gall to smirk at me just the night before as I made a fool of myself in front of Obidiah.

Poppa's chair creaked, followed by a more worrisome noise: the heavy scuffing of its legs against the floorboards. I flew to the front door and tripped, foiled by my ill-fitting boots.

Pipe smoke, sweet and leathery, preceded my father as he turned into the hallway with his arms over the indigo bib of his coveralls. "I think you best see if your brother needs help preparin' the load for the cart," he said.

"Yes, sir," I said brightly and hobbled out the door.

In only a few long steps, Poppa arrived at the wagon just behind me. The mesh of his hat cast a shadow over his face as the sun bore through its straw lattice, but it did not obscure his smile as he pulled a braided corn-husk hat from the cart bed. A gift! With a green ribbon tied around a flat top, it was not the least bit fussy, and it suited me perfectly.

"Looks spiffy," said Buddy, tightening the reins on our two mules tied to the wagon.

After quoting a list of chores requiring attention in our absence, Poppa gave my brother a pat on the back. He seemed to begrudge me none of my freedom and headed for the fields, where the corn was starting to tassel and our second crop of alfalfa was already blooming. Buddy was handsome enough, I had to admit, to catch the eye of a girl—even Caledonia Moore—though my concession did nothing to deaden the sweetness of my eavesdropped goody or the thrill of anticipating his torment at my interrogation.

Poppa clicked his tongue and gave the reins an easy slap, and Irish Bill and Harry worked their way up to a saunter. They were draft mules, strong creatures with straight necks and muscles prominent under their shiny bay brown coats. As they moseyed, they made an occasional snort.

We veered south onto Warwoman Road, named after my very own Cherokee ancestor from the Red Tail Hawk line. An arbiter of life and death, the war woman alone had had the authority to decide the fate of a prisoner of war. If she spared him, he was made an accepted member of the tribe. If she decreed his death, he was killed shortly thereafter. According to Granny, being a war woman was something handed down from mother to daughter, generation after generation. Had Lovelady known this too when she read my thoughts about Biggie Matterson the previous afternoon? I shut my eyes to see if I could sense my war woman blood flowing within me, but I didn't feel anything out of the ordinary other than the ache of my feet in my tight boots. Once out of Momma's sight, I tore them off and rubbed my toes through my knitted socks. With a sidelong glance at my father, I wriggled free of the socks as well. Poppa looked out the corner of his eye but said nothing when I dropped everything behind the seat.

We traveled in silence, the wagon seat bouncing on its springs as the wheels rolled onto Blood Mountain Road. As we approached the umbrella magnolia, I thought of Lovelady again and hoped she was thinking of me and our promise to exact revenge on Biggie Matterson. The cows grazing on the long grass and cranberry thistles made that same open pasture seem cheerful, even harmless, as if the previous day's attack had never happened there. But for me, the scene played out as if ghosts of myself and the boys still remained, and though I willed a better outcome, one in which I had the strength of three Mias and the Blood brothers never got ahold of me, I could not alter it. I shuddered as though someone had walked on my grave.

Poppa cleared his throat. "You're quiet this morning. Why don't you read our list out loud?" The sound of his voice pulled me back down to the ground, and I was grateful to be in the solid world of my father's company again.

Momma's order was written in round, printed letters: *oatmeal, rice, coffee (Peaberry, if they have it), tooth powder, matches, salt (sack), 24-inch oiled calico (turkey red, 2 and 3/4 yards), six-cord thread, lamp oil (one gallon), baking soda.* And then at the bottom in hasty script: *Please trade what you need for a pair of boots for Mia.*

My own boots!

I was just halfway through my outpouring of gratitude when an odd whirring interrupted me. Flying high above us, I spied a creature with double wings. Even the cattle looked up.

"What is it, Pa?"

He studied the sky as a thin white line puffed behind the thing. "Hot-toe-mitty, I believe that is a flying machine."

"A flying machine!" I bolted to my feet with such speed I almost toppled over the side.

Pa grabbed me by the waist. "Steady now," he said.

I clutched the seat and edged forward. "Where's it going?"

"I don't rightly know." The wonderment in his voice was unmistakable.

The wings seesawed left and then right, and the plume of smoke behind the machine's tail turned murky and ominous. Its drone was broken by a sputter and cough, followed by sudden silence. The craft seemed to float at a stop in midair. I was about to clap my hands in delight when the nose angled down without warning, and it plummeted as if someone had cut its strings, spiraling toward the ground with awesome speed.

"Pa!"

Just as the machine was about to meet its maker, it pulled out of its spin and soared up toward the heavens once more, whereupon, reaching its limit, the craft resumed its drone and gently rolled and banked, one wing skyward, the other toward the earth. It sailed north and lassoed the land, then returned, plunging below the tree line, again silent, first sideslipping, next leveling out, bouncing and coasting along the ground, only narrowly avoiding collision with the startled herd. The cows stampeded in response, bellowing complaints, and the grass seethed from the commotion.

With a taut snap over the mules' back, Poppa urged them onward. They ambled a short measure somewhat beyond leisure. "Giddy up, giddy up," I cried, eager to see the winged machine up close, but the brutes ignored me. Poppa tucked his bottom lip under his front teeth and whistled sharply, the mules' ears perking, as did their gait to a three-beat steady canter. "Be mindful, Mia, they're older fellas and doing the best they can," my father cautioned.

As we cut down the bias road traversing the pasture, two heads popped out of the craft like a double-headed cooter from its shell. A tall, slender man stepped from the front seat to the wing, and a short, portly fellow disembarked behind him. Both wore bug-eyed goggles and the most peculiar costumes I had ever seen. The portly fellow stood in tan and russet striped knickerbockers, which ballooned above glossy high-top boots with gilded buttons. He unzipped a long leather jacket and wiped his face with a duster. The taller gentleman's attire was even zanier, a panache of plum from head to toe; everything was the same color, from the cowl draped over his head to the tunic tucked into his baggy purple trousers—he even wore plum-colored boots that came up to his knees. The two men were deep in conference.

The cows resumed their lazy munching, though they kept their distance from the winged intruder, congregating under the shade of a chestnut tree.

Much larger than it had appeared in the sky, taller than a Clydesdale and at least three times the length, it was a tremendous, showy bird, its head and body gold and purple, its wings and tail a fiery red.

"Well, I'll be," Poppa said.

We'd pulled up just yards from the slowing wooden blades at the nose of the flying machine, and the slender plum fellow lowered his cowl and his goggles at the sight of us. He tugged his trousers from his boots and undid a seam of snap fasteners that piped down both sides of each leg. Then he resnapped them, transforming the trousers into a long skirt shaped exactly like a soda bottle.

"That's a lady person, Pa!"

"Good day," she shouted with a wave. From her pocket she withdrew a hanky and dabbed her face, which was spoiled by sooty spatter. Her features slowly emerged as she wiped the grime away: violet eyes so bright and beautiful I could see them from the wagon, along with a small black mole that hovered above the corner of her mouth. She tousled and smoothed her hair, which was as black as mine but cropped even shorter, a sharp, angular chop right above her jawline. My awe doubled.

The gentlewoman's partner shoved his gloves into his jacket and bustled toward us, crushing the cranberry thistles as he picked his way through the muddy craters left by hooves. He extended his hand. "W. P. Bartleby," he said, stepping with his flashy boots into a fresh cow patty.

My father suppressed a smile and leaned down to return the shake. "Thaddeus McGee."

"Allow me to present my sister, Miss Katherine Bartleby."

"Ma'am." Pa tipped the brim of his straw hat.

"You've stepped in manure, sir," I chimed in.

Mr. Bartleby turned his ankle and examined the bottom of his boot. "Indeed, I have," he said and scuffed his foot against the tall grass. "Nature's fuel, little lady, nature's fuel." A gold tooth tinseled back at me. "I don't believe we've been properly introduced."

I gaped at his tooth's spangle. "Amelia J. McGee, sir."

Mr. Bartleby removed his leather headpiece with a flourish. His hair was piebald black and white, curly, cut tidily, but damp and molded to the shape of his cap. The sun had tanned his face save a whitish ring around each eye, an owlish effect complemented by a narrow nose and a push-broom mustache.

"It's a pleasure to make your acquaintance, Miss McGee," he said. The man spoke in curlicues, exaggerated and fancy, and I giggled when he rounded them off with a bow.

My father wasn't impressed. "You all landed in a man's field."

"Do except our apologies, Mr. McGee. Is this your land?" Miss Bartleby asked.

"No, ma'am. Belongs to Nathaniel Bounds. I 'spect that's him yonder," Poppa said with a jerk of his chin.

The behatted head of Mister Bounds and that of his youngest son, Turner, bobbed across the rolling pasture as they approached us.

"Niggers?" Mr. Bartleby said, his voice piquing. "Niggers own this farm?"

"Now, W.P.," Miss Bartleby admonished.

"I am merely expressing surprise, dear sister," Mr. Bartleby said with a dismissive wave of his hand. "I have a tailor's eye when it comes to meting the square and survey of acreage from the sky. The breadth of this farm is considerably expansive for any man." He pressed his duster to his temples and wiped away a good pool of perspiration from the cleft of his chin. He studied our company once more, using his fingers to comb back his locks, which had already become unruly in the wet heat.

Poppa's eyes said to hold my tongue, but he had no need to be concerned. I didn't like how Mr. Bartleby was looking at Mister Bounds, as if he had just swallowed a mouthful of sour milk. So I certainly wouldn't be the one to let the wild horse out of the corral, as Granny would say, about our particular Hopewell history.

Mister Bounds arrived arms akimbo, wearing a soft-peaked hat and a sharp frown etched into his face. Turner had already tucked his own felt hat into the side pocket of his overalls. A boy prone to happiness, he found pleasure in all living creatures, and he was the gentlest fellow I knew. There was just something unnameable, some delectable quality that made us all want to touch him, as if the purity of his joy would rub off. But to embrace Turner was to learn a difficult lesson: He had the peculiarity of rejecting the most tender of hugs as if he had been dealt a powerful blow, and a noise would come out of his throat that was agonizing—a strangled silence, then a ragged, wet wind like the gurgle of a dying man's final breath. Only the Boundses' coonhounds could clamor about his legs without incident, and they did so now—a motley pack of tan and black, redbone, and bluetick, waggling snout to ground and flicking Turner with their tails as they chomped on clover, grass, and cow patties. I never found hunting dogs endearing, but Turner loved them.

Mister Bounds stroked the sides of his mouth as he rounded the tail of the flying machine, momentarily catching a glint of sun with the garnet ring he wore around his right pinkie—a family keepsake, according to Momma—but his frown deepened when he saw the two strangers.

Mr. Bartleby postured like a gamecock and stared at Mister Bounds as if daring him to speak first.

"Hail, farmer," Mr. Bartleby finally said.

"Good day," said Mister Bounds after several seconds. He offered his hand.

"It appears we've landed in your field." Mr. Bartleby let Mister Bounds's hand hang, unshaken.

"That so," said Mister Bounds.

Mr. Bartleby gazed frostily at Mister Bounds's hat, most likely waiting for him to remove it in his estimable and white presence.

"Glad to see you all in one piece," Mister Bounds said. "Saw you from the homestead. Those were some fancy maneuvers."

Mr. Bartleby nodded curtly. His stare grew animated, as if he were trying to knock Mister Bounds's hat off with telekinetic force.

"We thought you were goners," I piped in.

"Heh heh," Mr. Bartleby said with a cough. "That, my dear, is what is known as aerial artistry."

"Howdy, Nate, how are you today?" my father asked Mister Bounds.

From his front pocket Mister Bounds withdrew a handkerchief. "It's a fine day, Mr. McGee." As he wiped his head, Mr. Bartleby's forehead began to inflate and his push-broom mustache jumped as if it had a nervous tic. "If not a tad warm for the hour," Mister Bounds continued, tucking his handkerchief away. Without glancing at Mr. Bartleby, he then folded his hat into two halves and pushed it into his back pocket.

Mr. Bartleby's convulsing mustache came to rest.

It was almost imperceptible, but I thought I saw Mister Bounds grin.

Finding it intolerable to sit still any longer, and with a nod of approval from Poppa, I dropped from the wagon and scampered toward Turner, slowing to admire Miss Bartleby on the way. She had unbuttoned her fitted tunic to reveal a plum-colored blouse, and my face warmed as I noted her ample blessings, as well as her resemblance to the curvaceous bathing lady who adorned Buddy's secret postal card. It wasn't so much her appearance as her confidence and flair that were shared.

"Howdy," I said to Turner. He'd been struck dumb since birth but was neither deaf nor dim-witted. Still, he didn't attend the Washaway School for Negroes with the other colored children, so his brothers taught him his ABCs from their readers and a magazine called *The Brownies* by a Dr. W.E.B DuBois, a gift from their cousins in Harlem City. As a return greeting, Turner beamed at the sight of me, a gesture I accepted with a shrug of pleasure.

Mr. Bartleby huffed loudly, interrupting the silence of our exchange, and then turned his attention back to Mister Bounds. "In spite of our meticulous calculations, it seems a most wretched malfunction of our equipment requires us to retain use of your property while we seek out the necessary provisions, and given the prudential consideration of time and money, I'm certain you can be of merit in—"

"What my brother means to say," Miss Bartleby cut in, "is that we are in need of fuel."

"That a flying machine?" I asked. The hounds had settled, and I patted the bony head of one of the scoundrels.

"She most certainly is, Miss McGee. A biplane, to be correct," Mr. Bartleby answered. "A Curtiss JN-dash-4D, known to those who love her as a jenny." He leaned back into his heels and hooked his thumbs over his belt.

His tooth flashed. "But we have christened her *The Phoenix*. She's tried and true—we trained for the war together."

"You fought in the war? You a Yankee?"

"The *Great* War, my dear, the Great War," Mr. Bartleby said. "I flew a Nieuport 28, could ceiling up to seventeen thousand feet. Unfortunately, it had the unsettling tendency to divest its upper wing fabric if one pulled out of a dive too rapidly. Not like our *Phoenix* here." He caressed one of the spindles bridging the two wings. "And under Mitchell and Rickenbacker, I piloted a SPAD XIII." Here Mr. Bartleby sighed heavily and studied the sky with tenderness. "*That* can reach an altitude of twenty-two thousand feet."

"Mr. Bartleby flew sorties into German territory, even pursued the Red Baron himself." The lady embellished her story by pantomiming a scene in an imaginary biplane, complete with syncopated gunfire, much to my and Turner's pleasure. We clapped our hands and laughed, and Miss Bartleby bowed.

"You involved at Saint-Mihiel?" my father inquired.

"I was," said Mr. Bartleby. "Commenced service in reconnaissance back in August of eighteen and transferred over to pursuit shortly thereafter. You send any boys over?"

"County sent a hundred," my father said with some discomfort. "Got ninety-two back."

"My condolences."

There was an awkward silence, this time broken by Mister Bounds. "What kind of fuel you say you need?" he asked.

"Oh, just automobile gasoline. It's a V-8 engine, water cooled," Miss Bartleby replied.

Mister Bounds looked impressed and approached the biplane for closer inspection, undaunted by its presence or its former occupants. Mr. Bartleby watched him as a lawman does a vagrant.

"We're scarcely an hour from our destination, so ten gallons would suffice," said Miss Bartleby.

"I've got some kerosene, if that will do, but hardly what you need in the way of quantity. There's a fellow yonder, a right far piece," Mister Bounds suggested, pointing in the direction of Strummers Knob. "Owns a tin lizzie and keeps a steady supply of gasoline."

"Is it terribly out of the way?" Miss Bartleby asked.

"Not if you got the time," said Mister Bounds.

Turner tugged my sleeve and we left the adults to their negotiations. Like two barn cats, we crept around the flying machine, sidelong to make ourselves appear bigger and wearing mean faces to mask our apprehension. To my surprise, however, the craft was nothing more than wood and canvas held together by tacks, dowels, and glue. Why, it was an enormous toy, not a vehicle at all, at least not one worthy of useful transport. I reached out to touch it.

Turner grunted.

"What is it?"

He shook his head.

"Why? I ain't gonna hurt it."

Again he grunted.

"Aw, Turner, don't be such a nelly."

Turner stomped.

"I swan," I grumped, locking my arms in a huff. "It's a *bi*plane, Turner, not a rattler. It ain't gonna bite. I ain't never seen one in all my born days, and I know you ain't never neither and I'm gonna touch it."

Turner thrust both his hands out in a ball and smiled. I tapped one and he opened it, and in it he held a milk tooth. He grinned at me, tonguing the gum where his front tooth had been, and I forgot my irritation.

"Did it hurt?"

He shook his head and demonstrated the pulling of a string in one quick stroke. I rocked the tooth between my forefinger and thumb. It was brown at the shank, with a dot of blood at the root.

"I reckon this is the finest tooth I ever did see." I hooked a finger in the corner of my mouth. "I shed one too. All the way in the back, see? Got a brand-new one coming in."

Turner inspected the gap where my molar was erupting. I handed back his tooth, but he would not accept it.

"You want I should look after it?"

Turner affirmed with a nod.

He knew of my tooth collection, and I was honored, but how could I deprive my friend of any potential pecuniary prosperity? Whenever I lost a tooth, the tooth fairy, otherwise known as Momma, left a brand-new copper penny under my pillow. "Golly, if I do that you won't get nothing for it," I said.

Turner shrugged, content simply with my oath to treasure it.

Long as I could remember, I'd been drawn to this shy boy who disappeared behind the kitchen door each time Momma and I came calling. Since he was old enough to crawl that had been his hiding place. In my earliest recollections, I would sit on Momma's knee, helping her and Missus Bounds split cornfield beans while Turner stood behind the door, one eye and half a nose peeking out. Each time I glanced up, he'd dart from sight. Inevitably, I'd slide off my mother's lap, determined to coax Turner from his haven with whatever valuables I had nestled inside my pocket—a piece of leftover bacon, a broken shoelace, an eviscerated ant, a soda cap, a pear-shaped rock I had found in our spring—but nothing served to draw him out. It had been just two summers before, when Turner was four and I was seven, that I'd discovered the prize with which to lure him from his refuge: a fat caterpillar, striped black, yellow, and white, from a patch of milkweed, the bright orange blossoms squirming with the recent hatchlings, which I had plucked and pocketed as my pet.

When I deposited the wormy being into his hand, Turner seemed to forget himself as he caressed it. His jaw dropped, a dab of wet glossing his bottom lip. He laughed silently as the caterpillar undulated across his wrist and up his forearm.

I demonstrated how to make a bridge for the critter by bringing my hands together and then one over the other, an everlasting road of hands.

But Turner wasn't listening. He was stepping as fast as his four-year-old legs could carry him, out the front door. I flew down the front steps and past the immortal peach tree in the front yard, chasing Turner and my charge. Thief! I cried and sprinted after him through rows of apple trees that grew near the white-fenced corral.

Turner stood on the lower rung of the fence and leaped for a tree limb. Unpollinated applets and pink and white petals rained onto the ground, but he would not quit. Straddling the fence and holding the limb in one hand and my caterpillar in the other, he stood poised to release my charge back to the wild.

They don't eat apples, I insisted.

A horse snorted as if to belie my words, but Turner pondered my intentions and slid down.

Give it, I said.

Turner shook his head.

I offered to put him back where I found him.

He unfolded his hand. His palm was empty.

I wailed.

With a smile equal parts mischief and charm, Turner opened his other hand, and in it was my caterpillar.

I swore to him right then that I would never incarcerate or dismember another caterpillar for as long as I lived. In exchange, Turner Bounds became my biggest fan, and I his, except, perhaps, for the favor I'd begun to reserve for his elder brother, whom I hoped to spy on the horizon each time my gaze edged past the spectacle of the Bartlebys.

Turner and I shimmied on our bellies under the biplane until we found the perfect spot, shady and cool, to enjoy the growing theater of feet. Several cows had sauntered over, including a mother and her calf. The calf suckled noisily, its face buried and busy, and the two moved as one. Another set of hooves sidled up to Mr. Bartleby, whose polished boots were beginning to lose their luster.

"Oh my, my," Mr. Bartleby said with a nervous laugh. He backed toward the wing of his craft.

"She won't hurt you none. Sniff and slobber is just their way," I said as the cow nuzzled his hand. Holsteins are social to a fault, and this one, despite its impressive height and weight, was simply exercising its inquisitive nature. The gentleman allowed it with good-natured spirits, braving to stroke the animal's broad head. "Heh heh," he said, looking sheepish. "Just last week I was chased by a gentleman cow. Fellow didn't take kindly to my presence amongst his harem."

"You two get on out from under there," Mister Bounds ordered.

Turner and I had swapped hats and were each laughing at how the other looked, he with my green ribbon dangling in his face, me in his felt cap a size too small. We pulled ourselves to our feet and snickered as we gave each hat to its rightful owner.

Mr. Bartleby cast his disgust wide, catching me and Turner, our mirth, and Mister Bounds all in one swoop.

"Perhaps, then, you would be so kind as to point us in the direction of the nearest service station." Miss Bartleby offered, "We're due to arrive this afternoon and it would behoove us to telephone our sponsors, to assure them we've not encountered some calamity."

"Persimmon yonder is the closest town, about two miles as the crow flies," Poppa answered, gesturing southwest. Irish Bill tilted a hoof up and rested a leg. Harry shook his withers to disperse the flies. "Mia, time to go," my father said to me.

"Surely you don't intend to *leave* us here," Mr. Bartleby said.

Poppa's jawbone swelled as he set his teeth. "You all welcome to ride along."

"We accept," said Mr. Bartleby in a chipper voice.

Several cows more had come to investigate, one licking the biplane's body with short strokes of its long tongue. Mr. Bartleby looked at it peevishly. "I expect you will do your best to watch over our craft," he said to Mister Bounds. "As you can see, they have a proclivity for the dope that holds her together." He gave the heifer a sturdy shove. She swatted him amorously with her tail.

"Afraid I can't oblige," said Mister Bounds, with neither malice nor subterfuge. He was a direct man, a quality I appreciated, as I always knew what he meant when he spoke. "I can't spare the manpower. I'm already short a son this morning when his mother sent him to town."

"I am certain I misunderstand you, boy," Mr. Bartleby said, his words icy spikes along a winter-withered branch.

"Mister Bounds don't got no one to work for him 'cept his sons," I said, trying to be helpful. For all his land, Mister Bounds had no farmhands in his employ, as no white person would work for him, nor, for that matter, would anyone from Washaway Creek.

Mister Bounds didn't look pleased with me at all, nor did Poppa, whose mouth was set in a straight line, informing me I should let adults talk with adults and keep my remarks to myself.

"The sensible thing, I think, is for you to go without me," said Miss Bartleby, interjecting quickly, her warmth effusive and sincere. "It would be my pleasure to keep the cattle at bay." She caught a patty on the tip of her boot and flipped it aside. "Have no fear, brother, I can handle manure."

"No, Katherine, I will not allow it," said Mr. Bartleby. "I will not abide leaving my sister unattended."

I didn't know what Mr. Bartleby was afraid of, but I thought better of asking.

"Bosh! I am a grown woman, W.P., not a child." Miss Bartleby began addressing each heifer in her way with a firm shove.

Mr. Bartleby followed her. "Katherine! I insist we depart together."

Miss Bartleby waved him off as if he were a fly, but Mr. Bartleby jogged behind her anyway. The coonhounds, thinking it a game, chased after him, nipping at his heels.

My father caught Mister Bounds's eye and shook his head. Mister Bounds shrugged. Turner seemed enthralled by the spectacle of Mr. Bartleby chasing Miss Bartleby around the flying machine, cow chips flying, and began to hiccup, as he was known to do in lieu of laughter. Poppa released the brake, and the mules' tails swished in anticipation of our departure.

Mr. Bartleby ran ahead of his sister and cut her short, and with a wag of his finger commanded her to stand still. "Katherine, I beg of you, do as I bid."

"Honestly," said an exasperated Miss Bartleby. With a quick hitch to her skirt, she climbed onto the lower wing of the biplane and pulled out a leather book satchel from the front seat. Leaping down with equal ease, she then smoothed her costume and headed with clipped but elegant steps toward our cart.

Mr. Bartleby fixed his gaze on Turner. He spoke quietly, as if he wished to keep Miss Bartleby and Poppa out of earshot. "This young yet pleasantly sober fellow could attend *The Phoenix*, could he not, or is he so vital to your commerce that you find yourself unable to spare him as well?" Mr. Bartleby rested his hand on Turner's shoulder, but Turner dodged the effort, as deft as a rabbit in broom sage. Mr. Bartleby looked with a baffled expression at his hand, as if it belonged to another, perhaps confused by its attempt to touch Turner.

Recomposed just as quickly, he then withdrew a silvered coin from his inside lapel pocket and held it out for all to see, in the manner of a magician presenting a trick. There was no winged head of Mercury on the face of the coin, so I knew it wasn't a dime, nor did it have a feathered Indian head or a wooly-headed buffalo, so it was not a nickel.

"A quarter?" I asked, astonished.

"It's a half-dollar," said Mister Bounds in a guarded voice.

"It certainly is, farmer, a Walking Liberty, and a most beautiful lady she is," Mr. Bartleby said. He held the coin in his palm for us to see. Miss Liberty was wrapped in the Stars and Stripes, holding branches of laurel and oak, symbolizing civil and military glory, and stood facing a rising sun, striking the dawn of a new day, he explained.

"It has been my custom to compensate the youngsters of the past," Mr. Bartleby said. "What say you, farmer? Is the boy able?"

Mister Bounds seemed to be choosing his words before he spoke them, when Turner came from behind his father's legs, hopped up and down, and clapped. Mister Bounds squatted on his haunches and held his hands out, palms up, as if to say, "Is this truly what you want?" and Turner nodded with exuberance. I knew as well as Mister Bounds that it was not the value of the coin as much as it was the beauty that excited Turner. "He can stay," Mister Bounds said.

Turner beamed.

Mr. Bartleby held the coin aloft. As Turner reached for it, Mr. Bartleby flipped the half-dollar into the air. It floated head over tails, the silver shining onto Turner's eyes, lighting an excitement as brilliant as a sparkler on the Fourth of July.

Mr. Bartleby snatched the coin as it fell and pocketed it. "Let us see the quality of your performance before we anticipate the measure of its value," he pronounced with pleasure. With a quick look at Poppa and at Miss Bartleby, who was standing next to the wagon, he continued in a low voice, "It is, undeniably, most fortunate that these progressive times call for such diversity. I do hope, farmer, that you and your family cherish your privileges; it would be most tragic if anything were to jeopardize your contentment." He smiled a deadly smile, his golden tooth reflecting the sunlight in such a way that it appeared putrid and decayed. He shook off his flight jacket, folded it over his arm, and removed his duster with a cool serenity, and with an adjustment of his necktie and a tug of his vest, he sashayed his way toward our wagon, waving a finger at my father, calling, "One moment, Mr. McGee, one moment." The coonhounds bounded after him.

Turner's bottom lip trembled.

"Go with your daddy," Mister Bounds said to me, slipping his soft-peaked hat onto his head.

I hesitated, but Mister Bounds remained absolute.

"Don't you worry, Turner, you'll get your half-dollar," I said.

He shrugged his shoulders and gave a rueful smile, as if to say, "It don't differ with me at all," a quick and skillful tuning of expectations, and then he called the hound dogs with a slap of his thighs.

"Go on now, Mia," Mister Bounds repeated. "Your daddy's waiting for you."

Poppa was already helping Miss Bartleby into the wagon. She handed him her book satchel, which he tossed into the bed, and then her gloved hand.

"My, you are a tall gentleman," she said as he hoisted her up.

"Tallest in the county," I boasted, but only halfheartedly.

Mr. Bartleby plopped down next to a potato bushel in the back, where he preoccupied himself slapping cow manure off his knickerbockers and boots with his leather gloves. I ignored him as I climbed into the bed and sat cross-legged with my back to the seat.

My father clucked his tongue and the mules hit the grit, making a wide turn into the pasture until we faced Blood Mountain Road again.

"See you all later," I yelled as we bounced down the bias road, waving hard.

Only Turner raised a hand.

E. F. McGEE

For an angel went down at a certain season into the pool, and troubled the water.

—John 5:4

The sky cracks open and I jump. Brando slides off the sofa and sticks his snout into the seam under the cabin door. His ears turn out as if he hears something, and I listen too, but all I hear is the rain, and I start to wonder if we will float away like baby Moses in his wicker basket hidden by the reeds so tall and flighty, but Willie Mae says the cabin was built high up on stones and in all her years the rain has never been up to greet the porch.

She looks outside the window and pats Brando's head. "Where is that gal?" she says.

"Willie Mae?"

"Yes, child?"

"How old are you?"

Willie Mae's eyes crinkle at the edges, kind of like someone pulled a drawstring. "That is a very good question. Can't truly say, child. I gave up counting a long time ago."

"But everyone knows how old they are. I'm eleven," I say, pointing to my chest, "and Brando there is eight."

"Then it's safe to say I'm ancient."

Willie Mae drops the curtain and it falls back into place. She sighs and sits next to me. "Oh, child. Mary-Mary's a good herb collector, the best I ever known, but she's gone far longer than my comfort. She's my responsibility. You both are. I should of known better than to send her out in this rain, but it makes her happy to do it for me, even if she won't say, and I appreciate it, even if I don't always show it. Let that be a lesson. You ain't never too old to show your love." Willie Mae sighs again. "I got to go find her."

I get on my feet. "I need my coat and squirrel hat."

"No, child. You safer here, this house a sit-tight house, secure against ne'er-do-well haints and hidden hidey-hole-deep so no living being ever find it. I got my best protection powders buried in the earth around it and spells laid in the chimney to prevent the downdraft evils the likes of which I pray you never see. This where you got to persevere, this where you got to stay. She waggles her finger at the door. "Out there you vulnerable. Specially on a night like tonight, all blustery and wild. Something scoop you up, steal you away, and then we lose custody, we can't get you where you belong, and I ain't gon lose you, no I ain't." She pulls something from her dress pocket. A necklace.

I let her slip it over my head.

"The All-Seeing Eye," she says. "A most potent amulet."

And then she ties a ribbon with an Eye around Brando's neck.

"Prevents your soul from getting snatched. An all-else-fails."

We have two Eyes. Mine is cold against my chest. It glares up at me. A swirly blue ball with a white dot and a black dot in the middle. I hope it works.

Back at the hearth, Willie Mae jabs the embers with an iron poker. They tick and pop, and gray ashes tumble down. Then she grabs a cloak and swings it over her shoulders and lifts a lantern from a hook and lights the wick. Now she crouches in front of me and takes my hand.

"Remember, child, whatsoever you do, you stay away from the windows and you shun the door. You lock it behind me. And you open it for nobody, not a soul, not even for me."

With arms spread wide, Willie Mae presses her fingertips to the doorframe. She moans and chants, and I can hear tiny bits of her strange singsong: *We Fada wa dey een heaben, leh everybody honor your name. Wasoneba ting ya wahn, leh um be so in dis world, same like dey in heaben. Let we don't hard tests wen Satan try we. Keep we from evil.*

I want to tell Willie Mae to stay, but my words fumble, they trip from my lips and hide behind the swivel chair. After she leaves, I swing the thumb latch into the lock and run back to the sofa.

We sit inside the simmering silence of the house.

AMELIA J. McGEE

～～～

With sweat beading across his forehead, Mr. Bartleby resumed his sulking in our cart.

"I reckon you'd feel better if you were wearing a hat," I said.

"Oh, my dear, I think I require something more powerful than a hat." He sucked his gums and stared off into the pastures, brooding.

"You know, cows dance in the moonlight. I seen it."

Mr. Bartleby stretched his arms along the top of the tailboard and expelled a blowy sigh.

"They poop a lot too, fifteen times a day."

"All right, Mia, enough," my father warned.

I resigned myself to Mr. Bartleby's taciturn company.

Miss Bartleby, on the other hand, was effusive. Barns with tin roofs rusting orange, a weathering gray silo, sloping whitewashed chapels, the occasional wrought-iron weather vane—the most ordinary of scenes—all roused her interest. She chattered away, her comments sprinkled with cordial approvals—*How quaint!* and *Mmm, lovely* being her most frequent emissions. When at last we rode through the covered bridge over the Cuchulannahannachee, she quieted, as if the grandeur of the river overwhelmed her.

"Damnation!" cried Mr. Bartleby, breaking our short-lived peace. His voice reverberated off the ribs and panels of the bridge.

I turned just in time to see Miss Bartleby's book satchel open in a sudden gust and sheets of paper whipping out behind us like a long sail of white-winged butterflies. I clapped my hands to my corn-husk hat as Mr. Bartleby slapped at his body, swatting the papers, which covered him from head to toe like a churchman's vestment. He plucked them off, swearing oaths and blaspheming. Poppa shot him a look of reproof. I lunged toward the satchel, but as quickly as the bluster had begun, it subsided.

When we pulled out of the bridge and into the sunlight, more papers landed on the floor of the wagon bed. Staring up from the litter was a picture of Mr. Bartleby looking dashing in the cockpit of the jenny and Miss Bartleby sitting above him, on the middle of the upper wing, waving. Below their pictures, I read:

DEATH DEFYING FEATS OF AERIAL DAREDEVILRY!

See Captain Wilber "Wiley" P. Bartleby
USAS 94th Aero Squadron
Decorated Knight of the Sky
Recipient of the
Distinguished Service Cross

And

Miss Katherine Bartleby
"Queen of the Wingwalkers"
Accomplished aviatrix and acrobat

As they perform a program guaranteed to delight:
The Deadly Arabesque
The Corkscrew Maneuver
And much, much more!

Admission: one dollar per carload, regardless of how many in car.
Fill 'em up!
Bring the kids!

"What's a wingwalker?" I asked.

Mr. Bartleby, who was busy tearing at his collar, where several papers had lodged, at first smiled radiantly at his illustrated portrait—then recoiled when he flipped it over. "For the love of God, Katherine, we did not agree to this," he said.

Miss Bartleby swiveled on her seat and looked at her brother with feigned innocence. "Oh my, how on earth did that happen? You look quite a fright."

"A wingwalker is an acrobat. My sister, yonder, is a sky dancer, if you will. Although at this moment I would hazard to say she is a minx."

I stared at him blankly.

"I balance above the wings as my brother pilots *The Phoenix*."

"No!" I said.

Miss Bartleby laughed. "And I hang below from the skid, dangling by the back of my knee."

"Can't you get kilt?"

"I try not to. The secret is not letting go."

I turned the paper over. Two men stared back, one a grandpappy of a fellow with a large head capped by thick white hair, the other younger with an uncertain look in his eyes. Both wore suits and bow ties.

"It's a campaign flyer, and those men are the leaders of the Progressive Party," Miss Bartleby said with a touch of pride. "I am doing my part to see that they are the next president and vice president of our country. When we fly, we drop our billets from the sky, and I saw no point to wasting the reverse side. A most economical way of campaigning, if you were to ask me."

I stared at the paper. "On Guard for the People, Fearless and In . . . Incorr—"

"That's 'incorruptible,' dear. 'Robert La Follette and Burton Wheeler, fearless and incorruptible,'" said Miss Bartleby.

Mr. Bartleby's mustache began to quiver. "More like seditious and stubborn."

"W.P.!"

"Perhaps you'd prefer 'insane and inept'?"

"Freethinker and crusader!"

"Unprincipled. A satyr."

"You are treading a fine line, brother," Miss Bartleby warned. "Robert is a visionary; more men could afford to emulate him. I'll have you know it takes moral fortitude and courage to support an unpopular stance. What would *you* have done if marrying Gertrude left you dead in the eyes of the law? Frankly, I suspect my equality frightens you—heaven forbid you share your bounty. Just imagine if the country was the democracy it truly purports to be? I had to *earn* my right to vote, W.P., had to fight for it. And I'm proud of each and every day I spent in that prison, reminding my sisters that we women are *citizens* of the United States of America—*not* property, not *chattel*. We have a right to place our ballot in the box and have our voice heard." Here Miss Bartleby raised her fist in the air. "I am a convicted criminal and proud of it!" she said in a centurion voice.

Poppa gave the reins a vigorous slap and the mules' gait hastened. He stared ahead as if willing himself somewhere—anywhere—other than in the cart. I, on the other hand, was enraptured.

Miss Bartleby championed on, apparently inspired by her brother's cool silence. "Need I remind you that nine states have yet to ratify women's suffrage"—her eyes caught mine—"*including* this fine State of Georgia. An abomination. And what of racial equality, W.P.? Personhood is not a sliding scale. What do you know of that? What have you ever been denied?" Her voice was piqued now. "'It was we, the people; not we, the white male citizens; nor yet we, the male citizens; but we, the whole people, who formed the Union.' Susan B. Anthony."

"I'm not disputing your rights, Katherine. I'm not disputing anybody's rights. I salute the day you became enfranchised," Mr. Bartleby said in a weary tone. "La Follette's a traitor. The man doesn't deserve the honor of occupying the presidency of the United States. He stood on the side while his countrymen fought life and limb, while Germans bled the French dry at Somme—"

"That is simply not so! Yes, he voted against the war resolution, but—"

"—he is an anarchist, a demagogue in sheep's clothing. The Senate should have expelled him for treason," Mr. Bartleby bellowed, punctuating his words with the beat of a clenched first. Then, sighing a heavy breath, he regained his composure and spoke with a deliberateness I found unique to adults. "He did not defend your precious freedoms, my dear sister; your countrymen did. I will deny him my vote, as he denied us his support."

Miss Bartleby's face turned pink and she was almost in tears.

"'Neutrality is no longer feasible or desirable where the peace of the world is involved and the freedom of its people,'" Mr. Bartleby said with a tranquil air. "Woodrow Wilson."

"Your party inspires criminals and violence meant to intimidate the Jewish people, and Negroes, Catholics, anyone who—"

"Here we are, folks," my father interrupted loudly.

We had reached the crossway of three Cherokee trails—Screamer Hollow Road, Whispering Pines, and Blood Mountain Road—known as the Dividings, where Poppa always got out to check our cartwheels. Screamer Hollow Road led into the highlands of Hopewell to our highest peak, Blood Bald. It was impassable, reclaimed at least fifty years ago by the Takatoka. Whispering Pines wound behind town to Washaway Creek. Blood Mountain Road, the trail upon which we traveled, was our public road. It ran from the northeast through the Fertile Valley and into Persimmon, where it became Main Street. Back in 1842, the government hired overseers to command a band of slaves to extend the road on either end to Unicoi Route 101, Hopewell County's circumnavigating artery to the outside world. If someone chose, they could travel along the Unicoi without ever driving through Hopewell, and so the maintenance of Blood Mountain Road was kept to a county-prescribed minimum to discourage its use by outsiders.

After Poppa deemed our prized cartwheels in tip-top shape, he resumed his perch. To his dismay, the Bartlebys resumed their bickering as we rumbled down the hill and passed the weathered stone statue of Neville the Three-Legged Dog, Persimmon's long-deceased mascot. He was celebrated annually at the Neville Day Parade with roasted corn and fireworks for his deliverance of a loathed minister from our town a century ago. Poppa looked as though he wished he could invoke Neville's powers and strike the Bartlebys speechless.

The closer we drew to our destination—the mercantile—the more excited I grew. This landscape was far more fascinating than my backyard playground. To the right, in a small valley, was the cemetery where my McGee kin lay buried. Beside it was our church with its crooked spire, where Preacher Reverend Elias Front led his faithful following. Our county boiled with Baptists of all kinds: foot washers, half-pint, forty-gallon, dunkers, snake handlers, tongue speakers, stomp-and-singers, and just plain quiet Baptists. We were of the latter, belonging to one of the younger houses of worship, organized in 1882. It was a strong denomination with forty members, though we had no permanent pastor and so relied upon the visiting men of the cloth to sustain us. Preacher Reverend was our traveling man, and he led services once a month, while in his absence the laymen of God's army, the deacons and the elders, performed his liturgical duties. In front

of our house of worship, a small wooden sign hung from a post. GIVE THE
DEVIL AN INCH AND HE'LL MAKE YOU A RULER was this week's message, a
fitting one for Preacher Reverend, for whom temptation was kin to treachery, a scheme of the Devil. In a week, he was due to return to our cove. He
had a terrible way of observing me, as if through a peephole. I wondered if
he could see into my soul, even though he had taught us it was an invisible
organ seen only by God, oval and white, and with each sin it became more
disfigured and spotted until so pocked and so marked, it turned black, shriveled, and died, leaving the bearer beyond redemption, beyond everlasting
life. I couldn't help wishing such a fate on Biggie Matterson. But doing so
would blacken my soul too. The idea troubled me.

As we jostled onto Main Street, folks bustling along the brick sidewalks
nodded polite greetings, slipping glances over their shoulder to scrutinize
our colorful guests who were still arguing.

"For the love of God, Katherine, I wouldn't dream of interfering with
your mission. By all means, join the NAACP, why don't you. I'm quite sure
you would revel in mortifying our friends and family."

Miss Bartleby responded with a glare.

When we neared the bright red pumps of the service station, Poppa
eased back on the reins and we stopped along the curb.

"Mr. McGee," Miss Bartleby began, "I do beg your forgiveness for our
unseemly behavior.

My father stared ahead.

"And thank you most kindly for transporting us."

Poppa tipped his hat.

"Frankly, I become carried away, if only from the passion of my convic-
tions, which does not render it excusable." She hesitated. "If I may be so bold
as to give your daughter some advice?"

Poppa's face was pained. I could read his thoughts: He found Miss Bartleby ill mannered but didn't want to say it. "Perhaps another time," he said.

"Amelia—" the well-intentioned stranger began.

"Ma'am," my father said by way of protest.

"But Mr. McGee—"

"Katherine," interrupted Mr. Bartleby.

From the way Poppa's mouth was set I could tell he was struggling to find
a polite way to express his less-than-polite thoughts. Miss Bartleby quickly

chose to interpret his silence as consent. "Promise me you will never forget that your gender is not an infirmity. It is your esteemed heritage and your proud birthright. People will treat you otherwise. Do not allow it. Use your experience to fight inequality. You will be inspired." She spoke as if I were the only person in the world she could depend on and her message carried great weight.

I nodded because it seemed the right thing to do, and I rather liked the sound of her words, even if I didn't understand all of them. That would come later.

Mr. Bartleby buried his face in his hands.

Despite Miss Bartleby's entreaty, Poppa helped her off the wagon. Once Mr. Bartleby landed beside her, he bowed as he had earlier. Then, with a flourish of his hand as if to signal our dismissal, he departed, leaving his abashed sister to see us off.

Our visitors were steeped in dramatic gesticulation with the service station owner by the time we pulled up in front of Mr. Crisp's store, a front-gabled building with a porch just a short way down Main Street. I threaded my feet back into my boots while Poppa tied the team to a hitching post. He slipped each mule a raw beet and then scratched the back of his neck as he watched the Bartlebys' antics with the same look he wore when the sky darkened over our fields—a mix of concern and ultimate faith in God that everything would work out for the best. After lodging his pipe in the corner of his mouth, he took the twist from his pocket, cut a few slices of tobacco loose, tamped the broken cakes into the bowl with his broad thumb until it was full, and lit it. His eyes closed in tandem with the glow, and he shook his head as he savored the smoke. Then he began to unload the cart, lifting Momma's cherry-rhubarb pie from a crate, only to put it back just as swiftly. "Why don't we hold on to this a bit longer," he said to me with a grin and disappeared behind the store, holding, instead, a chicken upside down in each hand.

I climbed onto the wagon wheel and jumped down, tickled to be in town with its press of people all around, when someone shouted, "Kick it!"

It was Simon Blood. He was leading a charge after a tin can. Luther Blood and George Hailey chased after him. Biggie plodded a few feet behind them, his cheeks red.

I caught the rattling can under my foot.

"Kick it back," Biggie said, wheezing. He looked like a hog, roasted and freshly basted on the spit. But something was different about his face.

"No, here!" Luther cried, waving his hands overhead, his breath like a strong wind of tutti-frutti chewing gum in my face.

"To me, to me!" said Simon. His white-blond hair tousled over his eyes as he jabbed his twin with a sharp elbow.

Luther grunted but recovered quickly, licking his forefinger and jamming it into Simon's pale ear. "Say uncle!" he said. The glob of spit gathering on the end of his lips was a concoction I knew he intended to let drip. Not to be outmatched, Simon girded his arm around Luther's throat and both sprayed an impressive mix of cusswords on their way to the ground, where their faces disappeared in a skirmish of dirt.

I quickly side-kicked the can to George, who stopped it deftly with the ball of his foot. From under his gray twill cap he mumbled a *thanks* and then balanced the can on his left toe cap. With a quick flick, he flipped it into the air and punted it across the street, chasing after it with rhythmic cross steps and swinging hips, as if dancing a reel. I had never noticed George's grace before.

As for Biggie, he stuck a finger in his ear, dug out some wax, and rolled it into a brown ball, which he flicked at my chest.

Anger flashed through me and I clenched my fists, but for all my resolve and promise to Lovelady, I didn't move. He already had a black eye—that's what was different about his face—and it was fresh, if the ring of red, green, and purple was any measurement. Maybe I'd landed a lucky pop when I was fending him off the day before. I waited for a voice or a feeling inside to affirm the moment had arrived to finish him off. None came to me, and absent any messages or signs, it seemed best to ignore him, at least for now. When he didn't take off, I matched his stare with my most condemning look, but he only widened his eyes and stared at me even harder.

"Quit staring. It ain't polite," I said.

"Quit staring. It ain't polite," he said in a high-pitched voice.

"I have something of yours," I said, an impulsive taunt.

He eyed me with suspicion.

I reached inside my smock pocket and whipped out Turner's tooth. "It's yours, the one you're missing." I paused for effect. "The one I knocked out."

"That ain't mine."

"Sure is," I sang.

"No it ain't. I got a brand-new one. The best tooth in my whole mouth."

Biggie bared his teeth at me, and there it was, a porcelain incisor filling the formerly vacant gap.

I hadn't expected that.

He took a step closer and belched. "Stupid Injun girl."

"Yeah, well us Injuns got special powers."

"Right."

Caught in the excitement of my own bravado, I tied together all the Cherokee words Granny Blythe had ever taught me, making no sense whatsoever but hoping it had a frightening effect and concluding with, "A hex on you, Biggie Matterson, may the spirits of the war woman take your soul!"

Granny was surely spinning in her grave, but Biggie didn't look worried in the least. He poked me in the chest. "You're a stinking liar, missy, and if it wasn't for your no-good Injun stink of a mother begging that Yankee teacher, I wouldn't ever have to look at your ugly face. 'Oh, pleeeeze, Miss Crump, please let my half-breeds attend your fine school. Whatever can I say to convince you? Pleeeeeeze, Miss Crump, my children are almost as white as yooooooooou.'"

There was my sign.

"That ain't true," I roared and lunged at him, pummeling his ribs, but each strike had the dull thump of an oven mitt into a pillow, and he pushed me off easily, knocking my hat to the ground.

Biggie snickered, and then his smile dissolved.

"Charles," Poppa said by way of greeting, his shadow engulfing us both.

"Hullo, sir."

"Gentlemen," my father said in a loud voice, directing his attention to Luther and Simon, who lay on the ground, each one's head scissor locked between the other one's thighs. Biggie nudged one of the Bloods with his foot. They looked up from their pretzeled position. "Hello, Mr. McGee," they sang in unison.

"Everything alright here? You all are looking rather . . . compromised."

"We're not discomforted in the least, sir," Simon said squeezing his brother's face.

"Why don't you a-carry on with your horseplay somewhere else? I'm sure Mr. Crisp's customers would be most obliged." My father's tone left no room for argument.

The Blood brothers begrudgingly released each other.

"Charles," Poppa said, addressing the still-present thug. "How are you today?"

"Right good, sir." Biggie gave the *sir* an almost undetectable sneer.

"That's quite the shiner you got there."

"Yes, sir."

"How old are you now, son?"

"Going on thirteen."

"Thirteen. The years sure do fly. You know, I can't recall the last time I had a good talk with your daddy." Poppa took his pipe out of his mouth and raised his hand in greeting to Mr. Matterson, who had just come out of the service station and, together with Mr. Bartleby, was hoisting a fuel tank into the back crate of his apple truck.

Biggie's nostrils flared. He might have even paled.

"Why don't you catch up to your friends, as I reckon they need your help."

Across the way, I saw Simon and Luther wrestling again.

"Sure, Mr. McGee, whatever you say," Biggie answered. Before he plodded off, he gave me a knowing look, and I narrowed my eyes at him.

Poppa walked a few paces to my left, to where my corn-husk hat sat upside down on the brick sidewalk. He fingered the crown into shape and brushed the green ribbon with the back of his hand. "None the worse for wear," he said, fitting it back onto my head. He squatted on his haunches, took out his hanky, and wiped my nose with the soft, worn fabric. "Want to talk about how your pretty hat wound up on the ground?"

I shook my head.

"Don't let him upset you. Charles ought to know better, he's older. But so should you." My father wore a serious expression. "You're wiser."

I was? I didn't feel it. I had imagined my father grabbing Biggie and giving him a good throttle. That would make him think twice about tangling with me. Hadn't he heard what Biggie had said about Momma? "Is it true?" I blurted out.

"It sure is. Why, you're the smartest little person I know. I'd say smarter than some big people too, but I wouldn't want you getting too big for your britches," Poppa said with a squeeze of my shoulder.

"I don't mean that, sir."

"I see." He rose to full height and inhaled on his pipe. "Let me tell you about your mother: She wants the best for you and your brother, and you should never question that. Sometimes her ways are less than conventional, but that's part of her charm, if you ask me."

"But did she really go begging Miss Crump?"

"No, Maggie Mae. That boy, well, that boy has his own burdens to bear and he's simply telling tall tales to get your goat."

"I think he got it."

"It sure looks like he did. It won't happen again, now will it?"

"No, sir," I said, meaning it as best I could.

We climbed up the porch front, and the Blood brothers' "Give!—No, *you* give," faded as Poppa ducked through the doorframe, the door chimes tinkling their welcome to the cool sanctuary of Mr. Crisp's store.

The smell of green hickory smoke, from the colder months, had seeped into the dark wood walls and remained, like the scent in a sweater of someone you love. It lingered with us as we passed sacks of flour, cases of eggs, and piles of skins heaped on the floor and wove our way toward the glass counter where one Hiram Crisp, shopkeeper, stood framed by rough shelves stacked with Korn Kinks breakfast cereal and boxes of Aunt Jemima pancake mix. There were cakes of beeswax and butter, rolls of lace and ribbon, bolts of broadcloth, calico, gingham, and sheeting, bars of Ivory and Kirkman's Wonder Soap. A coffin, lanterns, a pickling tub, and wooden chairs hung overhead. Mauls, mattocks, pitchforks, axes, and grain flails were tacked against the walls; and overstuffed and overloved chairs clustered around the wood-burning stove.

Hopewell County had the distinction of being the remotest territory in our state; the imposing Anighilahi Mountains were our barrier, and the construction of a Blue Ridge Railroad had long since failed. Without Mr. Crisp, one would have had to journey half a day to the next town for the most basic of necessities.

Despite his appearance—he was a baby-faced man with a red nose and bushy white muttonchops—and despite being an old coot, he was never without a square-dance partner, which is to say he was particularly solicitous to his lady customers. This day, under his white apron, he wore green and purple plaid trousers and a striped broadcloth shirt secured at the starched collar with a lavender bow tie. He was making a sweeping gesture with his hand toward a display of Stillman creams, prattling on about the wonders of science to a well-dressed woman in a flanged cloche hat. He opened a small glass tub and dropped a dollop of cream into his palm, extolling its emollient qualities. "Like satin, Miss. Would you care to sample?" The woman shed her cuffed kid glove and allowed the salty granddaddy to massage the thick cream into the back of her hand. "By golly, in only one week, my niece hadn't a freckle, the honest truth," he said. And then in a confidential tone: "You have far too pretty a face, Miss. I promise you Stillman's will *e*-liminate your handicap or money back guaranteed." I couldn't tell out what was wrong with her; she looked in fine fiddle. Buddy had freckles and they didn't cripple him in the least.

My father cleared his throat and the woman reddened and hastily made her selection. Mr. Crisp wrapped her concoction in brown paper and then rang up the bill, the dimes and nickels slipping expertly from the coin troughs to his fingers and into the woman's hand. "Remember, satisfaction guaranteed," he said.

"Now, Hiram, you know you don't have a niece," my father said with a grin after the woman had left.

"Thaddeus McGee! What can I do you for today?" Mr. Crisp winked. "Saw you pass through earlier. I thank you for your patience." He whipped out a feather duster from his back pocket and brushed its plumes across his display counter.

"No trouble at all. I left two soup hens in the yard. Azaria promises they'd make a mighty good broth." Poppa patted his stomach. "Sends her regards, by the way."

I heard a shifting behind me: the scrape of shoes along the sawdusted floor. Standing against the wall was Obidiah. He was wearing a collared shirt I'd never seen before, and it made him look more handsome than ever. "Howdy," I croaked, jolted by the sudden rush of flutters in my stomach. "You here first?"

"Don't matter," he answered with an easy smile.

Normally Negro folks had to wait behind white folks, regardless of who was there first, but I wanted to prove my love. I wanted to be of use. I tugged on Poppa's sleeve. "Please, sir. Mister Bounds gotta need him back."

My father's jaw hinge clenched a moment, and then he spoke. "Hiram, if you don't mind, Nate's down to only one son today."

In the long pause following my father's request, the store fell quiet enough for me to hear not only the din of voices outside and the beat of hooves on the road but the water from the Cuchulannahannachee turning through the gristmill at the end of the block.

"What do you need, boy? We don't have all day," Mr. Crisp finally said.

The rims of Obidiah's ears were tinged pink. I gave him what I hoped was a winning smile, but he wouldn't look at me. When I finally did catch his eye in a mirror tilted overhead, he quickly glanced away and, taking his package from Mr. Crisp, left without saying good-bye. The door banged softly in its frame as the door chimes jingled.

Mr. Crisp had always before struck me as the pinnacle of humor and politeness, so I couldn't comprehend the pall that had come over his face when he spoke to Obidiah, or Obidiah's disquiet. I recognized only the sorrow at having done something that might evoke enmity rather than amity in Obidiah.

Mr. Crisp clapped his hands together and I jumped. "Mr. McGee," he said.

Poppa presented Mr. Crisp with Momma's list, and the shopkeeper peered over his rimless eyeglasses, reading to himself, confirming each item in stock with a sharp "*A*-ffirmative!" and a brisk tick of his pencil, normally worn behind his ear.

"New boots," he exclaimed. "Mia McGee, this is your lucky day."

While Poppa retrieved the bushel of potatoes and basket of eggs we had brought to trade, Mr. Crisp led me toward the back of the store, where rows of shoes, used and new, were displayed on raked wooden shelves behind the counter. He studied his supply, drawing a line with a pointed finger, and with a sharp breath paused to admire a pair of lace-up dress boots. "*Ex*-tra quality, these little darlings, with a vamp cut from *one* hundred *per*cent chrome-tanned patent leather." He polished them on his cuff and brought one to my nose. "Nothing like the scent of new leather. I'll take it over breakfast bacon any day."

I sniffed and thought: I'd a heap rather have the bacon.

"They're awful swell, sir, but I already got a Sunday pair. I need working boots. These don't fit no more." I stuck my ankle out. "I've done outgrown 'em."

Mr. Crisp tut-tutted. "Can't have you hobbling around on sore feet, can we? Ahh! Here's *ex*-actly what I was looking for." Mr. Crisp withdrew another boot. "*Ex*-cellent-grade leather upper, a durable heavy drill lining, flexible leather inner soles, and a last designed for growing feet, sure to please any parent." He took a moment from his shoe soliloquy to see if he still had my attention and added frankly, "What do *you* think?"

They were brown, which was a color I liked, and I said as much. I turned the boot over—the sole was black and bendy, not made of leather and not like anything I'd ever seen before.

"That," Mr. Crisp pronounced, "is a rubber sole. Made from tree sap. Much less costly to replace than the leather ones you're accustomed to, at one-tenth the expense."

Mr. Crisp came around the counter. As would befit a man who ran a mercantile, he himself wore an impressive set of shoes: yellow and black snakeskin lace-ups with brass toe caps. I thought them dazzling though somewhat incongruous to his otherwise amiable attire. I'd once come upon a yellow rat snake curled up in the rafters of our barn that looked not wholly dissimilar to Mr. Crisp's shoes. Rather than kill it, as I had hoped, Poppa had snagged it around the end of a broom and brought it back to the forest, saying we needed such snakes, as they consumed the pests that got into our feed or ate from our fields. I wondered now if that snake had instead met its fate as Mr. Crisp's boots.

He patted the seat of a wooden stool, and I sat while he adjusted a foot-measuring device he claimed he had invented himself, waving his fingers over the contraption as if he were about to pull a rabbit from a hat. Instead, he pressed my big toe against the board and adjusted the bars back and forth. I crossed my fingers for luck.

"Ah! Just as I thought," he exclaimed. "You, young lady—"

"Yes, sir?" I squeaked.

"—have the perfect size foot for your height, and I am willing to stake my farm they will stay proportioned that way."

I was awash with relief. It didn't occur to me until moments later that Mr. Crisp didn't have a farm. But by then he was atop the ladder and rummaging through a stack of boxes above the display. "Voilà!" he said and expertly slid out a box without disturbing the rest.

When Mr. Crisp rang up our bill, we were seventy-five cents short.

"They're designed for growing feet with soles you can change at one-tenth the cost," I said, appealing to my father and then Mr. Crisp, who winked.

Poppa frowned at the shopkeeper.

Not one to part easily with Momma's confections, my father nonetheless returned from the cart with the cherry-rhubarb pie wrapped neatly in wax paper, which we both knew he had been saving for himself. "I'll be expectin' back the tin, Hiram," my father said with a sigh.

"*In*-dubitably," Mr. Crisp said, admiring the pie and grinning as if he'd won the jackpot.

After we left the mercantile, Poppa determined he would pay a visit to the service station. Though he would never confess his dislike of the Bartlebys and if pressed would merely have said, "I can't rightly know them," his distaste for them was palpable. Still, it would have been rude not to offer them a return ride, and knowing my father, he had considered this undeniable fact: The sooner the Bartlebys were deposited in the Boundses' pasture, the sooner they would depart from Hopewell and from our lives.

When my father inquired if I wished to accompany him, I politely declined, professing I'd had my fill of strangers for the day, which was candid enough, and Poppa accepted my answer, leaving me to mind the mules.

When he returned, his broad smile preceded him as he strode toward the wagon. The Bartlebys had already left the service station.

We had not seen the last of them, however. As we rode past the Land of Galilee, Mr. Matterson's apple truck was parked along the bias road, the sharp scent of gasoline permeating the air. He stood in the back crate of his truck, a broad-chested man, short and squat, whom I'd once seen blow his nose by placing a finger over one nostril and shooting out a disgusting jet of mucus. Now he stood chatting in civilized fashion with Mr. Bartleby, who was turning a crank on the gasoline barrel in the crate. A yellow rubber tube ran from the barrel to where Miss Bartleby sat on top of the biplane just behind the propeller, to what I guessed was the jenny's fuel tank.

Biggie was leaning against the side of the apple truck with one foot perched on the running board, arms crossed over his chest, watching them. In the heat of the afternoon, the herd had moseyed again into the shade of the chestnut tree, where they lay in a cow heap, the only sign of movement an occasional flick of a tail. I scanned the land for Mister Bounds and Turner, but there was no sign of them. I hoped Turner had gotten his coin.

Miss Bartleby waved, and I returned her salute. When I looked over my shoulder for one last glimpse of *The Phoenix* before we turned the bend, Biggie pointed at me.

Maybe it was the way he held it, or maybe it was simply that everything about Biggie felt like a threat, but I pointed back with equal menace, convincing myself that all I had to do was be patient and wait, as Lovelady said, for the precise moment to strike.

E. F. McGEE

Beware of false prophets, which come to you in sheep's clothing,
but inwardly they are ravenous wolves.

—Matthew 7:15

This here room was so warm and friendly when Willie Mae was with us, and now the warm and friendly has got up and gone. First a flame fizzled. It stumbled across the floor all boozy and lost and jittered and quivered and died. Then the reds turned to yellows and the yellows turned to blues, and now nothing is left but a gray flurry.

We sit inside the cold.

Only the rain outside makes a sound.

I rub my hands and lean into Brando and think of hot things. I think of bubbling soups and the hearth in Cal's kitchen and the fires Buddy builds and how long they last, especially the night after we buried Momma and we all went back to his house, and Cal gave him a kiss with her pretty red lips. She said, Why don't you get ready for bed, Ella—I've already fluffed your pillow. But Thaddeus started to kick his legs and open his mouth like a baby bird, and Cal went off to nurse.

I did not get ready for bed. I sat on the bottom of the stairs.

Mia glared at the ceiling.

Buddy stared into his coffee cup.

And then they argued. They raised the roof. I put my head in my arms, and when Cal rushed back into the kitchen with Thaddeus stuck to her chest, she said, You want to wake the dead, never you mind frighten the baby.

Buddy lowered his voice. He said, Look where you live. Are you out of your mind? Whites live with whites, not with Negroes.

And Mia said, I'm not going to dignify that with a response.

It ain't safe, Buddy said.

And Mia said, What *is* safe? Here?

Look at what you do for a living.

And Mia scowled. Don't go there, Bud.

Traveling around pokin' your nose where it don't belong, he went on anyway.

Quit it.

Prying into folks' business and writin' about it in those flyers. You got no right.

And Mia whispered, I know what I do. They're called *anti*lynching pamphlets. I write facts. Accurate accounts. Not Hopewell hogwash. I make a difference. What do *you* do?

I mean it, Sis, don't take her.

Right. Where're you going to send her to school?

We'll teach her right here.

That's a hoot.

Callie will. She'll pick up where Momma left off.

And Cal said, I will, I promise. She slid her hand across the table to touch Mia's. Mia pulled hers back. She said, No, Bud, with me she can go to a real school. With kids just like her. Good kids from mixed families. Obidiah *owns* the house in Shaw. It's a great neighborhood. We have writers and poets, and even one opera singer living on our block.

The side of Buddy's mouth pinched like a bee stung him. We got all that, he said.

And Mia said, An opera singer?

You know that ain't what I mean.

Mia took a breath. I'm not doing the speaking tours anymore. I'm working from home. We've got a bureau in D.C. now, and I'm—

SLAM went Buddy's coffee cup.

And Mia stood up and threw her hands out and hollered, You already got enough on your hands with another one on the way.

And Buddy said, For Jove's sake, Mia, we worry about you.

Well don't. And quit judging.

And Buddy said, You're living in sin. Do you know how much grief you caused Momma?

And Mia said, Momma? She didn't judge me, not like you, Bud. She wouldn't and she couldn't. She made her own decisions to protect her family, just like I'm making mine. So don't you give me that holier-than-thou crap. And for your information, we are married.

What? How?

I changed my birth certificate.

To what?

Indian.

Jesus! said Buddy.

Watch your mouth, Cal said, hoisting baby Thaddeus to her shoulder.

And Buddy said, She'll never fit in.

And Mia said, Like she fits in here. Momma practically kept her locked in the house.

She wasn't a prisoner, Mia. Don't make like she was. You're the one who walked out on a three-year-old.

And Mia stared into her coffee. I went to college, she said.

And Buddy said, She's got family here, folks who know her and care about her. Cal knows the foods she likes. You gonna give her all that?

And Mia said, I'm her mother, Bud. I want her to know me.

That's when Cal saw me. Ella, how long have you been sitting there? she asked me.

Mia looked over her shoulder and said, Come here, baby. Don't you cry. Everything's alright.

I hugged myself tight.

And then she said, How would you like to come live with me?

And when I asked if Brando could come too, she said, Of course he can. Don't you remember I picked him out for you? Right before I left for college?

And I said yes, I would come and live with her in D.C., where Mia was a writer for the NAACP and W.E.B., and I told her to call me E. F. McGee but she said don't be silly. She named me after Elisabeth Freeman, a great suffragist and speaker.

Elisabeth Freeman doesn't sound like my name at all.

I wish my name was Wanda.

And Buddy said, Do you understand? Do you understand that you won't live with me and Caledonia anymore, that you'll go with Mia in the big city?

I asked if the big city was far away.

Buddy said yes.

And now I am alone.

If I squint my eyes I can still see Willie Mae by the door, like the last glimmer of shimmer on the silver screen. I trace her shape with my mind.

Brando lifts his head when I slide off the sofa. His eyes are smart, as if he knows what I am up to.

"I'll be right back," I say and pick up the candle.

It is not nice to poke through other people's things, but the wardrobe is locked anyway. I put the candle on the nightstand and try the trunk at the foot of the bed. I want my coat. I want my squirrel hat. I pull out a pillow-case. It is heavy and I open it. I touch something soft inside. Someone's hair all cut up into twists. They look like snakes. I pull my hand out, and I see they are only braids. I stuff the pillowcase back into the trunk. And then, there! Tucked in the corner. But no. It is only a rag doll. She is bald and wears a stiff red dress. I pick her up and cradle her in my arms and hear a *tee hee hee*.

I look at the doll. She does not make a sound.

So I creep to the bed stand and peer out into the gauzy gray. The clouds fly through the sky and the moon shines and lights up the rain. Below, tow-ering trees sway sway sway. My breath turns the glass cloudy and I spell my name in the fog, my finger squeak-squeaking across the pane.

I see a flash of white. A girl in a white dress. Dancing in the rain.

"Oh!" I say.

She looks up at me.

She curls a finger. "Come play," she mouths.

I back away. I turn. "Brando, come," I say in a hush hush hush. He pads into the room. He barks. And there. Hovering outside. In front of the pane. The girl. I can see right through her to the swaying trees.

I scream.

I drop the doll.

I clutch my Eye.

The chain breaks.

The girl's face mirrors mine and she yowls and flies up into the air, twisting into a tangle. She disappears.

I pant along the floor and run my hand over the boards. I must find my Eye. Then a chill runs up my back. Brando is nosing the window. His nostrils twitch and flare. And now I smell it too. Something sour. Like dead roses. I blow out the candle and peek over the window ledge.

Deep in the forest, a gray white fog curls through the trees. It is its own light. It billows into the yard and snakes around the puddles and twirls and twines, and now there is a lady in a long cape and a hood draped over her face, and she starts and stops, running and clawing like someone who cannot see. "My baby? Where is my child?" she wails and tramples through the mud, treading from tree to tree.

"Momma?" I whisper. "That you?"

Her head snaps toward the cabin at my sound.

She bustles to the pane. Her cape drags across the ground. "I'm ever so hungry," she says, bunching her hands. "Let your mother in, let her in." All but her mouth hides in the folds.

Brando curls his lips and starts to growl.

"Please," she says. She presses a hand against her big belly. It squirms as if something is caught inside. "Now," she begs. "Now!"

I push hard and make the window move up a crack, and she seeps into the room.

"*Chère enfant*," she says and slithers toward me. "Come here, my darling." The room swells with her rotten-rose scent.

My feet scuff the floor as I back away. Momma always smelled like fresh lavender.

"No, no, dear, stay," she pleads.

My legs turn to jelly and my belly flip-flops as the shawl drops back from her face and gathers into folds on her shoulders. Where Momma's eyes should be are dim white orbs. Her skin is pale and waxy. Clumps of blond hair straggle down her head.

"You are not Momma," I say in a small voice.

Her fingers nibble the air. And then her white orbs shift over my head.

"You!" she hisses.

A silvery glow lights up the room.

"Get down!" Willie Mae shouts. I crawl under the bed. Something warm and furry snuggles up to me. Brando!

"You took what's mine," the rose lady snarls.

"I ain't done nothing of the sort, you troublesome wraith."

The lady roars a misery that rattles the cabin. "Hell hag! Harpy! *Goule!*"

"Pitiless names, them pitiless names!" Willie Mae hurls back, all fire and flint, and begins to chant under her breath. Her arms branch over her head as if she is holding up the sky.

The woman howls. The winds screams. Her bulging eyes sink into her head, her face inflates, and her wide mouth ripples and quakes. Her jaws spread like a timber rattler about to eat a mouse.

The cabin starts to shake.

"Here!" cries Mary-Mary from the other room. She holds a green bottle with a branch in its neck. She waves the lantern high as she rushes in.

The lady gurples and gasps, her cheeks go slack, and then her eyes push back out. They fix on the sparkling glass. And then she shrieks.

I clamp my eyes shut and bury them in my hands, and when I open them Willie Mae and Mary-Mary are bickering over what to do with the bottle. It beams bright as a frog full of glow flies.

"Let her go once you beyond the Spring of Woe," Willie Mae is saying, "and I don't intend to hear no more of it."

Mary-Mary's eyes blink-blink. She looks pleased with herself. She tinkles the glass with a fingernail. "Isn't she better off we dip her in the Pool of Forgetfulness. One quick plunge . . ." she says, her voice trailing off. She tugs at her hair and scratches her head. Mary-Mary is slathered in mud from tip to toe.

"Then we leave her with no past whatsoever, and that's a mean-minded thing to do. She'll never find her way home then. You bottle your first one and now you an expert."

"Maybe it's better, no memory?" says Mary-Mary softly.

"I ain't dignifying that with a response."

The bottle grows brighter and Mary-Mary grasps it firmly between her hands. "We could set her out in the garden. Let the sun undo her after the storm has its say?"

"No."

"She wouldn't do the same for you."

"I'm gon do it myself you keep this conversation flowing in a direction I don't appreciate."

Mary-Mary clucks her tongue against the roof of her mouth and carries the bottle out.

"Look where you running this time," Willie Mae shouts after her. "Stuck haints. Downright pests," she mutters to herself, hands on her hips. She bends down and peers under the bed. Her face is tired. "Okay, child, time for you and your accomplice to reveal yourselves."

Me and Brando scrabble out.

Willie Mae pushes the window down and lights the candle with a long match. Then she picks the rag doll off the floor and holds it in her lap. "Now, I thought I told you to stay put."

I do not look at her.

"I see I got to be double specific with my instructions," she says, tight-lipped. "You all in one piece?"

I nod and sit on the bed and let my legs dangle over the edge. "I wanted my coat," I say. And then I realize. The house is warm and friendly again.

"That's my fault, child. I should have furnished you with more quilts."

"Who was that lady?"

"A haint, that's who," says Willie Mae. "The worse kind. She got a strong taste for other people's children cause she lost her own. You pass by the window?"

"Yes, ma'am."

"Who else come for you?"

"Ma'am?"

"You see anybody else?" she asks, sharp and loud.

I am quiet.

Willie Mae draws in a breath and in a calmer voice says, "I need to know, child. There anybody else who come?"

"There was a girl."

Willie Mae sucks in her top lip and nods.

"Why did the lady want to come in?" I ask. "Why did she say she was my momma?"

Willie Mae's sad eyes rest on me. "That one is unfortunate in death as well as in life. And now she stuck like nobody's business. She got nothing left of conscience or reason, just painful rememory and terrible want. That's the worst state a haint can be in—wandering so long, there ain't nothing left of their humanity." She shakes her head. "Haven't seen her in a powerful long time. Thought she finally made peace with herself. She proved me wrong, hoo! She a strong one, and cunning too—all the words on the walls won't stop her. You got to listen to me when I tell you what to do. I got powers to protect, child, but they ain't impenetrable. All we got between us is trust, and we need it to keep you safe." She wraps her hand around mine. "When she was a young woman, she come undone by grief. Her only born child died. It chewed her up from the inside. Took to blaming everybody, even if it wasn't nobody's fault. Now she got a strong taste for other folks' children to make up for the one she lost. She prone to following on the footsteps of child spirits, but she don't quit there. She's drawn to lost children and newborns, hunts them all down like a bloodhound—no offense to your kin, Mr. Brando. And then, well, I'm sorry, child, but you got to know so you'll be more careful: She swallows them. See that big fat stomach? That's what she got inside. A regular symphony of grief. She got a perpetual hunger than ain't never satisfied."

Willie Mae sees I'm missing my All-Seeing Eye. My face gets hot.

"It will turn up. It done its job. I heard it singing the moment you went roaming where you didn't belong. It nearly set my head on fire when it dropped," she says. "You got to promise me: When I tell you to do something, you honor it, you hear?"

I nod. "Am I a lost child?"

At first, Willie Mae doesn't answer, and then she grunts. "No, child, you ain't lost, you just momentarily diverted." She looks out the window. "Haints are a sorrowful thing, really. It's best to have empathy. All us gon be haints one day, but not all us gon be stuck, and even if you stuck, it ain't necessarily a tragedy. You ain't condemned to wander for eternity. You got a choice to be free. But the last part of the journey, we alone, and for some, it's unbearable. They don't trust in the Lord, they don't trust in Home. This where a haint got to hold strong. We all a map—all civilization one giant map—every life, a road, and sometimes it merges with somebody else's road, and sometimes you on a huge big road, so wide fat with so many folks ambulating, til one by one, they leave you or you leave them, and you trablin' alone again. For some, the road long, but it's direct, and for others, well, they got to turn back. The Almighty say, 'You ain't done yet!' The Lord return you to the living with a new job, and then you got to find your away again." She props the rag doll against the pillow and presses two fingers to its lips. "Death be the most alone business there is. When we get lost, hope and faith all we got to guide us. You got to stay the road. Hope is God. Faith is God. You feel that, you feeling God. Not some man pie high in the sky."

"Do you?"

"Do I what, child?"

"Do you know if there is a Home?"

"Like I say, I hope to be heaben bound, once my work is done."

I frown and bunch my lips. "What about dogs?"

"What about them?"

"Do they go to heaven?"

"I don't see why not. Animals got souls. Never met one that don't. What do you think, Mr. Brando, you gon be heaben bound?"

Brando wags his tail.

"You got your answer, child," Willie Mae says, stroking Brando's head. This makes me glad.

"Willie Mae?"

"Hmm?"

"Are you God?"

Willie Mae is quiet, and then she laughs big and loud. Her smile climbs out and fans across her face. "Now, wouldn't that be something if God was an old black woman. I'd like that very much. No, I ain't the Lord," she says. "But we off track. I want you to think now and push your fears aside. The girl at the window—what did she look like?"

I close my eyes and look at the pictures in my mind. "She wore a white dress and had lots of ribbons in her hair."

"Thank you, child, thank you very much," she says, although I do not know why.

"Willie Mae, why do you glow?"

"Do I still glow?" she says, with a funny sadness in her voice. "That nice to know," she says. "It ain't something I can explain, but it's there, protective and fierce—like mother love for a child."

She lumbers to the door. "Let's us have a snack and get you to bed, been a harrowing night for all."

We follow Willie Mae to the big room. We climb onto the sofa and sit as she lights a new fire.

From INSTRUCTIONS TO MARSHALS AND ASSISTANT MARSHALS U.S. CENSUS, 1850 QUESTIONNAIRE

Explanation of The Schedules

Schedule No. 1—Free Inhabitants.

3. Under heading 3, entitled *"The name of every person whose usual place of abode on the 1st day of June, 1850, was in this family,"* insert the name of every free person in each family, of every age, including the names of those temporarily absent, as well as those that were at home on that day. . . . Indians not taxed are not to be enumerated in this or any other schedule.

6. Under heading 6, entitled *"Color,"* in all cases where the person is white, leave the space blank; in all cases where the person is black, insert the letter B; if mulatto, insert M. It is very desirable that these particulars be carefully regarded.

Schedule No. 2—Slave Inhabitants.

1. Under heading 1, entitled *"Name of slaveholders,"* insert, in proper order, the names of the owner of slaves. Where there are several owners to a slave, the name of one only needs to be entered, or when owned by a corporation or trust estate, the name of the trustee or corporation.

5. Under heading 5, entitled *"Color,"* insert in all cases, when the slave is black, the letter B; when he or she is mulatto, insert M. The color of all slaves should be noted.

WILLIE MAE COTTON

I COME INTO THIS WORLD.

They called her Easter. Her real name I never did know.

The force of her water was an ocean, a regular gush of brine, and out I slid as slippery as a goatfish and just as wide-eyed, born along the Oconee River in a cotton field at cotton-picking time. A granny woman fixed her up good, and she was back toting baskets fore the sun reprised. Mother was stronger than ten oxen, and that was just her mind. Unless she needed, she didn't speak, and I grew up thinking her voice chafed her cords or burned her throat the way she pained when she used it. I clung to any word that fell from her lips.

"Nyam, nyam!" Eat!

"A wohkoh!" Come quick!

"Tie 'e mout'!" Hush, stop talking!

When they weren't catching babies, them granny women worked in the spinning house, pedaling their wheels and talking steady, carding four cuts of thread a day. The overseer was a white man with well-built shoulders, and he'd lay on the lashes if they weren't done by sundown, but most of them grannies never fell short.

They never quit fat-mouthing, neither, not even when I come in with a mess of fresh-ginned cotton: "Who do she think she is with all that coral, gold, and glass under her head rag? Don't she know she got to tie her hair and train it right? I'd like to burn that curl out with lye myself. She too bigheaded, that saltwater negro."

From the way they were looking at me with everything but their eyes, I knew they were smacking Mother around again.

"How long she been on this farm?" ask a rented granny, not with us a week herself that summer and already acting like head bee. Round her neck she wore a copper tag that say who owned her and the county she from, making her a badge-holding slave, the fearsome kind with her comings and goings from place to place and on her own, seeing how other folks, negro and white, got public and private done. She had opinions, she had knowledge, and she had thoughts for trade and influence.

Course, I never should of done what I done next, but show me a child that knows to be wise and keep her chest of love firm locked.

"How old is that one?" ask a skinny granny, chinning her whiskers at me.

"I'm born in 1845," I say real loud, dropping my burden basket, too mad and too proud to keep my peace another day longer, meaning to show off, meaning to put them in their place for down-talking my mother, touching the tip of each finger, counting, counting, each one a year, until I got to 1853. "Eight," I say. I wasn't just good at figuring, I was a damn talent and intended them to know it.

All them eyes busy looking at everything but me shot at my fingertips. "Don't you never do that again," say the granny who cut my birth cord, the lines around her lips bunching ugly. "Don't you never." She far-reached from her seat and swatted my hands down.

Just fore sundown that day, right after the blast of the driver's horn, this very same granny grabbed at my elbow and towed me round the side of the mess building, away from the other youngsters swarming for the twilight meal.

"Tell me," she hiss. A glare that could singe the eyebrows off your face she fixed on me. "You tell me who's teaching you."

You would of sold your right arm to save your friend or sold your friend's right arm to save yourself on that farm, never knowing which person you were til the time come.

I kept my tongue still, my eyes on the gin house, where folks were pouring out, their sacks of cotton weighed, and I strained for a glimpse of Mother among the hands steady flowing across the yard.

"You keep it that way. You keep your mouth shut," say granny-who-cut-my-birth-cord, hunching low over me. She stank the way she always did, like something that needed burying a long time ago. "And you tell Enoch, you tell him he better mind who he's teaching and who knows about it. There's folks envious of his station," by which she meant manservant in the big house. "If we were on speaking terms, I'd warn him myself. So you keep your learning to yourself. For both your sake."

She say she seen me in her dreams, and I was gon find myself in the Promised Land one day, but I ain't gon stay. I was gon swing low and carry folks over the River Jordan, was gon carry trablers home in my chariot, so I better do as she say. I didn't argue, for granny-who-cut-my-birth-cord was a powerful conjurer. She could see your future and you didn't cross her, and if you did, well, you best guard your toenail clippings, your strands of loosed hair, your undergarments line-drying, even your own shit, for she'd lay her tricks against you using whatever you got that's personal. I promised to keep my mouth tight, though I wasn't sure about driving no chariot, and she let me go. Lucky for me. But lucky for granny too, for Mother was more than halfway across the yard, barreling past Auntie Sparemade tending the grub kettles when granny quick-slipped away.

Enoch Golden was a tripled-headed negro, meaning he could sum, read, and write. A courteous man. A kind man. Gaunt, but was he spry! We would sit on a low bench outside my cabin, old Enoch talking Bible. He spoke of the New Testament and say it got *four* gospelers: Mr. Matthew, Mr. Mark, Mr. Luke, and Mr. John. He say Jesus story got *three* parts: living, dying, and redemption. He say Mother got *two* beautiful eyes and she the *one* for him. He smiled when he say that and rubbed his beard all smattered with gray. And then he worked them numbers into the grit with a whittled pointer, showing how addition was like multiplying loaves and subtraction like dividing the sea. He roomed in the back of Marse Tom's big house, alone in a slim closet next to the pantry, but when he talked words and numbers, the expanse of him was infinite.

Once I took a dare from a house girl about my own age: I crept up to the big house, close enough to see the paint scabbing off its sorry frame. Marse owned better than one hundred folks, all them working solid hard, but fixing cracks, he didn't care for those kinds of details. Not when you couldn't see them from far away. From far way the house was fine, more than large, mashing down on you with its one-two-three sagging stories and its winding wraparound, where the whites had time to sit and rock in the cooling shade and watch the day poke by. When I looked in, old Enoch nodded to me from the inside, curt and erect with one hand under a silver server, nothing like his teaching self.

Everybody knew granny-who-cut-my-birth-cord blamed Mother for turning Enoch's head. Granny been counting on Enoch for herself, and she been campaigning for quite some time. She was a double-sad woman whose husband long been sold off, along with her children, and her days were filled with nothing but cotton and catching. Don't matter how much folks sought her wisdom or her mojos, don't matter she was the great queen granny woman, the master hoo-dooer, she had an ache for love, the one thing she couldn't muster. No anvil dust mixed with sugar and a double pinch of salt, no graveyard dirt or dried rattle-snake head would bring him to her door. I'm saying her heart was cracked by the lack of Enoch and her pride shamed by Mother being a foreign negro and half Enoch's age and everybody knowing her love charms don't work.

But I must of rattled them good the day of my big show, for none of them granny women never said no more about Mother, least not in front of me. Course, by the time they quit their loose talk, my mother's story already been knitted right into my head without her ever telling me.

Stolen from the Lion Mountains, my mother already was a mother to five daughters and one son fore a band of pirates snatched her from her tribe. Took six of them freebooters to pin her. One lost an eye.

She left the Windward Coast in an iron coffle, smuggled below in the hold of a slaver ship. Three moons sloughed as she sailed across the Great Waters.

In Charleston, a Beaufort planter bought her on the sly.

She ran away and hid under the mangrove swamps.

They hunted her down til she was found. The planter whipped her with a rawhide quirt and seasoned her blisters with pepper and salt. But Mother didn't quit, no sir. The next time, she paid for it with an earlobe. Took three years of her smarting up, learning that old-world-new-world speak she spoke that even the grannies knew wasn't no Africa but wasn't no gibberish neither, listening to what folks say about the seasons, the territory, how far the pat-tyrollers circled out, til again she ran off, getting as far as the Edisto this time, where she jumped into that slow-moving black-water river, riding past cypress and tupelo swamps. Her plan was to wash right out into the Atlantic. She didn't want no Ohio River, no Canada, no drinking-gourd-big-dipper, no moss growing on the north side of the tree, no ciphering which house got the Friends and which house don't. Mother didn't want none of that. She wanted her home, her children, and her life, and if she couldn't have it, she'd rather join her ancestors, a dead soul free better than a living one caught.

Instead of the ocean, she wound down a channel to a dried-up stink marsh. She slept in the reeds and when she woke, she was staring up at two pattyrollers matching a drawing on a flyer to her wide-like-mine eyes and the scars around them—high markings of the home she come from. I loved them scars, smooth and raised. They dressed up her face, the music of a glory song.

Them pattyrollers sniffed her and then they did her, and the planter sold her, and so she goes from winnowing rice in South Carolina to double-fisting cotton in Georgia.

When I come along, Marse Tom Darling was delirious seeing how he got two for the price of one. Marse was a cardplayer and he worshipped bargain almost as much as he loved luck.

If you weren't "wild or refractory"—if you never gave Marse lip or dragged your feet, never looked him in the eye too long or not long enough, never cried or laughed too ha-ha hard, never showed pleasure in the honeybee air of a bee-buzzing summer, never refused to take up with who he say, and if you didn't pick fights, run off, gather in numbers too great, destroy his crops, thief his shoats, malinger, get dead-dog tired or die before he say it was alright—he granted you a scratch of land to grow whatever you could in whatever time you didn't have left. We called it Lower Town, the place we lived, a double string of log cabins behind the big house, surrounded by a grove of crown-rounded buckeye. Our place was simple. It had a hole in the wall where a window would of done nicely. Rats used it as a door. We had no floorboards, but a dirt floor gets hard and smooth if you know how to pack it right. Mother did.

Folks did the best they could, minding their scrawny patches of Gethsemane, broadcasting ash from their fire pits over the tater ground, shooing the flea bugs away, making do, making do.

Either way, despite the best efforts of those who give a damn, it was squalor.

This how it was, the way of loving.

Mother kept me fed.

With a single look, she could stop a hand from swiping my portion of greens or fried salt meat. She gave me the coon off her own plate, for it was more delicate than possum and the hair didn't funk up the meat.

Mother kept me clean.

She picked the crust from the corners of my eyes with her finger and spit. She rubbed cornmeal into my head and rinsed it with larkspur tea to keep it free from ringworm and nits. On hair-doing day, I sat lodged between her knees as she undid my plaits, never mind my complaining as she ran the card's metal teeth through my frizzled locks. With tabs of sweet butter she oiled my scalp and dabbed elbows, my knees and my feet, rubbing shine back into my rust. And when she finished weaving my hair, she kissed the nape of my neck, every tender-headed spot. I knew bad hair was what I got, that good hair was straight and thin, yellow the best, but Mother say to stop up my mouth, my hair was no shame.

Mother kept me dressed.

Marse made you earn your togs, and you had to make them last. When my shimmy tore, Mother fought back with a bold needle and heavy quilting thread. If she needed a patch, it come off her own dress. No way her child was running around with holes in her garb or half naked.

Now, socks were another matter. They ain't immortal no matter how you try to resurrect them, and the first day of my ninth year I woke up to find Mother had turned her only pair into a doll baby. And when Miss Katie Darling, Marse's wife, gave Mother scraps from a gay red calico, ha! That doll baby had a dress better than me.

Lord, how my dolly scared the other children. They thought she would gnash them up with her teeth. Mother didn't have any time to sew them round and neat, see. And I knew dolly was ugly—she had no ears, no nose, no hair, no lint to grace her head, nothing but the thread outline of her eyes. Them teeth zigzagged jagged white across her bold black face, and her red mouth gaped. But I loved her, this thing my mother made just for me.

Two months after she come, rented granny left us. She say she was heading back to her marse, but she looked too damn chirpy for it to be true.

A day later, the horn blew double.

We dropped our file, our hammer, our pick, our glut, our tongs, our chisels, our wedges; we doused the fires and quit our baking, put down our brooms and our shining cloths; we stabled the geldings and the fillies, the jacks and the jinnies, and penned the swine, the heifers, and the calves. All us come running from all directions, all us gathered in a round, from house servants to field hands, from smithies to coopers, from tanners to stonemasons, sawyers, founders, and wheelwrights. Every last one of us, from little ones to middle ones to the full-growns, including the grannies, filled the yard knowing what the double horn meant. Someone was in trouble. One of us was about to get messed.

From folks which-ing and why-ing under their breath I tweezed words out of the tangle and tried to stitch together some sense: Who's getting it? What did you hear? Something been stolen? We don't need no trouble. We got plans. Ain't about that. How do you know? Who you been talking to? She say what? That snitch. They say this dancing in place to keep from freezing.

Snap come the crack of a whip, and folks tied their lips.

The overseer led the march, followed by Enoch, his hands bound, his ankles shackled. The snake-eyed driver shoved him in the back.

Next come Marse, swaggering into the yard and shaking a book over his head. "I bring you the alpha and the omega," he say, pursing his lips, warming up his fiction. I shrank into Mother. She pushed me off. "*Wa gal wa, oonah stan' tall. Don' onrabble.*" Come, girl, come, you stand tall. Don't be scared, she say.

Mother didn't know about my learning.

Marse flipped his book open and stumped a greasy finger to the parchment. When he looked down, a grin broke out on his face like he wrote them words himself and he was real proud. He say, "Why don't we have Enoch read it for himself?"

"'Wherefore if thy hand or thy foot offend thee, cut them off, and cast them from thee: it is better for thee to enter into life halt or maimed, rather than having two hands or two feet to be cast into everlasting fire,'" read old Enoch, Enoch with hands trembling, his face a sad sorrow, tears slipping down his wrinkled cheeks, weeping with joy, holding a tome he ain't held for the longest, reading the teachings of Jesus with his very own eyes, and maybe for the last time. He held his head with dignity. That is, til the overseer knocked him down, and then old Enoch was so low he was breathing dust off the ground.

Marse ordered Enoch to lay his right arm over the block.

"Marse Tom," say Enoch, his voice real soft, as the driver untied him.

"Someone else care to offer his arm in your stead?" say Marse, like he was making a genuine offer. Mother pulled solid on the back of my collar just as granny-who-cut-my-birth-cord stepped from our ring. Marse laughed. "Get back in line, you old nigger."

The driver wrenched Enoch's arm over the block.

Then there she was, Miss Katie Darling, raising revolution and lathering into the yard, urging Marse to "belay his order," saying Enoch was her faithful servant and friend, reminding Marse he was a gift from her father. "Desist!" Marse say. Her voice was "the buzzing drone of a one-note hurdy-gurdy," and he would not allow her dowry to infect the rest of his property. He ordered Miss to the big house, but she only swallowed gulps of the cold air and begged him to reconsider. "'Tisn't his fault that he is learned," and you could tell she was straining for a sweeter note. She say it was her own daddy, may he rest in peace, who had done it: When Solomon and Enoch were youngsters, he'd taught Enoch the Word of the Lord Almighty, creator of heaven and earth, and Enoch become his first convert. That inside Enoch was her father's loving kindness, some Other who bore witness to and held the memories of her past. Then she got low-down on her knees and pressed her hands together, pleading with the Lord to "spare Uncle Enoch from the barbarism of my husband."

Marse say, "Go back inside."

"He is not yours to mutilate," she say.

Marse's nose flared. And then he slapped her.

Our eyes shot to our feet. He did it to shame her in front of us and we knew it. But Marse wasn't getting what he wanted: The slap only trenched her deeper. "You will not harm him," she say. "No, you won't." Nothing, not even her lips trembled.

Maybe one of us wanted to jerk her to her feet and say, "Miss, you only gon get yourself beat." Maybe another hoped to see it. Either way, not one of us moved.

The overseer stood over the miss. He say, "Let's get along, ma'am, and let Mr. Darling do what he needs." He reached down and took her by the arm, but she yanked it away.

Marse lifted his hat and ran his fingers through his barely there red hairs. Then he rubbed his mouth. He bent over the miss and say, "If you don't go, I will kill him myself."

All us took a step back, small enough not to be seen by anyone but us, our souls edging away while our bodies stayed put. And Miss began to shake. She ain't gon cry, no she ain't, you can see it in her face all that holding back, and she looked over at Enoch, who wasn't looking at her, just holding his head steady as he knelt next to the block.

Miss Katie say, rising to her feet slow, "And if you do I shall take you to court. I will bring a bill of complaint against you tallying every detail of cruel punishment you have ever dispensed, every law you have broken, including the destruction of my property. Then we'll see what you'll have left of your precious estate."

"Now, Katie," Marse say with a laugh. "Lester," he say, and the overseer grabbed Miss and started hauling her off.

"You shan't treat me as an unruly child," Miss Katie shouted at Marse, and then her face come awake, like someone just dealt her the card she been long waiting for. She stopped fighting the overseer, and say dead quiet, "No, I am your wife. And your child is in that house. Where I presume you wish him to remain in residence with his loving mother."

Thomas Darling, Jr., Marse and Miss's only child, was nearing two years. I'd seen him nursing at the tit of a house girl. He was the spitting image of Marse: Both had fat pink lips and a head starving for hair.

"You're shaming yourself," Marse say through his teeth.

But we all knew she was shaming him with her outburst and cheek.

He strutted over to Miss, Marse did, and bent his head down. The brim of his hat hid both their faces. "Behave," we heard him hiss.

We watched Miss and Marse low-talking, the overseer hovering next to Marse. Just a few feet from them, old Enoch stayed rigid on his knees beneath the snake-eyed driver. Never thinking Miss Katie could possibly win, we pocketed our hands and shuffled our feet, fighting to keep what was left of our heat, rubbing at nipped earlobes and noses, folks wanting this show over, to go back to work and warm up. We weren't heartless folk. Just folks needing to save ourselves.

And then Miss Katie stepped back from Marse. "You shan't kill him," she slow say.

"Right." Marse's voice was flat, and you could see Miss trying to read if he was lying.

"You will leave his arm intact."

"Agreed."

"I think I hear little Tom calling me," Miss say, even if the only sound around us was our own breath, and with that, she left.

But Marse was a capricious man, one who didn't care to have his might watered down by his missus.

Once she rounded the big house, he nodded to the driver, who forced Enoch's palm to the block. Marse say Enoch should be grateful—he was getting off cheap, only one finger for each sin. The overseer walked over with the hatchet.

"They were on loan to you, Enoch, you know that," say Marse.

I flinched with each chop, keeping my eyes steady closed.

Course, old Enoch and I never did no more learning. And he didn't come courting Mother no more, neither. He been broke too many damn times.

One night not long after, Mother was rocking restless beside me on the pallet, something chewing her mind. Her eyes were red like she been weeping, but Mother didn't weep. She had a look like she was scared, but Mother never been that. I hugged dolly, not knowing what to do, when Mother pressed two fingers to my lips.

"*Oonuh,*" she say. You.

"*Daa'tuh,*" she say. Daughter.

"*Swit,*" she say. Delicious.

Two years passed.

In April, we planted. By June, cotton blossomed. Come August, the heat made the boll expand and burst open. No more chopping or picking trash, no more toting baskets—I was a field hand now. I waded into the cotton long fore the sun boiled up. With a burlap sack slung over my shoulder, I plucked the white fluff and worked steady: ten years old and I could pick a hundred and fifty pounds by noon. Fear moved my feet. It didn't matter the dry husk pricked my fingers, it didn't matter I got a cramp in my side, a crimp in my foot, or the boll was stubborn and only half open—I pulled cotton. Sweat dribbled from my underarms, it welled in my collarbone, it trickled down my spine, my body wringing every last bit of water out.

A person can survive even when they afraid all the time, but terror is one thirsty thief. He takes his toll, he's crafty, he spreads his wings wide and soars across the sky and you don't hear a thing. He's blind, but he'll find you, he got a fabulous sense of smell, and when he do, he will drink you in, drop by drop.

But then, terror a cursed fellow. He ain't never satisfied.

The second week of August was the alpha and omega for me. From the fields we saw Colonel Samuel Bounds approach in his wagon drawn by two high-stepping Arabians. They come up the wide drive, Colonel Bounds as fancy as usual in his linen duster cutaway and long white tails, his wife flounced in lilac silk. Perfect yellow ringlets covered her ears, her bitty head capped in a steeple-crowned hat. That Miss Emmaline was as pasty as a bisque dolly. Nervous too, the way she fanned herself, like a hummingbird crazing around her head.

Colonel Bounds was Miss Katie's brother, but they weren't tight, so went the chatter on the farm. It was Miss Katie who come flying out of the big house, hot pepper in her step, guiding Miss Emmaline up the stairs like those two were closest of sisters.

The next morning, they made a table of four and the cards began to flow.

In the game of hearts, a player got to avoid winning tricks containing hearts, for each heart got one penalty point attached to it. None of the other cards got value, only the queen of spades, and if you get her, you in trouble, for she worth a whole load of penalty points. Discarding a heart called breaking hearts.

If you get all thirteen hearts and the queen of spades, you shooting the moon.

Means you win.

Later that day, Enoch come huffing into the fields. He say for me to go with him. I knew if I didn't keep up with the other hands, Marse Tom would sell me right off the farm. But old Enoch wore a face that meant business, so I dropped my sack. I saw Mother ten rows up, and she was looking right at me, and then at Enoch, and then at the driver up on his horse. He flicked his snaky eyes and made a motion with his head for me to go.

Old Enoch scratched his beard with the two fingers left on that hand. "Don't you tarry," he say.

Marse Tom stood in the yard with Colonel Bounds. He clapped Colonel on the back and say, "Her mother's a field nigger, a real workhorse, good with the hoe, splits rails like a man. This here is her only offspring, but she's just as hearty. Homely, but her mother's even worse. Darker than rabbit turd. Now, you'll find her demeanor supple, reared her entire life on my farm."

Colonel Bounds frowned.

"She's one of my best. Those hips will broaden when she ripens in another season or two," Marse say with a smile.

Colonel Bounds crooked a finger under my chin. He was a slim man with a large head that shielded me from the sun. He pinched my jaw open and rubbed my gums. He prodded my ribs.

I froze, scared spitless.

"She'll do, Tom, she'll do."

Turned out Colonel Bounds had shot the moon and his prize was me.

A house girl brought out a tray of sweet tea.

I saw Mother running. Her eyes so wide I could see the crazy in them.

She was running and tripping and running.

The earth failing beneath her feet.

Her arms flailing through the air.

She was screaming. She was screaming, "*De gal, she b'long tuh me, she b'long tuh me!*" She beat her chest.

"A wild one," say Colonel Bounds.

"The mother," say Marse, sipping his cooling drink.

The driver chased after Mother, hard-heeling his horse. He reached down and grabbed at her, but all he got was her head rag, and now Mother was a blaze of coral, gold, and glass. Then he jumped. He slammed her down and pitched his spur into her neck.

I ran for her, but Marse caught me by the wrist, and his grip was as good as shackled.

He say if I go with Colonel Bounds he'll spare Mother, but if I stayed, he'd shut her in the nigger box. Which did I choose? His eyes smirked, and I knew he wasn't offering me no real choice. Not with the overseer ripping open the back of Mother's dress. Dragging her to the strapping log and wrenching her arms over her head. Unleashing his bullwhip.

And I bawled and screamed for the onliest person who loved me.

A person got to wonder at the misery one human being inflict upon another. Got to wonder what the Lord intended.

Enoch Golden had his Father, Son, and Holy Ghost. Mother prayed to her ancestors.

I worshipped at the feet of Mother.

Her back all shredded. No one hiding his face at her pain.

I crawled inside all that red and closed my mother back up.

That night, I curled next to her in the sick cabin.

She didn't move, and no one come to tend her. She didn't wake neither, when I left our pallet in the morning.

Nothing is hopeless when you a child.

I kept pace behind Colonel's wagon, burning each turn into my memory—like this bridge got five knotholes in the treading and stink of horse piss, and that one got a long window cutout where I could see a string of white boys all lined up. At the end of their fishing lines, green gray frogs—ever so small—skittered across the water surface. I pitied them croakers, all tied up.

But the world got to be so far wide it set my head spinning dizzy like I was a tin pump top and the outdoors a carnival of colors. The sun was boring a mean hole into the top of my head—Marse sent me off in nothing but my shimmy—and after a long while, I couldn't keep from slugging my feet. Miss Emmaline say they would never make it in one night at that rate—she wasn't looking to camp and she hated to sleep in a foreign bed, so Colonel made room for me in the wagon.

Burlap and straw never felt so good.

Miss Emmaline offered me a dram of water and then some cornbread coddled in a clean pink towel. The smell of fry bacon so savory hit my nose the instant she unfolded its swaddling cloth, showing that cornbread off like she was so damn proud of its butter color, holding the loaf like a newborn, and I swear she was humming a lullaby. I admired it for her but fought the urge to take a piece. I didn't want nothing off her.

She shrugged her dainty shoulders and stared at me with eyes like broken china, shattered blue and white.

"Suit yourself," she say. "We still have a long way to go."

And she was right. The road turned from flint gray to rubble brown to soft red clay, mountains rose, the air chilled, and trees with blue quills—the likes of which I'd never seen before—narrowed the causeway.

By the time we got to the colonel's, everything was slathered in shadows but the big house. It burned bright with candles in every window, and I marveled at what kind of magic this colonel worked that his tallow didn't stink of rotten feet.

A burst of folks come running to help Miss Emmaline from the wagon. Colonel handed his hat to a servant and left, nobody saying nothing to me. I sank my chin over my knees and got to work on my mapping. Oh, I panged something terrible for Mother, but I was gon find my way back, and I found comfort in every river—this one with the tree of songbirds, that one running wild with brown foam—pasting them together, river to bridge, road to river, the bridge with the cutout, the one with the stink, only to find a panic slow sweeping me. I had a river running upstream when it should of been running down, a road turning east that should of gone south. I was missing more than one bridge, more than one crossroad.

I had no idea where I was and no way back.

My stomach twisted and I gagged. Green—nothing but—come up, my throat stinging from all that empty.

What a hard thing to rememory. This child, my child, my mother.

I didn't shed no tears on the trip and I wasn't gon start now, so when this ginger-cake face come running at me wearing shoes so shiny they kicked up the candlelight and trousers without a single patch, a boy swinging his lantern like he was Mr. Jaunty or somebody, and he say, "I'm Alger, and I'm to show you where you live," I just let him tuck his hands under my arms and help me out.

"You don't weigh a thing," he say in a voice that cracked.

We went along a brick path around the side of the big house and into the back courtyard. Mr. Jaunty say, "This way," and waved his light at a small community of weatherboarded places. They were one-roomers, looked like, wood shingled with raised-up porches, stone slab chimneys, and windows shuttered closed. Each one had a garden patch of green peas and pole beans, corn, and potherbs.

"Who stays there?" I say.

"You do," he say.

I just stood staring at them quaint houses, all six of them with light spilling out of the shutter slats. When Mr. Jaunty saw I wasn't with him no more, he come jogging back.

He raised his hand. I jumped away. But he only say, "Hey," soft like, and plucked a blade of straw from my plaits. He tossed it casual and it floated away.

I looked him in the eye for the first time, this boy with a frame aiming for manhood but with a face caught in between—it was a balance of pleasing, you might say, if you liked eyebrows that peacocked blue black and oily, a chin marred with tiny carbuncles, and a top lip smudged with some sad fuzz he probably took for a mustache.

A horse nickered and another grunted. In the stable a groom was rubbing down the Arabians. "Manasseh and Ephraim," Mr. Jaunty say, nudging his chin their direction. "You have any belongings?" Then he looked sorry for asking, so I didn't bother telling him what he already knew.

He took off toward one of them quaint houses, and I trailed after him when all of a sudden my skin broke out into a sweat, and I'm bending over, cramping up inside like I'm a snuff pan filled with grease and fire lit.

"What's wrong?" say Mr. Jaunty, and I tell him I got the urge powerful bad. He grabbed my hand. We ran to the outhouse directly, but I soiled myself fore I ever got inside.

I sunk to the ground full of something—shame most likely, followed by defeat, as Mr. Jaunty and his lantern sped off.

When he come back, he was lugging a bucket of water and holding out a brown soap. He gave me my modesty while I scrubbed.

A flavor so frightful coated the inside of my mouth and I wasn't sure if it was anger, or hate, or rage, and who at.

Next thing I know I got this woman standing over me, telling me to stand up. She toweled me dry—not rough, but efficient—and tugged a homespun dress over my head. She say she was the housekeeper. She wore a head rag, knotted high and tight, and it pulled my eye up. And I do mean up. That woman soared treetop tall. She led me inside one of them quaint houses where two double-deckers lined either side.

I don't memory falling asleep in the bunk she showed me, and I got no idea how long I been out, but when I wake I'm shuddering with cold and sweltering with heat. From the way folks look at me, I'm certain I'm gon die.

Faces swarming over me saying, "You got a plague of miseries, gal" and "You got to sup this" and "What are they thinking, putting her in here?" Someone greasing my chest with turpentine and camphor and rubbing thick scoops of menthol jelly into my back til the soreness passes into a dull throb. Spoonfuls of hot water and vinegar pouring into my mouth and voices saying, "You got to keep this down," while others whisper, "Breakbone fever" and "She done for." Teas of boneset and butterfly root keep me soaked in sweat, and a pair of hands swab my body with cool rags. Balmony, queen's delight, life everlasting. Someone doctoring me, and I don't know who—my eyes won't lift—they sealed shut—and I pray they stay that way.

The room mum as a water snake cutting downstream. Outside, tree frogs trilling something high-pitch and eerie. Nighttime. Someone tossing on the bunk above me. Another one snoring. A breeze as soft as a ballad rustles my sheet, and a woman sits in a chair next to my bed.

She say, "*Oonuh* forget" or maybe "Don't *oonuh* forget." Hard to tell, her voice so raw.

Mother.

She presses two fingers to my lips and nods at me like she sure of something now, though I don't know what. The grief in her eyes cuts like a noose around my neck and it's too much, I can't breathe. I shut my eyes and quake. I got joy flooding out my sockets, my throat, my nose, I'm so happy to see her and so terrible sad, and when I open them, Mother's gone, but I know she coming back for me, I know she knows where I'm at. After all, she left my doll baby right there on the chair.

"Psst." It come from afar, from behind my ear, or not at all.

My lids lifted, weightless. The death damps were gone, and I felt clean and fresh, like I always imagined the baptizers in Marse Tom's pond felt after they got sprinkled. I breathed free, only to draw in one foul stench. Woooo, how that room odored and the walls sweated. It was the dank fester of us gals sleeping in air too damn heavy and still.

"Who that?" I say, my voice husky.

I listened to the women in their cots, slumbering still, slumbering deep. From one corner, light snoring, from above me, dream talk.

"Psssst!"

Wasn't delirium or incantation, no sir, I was fully awake, clearheaded, and sure it was blowing in from the outside. I planted my feet on a puncheon floor. Been down long enough they'd softened some—and I caught a splinter in my sole. Sometimes pain is sweet.

Now, this morning I'm talking about was the first time I ever noticed the glow—*my* glow. There weren't no lanterns burning, no candles neither, but the room sure did brim with silver. It was an unearthly color. Made me uneasy, the way it dogged me: I stepped here, it stepped here, I stepped there, it stepped there. I tried to outwit it, but it kept on following me with its dazzle. Found myself thinking maybe I'm a haint, I ain't really alive. But when I caught another of them damn splinters—in my main toe this time—that sure brought me to my senses. Sometimes pain just pain.

Still, all that silver was making my head tingle, and I didn't take kindly to the inconvenience. What was Colonel Bounds gon do with a slave who glowed? Don't nobody need that. I grabbed a blue madras handkerchief hanging from a peg and tied a turban. Near as I could tell, the silver didn't leak.

"Pssssssssssst!"

I was gon find the creature culling me from my bunk with it sneaky sound. And I was gon do it fore the whole place began rising, fore the overseer bugled his horn, without no one catching me. There was a dark blue dawn sitting on a mountain ridge, but no sun yet. Mist swirled around the grounds, rising in plumes and disappearing. Scared me a little, the way they looked like ghostly creatures, all hazy and animated, but I didn't let it stop me. I passed the work buildings and the big house. No candles burning now. Too early for whites. Hoo, if I had a place like that—wood framed with green shutters and painted hello-yellow like someone gave a damn—I wouldn't get up til long after dawn neither. Nothing flaking off like Marse Tom's place, but it was smallish, with only two floors. Scattered along the porch were rocking chairs and log benches for all that sitting the white folks did. Flowers grew everywhere, like someone was suiting this place up with life: morning glory on the trelliswork, giant moonflowers on the columns, honeysuckle on the lattice under the porch, and all along the front a rose garden. Not just any old rose garden, either, but roses so pale pink they were almost white, each one the size of an infant's fist but with a scent so strong it was big-man punchy, enough to knock you flat. To my right, fields of tobacco grew bushy and fat. And up on a hill a herd of stout brown sheep with droopy necks was napping standing up. Handsome critters, sheep. Beneath the hill, the moon wavered across a pond. I heard a cow lowing. Found it peaceful. And then something took over me, I got snappy in my feet, and I'm heading down the drive lined with dogwoods, running for the two log gates. I got this feeling in my knees, all hollow like, and now I'm standing outside the gate. I'm shaking, the feeling in my knees so bad. I'm daring these legs to stand it. I take a step forward and then another. My whole body starts to go, and just as I'm about to fall apart, I pull myself back inside the gate.

Can't know what free feels like when you never been it.

I didn't know what to make of my short-lived fugitive state, wondering if I had my mother's running blood inside me, scared of what it meant, for all of mother's running led to nothing but defeat. With the first rays breaking over the mountain, I dragged my shaking self back to my quarters.

"Pssssssssssst!"

It was coming from inside the kitchen house, a two-roomer with gray and white smoke flying from a stone chimney. The top of a head and two oily eyebrows popped above the windowsill, and then I knew who was hiding below, pestering me. Mr. Jaunty.

I made it to my door just as a shrill cry sliced through me. This big banty was strutting along the roof of the kitchen, prancing back and forth, his neck straining, his red wattle and comb shaking. Lord, I still distaste them tuneless birds. Anyway, Mr. Jaunty didn't make his sneaky sound no more, not with the housekeeper shooing him and his eyebrows away from the window with the snap of a towel.

The overseer stepped out blowing on a ram's horn.

He shouted, "Wake up!"

Folks called back, "We is."

This overseer was a stout but powerful built man who walked with a hitch, one leg shorter than the other. He rubbed his face like he just rolled out of bed, and his body looked it too, the way his braces hung slack from his waist and his nightshirt flapped out of his trousers.

I'll confidence you what else I saw. He didn't come shuffling from his own house, no sir. He come clean out of the housekeeper's.

Inside my quarters, the four women yawned and scratched, brushed their teeth with spearmint bark, and washed their grimaces in face bowls.

"Morning, gal."

"Sure good to see you awake."

"Welcome to the living."

This was what the women say.

The older three rustled about wriggling quick into a grand heap of clothes. Woo, real fancy garb! Stockings and garters and knee-length flannelettes, stiff petticoats and bind-up bodices, each one looping buttons up the back of the next, finishing off with high-necked dresses. They were jewel-winged damselflies, these gals, sunshiny amber and stirring alive. Over all that fuss they tied white aprons. I judged them relations, close in age but none the same, each one a forecast of how the next one might look. The fourth gal got ready on her own. She wasn't no bright yellow and she wasn't no delicate. She wasn't no woman, neither. She was a youngster like me. Shifty looking. Skinny. Gap-toothed. A runt.

Now the house girls on Marse Tom's farm, they sure were a standoffish lot, and here I was right in the middle of a covey.

I got to say, they weren't nothing but civil, the tallest one saying, "I'll tell Miss Lossie you're alive," and then those three look-alikes filed out, followed by the runt, who blinked twice and say all saucy, "That's mine," aiming a thumb at my blue turban.

I folded back a shutter and watched all four bustling up the back of the big house like they were glad to be awake. Can't nobody work off an empty stomach and be happy about it, not even a saucy house girl. Yet no one was walking to the mess hall. There wasn't one, least none that I saw, but my nose wasn't lying. I knew I smelled some swirly-good scents: fried eggs and grease taters and griddle cakes as rich as Christmas oozing out of Marse Tom's place. With each rattling pan and clanking plate, I made a case for folks taking their meals in their own quarters just like the whites.

If that didn't shock.

I began nosing around for something to eat myself, and that's when I saw her. My doll baby, sitting on the chair. It wasn't no dream, no sir, and I clutched her to my breast, my nose shoved into that baldhead.

"Put that down," say the housekeeper, breezing in and towering over me with a face that say, "This my face but it ain't," like she was hiding something deep in the hayrick. She wore a violet shawl tucked into her apron belt and a jumble of keys on a ring that clanged against her thigh as she walked.

She praised my waking state and held out a drinking gourd. "Drink this," she say. As I supped, a glory-hallelujah-rising-sun ran through me, waking my organs and stirring my blood. Hoo, water never tasted so good.

Then she say, "Look up, look down, open your mouth, stick out your tongue, cough." I did everything she say, for I rememoried the touch of this tree-tall woman who was barking at me. She was the one who brought me back to life.

"Once I tell Miss you're awake, she'll want to see you first thing. She's been praying for your recovery. Get that nightdress off. You need a good cleaning." Dry sparks cracked under her shoes as she left.

I wasn't gon argue with no tree-tall woman, specially one who took care of me when I was so bad off. I stripped to my skin. Through the window come the sound of folks bidding each other good day, stable doors swinging open, horses whinnying, chickens clucking, those fussy cocks crowing, even someone laughing in an appreciative way. What I didn't hear was the cracks of a snaky bullwhip and snarls from an ugly-mouthed, pink-faced, pointy-nosed, snake-eyed driver.

When the housekeeper come back, she had an armful of togs and a bucket of steaming water. "Take off that rag," she say and tapped the door closed with her boot.

I thought up excuses, but "I got myself a shine so bright it will blind your eyes" didn't strike me as wise.

"Don't test my patience. I have none," she say.

I took my turban off and held on for her shock.

"Now that wasn't so hard, was it?" She got to work slopping at my neck with a fat yellow sponge. "What are you looking at?" she say, eyeing the ceiling.

"My glow," I say as the light filled the quarters. My head tingled something strong, so I gave it a good scratch.

She sniffed at my scalp. "That's no glow, that's luster. Your hair is dirty."

If she didn't see it, I wasn't gon argue.

She held open a pair of drawers and rolled some stockings up my legs. "You from Marse Darling's farm," she say, like she was trying on casual. Wasn't no question. More like a leak. "You know an Enoch Golden?"

"Yessum."

"And how does he fare?"

"He managing. How you know old Enoch?" I was impressed with the connection, someone knowing Enoch from so far away.

She ignored me, all the while tying a shimmy and petticoat over me, tugging and lacing and finishing me off with a full-length dress and an apron. I was real glad when she fixed a round cap on my head. Though it wasn't as tight as the turban, it stopped my glow from showing up the place.

"Put these on," she say, holding out some ankle boots.

"I never worn nothing on my feet."

"You can't enter the house barefoot. Miss Emmaline will throw a fit if she sees feet."

If that ain't peculiar.

She say for me to sit on the bunk. "Miss tells me you're ten." She shook her head and started lacing up my boot. "I suppose that's one way of keeping a hanky in your pocket. She says your name is Willie Mae."

"Yessum."

"I'm Lossie."

"I don't know nothing about maiding, Miss Lossie."

"You'll learn."

"I pull cotton."

"We don't have cotton. We have bright-leaf tobacco. Now stand."

Them boots were damn big. I didn't walk, I clomped. And all them togs—I couldn't hardly move I was wearing so many, enough for a whole passel of gals. The dress wasn't half bad, if you liked useless, made of nothing I never touched, no cotton, no lowell cloth, no linsey-wool, but something cushy and soft, the color of dried blood. It rustled when I moved, a regular racket, and I could smell someone, the last gal most like. Wasn't a funky odor, but a heavy one. Something woeful sad seeping deep into the fabric. Made my chest hurt.

"Pick up the hem when you walk," say Lossie, "and you won't trip."

Fore we pushed out of that quaint house, she stopped short. "My daddy's well," she say, more to herself than to me, and for a moment, her mask melted off and she was a small girl, not a tall, strong woman.

"Old Enoch your daddy?"

Lossie sucked in something uncivilized, the way heartache can be, and covered her face with a cough. Then she clamped her mask back on and we walked to the back of the house.

Moist, cool earth, the kind that been dry for a spell and newly showered: That ain't how I imagined forbidden to smell. Quiet, so quiet, everything outside a harmless thrum. I was inside a big house for the very first time, and I thought it supreme.

We passed through a scullery into a hall. On the right, Lossie pointed out a parlor and on the left, a drawing room, where she say Miss Emmaline spent her day. Sweating strong under the weight of my costume, I managed to clumsy up this grand staircase, trying to keep up with Lossie as she gusted down a sunlit hallway.

When we got to a carved door with a glass knob, Lossie say, "Don't you forget to curtsy," and rapped.

"Enter," come the voice of Miss Emmaline.

Lord, I never seen so much pink. Never fore, never since. The whole room, just one hellish haze of blush right down to the wallpaper with a pattern so busy it could scare a madman into sanity. Next to a four-poster, Miss Emmaline lay on a lounging chair, her head flung back, her tiny self lost in a mess of frills and lace, one hand limping over the armrest like the garnet ring she was wearing was weighing it down. Her face was as gray as boiled goat meat, and pinched, and her yellow hair was dull. This miss was a wreck.

Lossie cleared her throat. I dropped my head and curtsied.

"That will be all," Miss Emmaline say.

Just me and Miss now.

I curtsied again.

"The server," she say.

I looked over to a bowfront where there was this server piled high with tarts, cakes, sugar, jams, a stack of pink and gold cups and plates, just a whole load of fancy.

"Bring it hither," she say.

The whole server this miss wanted. Not just a biscuit and a plate. Lord.

Now, hauling heavy didn't daunt me, but this was a matter of grace. I grabbed the server, knuckle nervous, and lifted it steady and poked along that wove carpet, kicking my hem out in front of me with them awful boots, praying I didn't trip.

"Set it on the ottoman," say the ghastly miss, tapping on a puffy lump looking more like an oversized pincushion than something proper for your seat. She leaned forward in her lounging chair, shadowing me with her hands, like this was some kind of help.

"You may serve yourself," she say. "Try a *brioche*."

Eating my miss's food in her house with her watching me. Didn't get stranger than that.

"Go on," she say, pushing a plate at me.

I picked up one of them shiny bread buns, my mouth watering as soon as I touched it.

"No, no! Not with your hands," say Miss Emmaline, plopping off her lounging chair and onto the carpet. She curled her legs under her frills and lace and patted the space next to her. "Sit," she say, her lips arching foxy. She draped a linen napkin over my lap and picked up a silver tong. "Butter," she say, "or preserves? Blackberry or blueberry? Or perhaps some orange marmalade? Do you take tea? Sugar or cream?"

I say yes to whatever she got.

Then Miss fed me, breaking off crumbs and buttering each one, insisting I eat from her fingers, the whole time smiling at me with a mouth full of merry and a look more fitting a hawk. And she wasn't the only one watching me. There was an eye blinking at me through the keyhole of the carved door.

"*C'est bon*, is it not," Miss Emmaline say, "to break bread in such a way?"

"Miss?"

"'Tis good?"

I could of hurt that miss, the way she was looking at me like my say-so mattered. "Yessum. Real good," I say instead.

She lifted a gold bell from the server. The eye moved off the keyhole and in come Miss Saucy. She took the tray away, but not fore giving me a look of pity.

About an hour later I was standing in the backyard, filling a pitcher with water from the well. Miss Saucy come over to me and say, "Don't give her any. She'll only pour it on the floor."

"She told me to bring it."

"It's not for drinking," she say and stalked off.

I wasn't taking no orders from that runt instead of my miss, so I brought the pitcher to her chamber, and sure enough she poured it right onto the floor. She opened her mouth and low-toned that puddle like she was chatting with a dear old friend, her face getting soft and gummy. Lord.

In the scullery, I found one of them damselflies, the eldest, and tell her I needed a mop rag, and she say, "Why?" and I say what Miss Emmaline did. And she say Miss was always talking, did she ever, to folks who weren't ever there. That she been doing it ever since she was a child. She say it was best to ignore it. I say, "How you know she ain't talking to someone?" and Eldest say, "All you have to do is look—there isn't anyone there, there isn't." I say, "Maybe you just can't see them." Eldest say nothing, just looked at me queer.

Back in her chamber, Miss wasn't standing over her puddle no more. She was sitting pert on the side of her four-poster, ankles crossed, face pink as her decor, and it wasn't pinched no more. This miss was plum cheery.

That night, I ate with the three gals and the runty one in our quarters.

"You can take that cap off," say the youngest sister, scooping mutton stew and boiled carrots onto my plate, real prime-smelling grub.

"Yes," say the middle one, "why don't you. I've cleared the bottom drawer for you in the chest."

"Let her be," say Eldest. "When she's ready, she'll take it off."

Miss Saucy just big-spooned a carrot into her mouth and looked at me like she knew I was hiding something. When I scratched at my head through my cap, she tongued the gap between her front teeth and scratched at her own head in the exact same place.

"Stop scratching at the table," say Eldest, her watchful eyes on me. Middle say my hair needed washing. Youngest say she would do it come Sunday.

Miss Saucy gap-tooth grinned me like she won a game.

The next day, I did something I never done my whole life. I stole off my mistress. After sundown I didn't go back to my quaint house, no sir. I made for the hill of handsome sheep and over to the pond. Once I got there, I didn't waste no time pulling out Miss Emmaline's garden shears from my apron and taking off my cap. Woo, how my glow kicked out, smacking the blades of the shears and bouncing up. It felt good—all that glow pent up and now it was free. The farther it shot, the more it faded. But there wasn't no time for rejoicing. Like a baby bird it flew right back, resting on my noggin, my very own personal fowl of silver. I ran behind a tree, praying folks were too hard thinking about their empty bellies and tired feet to notice. Then I got to work on my hair, snipping. The only way to keep folks from asking why I never wanted my hair done was to have none to do up. Be simple to keep fresh, now, too. Just give it a good dose of soap and water, just like the men with their hair close cut, which is what I did standing on that shore, scrubbing.

As soon as I got back to my quaint house, I stuffed them plaits in my pillowcase.

That next morning, just as I took them shears out of my apron like they never been gone, Mr. Jaunty come strolling into the garden saying he wanted to introduce himself proper. He took off his cap and say with a low-sweeping bow, "I'm Alger Young. A pleasure to make your acquaintance."

"Nice to greet you, Alger Young. So which one of you is Alger Old?"

"There is no Alger Old." Young was his daddy's name.

"That so?" I say.

"Sure is." He say his daddy was the overseer Riddle Young, he was in charge of running folks, and his mother was Miss Lossie, the housekeeper and cook.

"How come I ain't seen you working in the big house?"

He snorted. "I don't. I'm a boot and shoemaker. All the boots you see folks wearing, I made them. Except for Miss Emmaline. Hers are imported from Paris." Then he say like he didn't care, "Miss Emmaline is my daddy's sister."

So I was talking with the kin of big-house royalty. "Humph," I say. He was puffy, but I judged he got the right.

Alger was quiet for at least ten long seconds fore he boast his father was gon buy him and free him, and when he did Alger would trable all over the world, maybe even as far as China. The Orient was right under our feet. "We could tunnel straight down and pop up in the middle of a rice paddy," he say.

It was my turn to snort. "That ain't so."

With an armful of fresh cuts from the garden, I dropped them shears in my apron and headed up the narrow brick path.

"Hey," Alger say. He handed me a rose that fell by the way. He say when he got to China he was gon export silkworms and become a very rich man.

Sounded outlandish to me, but I wasn't gon be the one to tell him.

From AN ACT TO PROVIDE FOR TAKING THE FIFTH CENSUS OR ENUMERATION OF THE INHABITANTS OF THE UNITED STATES

Twenty-first Congress, Session I, Approved March 23, 1830

Be it enacted by the Senate and House of Representatives of the United States of America, in Congress assembled, That the marshals of the several districts of the United States, and of the District of Columbia, and of the territories of Michigan, Arkansas, and of Florida, respectively, shall be, and are hereby, required . . . to cause the number of the inhabitants within their respective districts and territories (omitting in such enumerations, Indians, not taxed), to be taken according to the directions of this act.

The said enumerations shall distinguish the sexes of all free white persons, and ages of the free white males and females, respectively . . . and shall further distinguish the number of those free white persons included in such enumerations who are deaf and dumb . . . and shall further distinguish the number of those free white persons included in such enumeration, who are blind.

The said enumeration shall distinguish the sexes of all free coloured persons, and of all other coloured persons bound to service for life, or for a term of years, and the ages of such free and other coloured persons, respectively of each sex . . . and shall further distinguish the number of those free coloured and other coloured persons, included in the foregoing, who are deaf and dumb, without regard to age, and those who are blind.

RIDDLE YOUNG

HUNTER'S MOON

I didn't want to be saddled with her for life.

Like a she-devil my sister arrived, a shrouded fury, a spitting spawl. She slew our mother first, you see, killed her in the birthing when I was twelve winters. The old man held himself together for a time, just barely, though. As Da grappled with Lady Despair, the hag leeched his vitality until, hollow eyed and skeletonized by grief unstoppered, he gave up the ghost, bequeathing me a one-room cabin and a meager parcel of vertical land. High-bush blueberry, rock, and rubble composed the lion's share, a stubble field of maize and a swath of bluegrass the remainder. I was sixteen and the girl four when Da went the way of all earth.

In the harsh daylight wheeling through the cabin's lone window, I read his will with care, recognizing the names of all things, as my mother had taught me to read by way of a compendious dictionary, the Holy Bible, and the works of a William Shakespeare:

In the name of God, Amen.

Know all men that I, Duncan Young, of sound mind and disposing memory but weak in body, know that it is appointed to man to die, so I make and constitute this my last Will and Testament.

ITEM FIRST. I do give to God my Soul who gave it.

ITEM SECOND. I do hereby bequeath unto my son, known as Riddle Young, the following property to Wit: all my Sharyes of lot 42 in Screamer Hollow in the county of Hopewell, whereon he now dwells and has made improvements, containing twenty-five acres more or less hitherto, and beginning at the Takatoka Woodland and running thence south to the old Indian path, and bordered by the Glassy River east to the Wilderness west; also my corncrib, springhouse, smokehouse, and hog pen, and real and personal property of every sort, including the following goods and chattels to Wit:

1 old sow
1 Kentucky rifle, patches, flints, and balls held therein
1 powder horn
1 canteen
3 globe lanterns
1 canvas saddlebag
1 ax
1 lathe
1 brier scythe
1 foot adze
2 hoes
1 hatchet
1 froe
1 mattock
2 plows
2 tin buckets
1 pickling tub
1 walnut table
2 ladderback chairs
1 swivel chair
1 bedstead, furniture, clothing, and quilts
1 chest of drawers
1 cedar trunk
1 washstand
1 looking glass
1 set shaving instruments
1 fire shovel and hand bellows
1 Dutch oven
2 cast-iron pots
1 skillet
1 stoneware jug
1 lot crockery
1 lot tinware

1 lot tea ware
1 set white-horn handled forks and knives
1 Family Bible
1 Dictionary of the English Language
1 Set of Drama, Wm. Shakespeare

ITEM THIRD. I do hereby devise my son, Riddle Young, bound by the ties of nature and by this, my Last Will and Testament, to care for my beloved daughter Emmaline Young. Should Riddle Young's death supersede that of his sister, the balance of property shall be distributed to her.

ITEM FOURTH. I, Duncan Young, lived in the bounty of love with my dear wife Blathnaid Nunne'hi for fourteen years, and know that she awaits me wherever the dead await the living, and wish to be buried beside her in a Christian manner.

ITEM FIFTH. I hereby appoint and constitute my son, Riddle Young, my true and lawful executor and charge him with the faithful execution of this, my Last Will and Testament. Thus having disposed of my earthly treasures, I close in hope of a more enduring substance in heaven.

But these particulars were not my measure. All these I bettered in one general best. Though I'd no oil-painted miniature, no lampblack silhouette of my mother's likeness, there was no need, you see. I'd a trove of untainted remembrances that no one could filch from me: memory, the warder of the brain. Ah!—my very first, standing upon the seat of a ladderback, eye above the sill, watching the players of a dramatic storm charge the stage: a shower of sparks, a churning sky, clamorous claps and peals, rain falling slantways, the weighty drops tapping a midnight revelry, and then, my bonnie young mother tucking me into her warm and ambrosial bosom, her dark hair lapping against the side of my face. Was there any better place to be? Nay.

It was right upon that very bald, my mother said, pointing at Blood Mountain's grassless peak, where the People's giant canoe came to rest after the Great Flood.

Like Noah and the Ark?

Mmm, yes, very much like that.

And another, when I was a cub of six or seven, trailing my supple mother over the autumn-tinted knobs and crests of the mountain, which she traversed confidently, more at home in the wild than at the hearth. Nigh a long-needled evergreen, she stooped to gather fallen cones into the scoop of her bonnet.

What do you smell? she asked, holding the crushed fragrance beneath my nose.

Pine, I answered.

Very good! she laughed. And what else?

Again I sniffed, and an impish smile bloomed upon her lips. Ah, I thought, she was being mischievous.

Can't you smell the stars? she asked.

Nay, I said, pleasantly bewildered.

She brushed the stuff off and guided us toward a broad bed of sun-warmed boulders. Shoulder to shoulder, we gazed up into the bosky bower as she unfolded a story.

Long ever ago, when the world was still young (as her stories always began), there lived seven boys, and each boy was a very good boy who was loved dearly by his mother. Every day the boys gathered to play the *gatayu'sti* game, and they played with such joy, chasing after their small stone wheels with long hickory sticks. But one day, when it came time for supper, the boys refused to come home—the game was not over, no one had been declared the winner! We must teach our sons a lesson, the mothers said, for it is not wise to ignore their mother's call. That night, while all seven boys were asleep, they gathered up all the stone wheels. The next day, when the boys went to play, they could not, not without their stone wheels! The boys were very cross and sulked all day, but when it came time for supper, they had no choice but to turn home. When they sat down to eat, each boy's mother lifted a heavy lid from a steaming corn pot, and do you know what was inside? The stone wheels! The mothers had boiled them for supper! The boys were furious. They stomped out and were not seen the rest of the afternoon. That night, the mothers grew worried when their sons did not return home. They searched for them and found them nearby, dancing around a council house. They were dancing the feather dance, toe to heel, heel to toe, waving their arms in the air, faster and faster until their feet flew off the ground. No! cried the mothers, running toward them. They grabbed at their sons as they rose in the air, higher and higher with every round, but only one mother was fast enough to reach her son in time. She hit him with a *gatayu'sti* stick, and he fell, oh how he fell, with such force that he sank into the ground PHUMF! The earth closed over him. As for the other six, their mothers could only watch as their sons spiraled into the heavens. At night, we can still see them, the shine of their souls in the constellation we call *Ani'tsutsa*. Oh, how the People grieved for their children. Every day and night, the mother of the seventh boy wept over the spot where her son had fallen, so many tears, until one day a green shoot sprouted up from where he had disappeared, and that shoot became the tall tree we now call the pine. So you see? she said. The pine, the stars, they possess the very same essence.

She tickled my nose with a tail of pine and happed my face with her kisses.

My mother claimed these were the stories of the Cherokee. How she'd been privy to the red man's faith'd been a mystery to me. At the time, I'd thought that they were a fictitious people, a folly of my mother's imagination, you see, for she was the kind of person who would've made them up just to please me.

Blathnaid *Nunne'hi*.

I fine-tuned the cadence set forth in Da's will, pronouncing her name trippingly on my tongue and without murdering it with my breath. I posited a question and answered it thusly: My own mother must've been a member of the vanquished Nation excised from this northeastern quadrant, and this land bequeathed to me was not of my father, but that of my beloved she.

Why did he, they, withhold this from me?

By my troth, my mother's love had been sweeter than the clearest water, better than high birth, richer than wealth. With her death had come the most disturbing sound to befall my ears: nay, not my father's racking sobs, but the hardened clumps of clay rapping against her coffin as he shoveled her and her stories away.

If a fine marksman can strike a turkey between the eyes with naught but a slingshot and stone, then Da was a sharpshooter, which made his firing a Kentucky rifle akin to cheating. Carved from tiger-stripe maple, it was a consummate beauty, from the sterling-dipped nose cap down a magnificent forty-six-inch iron barrel to the scrolled flintlock and graven stock that ended in a crescent-shaped brass butt plate. On the right side a hinged patch box, its cover inlaid with silver, bore a Jacob's ladder and a cherub. On the left a peel of moon, six stars, and a rising sun were rendered into the cheek piece.

Surrounding our hollow, a forest thick with gluttonous shade made the long rifle, with its open gunsights and spiral bore, a necessity, even for Da, as it could fire an arc across three hundred yards to accurate death. Game was aplenty, and with Da tracking it, whether boar hog or white-tailed buck, black bear or catamount, it mattered not; Da would triumph.

Stalking requires patience, of which he suffered no lack. Why, he'd easily spend half a moon up mountain, cloistered in the woods.

I'm off, son, I'm off, he said.

He'd never afore looked so white haired. Feeble. Bent. Old. His eyes sunken. His voice a macilent whisper.

Are you certain, Da? You don't look well.

I reckon I ain't.

He set the long rifle along the walnut table to prepare himself for the hunt. Many a day as a boy, I'd arisen to watch him afore he left; waiting for the moment my company'd be requested. When at last that time had commenced, it'd been as pleasurable, more, than I'd ever expected. Since our mother's passing, however, he'd taken to setting out more oft in solitary.

I kept my sight on the hearth fire as a blackened log cracked and broke apart. I'd no need to watch his maneuvers, you see, as I possessed them in my heart. Instead I bent my ear to the slow opening of the hinged patch box, the clack against tabletop as he surveyed his collection of knapped flints. From the shadow cast along the floor, across wood shavings and scattered nutshells, I knew that he was studying them in the yellow drape of the autumn daybreak, fingering the edges, culling out the dull, seeking the sharpest. I heard him loose the cock and slide a flint between the worn, leathered jaws of the hammer. I lifted my eyes at the precise moment to catch his satisfaction with the flint's placement. He tightened the jaw screw.

From a peg he withdrew a broad-brimmed felt hat. He slung his knapsack and powder horn over his shoulder and made for the door.

Da, you've forgotten thy canteen. You'd not want to leave without. The weather might turn a spatter and chill. (The truth was, you see, the old man kept it filled with corn whiskey.)

His shoulders sank, and he eyed me briefly afore shunting his gaze. He appeared to recede into the swaths of spindle light splitting through the seams of our log home.

Before me he stood dressed in streamers bright. A broken man.

If I'd seen his eyes water and trickle, as tallow dips do gutter in wuthering wind, would it've been unkind to relieve a ravaged man's suffering? Why, I'd've shot a common dog for less. Would I've been mistaken? Would it've been ungodly to spare us—him—of his misery?

Reckon not, he said.

Pardon?

The canteen. He shoved the thing at me.

Ah. Sure, Da, sure.

I reached below the walnut table, hoisted a cool and capacious stoneware jug to my lap, and wedged the corn stopper out with my thumb. I topped the canteen and passed it back.

You fixed for black powder? I asked. I'd not seen him refill the horn.

Yep.

Alright, then, I said.

Well, said he.

I tucked my hands in the warm pits of my bed woolens.

Take care of your sister, he said, jerking his head at Emmaline, asleep in the chimney corner. The girl lay curled, a larval worm under a muted palette of thick calico.

Sure, Da, sure. I'll keep her by my side all day if she'll have it. (He coddled her too much, you see, and what use was that? A body must earn its keep.)

I mean it, son, swear to me this day. Vow you'll look after Emmaline.

I'll not let her from my sight.

She's the spitting image of your ma. Have I ever told ye?

No, Da, no.

But of course he had. Nary a day gone by, the same script on and on, as if the girl were a mirror'd reflection. The qualities he gave as evidence—her wistfulness, her scowl—I found peculiar, and I'd remained unimpressed. Why, my mother had hair of lustrous black, her brows were inky, her lips the rich red of wild raspberries, her flesh the tawny sky of a summer sunset; she'd been no feinted beauty. My sister was but a faded specter, a babe barely made in her image, a thing as white as a hoarfrost, skinny lipped and chappy fingered, her eyes the chilled blue agates of our father, her hair as brittle as old straw. The only swarthiness the girl bore was the tempest beneath her pale frontage.

A change came over me, and though I knew it would ignite him, I chanced hurting the old man's pride: He did not look as if he ought be off on his own, and so I told him.

Aye, son, are ye prepared to hunt? he asked in mock surprise. Your leg have a miraculous recovery, did it now?

My old man was still quick to parry.

I've mended well, I said, and stretched my crooked leg toward the dying fire as proof.

You're growing too fast, that's your problem. Turns a lad clumsy. He cleared his throat as if to say more, his hand on the latch.

I made no effort to detain him. Take care, Da, I said.

He slouched out, a slanting heap of man.

I boiled cabbage and fried speckled trout, for once without Emmaline's antics, and cracked open the last crock of pickled corn relish. The following day, I trapped a rabbit, cooked a brown stew, and spooned it over a wedge of pone. We ate, we slept; the sun came up, the sun left. The sky brooded, sent a mizzling rain, and cleared. The days bled one into another as I felled a burly red oak, cut wood for kindling, split shingles, repaired a breach in the roof (without falling off this time) where sizable rats had been squeezing in (causing Emmaline fits of laughter when they ran over her toes), daubed mud in the wall where the chinking had dried up, caned a chair in dire need. I chased the girl out of the corncrib (tears), where she'd sat conversing with grain moths (antics), and when she tumbled onto her knees (more tears), I lifted her overhead and whirled her around until she shrieked and laughed. Together we shook the old cobs out of our mattress and replaced them with fresh. Mark my words, I told her as white breath streamed from her mouth, a working body is a blood-warm body.

I battled our clothes when they grew overripe and bathed the girl when she grew far too foul, and other such women's scut.

All same as usual.

It took the girl sniveling one morn about her daddy being gone too long for me to concede something might be amiss.

Ah, Emmaline, I said and wiped her snout with my neckerchief.

With a twist of dogbane I tethered her to a chair to discourage her from wandering the riverbank in my absence. Why, the sound of living water held the girl entranced; it wasn't natural, and I'd not allow her to drown. The Glassy River was nigh a hundred paces east of our dwelling, you see. Fed by the Spring of Woe, it meandered down Blood Mountain, rushing over rocky escarpments, bending past our homeplace, widening and gathering speed until it split into Bridal Veil Falls and plummeted down the Great Gorge into the Pool of Forgetfulness.

I donned a pelt coat and beave hat, shoved my hunting knife into my boot, stoked the logs. I offered the girl a jar of blackberry preserves, which she greedily accepted, tearing the beeswax and scooping out sweet gobs with her paws, and set off.

I found our Da.

I found him slumped against a grizzled hemlock, a blanket of moiled foliage glazing his body. One foot remained clad in a wet woolen stocking and hobnailed boot, whilst the other was bare. The long rifle lay across his chest, the muzzle caught, caught in what remained, what remained of his gray face.

I tugged at the stock.

A dried scum of blood and bone parts cracked off the hemlock's bark. Adding to this misery, his stench, a cloying sweet of putrid fruit, must've broadcast his death, as he lay filleted from nave to chops by a woodland beast.

Is the Almighty nigh to them of broken heart?

Did Da call out ere the hammer struck?

And where was God in His infinite mercy? Who was this, our Savior? If we were made in His image, then what kind of man was He?

I stumbled back and heaved the contents of my gut.

Ah, Da, I said with a swipe of my mouth. I stared into the trees and trained my eye to the single shaft of sunlight piercing this fortress. Within it, dust, a slow-wheeling movement, took possession of my gaze. Life continues, despite our withdrawal.

I broke from my stolid pose.

I collected the powder horn, the Kentucky rifle, the saddlebag. I eased his boot off his cold foot, momentarily, unavoidably drawn to the other, already bare and marked with gunpowder, and no less unsettling than his carcass. Yet I crouched transfixed. It was translucent. It moved, squirming from within, to be exact. Maggots feasting on Da's meager fat.

Dear God. Havoc wrecks the flesh when its vital force hath left it.

With my knife I tore my shirt opposite my heart and stabbed the earth, and without pause dug a trough waist deep, the pungent smell of earth a small comfort.

I allowed him the final dignity of his hat and poured dirt over his remnants.

I wept. With relief. In shame. In sorrow.

I said a prayer petitioning the Deity for forgiveness. For myself.

For Da.

Aye, I raised her. Someone had to act the girl's nurse.

I crooned the only cradlesong I knew, a gloomy verse about a broken bough and a fallen babe, in the tenderest cantabile. I read, from the impressive works of William Shakespeare, a play by the name of *Macbeth*, affecting a different voice for each member of the dramatis personae—the king, his lady, the son, the three weird sisters, the murderers, and so on. She took to it, eager to sound the words for herself.

She'd always been a fussy tot and feeding her the work of a buffoon, with my aping around the room, pulling faces and clowning until she laughed, too content to mind the sog I'd just shoved into her twee mouth. Now, with Da gone, I deemed it time to promote her to self-ability. I treated her cautiously, as one would taming a whelp. To begin, I insisted she feed herself. I ignored her baseless fits of refusal.

You will suffer thy hunger anon, and you will be made to wait until supper, I warned her.

When the agony of hunger finally seized her, I did not relent despite a fury so pure it was dear: her miniature fists clenched, her cheeks a study of heat, and tears so rich they clung to her pale lashes in the manner of old syrup. I nigh flew into a fit of laughter at its intensity, but was not so cruel as to show it.

The very next morn, she sat, spoon in hand, ready to wolf down whatever I served her.

She'd ask after the old man, and I'd tell her the Divine had called him to the sweet thereafter. Then she'd ask when he'd be coming back and would he be bringing our mother?

Nay, Emmaline, I said, both our parents have flown this world and neither one shall return to it.

Her lips trembled. I'm upset, she sniveled.

Aye, I can see that.

Despite my brusqueness, the girl sulked if I wasn't inclined to speech and delighted if I was. She'd a way of clinging to my every word, watching me with her peculiar blue eyes, mutely, never looking away.

A person ought to look away.

WINTER'S TAIL, 1835

DA FIVE MOONS GONE.

I lay rudely roused from well-earned sleep to find Emmaline standing nigh the bedstead, her lips burbling nonsense. A slash of lurid moonlight cut across her fretful face.

Wha—Emmaline, you near flayed me flesh of skin, I said. (Verily, this was my heartfelt desire. Whilst the girl fell into an enviable sleep, my skin would creep with a vengeful itch for which there seemed no relief, and I'd lay awake clawing the bedsheets, my nightly discomfort swelling. I could not recall when the malady'd commenced, and my mind, half awake, would glom upon an endless catalog of efforts and wagers meant to keep us alive, until exhaustion prevailed and I'd finally drift aloft.)

I heard someone calling, she said.

'Tis the wind, I said.

Why would the wind call me?

'Tis not calling you, Emmaline. 'Tis only the sound it makes.

I want to be the wind.

When you grow up, you can be the wind.

Promise?

Aye.

Truly?

Nay.

Her face fell.

Now, don't you weep, you know I can't abide thy weeping, Em.

I reached for her. She stepped back.

Wha? I said.

She shuffled closer and placed her grubby paw atop my head.

I allowed it.

She cupped my chin.

I took her paw away and held it.

Forgive me, Emmaline. Return to bed.

She squirmed from my grasp and kissed the tip of my nose and my cheek. She crawled over my chest and laid her head against the pillow, her tiny paws clasped beneath it, her knees snug to her chest, her wee cold toes tucked under my buttocks for warmth and, with a yawn almost innocent, fell asleep.

HEIGHT OF SPRING, 1835

PLANTING MOON

A prismatic day. The sun strong. Six hours nigh sunset.

From my vantage upon the bank, I studied the rain-gorged fleam as stark gems of light hopped across its surface, and waited for supper to bite. For the vast part of the year, the river ran untainted, and I required no more than my eyes and a keen spear. After a lengthy spring shower, however, it would surge brown, and a fishing pole and patience were without a doubt essential.

We now relied upon the fish I caught for our meatly needs, you see.

The old sow had croaked, emaciated and choleric, and I'd trapped not one creature, not even a vole, in my deadfalls. 'Twas as if the land had been abandoned by all species of rodent. Soon we'd be depending upon the twigs and catkins meant for a ruffed grouse rather than eat one, for there'd been no sign of the bird, whose breast mixed nicely with pork grease and ramps. Nay, not a single beat of its mating call, the wings drumming against felled timber, a deafening sound that formerly, dramatically, reliably marked the spring commencement.

As for large game, I stood no chance, not since the Kentucky long rifle'd become of scant and shameful use to me. I'd not felled a blessed creature since our father's demise. Never afore had I been so off my mark, unable to align the sights, shooting over the heads of my prey or into the soil as if the thing were hexed. I'd flinch, I'd fumble and anticipate the recoil, or I'd shoulder and squeeze the rifle too tightly. I'd lost what stealth I'd ever possessed and slogged along noisily despite my best efforts, announcing my presence to every beast within remote earshot. I was sluggish with the thing too, managing only one cumbersome load over a prolonged minute. If my old man could've seen me, he'd have found my incompetence a leg-slapping hoot and shaken his head knowingly at my hobbled gait. Adding to my shame, the one time the prey'd been delivered to my very feet, I'd not had the power to lift the rifle.

It'd begun with the rustling of leaves, you see, and rose to a skirping hiss, until the clabber underfoot shook with the weight of tremulous hooves. A herd of deer thundered forth, gracefully dodging my being as they threaded through the trees, until all had passed but one—a youngling, this winter buck, a lone straif bearing witness to my craven posture. I could tell you not what'd flushed them in such numbers unnatural; I could tell you naught, as I'd sunk to my knees like a woman, skirling with fear. If I'd not had the girl to care for, if I'd not avowed her protection, I'd've done my own self in.

And now, adding to my defects, my fishless hook. I pulled up my line in disgust. Again, small scrappers had nibbled off the bait.

As I passed the metal barb through another night crawler, the girl sat spraddle legged upon the slope of pointed bluegrass, breaking stems of sow thistle and braiding the violet flowers into her faint hair. She gasped and suckled her thumb, having pierced it upon a furzy prick.

Wheesht, I said, casting her a sideling glance. You'll spook the fish.

I felt her arms lace around my shanks.

Emmaline, quit it.

And so she did. And when it grew far too quiet for too far long, I knew it meant no good as well. A glance to my right confirmed it: The girl was creeping down the bank, her sight trained to the water.

Come now, Emmaline, step away. Be a good lass.

She ignored my entreaty, unwavering in her concentration in a manner all too familiar.

Look! she finally said, down there! She pointed at a stirring in the middle of the fleam. Don't you see him?

See whom, Emmaline? said I, tiredly.

Da, she said and clapped her paws together.

This was her most recent fatuity, manifesting our father, most oft in puddles of still water or slow-moving rills ginned by the sun. I'd endeavored to explain these were her own reflection, but here in these rapid-moving waters, reflection was all but an impossibility. Battling her imagination would be the end of me if I could not put a stop to this foundless haunting.

That will do. Begone from there.

'Tis! And there's another. Hello, she waved. Is that Mama? She shielded her eyes as if from a blinding glint and then squinted at me quizzically.

A new claim. I grunted my displeasure.

The girl dipped a toe into the water.

Nay, Emmaline.

She walked into the fleam, her dress belling out in the rush.

Get out right now, I said as my twine pulled suddenly taut. So strong was the pull, I trenched my heels into the moss. Don't play deaf with me! Emmaline!

When she sank up to her waist, I chose my sister over repast and dove in after the minx, yanking her from the churning waters, ignoring her snarls and protestations, dragging her tangle and limb the hundred paces back to our homeplace. I tied her to a chair and threatened her with the strap should she ever wander into the river again.

To sleep—perchance to dream.

Deep in the bowels of the night, I began to despair. Sweat drenched my bed woolens. The room smoldered with a preternatural heat more suitable to a hellish summer than spring. I untangled my legs from the bedsheets and gently lifted the girl's arm from my chest as she burbled in her sleep.

With lit candle, I stood afore the washstand, naught more than a shadow in the looking glass. My cheekbones soared higher and my nose seemed more pronounced in the hard-edged moonlight. My hair—once long, brilliant, and oily—had lost its sheen.

Fingering a brown crust under my chin, the aftermath of a shaving, I searched for relics of my father in my aspect.

Emmaline resembled him, not I, I reminded myself, when suddenly I saw the old man glaring back at me from inside my own pulled skin. I rubbed my face and glanced again. I found dark eyes and darker circles beneath them, but they were my own. A dagger of the mind, a false creation, proceeding from a heat-oppressed brain, no doubt.

At the table, I sat and rapped a nervous tattoo. This served me not, and so I rose and paced. On the brink, I was, of some terrible precipice, and so I sat again to steady myself. I stretched my legs, only to encounter an impediment. The stoneware jug. Half full, just as the old man'd left it. I poured a dram into a tea saucer and sipped. Despite the bite, I scudded another down my throat. There was a strange pleasure in this pain, and I drank directly from the jug until naught was left but curdling vapors.

Soon after, my shoulders loosed, my eyelids drooped, my jaw unclenched, and my head began to drift from side to side. I viewed the room as though from a gently rocking skiff. In this condition I deemed it wise to take a walk.

Once outside, I wove my way toward the fleam, but somewhere between, I sank. With abject pleasure I moaned in the dewy bluegrass. I rocked like a child and pissed myself. I laughed. Emboldened, I rolled down the slope and lay prostrate, grinding myself against the nubby peat until I shuddered with an unexpected pleasure and relief.

I ruminated: Who knew the earth could bring such satisfaction?

Overhead, a flock of flitter mice flew against the light-gorged celestia, momentarily obscuring the moon. Behold, such sights! I shouted and staggered to my feet, casting myself among their kind with the gait of man struck spastic, flapping up the bank and racing over an earth that seemed disturbingly not firm set. To my amusement, I found myself on my back again, watching the dark-winged flock as they flew a dizzying figure eight. Nay, eighty-eight! Uninspired to rise from this horizontal repose, I fingered a small stone and hurled it skyward and, with a sense of smug satisfaction, watched the nightly creatures pursue the false lure. They darted silently toward it. I snickered, I laughed, and I laughed louder still, until I noted with a kind of heightened awareness, you might say, the stars spinning a twee unpleasantly. *Tsistu. Selu. Kana'ti.* These sprawled across the sky, blinking coquettishly. Each held a story told to me by my mother, though I could not, in that moment, recall a one. As I traced their shapes with a limp'd wrist and finger, I heard a voice speaking. I listened to its tenor rumbling along, unintelligibly, desperately, until I realized, aye, indeed, it belonged to me, and what I took for notions pronounced inside my head were, in truth, spoken outside of it, one thought rolling into the next without boundary. And so it was I found myself chatting to my old man with a false amity.

What do you think? I asked. Are you pleased? See how we fare? Weary of life, were you? Better off, aye, better off dead. I tend to thy daughter better than you ever did. Wha? Do you speak? Aye, speak, I charge thee.

I cradled an ear.

When I heard naught, a sloppy rage grew within me and I surged to my feet, tripping along the bluegrass down the mossy scarp and into the rushing water.

Bury you beside my mother? Nay! Not worthy, I shouted, walking deeper into the fleam. I turned on the Deity, I scorned the heavens and rattled a fist, I spewed a sluice of acrimony: What of you? Do you too not speak? Muted minister! Mongrel! Mutt! Speak, I say, speak, I prithee. Prove thyself to me. A word. A sound. A noun, aha! A miser of miracles is what you are, I said, slashing with arms wild until I could seethe no more. I submitted to the current.

As I sank, I felt the thrill of submersion.

At first the silence engulfed me, and within it I could hear the lull of my own heartbeat. Enraptured by its faithful rhythm, I was soothed, happy until, too long deprived of breath, my joy turned to bile and I felt only the terror of my watery sarcophagus. I fought my way through the river's skin, straining against the current as it assailed. I flailed, sputtering for breath, and floundered down the winding fleam, nigh drowning until fortune provided a miracle in the form of a dead birch. Girded against its weight, I flung a leg about its generous circumference, and with frozen fingers I scraped my way up, clutching the birch, a thing most dear to me. What remained of its root plate lay anchored in the bank at half fulcrum, its trunk levered over the churlish water, and I was most grateful to whatever fungus or fly had caused its demise, even as I spewed up the river's dregs, provoked by the stench of infected bark. I shuddered, my chilled limbs numbed and dangling, and clung to the tree for a timeless quantity, ashamed of my polluted nightshirt, my flesh mongering, and my depravity, until, with great effort, I fumbled my way back to sanity. Upriver I slogged in my shambled state, at last finding my faithful swath of bluegrass, and collapsed in a heap.

Show thyself, I shouted into the heavens. Speak!

I listened for the voice of either father.

Leave us, then, I said. Let us be.

CUSP OF AUTUMN, 1836

HARVEST MOON. DA TWO WINTERS DEAD. MY DEAR MOTHER SIX.

When the maize refused to tassel, we nigh starved.

Aside the bed we knelt, petitioning the Deity with elbows (dutifully) perched, fingers (desperately) laced, heads (deferentially) graced; we were two supplicants (one false, one true) bent in prayer, until one providential day, a family of wayfaring proselytizers arrived in search of lodging and our luck began its hesitant shift.

The girl, unaccustomed to visitors, was at first terrified by the appearance of these others—no mere reflections, you see, no supernatural solicitors of her fantasies, but a caravan of living folks in seven skinned wagons arriving in the flame-tinted light of midday. She sat at the bottom of the hill, next to a gnarled persimmon tree, and watched the foreigners through swiveling eyes, the look of a wildcat upon her face.

I too watched them. Down the sights of the long rifle and, I hoped, to great effect.

The caravan waited on the rutted path as a foppish man of roughly twenty winters broke off.

May I approach? he asked, his gloved hands in plain evidence, fingers fanned and open faced, as though to promote their innocence.

I divined no weaponry (though I could conjure six niches on a man's body to conceal such device), nor did his manner seem malignant.

We are pilgrims from the high country, he said, and in need of respite. We, sir, mean neither harm nor to disturb your quietude. He removed a ridiculously plumed hat.

Aye, I said, shouldering the rifle and leveling it at his chest. (Better to posture than be mistaken.)

As he lifted the loop from the fence gate, the girl ran squealing up the hillock and over the three flagstones leading to the porch. She scurried into the cabin, hiding under the bedstead, until the lanky lad (after polite introductions and acceptable apologies, and with my blessing) knelt on the rag carpet beside her cave. I expected (with a perverse pride) Emmaline to act the fiend, but he expelled her easily (to my dismay and relief) with a low-sweeping bow and a mere palliative, Please?

His name, he said, was Samuel Bounds.

He was an oddly compelling lad with a clean-shaven face, and I credited him for Emmaline's unusual tractability. She followed him about, wagging her tail like a spaniel at the heels of her master. I stifled a laugh, as the young fellow himself was such a sight. His slender personage, I wagered, was unfit for labor, and he possessed a most ill-fitting head; by this I mean a volume too large for his stringlike neck. His fair hair curled loose without thong to restrain it, and his ruffled cuffs extended degenerately beyond the arms of his plaid overcoat. Indeed, I'd've found him a trifle womanly were it not for his broadfalls and coarse leather boots.

His father, by way of contrast, was an austere-looking gentleman of roughly two score and seven, with long muttonchops and a chin beard of gray: Down its center ran a strip of white, evoking the pelt of a weathered old skunk. He wore a preacher's round-brimmed hat, whilst his complexion bore the deep routs of the pox.

He dismounted and withdrew a filigreed walking stick from a tote behind his saddle and tapped it along the ground. He was their leader, this blindman with clouded eyes, a pulpiteer by the name of Solomon B. Bounds.

The group included his dour and wordless wife; their son, Samuel, heretofore described; a homely daughter named Katie, several winters Samuel's junior; a menagerie of hounds, horses, cattle, sheep, goats, and swine; and a small community of bondmen and bondwomen of all ages, including a trio of high-spirited toddler girls who appeared to be no more than two, three, and four. They gave the wife substantial berth, ducking her swats when they came within proximity and clinging to the preacher despite his repeated rebuffs.

Intrigued by this motley bunch, I welcomed them all with mild reservation to our homeplace.

An authoritative negress was the family's cook and housekeeper—and, it would be fair to say, a giantess. Her name was Lossie. I judged her a hard decennium older than myself, a middle-aged woman of twenty-eight. Her bosom was plentiful, her seat round, her waist trim, her legs conferred the bulk of her height, and in the light of the pit fire, her face shone with mark'd beauty.

Assisted by the preacher's manservant, an older black by the name of Enoch, I transferred our walnut table outdoors. Several paces away, a pair of young bondmen crafted makeshift tables from my supply of cut lumber and undressed planks.

We sat with the preacher and his family under the cheer of sun and were served a veritable feast of roasted goat shanks, golden beets, and dark rounds of fragrant bread, prepared by the giantess, who neither bent her head nor temper'd her eyes as I stared at her with amicable curiosity.

After supper the preacher inspected the quality of my workmanship, his hands sweeping across the chestnut logs and dovetailed joints of our home, his walking stick tapping the solid masonry of its foundation—eighteen inches of flat river stones, as termites will climb no higher than this—and the chimney of fieldstone slabs and pure red clay, which not only stood perfectly upright but possessed a powerful draw. Inside, his easy gait measured the evenness of the chestnut floorboards.

He nodded, impressed. You have reared a fine cabin. As tranquil in ambiance, he imagined aloud, as a monastic cell.

I offered him our most comfortable seat on the porch, a swivel chair, whilst I took up residence in the ladderback. When the bondman Enoch brought his master a weasel-pelted coat, I proposed we remove inside where he would find great comfort by a fire, but he said he found the night air invigorating, the most exotic he'd ever smelt, and the lull of voices around him as his bondmen set up camp brought him great comfort, and so we lingered, the brightness of the caravan's brass fittings and buckles fading into the darkness as the sun extinguished.

Over the course of the evening, I learned that Solomon B. Bounds hailed from Plattsburg, North Carolina, where some years back he'd entered a land lottery and won title to a substantial plot, sight unseen, in the valley of these mountains. Now that Old Hickory had finally removed the remaining Cherokee from the parcel, it was his to claim. He'd been content with his lot back in Plattsburg, he insisted, but saw opportunity in this new venture. He'd heard much about our bottomlands and their fecundity.

From an inside pocket he withdrew an embossed leather case, the holder of five stoutly rolled cigars. Extracting one, he cut it and plugged it between his lips. With a quick strike of a lucifer, he leaned into the cupped blaze, twirling the roll until a black ring formed around its end.

I wondered aloud how one could negotiate so confidently without any sight. He sucked and puffed the smoldering thing with an appreciative expression.

Faith, he answered wryly.

He offered one to me, and I, unfamiliar with its ritual, mimicked his motions and soon found my lungs filled with burning soot. I coughed and hacked as the preacher whooped.

One is not meant to inhale, he said, but to relish the smoke as it infuses the palate.

Indeed, I said through charred throat.

He admitted the flavor was robust, an acquired taste, an oak-fired dark leaf. He then leaned on the arm of his swivel chair in the manner of a man intent on sharing a clever conspiracy. I have brought with me an item, he said, more valuable than all the gold of Hernando de Soto.

It was tobacco seed, a new breed of the weed that had taken him three harvests to develop, more aromatic than the average leaf and sweeter than a sultana grape, and with a wider appeal, he wagered. He would cultivate this new strain to rival all others (his ambition) and resume preaching (his predilection and joy), praise the Lord. He raised his chin and sniffed.

It is intoxicating, this rawness of nature, and no doubt will have a medicinal effect on my health, he said.

He'd suffered a panoply of blights, including ague, melancholy, neuralgia, and flux of the bowels, and spoke as if each plague were an inhospitable territory that he'd dared to explore, and having survived, relished in the telling of it.

Fear not, he said, as if sensing (rightly) my impulse to retreat from my visitor. I bring with me no contagion.

He claimed his housekeeper, by which he meant the giant negress, prepared solutions that could compete with any doctor's antidote, and with that my interest in her piqued.

Is she able to cure insomnolence? I inquired.

I'm sure of it, he said, as I myself no longer suffer from it.

You are fortunate to have her, I said.

Worth every cent.

She is (and here I faltered) quite tall.

He laughed amicably. Yes, she is that.

The bondmen'd set up camp under a grove of chestnut trees nigh the southwest border of my homeplace. Several sat around a smoldering fire, warming their hands where earlier their women had fixed their meal. Engaged in a gathering of musical collaboration, one jounced spoons against his knee and another rattled a gourd. A variety of inventive instruments soon appeared: a skinned drum held under an armpit, two large rib bones of a bear or catamount, and the simplest—clapped hands and patted feet. A hypnotic percussion filled the hollow, and I welcomed it with a moved heart, as one does a relative one hath never met. If the preacher had not required my company, I could envision a scene in which I joined these talented musicians, if only to sit in their company. But alas, it was only within my mind that I could acquit myself in a manner so emboldened.

A fair distance from the campsite, the tent of my giantess sat in isolation. With a hand to my forehead, as if to scratch at an insect bite, I watched her ample form, gloriously lit from within the taut skin. I could not interpret her languid movements—was she unwinding her shawl, her generous over-skirt, or wrapping herself in a long blanket? It mattered not, as my mind began to manifest an answer that pleased me: Her shadow glided like a fluted note as she disrobed.

And what of afflictions of the flesh? I asked through tightening throat. Doth she heal them with equal prowess?

Of what nature do we discuss? the preacher inquired.

A general one, I said, ignoring the prickling onset of my skin's familiar itch.

The preacher commenced a reflective silence, rolling his cigar between his thumb and index finger. If it were an appointment with my housekeeper you desired, it would be my pleasure to arrange it, he said.

I said I would welcome it. (The thought both terrified and excited.)

He leaned in. I once suffered such an affliction, he said. A stab of pain crossed his face.

Fearing he might divulge matters ever more personal, I spoke extemporaneously. What did he think of our land? I inquired.

Most mountainous, he responded heartily. With its steep climbs and harrowing descents, narrow ridges and hidden coves, such treacherous terrain as this he'd never afore encountered. And well it should be, he said. A treasure must not be made easy to reach.

I agreed with this logic, and his passion for talk continued.

How old are you, son?

I am eighteen. Emmaline yonder is nigh six.

I watched her with a protective eye as Samuel Bounds dandled my sister upon his knee. He sat near the pit fire (which the bondman Enoch kept alive with logs of green hickory) on a handsome leather chair mounted on brass casters, removed earlier from a furniture-laden wagon.

You have had the great fortune to live here all your life? asked the preacher.

Aye.

Tell me, then, where is the local prayer house?

There is one in the town.

And if I may inquire, of what faith?

Presbyterian, said I.

Ah, he said with a note of dismay.

Abandoned, at last count, I said.

Oh?

I related the tale to the best of my youthful recollection. Four winters past, the minister had quit, expelled from town by a three-legged mutt named Neville, who'd taken a nigh maniacal dislike to the man. The townsmen, who'd not cared for the minister (a spoon-faced fellow rumored to accept tithes), had given the cur an unusual amount of latitude for a stray. Left to his own liberties, Neville had tormented the minister whenever the man set foot outside his parsonage. Upon the minister's expulsion (Neville finally chased the man to the county's southern border), they'd erected a stone statue to the now-deceased canine. 'Twas the first thing one would see entering Persimmon from the northeast, this monument. Neville himself lay buried in the church cemetery under a headstone that pronounced, HERE LIES NEVILLE THE TOWN DOG. Without a minister, the prayer house had fallen into disuse and the Presbyterian faith, to the best of my ken, had all but faded as breath into the wind.

I see, the preacher said with a cautious laugh. And what of you, son, what is your relationship with God?

Indeed, I thought and cleared my throat. Emmaline's laughter grew boisterous as Samuel chased her around the fire and into the arms of the sister, Katie, whilst the preacher's wife looked on without affect.

My companion waited with marked patience for my reply, his sightless eyes seeming to gaze at me with curiosity, until silence became my answer.

Ah, well, we all wander through pastures of doubt, he said. Take solace, son. God is a tender shepherd. You would not be the first to drift. Perhaps you will allow me to be your compass.

What is it, exactly, that you preach?

I am a Baptist, he said.

Ah, I said. I am unfamiliar with its nuances.

Then you must join us. Allow your soul to make its own decision, he said.

As if sensing my discomfort, he deftly changed the subject.

If I may, how have you come to live alone in this cove, a young man such as yourself? he asked.

I told him both our parents had passed.

I am sorry for your loss, he said.

It was quite some time ago, said I.

Forgive my forwardness, but you have no other family?

Nay. Da hailed from Pennsylvania. He pioneered here alone.

I see, he said. He tapped the ash from his cigar.

Emmaline's pleasure rose to a shriek, and I called the girl. She dutifully left the foppish youth and panted across the yard.

Have you had any trouble with lingering Indians? the preacher asked.

You would be our first visitors, I said, blood riled. I pulled Emmaline to me and set my cigar on the rail, as its flame had long extinguished.

It is not my intention to alarm, he said, mistaking my tone. I've had word they still hide in these secluded coves, burrowing into the land like scabies, despite reports confirming this area cleared, and I am grateful for your firsthand evaluation. He sighed. If only the government could be as effective with removing the savages from the northwestern part of the state.

And you, sir, I said, thy faith in God must be quite profound to risk traveling through this territory when there exists a palatable turnpike only miles west better suited in terrain and inhabitant to transferring one's family.

He narrowed his blind eyes and drew deeply on his cigar. A man must take certain risks to ensure his family's survival, he said, and some may seem counterintuitive. I pray and listen to the Lord's guidance.

Upon their leave the following morn, the preacher presented us with a handsome woodcut, royal folio in measurement, depicting a golden-winged view of John the Baptist. I said I'd treasure the artifact and handled it as one would a rare red trillium, until informed I was meant to post it to a wall and apportion my time by it. Indeed, below the portrait of their robed prophet hung twelve woven sheets, each one a collection of days, a month with its proper name, and which, by invention of commodity, could be replaced after the set played out. It seemed a most static interpretation, each day measured by a vacant, empty box, each month with naught but a title to set it apart. A sad view of the zodiac by my estimation, though I did not disclose this sentiment. A gift it was, whether to my liking or not.

I accompanied the preacher to his caravan, where he bestowed upon us a wealth of marvelous foodstuffs: milk, butter, salt, sorghum, sugar, flour, and salt pork, as well as a pair of honey-colored tapers with the enchanting scent of beeswax and bayberry. He grappled my hand and secreted a small vial therein, instructing me to drink the tincture on a vacant stomach with promises of relief of my insomnolence. As for any other disturbances, you must seek the services of my housekeeper, he added.

If a blindman should wink, I'd attest he'd done just that.

I thanked him for his largesse and offered, with sincerity, my labors in return, to which he replied he could foresee a future in which he would accept my offer, but that these gifts required naught of me.

In parting, he invited us to attend prayer meetings, and I said we'd be obliged. I did not wish to appear irredeemable.

Their horses were a pageantry of colors: bloodstone with silver mane, dun and eel striped, roan, buckskin, bay, chestnut, sorrel, and coal. Nary a one suffered from blemishes or unsoundness of hock. Aye, they were an impressive lot, glossed and heavily muscled, good sized, with solid feet, easily fifteen hands apiece. They led the seven skinned wagons down the rutted path at the bottom of our hillock, destined for the valley.

I'd offered the man a crudely drawn map outlining a course that would achieve their destination in less than half a day. There was a swifter route to the west, but travel over the truss bridge that spanned the width of the

Cuchulannahannachee River was not prudent. The bridge was not meant for a wagon train of such heft, you see. Instead, I instructed him to follow an old trail that twisted down the mountain in an easterly direction, thereby surpassing the Great Gorge to where the river bent at a passable depth. Once he reached the ford, he'd continue west, where he'd find the wagon road running a bias across the valley. A stone cairn marked the mouth of the trail, which I'd described to the preacher in short length, as its entrance was not easily deciphered amid the heavy weeds and teenage saplings. The preacher did not ask how I'd come to know of the trail, perhaps thinking it common knowledge to all rather than to a son of Blathnaid Nunne'hi.

As I watched the convoy depart, I drank in the giantess, who sat alone in the back of the kitchen cart, and my chest filled with a languid, honeyed warmth.

In the space of fourteen rectilinear days, the preacher'd roused a spry church following.

'Twas not the tomblike confines of the chapel's sanctuary that made my palms clam, nor the climb down the mountain's southwestern switchbacks that overheated me, but the unexpected gathering of bare necks, napes, and rump-fed ronyons, of exposed wrists, slender ankles, and sturdy hips—all at once, and in numbers far too great for one small edifice.

During one somber psalm, the congregation rose and I with it. They swayed with arms raised and sang of wretchedness, of being lost and now found. It was called "Amazing Grace," and I found the tune loathsome.

I held nary a thought of salvation, as my mind was elsewise preoccupied by a lass of the chorus, her solitary flaw a constellation of caramel-colored freckles spanning the sky of her face. She stood upon a raised stage, reading a shape-note tune book. (She was no Lossie, whose brew had brought me a sleep seven leagues deep. Since my cure, however, I'd not found the courage to keep my appointment with her. Now, I found, my cravings did not discriminate; any woman'd serve a likely surrogate.) My blood galloped with each elongated vowel (such ovals! such lusciousness!), my skin itched with an inferno, until she unexpectedly raised her pious chin and ensnared my gaze. My unsavory thoughts roiled within me like a tempest tossed, and the lass read them as easily as her hymnal. Her cheeks rubified and her eyes rolled into her head as she swooned to feverish shouts of praise, the congregation believing her touched by the hand of God.

I slunk down the aisle and into the autumnal air, forcing large quantities of its smoked and piggish scent into my lungs. I was the monster, a moniker I'd heretofore ascribed to Emmaline. That very morn I'd had to wrangle the girl from her procreant cradle in the corncrib and bribe her with promises of indulgence. But here she'd taken naturally to the other children (not biting a one) and charmed her elders with poise, whilst I myself could not abide them.

To wit, my churchly attendance remained sporadic.

The preacher, however, was not a severe judge. He did not challenge my ecclesiastic impediment, and when he sent an emissary up Blood Mountain with a request, I did not hesitate with my response. There was naught required on my own place, no hog to scald, no maize to harvest, nay. My scrap of land lay fallow. Mind and body hungered no less for industry, and thus I accepted his challenge: to race the climatic elements and raise the man a homeplace afore the shortest and coolest days were upon us.

That evening was a full harvest moon. It emerged from the dark horizon a globe of red.

Someone's set the moon ablaze, said Emmaline.

Indeed they have, I said.

The following day, in the bracing cool of dawn, I trekked down the ridges of Blood Mountain.

I convened with the father in his valley plot, where their caravan'd been living by way of makeshift campsite. As the sun swept over the landscape, it smoldered umber and ocher, a palette of turning leaves, revealing a rambling brook alive with sparks of light that collected in a giant fishing pond. Verily, the parcel's breadth and length were six sum of my own plot, and in the plat where I was meant to erect the preacher's homeplace there were no trees to clear save a chinquapin, a walnut grove, an arbor of dogwoods, a magnolia, and a peach tree. Such magnificent and unusual specimens to thrive in our climes, I suggested that they preserve them.

A slow-rising ridge below us gave way to a forest of softwoods bordered by sassafras, which he intended to clear for crops and pastureland.

At their campsite, I relieved myself of the stunned girl (neither the early-hour journey nor the nipping temperature had pleased her), placing her under the wing of the dour wife. Emmaline left me with great willingness and disappeared through the door flap of a large calfskin tent, which functioned as the family's temporary habitat.

The preacher stood beside a heavy mahogany table a dozen paces away. He had walked the land, he said, assessing its topography and measuring its plats by degree and breed of use, describing with startling accuracy the land's physiognomy. By aid of his son, he'd drawn an elaborate plot plan.

Inviting me to join him, he tapped the tabletop with the head of his filigreed stick to draw my attention, but there was no need, you see, as I'd been intrigued by the spread parchment from the moment I'd sighted it. Weighted on opposite ends by silvered candelabra, it illustrated each planned structure in elevation and orientation, meted to exact location. The sun shone in the manner of a scoping light upon this detailed map, and I leaned over to study the graphite-lined figures.

When Samuel arrived with a spread of floor plans and cross-sectionals, I launched a series of questions to ensure my comprehension and thereupon was submersed in an expedient lesson in clapboard construction and found, though the end product was more evolved than my own, the principles of home rearing remained equivalent.

By midmorn, the line of command was set: Samuel would act as manager and I as his foreman. In a clearing to serve as our base, a crew of ten able-bodied bondmen and bondwomen were placed under my surprised direction. And the giantess, oh, the giantess!

She was clad in a waist-fitting overcoat that dusted the ground, adding ever more height and dignity to her general aspect. She left with the preacher, his arm crooked through hers as she led him over the terrain. My heart dropped. She was not to be included in my crew's number. I drew in a jigger of air as crisp and sweet as a Limbertwig apple, exhaled, and conveyed it to her with the hope she would partake my breath and turn my way. She did not.

When they were midway back to camp, the three toddler girls ran flocking to the preacher. He did not drive them off. As the five walked, they projected the tableau of a family, and my chest pinged unpleasantly, a bitter taste flooding my mouth. I turned away from the vision.

After Samuel issued his instructions, he too retreated to the warmth of his campsite, whilst I was left with the ten. They wore a cornucopia of expressions of which doubt was most predominant. I'd no quibble with any of their number but sensed from them an unprovoked hostility. I sought an alliance with the preacher's favorite, nodding my head at him.

Enoch, I said. I lifted my hat.

Mr. Young, he said, by way of acknowledgment.

I then aligned them by height and heft. Equipped with an expanse of tool stock, including ax, hatchet, and my own foot adze, we headed toward the woods on the northern border of the preacher's plot. A young bondman with broad-hanging lips sidled up to me as we walked. He introduced himself as Stephen.

Best not let Marse know you a red, he said.

I serviced him with a stern look. I claim no allegiance to the native, I said, though within I cringed with this betrayal.

You sure do look like one, he said. The son don't care, but you best look out for the daddy.

We cleared the land assigned to the house and its cooperatives in the space of one calendar week, scything and burning all brush and scrub. By the end of the second, we'd felled and bucked the required oak, pine, and poplar from the surrounding wood. In three weeks we had the trees debarked and canted, by four we had it seasoned, by five the boards were rived and planed, and by six we'd braced the frame and pegged it together.

From cruck to king post I raised a wondrous clapboard structure for the Boundses to call their home, beveling each board with alacrity and high spirit. We gave the place two stories, the top with four rooms dedicated to naught but sleeping, and below, a room each for sitting, drawing, and dining, plus a serving pantry.

Between the two levels I framed a staircase of oak treads and risers, turning each tapered balustrade on my lathe, chiseling and knifing the railing myself, undeterred by the preacher's outlandish assertion that he could order such parts from a company in his native state by way of catalog. When the job was complete, the preacher set his hand upon the newel post and walked the length of the banister without missing a step. Speaking to me from the top, he proclaimed the staircase a masterpiece.

When I suggested a porch to run the length of the housefront and the back with whitewashed posts and railings, the preacher agreed, and why not? At any time of day, one could bask in the sun. So I built grand rocking chairs and a sitting bench, cutting, sanding, carving, ornamenting each with fruit-shaped embellishments in bas-relief, a cornucopia of apples, grapes, and pears.

When Samuel pried open crates of red bricks made on the European continent (were Flemish kilns of such superior quality?), I leveled and laid a tidy path running from the front of the house around the side to the back-yard, despite the preacher's claim of qualified bondmen to perform such labor. I'd not allow it. Had not the preacher commented on the evenness of my own home's floorboards? I considered the brick path my testimony to his trust.

Samuel'd taken five of my ten to build the stone foundations for the farm's outbuildings, each one a replica in construction of my own simple-hewn log place and modified to specific function: a springhouse, two barns and a stable, two smokehouses, a cure house, a loom house, a toolshed, and a blacksmith shop. Emmaline served as my miniature helper, handing me maul or froe, hinge or latch (the preacher'd brought three crates of iron pieces, wrought by a Plattsburg blacksmith, bean swiveled and heart cusped, and I had to admit to their elegance), or a hot cup of Spanish cocoa (such decadence I'd never tasted). In spite of the wife's protests that such work was not fit for a girl, I did not relent, until she suggested I might render Emma-line unmarriageable, and then I did not hesitate—back into the Boundses' tent the girl went.

When it came time to construct the dwellings for the bondmen, I took the assignment of the giantess's home for myself, building a covered passage from the main house to her quarters. What was built by my hand—a two room weatherboarded cabin roofed with chestnut bark, the front a kitchen, the back for recuperation—would be touched by hers, and in this manner, unknown to her, we would conjugate.

The weather, more temperate in the valley than in our hollow, did not defy us, and afore the year'd run out the last louvered blind and final roof shake was in place, in time for the celebration of the birth of their Jesus.

The girl and I returned to our home by way of borrowed horse, a young broodmare with an elegant neck named John Joseph. I'd signed a contract with the preacher to lease the creature for the distance of twelve months, though the preacher would accept no payment. When I professed it was overgenerous, he claimed it appropriate recompense for my labors, adding he would entertain repayment should I desire contract renewal upon expiry.

We took with us a gift basket adorned with green and red ribbons, filled with dried apples and a smoked ham, a stook of peppermint sticks, and a new twelve-month set for the Baptist calendar. The reward, in truth, was something far less tangible. Pride, it was, in part, but to the greater extent, I discovered, it was contentment.

NEW YEAR DAY, 1837

BLUE MOON

In my absence my land had grown ever more pitiful, my mother's grave a disgrace.

I awoke the first morn of the year inspired to transfigure my paltry plot.

And so I did. By whom, if none other than myself?

'Twas I who brought forth a bounty of edible textures and vibrant tones. 'Twas I who furnished the girl, who sheltered and clothed her. What did the Lord provide? Inclement weather. Pestilence. Frost. A blight worthy of Job.

By the month of May, we plucked strawberries and rhubarb; June, succulent cherries; July and August, clusters of blueberries and blackberries and tender pole beans as long as the span of my hand. In autumn the harvest was plentiful; the maize tumified, robust and vibrant with its myriad colors. When the chestnut trees dropped their spiny-burred fruits for the first time in years, I noted the day on our twelve-month sheath: *Chestnuts falling. A good day. November 15, 1837.*

When the following year brought an all-hallow'n summer, our crops thrived beyond measure. Emmaline grew gilpy and strong; she consumed her meals as if driven by perpetual hunger, and I found great satisfaction in her satiated torpor. Her sallow appearance grew rubicund, her smile sanguine, and her body gorbellied, filled with gourds and grounders cultivated in our garden, once barren and now nursed back into fecundity.

The final evening of 1838, we celebrated with roasted chestnuts and maize, after which I read to the girl from the bard's *King Henry V. Once more onto the breach, dear friends, once more!*

I was now a man of twenty, and Emmaline had lived eight winters.

AUTUMN, 1839

TRADING MOON

The girl loved chickens. Nobody loves chickens. Simply put, they're meant to be eaten.

I'd acquired a flock from the preacher's son, who raised the fancy birds as a hobby. 'Twas with nigh unbridled relief I'd expelled the Kentucky long rifle and its taunting presence from my home in exchange for eighteen spring chicks and the promise of a cock, come breeding time. Dominiques, he'd said, were an instinctive bird, and hatching and rearing came to them naturally. I would raise a fund of eggs and roasters. This much I could supply by way of meal meat.

When the preacher learned of the trade, however, he chastened his son for taking a family's memory piece and forced him to return the thing.

Despite my efforts, the godforsaken rifle remained over the hearth, unfurbished, uncharged, and unwanted.

It would be fair to say Emmaline fell all over those chicks, lifting them out of the brooder, coddling them to her breast, insisting on taking a different one to our bedstead each night, not wanting to play favorites. They were ugly things, pink skinned, scantily feathered, and weak, exhausted from pecking their way out of their shells by way of a lone egg tooth, and I feared I'd roll over and smother one and we'd have one less for supper.

Two square months later, they feathered out, and I moved them into the coop. Emmaline's devotion wavered not. She relished tossing them scraps in the morn and at night, gathering grit for their feed, and changing their soiled hay. She kept the henhouse clean as if tending her own homeplace, stringing jasmine vines over the roof to overcome any scent she was unable to prevent and to protect her brood with shade.

To my mind they were all alike, red combed, black and white barred, with nary a feature to set them apart. Not to the girl. She could distinguish one from the other, you see.

This lovely black one with the fluffy feet and white frizzle is Fred, and over there pecking the grass, no, not that one, next to him, yes, that's Gilbert, and this little sweetheart pulling up the weeds is Barnabus, the girl said, petting a meaty pullet and giving it a kiss. Isn't he a darling? He's my favorite, though I try not to let the others know it. And here's Katie and Solomon and Gay. And this fusspot is Samuel, she said, stroking its head. I thought to tell her they were all hens, nary a cockerel in the bunch, but I didn't see the sense. 'Twas somewhat humorous, her christening them after members of the Bounds clan, especially as they came running at the sound of her voice, greeting her with soft whistles and coos. They enjoyed her society and she theirs, jumping onto her lap when called, cackling and clucking as she shoveled their excrement out of the coop.

Emmaline, you'll confuse them, you're wreaking havoc with their pecking order, I said.

When I found her nesting with them, right in the coop, I insisted: Not until you sprout feathers and a beak, Emmaline Young, shall you ever do that again. I put her over my knee and slapped her seat.

She was insulted and said as much, rubbing her rump.

Emmaline, I said, I've not been overharsh. Now eat thy porridge.

She pooched her lip and shook her head with defiance.

It could've been worse. I might not use an open hand next time, but a switch, I said.

What do you know? she answered snottily. When have you ever received such a beating?

Many, and more than you can imagine.

I don't believe you.

'Twas ere you were born, and it matters not. You shall do as I say.

And why must I obey you?

I am thy elder, Emmaline.

When shall I have rights, then? she pouted.

When you're grown and married, you shall be mistress of thy own home.

Then might I do as I please?

That would depend on the generosity of thy husband.

And where shall I find such a husband? she asked, wiser than her nine winters.

Where indeed.

On the first of November, I sent the girl to the Boundses'. The sister Katie'd taken her as a plaything, and off Emmaline went with defiant happiness in her step.

What freedom to be released, if only in a short spell, from my sister.

She'd been instructed to return with the family the following day to partake in a feast. I admired how the preacher shared his wealth. I wished to demonstrate my thanks.

Aroused by this, the impending role of magnanimous host, I could scarcely sleep, and yet I arose afore daybreak bewildered with excitement and possessed by sharp clarity and singleness of purpose. To my pleasure the air was balmy, the sky clement. I set to work building a pit a fair distance away from the coop, and over a fire of hewn pine logs I filled my largest cauldron with spring water. In the slippery light of a tallow-burning wick, I attended my hatchet with boar bristle, brushing the blade free of wood sap and rust. At the whetstone, I counted under my breath ten strokes to the outer bevel, one stroke in, until the cutting edge was sharp enough to reflect the lamplight.

Inside the coop the birds slept nuzzled together in their nest box and alone on perches. I grabbed the plumpest pullet by its shanks and carried it to the log stump. I'd expected a fight, but the thing was coolly stoic—that is, until I swung my ax. At this untimely moment it chose to flap its wings. I missed its neck and caught it precisely below the comb, debraining it. Again I struck, and quickly—a lethal blow. The headless hen wobbled about the yard and collapsed. With morbid interest, I examined the mess: its spinal cord (shattered), its jugular (severed), its windpipe (glutted). The bird bled in dark, phlegmatic glubs. Shoddy work at best.

To the coop I went for another. This time I took off its face and beak ere landing a killing blow. Such a maiming no creature deserves, not even a chicken. 'Twas a most pitiful sight, and formed by my own hands, to my shame. What more, without an easy beheading, one of mercy and single stroked, there be no tasteful feast, not with the lungs filling with blood and ruining the meat.

With resolve, I altered my tactics. I grabbed a third. I gripped the head and forced it back until I heard a snap—aye, the neck. The thing shook with spasmodic shudders. It ruckled and expired easily. At last, success!

Twisting a coarse twine around the hocks, I hung it from a chestnut tree and sliced its neck, allowing it to bleed with a satisfying pling into a tin bucket. In this manner the flesh would remain pristine. I finished off the fourth and fifth in the same wringing manner.

What a wondrous sight was the sky as it began to ignite over Blood Bald!

I worked quickly, scalding each bird in the cauldron and plucking its pinfeathers, eviscerating, butchering, parsing fragments of the spoiled birds into a large crockery post—flesh not worthy of my impending guests, but for me they'd serve a decent munch. I'd fry their organs with an egg and have them for breakfast; the muscle I'd salt cure and jerk.

To the springhouse I set off, first with the crocks of spoiled parts, next with the blood-darkened buckets, and at last with my pristine three. I drew in the cold odor of a damp and mineraled earth, the stillness of the place, and recalled a time when it'd once been filled with jars of fruit and garden vegetables raised by my mother.

If I'd been a softer man, I'd've admitted to a longing for her.

Upon my return I surveyed the yard and set about rectifying it. As I raked viscera and wet feathers into a pile, I considered the gracious manner in which I'd invite my guests to sit around my table. I'd warm the cabin with a hickory fire, light the beeswax and bayberry candles, and serve them fragrant slices of the slow-roasted birds on a heavy tin plate, a horned-handle fork and knife beside it. Verily, the thought of three succulent birds skewered along a green-limbed spit, the vision of crisping golden skin and dribbling fat sizzling into the fire, caused me to salivate.

'Twas then I heard an unmistakable cluck.

I'd neglected to close the flap to the henhouse.

Whom do we have here? I said to the downy wanderer.

The bird trundled toward me and stopped as it reached the pile of feathers. It canted its head and complained. Then it toddled away toward the road at a decent clip.

I followed it. Slow down, now, I said. Where're you off?

The bird scratched and pecked at the ground, pulled up an earthworm and swallowed lustily, ambled back to me and crapped.

I sighed.

It cackled and cooed as if pleased with itself.

You truly are an ugly thing, I said, and bent to stroke its back as I'd seen Emmaline do. I stared at the bird, unable to discern which one it might be. Hannah? I tried. Gay?

When its wings closed around its soft body and its eyes narrowed to slits, I thought it content. That is, until it cocked its head back, flared its hackles, and jabbed me with its beak.

A small puncture adorned the meaty round of my palm. Blood did not dribble, yet the pain radiated deeply, and I folded my fingers over it.

Six is a fine number, would you not agree? I said.

I tackled the deviant and we skirmished in the dirt. It squawked, lunged, and clipped my ear with its beak, pinchering the lobe. I hollered and clamped a hand to my head, hammering at the bird until the stubborn miscreant released me. Off it went, squawking, feinting left and right. Who knew chickens could run with such velocity? I gave proper chase. We sprinted about the yard—that is, until finally, murderously, I cornered it inside the empty sow pen. It glowered at me with a yellow eye. Winded but not defeated, I rushed it once more. Triumph!

I secured the malevolent thing under my arm, slapped it over the chopping block, and swung my hatchet.

I thought I heard it gasp.

It had not.

'Twas Emmaline. 'Twas the girl. Walking up the path, primped as I'd never seen her afore: a vision of pulchritude, her hair no longer straggled but pressed into clean curls, her frock not her own but a pink and white pinafore unlike anything she possessed.

I looked down and the bird was headless. I'd not missed this time, but my stomach seized as the feathered creature ran toward her. She screamed no scream, and yet my blood did curdle when the bird crashed against her chest and spluttered its guts across her pleasant dress.

She stared down at the bright red clots, at the toppled hen at her feet, and back at me. Her little body shook as she bent and lifted its carcass. She searched for and found its grimy head in the dirt. She walked past me and sat on the second porch step, the dead bird clutched against her chest.

Em, let go.

The girl sat and rocked. Flies gathered. The blood on her pinafore turned to rust.

I set about righting the yard, and afterward, though I longed to bathe, I could only dust the curd and crust off my trousers with the back of my hand and work the gristle from under my nails as best I could with a file, for I dared not leave the girl and her flop-necked hen unattended.

When the preacher and his family arrived nigh the marked time, still she would not release it.

Em, it's not right. Give it here. Please, I said with an apologetic smile.

She shook her head. You killed him.

Aye, I did, I said.

The daughter Katie sheltered her face as the flies swarmed. The preacher's wife cuffed the air. The preacher bowed his head.

May I? Sam asked me. He removed his top hat and crouched by her feet. Does your little friend have a name?

The girl nodded and mashed the bird to her chest.

Dear Emmaline, why won't you tell me?

She cupped her mouth and leaned into his waiting ear. The flies scattered.

Barnabus, said Sam quietly.

(I sighed and rubbed the side of my face. Barnabus. Aye, of course.)

Perhaps we should bury your dear Barnabus, said Sam. My father will say a prayer?

Why not? We are all God's creatures, said the preacher.

The girl tugged at Sam's flounced sleeve, and he looked down at her with a sympathetic smile. She reached into her bloodied pocket and drew out the bird's head.

Will God put it back on? she asked. I'd not want him walking about heaven without his head attached.

Yes, Sam answered, God can do anything He wishes.

Sam offered his hand, and together they mounted the hill. I grabbed a mattock and followed this ridiculous processional. We climbed to the northwest, over the bluegrass and up a rocky scarp. When Sam arrived at a high, grassy knob only fifty paces from my own mother's resting spot, he said, Do you mind? and indicated where I should dig.

(Mind. Aye, I minded. And yet he could handle the girl. Who was I to lament?)

Not at all, I said.

I swung the chiseled blade and tore at the ground until I'd carved a trench four feet deep. I did not want evening rovers digging up fair Barnabus for a nighttime snack.

The preacher sang a psalm of salvation as Sam somberly placed Barnabus into the hole, puzzling the bird's body to its head, which he draped in a linen handkerchief. The preacher extracted his Bible from his long-coat and thumbed the gilt-edged text, running his fingertips from left to right over the raised type. He spoke sincerely, extolling the virtues of fowl, and concluded with *"For dust thou art, and unto dust shalt thou return. Amen."* The wife and daughter emitted a high, nasal sound, and Emmaline bawled out her anguish. I thought them all mad.

After the preacher and his family left us, silence set upon my homeplace.

Verily, no words exchanged between us, day after autumnal day, sunrise to sun rest. Emmaline minded the cabin and I the land. I fished our dinner, and she prepared it. We sat and ate. We slept in the very same bedstead. But lo, we did not speak.

She no longer interfered with the chickens, and this pleased me.

When at first she began to slip away, it was for short spells, and I was not harried. She was never long out of sight. Soon after, however, she began to remove herself thrice a week, lengthening the time with gradients meant to be imperceptible. Ha! I denied the fool-begged urge to search for her.

When at last she returned, she'd find me with my feet to the fire, reading *Hamlet*.

Until one night, the red planet with its dim winter light rising in the eastern sky, I could withstand her absence no more, and I rushed up and down the fleam, blaming myself, mourning her loss, blathering her name, only to find her at last, at home, bedded down, feigning sleep.

'Twas then I judged the girl more than capable of looking after herself and summarily recused myself of her care.

THE BIRTH OF SPRING, 1840

WINDY MOON

I was in slow courtship and took pleasure in the temerity of every moment I dared to snare the eye of my inamorata.

When the preacher hired me as his carpenter, out of the hollow I ventured with greater frequency. I received a practical sum for my labors and became acquainted with the balanced temperament with which the preacher handled his bondmen, in contrast to the military manner of the son. As Sam barked his orders, foppishly brandishing his new Colt pistol, I took him for a man practicing his form, as he'd soon join the ranks of federal men in a war in the Everglades. From his talk I gleaned that a group of Florida Indians refused to take their so-called place in the hinterlands west of the Mississippi. He seemed not to care for sides or allegiances as much as the opportunity to escape his own father's command, or perhaps his destiny. An opportunist, he was, by my measurement, a lad of no palpable industry.

He departed the fourth week of January. Emmaline, who oft shadowed me through the wintering trees as if I could not hear her tramping on frozen leaves, was bereft. I did not counsel her, nor did she seek it. Our war of silence remained stalemated.

In the son's absence, Solomon's use for me expanded, and I soon discovered I was not a man designed for constant solitary. I found I thrived in the company of others, though not without expense; it left me charismatically depleted, and I spent self-enforced days of recuperation upon my own homeplace, cabin'd, cribb'd, confin'd, and aside my mother's grave, where nary a sound of humanity existed.

Once restored, I resumed my duties and leveraged them to espy the object of my desire, be it from the roof of the Boundses' yellow house, from the rung of my ladder, from the toolshed, or in simple passing. In addition to running the household, the giantess served oft as the preacher's guide, leading him about his farm, and I enjoyed gazing at her outright whilst the blindman spoke to me, quoting lengths of wood and brats and nails required for this or that repair. She'd not be flustered, and this drew me to her ever more.

I had begun my romantic campaign with a kindly nod the first day of the new year.

The second week, I smiled.

The third week, I smiled again.

At each overture, her face remained unmoved.

But come February, she raised an eyebrow. By March, my greetings seemed to vex her not, and one unseasonably warm Saturday evening (and I was certain my eyes were true) she removed the parsley from a plate of beef gobbets afore it was served me, as she knew I disliked the bitter herb.

From thence, I supped daily at the Boundses' table, as did the girl, the clan too polite to remark upon our mutual silence. Lossie simmered and stewed elegant meats (goose, lamb, ham, and roast beef) that aroused the sleeping beast of my appetite, while her sweets too unraveled me: gingerbread, buckeye pudding, and solid syllabub! Ah, balms; ah, nectars; ah, elixirs of life.

THE ENDURANCE OF SPRING, 1840

FLOWER MOON

Accompanied by the dawn's first birdsong, I bathed.

Dressed in a fresh cotton shirt, vest, and trousers, my best leather braces over my shoulders, my hair combed, its long length fettered in a leather yoke, I set off to gather wildflowers. Down in the Great Gorge I ventured until I found my intended, a broad reaching bed of red trillium. 'Twas not merely the color—a sumptuous burgundy—or the shape—a perfect symmetry of curvaceous petals against diamond-shaped leaves—but its odor—cloyingly fetid and yet not repellent, a scent akin to a favorite wet mutt—that drew me to these fleshy whorls. I counted every third blossom of this majestic flower and requested its permission ere I cut it, recalling with poignant heart the custom of my mother, who'd taught me to gather in this respectful and conserving manner.

The blue mist of the gorge intruded coldly inside the collar of my shirt and in no time wilted the brim of my hat. The rocks sweated, the ferns dripped. Still, it was a damp and beauteous Avalon. I offered my thanks, not to the Lord but to the forest, for this floral gift.

Arms laden with enough April blooms for a dozen Lossies, I arrived at her well-built kitchen door, which was ajar, and leaned into the shade of the roof's overhang to steal a glimpse through the window. Her pendulous curves formed gracious arcs as she bent over the fire and fried a fragrant meat. At the sound of the great number of skeleton keys tinning against her thigh (they hung from her apron belt), I sprung erect.

Presently, she stood beneath the doorjamb toweling her moist neck.

Good day, Mr. Young.

Alas, my tongue would not release.

Shall I prepare them for the mistress or are they for Miss Katie?

Miss who? I expelled.

Miss Katie. She placed a strong hand on the full of her hip.

Why, nay, nay, they are for you. I thrust the wildflowers forth, nigh losing my gift as several blooms fell at my feet.

She took them and said under her breath, What are you doing, Mr. Young?

Wooing you.

Wooing me?

Aye. Courting. I am in love. I managed to somehow remove my hat, still damp from the gorge's fog, and place it under my arm.

In love?

Aye. I am in love.

With who?

With you, of course. I unfurled the sheet I'd prepared and began to recite:

> So are you to my thoughts as food to life,
> Or as sweet-seasoned showers are to the ground;
> And for the peace of you I hold such strife
> As 'twixt a miser and his wealth is found:
> Now proud as an enjoyer, and anon
> Doubting the filching age will steal his treasure;
> Now counting best to be with you alone,
> Then bettered that the world may see my pleasure;
> Sometime all full with feasting on your sight,
> And by and by clean starved for a look,

Possessing or pursuing no delight
Save what is had or must from you be took.
Thus do I pine and surfeit day by day,
Or gluttoning on all, or all away.

She puckered her lips. It's not the clumsiest thing I ever heard. You wrote that?

No, madam. William Shakespeare.

Don't madam me. I'm Lossie. Or Cook. Either one will do.

Lossie, I said, tasting her name.

Her eyes sparked, but I did not break my gaze.

You can tell Mr. Shakespeare thank you for the poem, but I believe you've been cheated of your money. She frowned. Take these to the mistress before they wilt, she said, wrinkling her nose. If she'll have them.

I reluctantly received them. I can be discreet, said I, my chest tightening.

No, Mr. Young.

She swiped the trillium I'd dropped from the dirt and closed the door on my face.

I left, elated.

My next encounter occurred seven days anon under the guise of a medicinal visit.

You're late, she said from within the room of her kitchen.

My appointment is at two past noon, is it not? I'd gauged the angle of the sun, noting its degrees relative to the globe's arc and ascertained my visit timely.

I prepared a potion for you, she said.

Aye? I said, looking about the place.

Several years ago, she said with mouth set.

Aye, I said, delighted she remembered me. For insomnolence. 'Twas most efficacious and enduring. I sleep now undisturbed.

Undisturbed. She breathed out her nose like a horse. I like that. I seem to remember Mr. Solomon offered you an appointment.

Aye, I said.

Too good for my services? she asked, arching her back in the manner of one self-possessed.

Nay, I said with utmost respect.

I'd say you don't take my medicine or yourself seriously, Mr. Young.

But I am free.

Free? Free of what? Mr. Young, what is it that you are free of?

I am . . . self-cured, I stammered.

Ha. I'll be the judge of that. She widened her door.

I did not care for her tongue-lashing, nor her gaming, but if it gained me entrance to her sanctum, I'd allow her tongue to lash me, her mind to game me forever. I quickly mucked my boots along the gourded mat and entered. My mouth watered as I drank in the scent of yeast, dampness, bread soft and dark, and then a note of something beneath it, an earthly odor of something well fed and guarded.

I understand you suffered an affliction of the flesh, she said in a manner professional, indicating I should arrange myself at her harvest table. It was a furnishing I knew well, having hand-planed its broad chestnut top and having carved, under a spell of besotted boyishness, our initials, grandly hooking the leg of my *R* through the loop of her *L* and linking them both to my *Y*. I pulled out a chair and sat. With a cant of my head, I noted with a particular satisfaction the glint and dents of her copper skillets and pots that hung overhead from a circular device of hammered iron, which I'd crafted myself.

Aye, I answered. I'd no intention of playing patient to her doctor. Nay, I'd raise the stakes. In describing my condition, its crawling and throbbing nature, I did not mince words, but she neither recoiled nor softened her face. I did not wish to overplay my hand, nor did my sense of decorum allow it, so I told her not my most heinous act: More than once, I'd served as intimate partner to myself, which pleasurably intensified and momentarily mollified but never sufficiently cured the base sensation. I am the personification of health, said I, and flexed a bicep, intending to evoke a smile, some levity, or at the least remove her look of scrutiny.

Speak English, she said.

I am no longer in need of relief, I said. As if to mock me, my skin chose this moment to resume its infernal itch.

She read it upon my face. Ha, she said again, triumphant, and drew a bluish curtain across the window, subduing the clatter of voices and hoof steps outside.

You might loose your collar, Mr. Young. You're looking faint.

My heart was pounding. Was I having a fit?

She brought over a dram, and I quaffed in quick gulps, then sputtered. 'Twas not water but a meaty brew, familiar to me in its potency.

Highland scotch, she said. It's meant to be sipped.

I thought it a remedy, I said.

It can be, said she.

Indeed, I felt the liquid's agreeable effect as its warmth spread through me.

You suffer no malady, Mr. Young. By my estimation, you're a normal man who's been jammed up on a mountain too long with no one but his sister for company. A hermit with an appetite and no one to feed it. It's not healthy. How old are you?

I am twenty-one.

You say it like you're a man.

I am.

We'll see about that.

She popped the button of my shirt collar.

Again my heart palpitated.

May I inquire as to what age you possess? I asked.

No, you may not. She untied the top of her dress. I'm thirty-four.

With a newfound steadiness, I loosed her corset, and after the fair obstacles of wool cord and grommets, my nose stood level to her gracious chest.

Mr. Young, she said. Get ahold of yourself.

I've never beheld such beauty, I gasped.

I appreciate that, she said with a tug at my braces. You planning to take them off?

Aye, I said. I could not help but grin as I stood, at last, from the waist down, liberated.

The giantess took measure of me, and in her gaze I saw nascent approval. Not in my kitchen, she said. To her bedroom we made haste.

I gripped her hips and attempted to turn her from me, prepared to mount her as I'd seen in all manners of barnyard rutting, but she stood firmly rooted, and asked me with her jaw firm set if she looked like an animal. I told her, Aye, with the strength of a bear, the coarse hair of a boar hog, the sueded skin of a mare horse, the—

She interrupted. Mr. Young, this will go better if you keep your mouth shut.

I obliged and used it instead to tend to her every inch, the household keys jangling a tune of loving accompaniment. When I finished, she said to me, Mr. Young, consider yourself courted.

I soared home to Screamer Hollow the following day, buoyed by the sensation of utter elation. Verily, if I'd been an eagle aloft above Blood Bald, rather than upon the sturdy back of John Joseph, I'd not've been a lighter person.

When I arrived, I found Emmaline inside, poised on the tips of her toes atop the compendious dictionary, which she'd placed upon the seat of the ladderback, lifting the long rifle from its place above the hearth. I had to stifle my laughter at the picture she made, this diminutive woman-child of nigh ten winters wielding a rifle of the same height. She managed, summarily, to displace it. Her mouth crooked in half smile, a thief caught in the act.

Samuel has returned, she said, breaking our long-held silence.

I am aware, I countered. (From the Florida jungle a decorated officer, no less. As to what feat he'd accomplished in his brief absence of twelve weeks to attain the rank of colonel, other than to survive, I'd no knowledge. Verily, I'd not've been surprised if the resourceful lad had purchased the title.)

He's teaching me to hunt, she said.

That so.

'Tis.

I forbid you to cross that threshold, Emmaline. It is not thine to take.

She continued down the steps.

If you should leave, don't ever you come back, I said.

You don't mean it, she said without turning.

But I do.

No, you don't.

She was right.

THE BUDDING OF SUMMER, 1840

GREEN CORN MOON

Oft I lay with the giantess. As promised, I was discreet. After, I'd stroll in the dark along the preacher's grounds, gazing up at the window lit by flickering wick, my sister's nightly light. The girl was now a sponsored member of their family, returning to our homeplace with rarity. Neither the preacher nor his wife ever mentioned her overnight roosts with any sense of their peculiarity. That she should shun her own kin (never mind the sentiment was mutual) and replace me with these others was not once brought up in my company.

Keep her, then.

July, July! My woman was with child.

Yet not one eye winked nor smooth brow wrinkled at the rising moon of Lossie's belly. No mouth poured with gossip, not from her compatriots nor the Bounds patriarch nor his family.

Late one August evening the preacher arrived at the kitchen door to take an impromptu stroll. He stood under the lintel and waited for his housekeeper whilst I remained half-mast upon her bedstead.

Have a good evening, Mr. Young, he said as they left.

Was I an exposed libertine?

With haste I pulled on my trousers and left the cabin, shirtless, the heavy air of summer seeming ever more heavier in my half-cocked haste. I'd not abandon my woman. I'd take her punishment in her place. I surveyed the ground for figurative evidence of their retreat; I listened for the sound of the preacher's tapping stick. A fair minute passed and lo! I heard it; yet afore I could ascertain from whence it came, I saw them round the homeplace. 'Twas the preacher leading Lossie by the elbow (rather than the contrary), for her outstanding stomach oft capsized her well-shaped vessel. She walked with her hand tucked in the small of her back, leisurely, pleasurably, sonorously laughing, as if the preacher had told a mirthful anecdote. When they reached the back quarters, he bade her good night, tapping to the front of his home on his own.

What did he want of you? I said upon her return. As she passed me, I noted her scent, or that of her garments, not native to her but to the preacher. 'Twas the tang of his rank tobacco.

He was having trouble sleeping. Get back inside. You're half dressed. Her gaze was amorous.

So he sought to ambulate? I asked, following her inside.

If you mean walk, then yes.

'Twas quite brief.

Lucky for you, she said as we crossed the threshold into her bedroom.

He is not angered by my . . . intrusion? I stretched myself upon the bed-sheets, now cold. She quickly disrobed and resumed her position along-side me.

If he didn't want you doing what you're doing, he never would have offered me to you in the first place, said she.

She rolled onto her side and fit her copious seat into my crotch.

And what is it that I'm doing? I said. I reached around her and cupped a weighty bosom.

She removed my hand and placed it upon her belly. It does something to the appetite, she said.

Aye. I am well aware. There is no part of me that doth not ache.

She laughed, turned toward me, unbuttoned my trousers. If ever a man was spent from lovemaking, I admit without dishonor, I was he. Her condi-tion inspired her needs, you see, and a regiment of one hundred well-hung men would not've satisfied her.

A pause, and then I said in a way meant to evoke no effrontery, Have ever you joined with another?

Certainly more than you, she said, and peppered her warm-lipped affections onto my neck.

Aye, but none is not hard to trump. I ventured again. The three young lasses . . . (My mind blanked as her hand traversed the map of my lower complement.)

Must you speak? she asked.

I continued, driven for an answer. Anna, Cassia, and—

Galilee, she said, releasing my dividend.

They are yours? I asked, at last expelling my long-held inquest.

She folded her arms under her head. Why?

They flock to you with great affection and even greater to the preacher. Are they yours?

She cut me down with a burning glance. They're alone, those girls, if that's what you're asking.

So this child is thy first? I asked, a whit too joyfully. To make amends, I turned my head on the pillow and nuzzled into the dark swamp of her fur-ried pit.

She swatted me off. To live, she said. Now get out. She stared with ill-humored expression into the timbered roof.

I meant you no insult.

You have a lot to learn, Mr. Young.

About you, I affirmed.

Yes.

I will never tire of learning.

You could start by finding the door. She gave me her back.

Nay, I said, do not spurn me. I rolled over to hold her.

No.

I wish to know you. Allow me. Lossie?

Get out.

After considerable time, I rose to leave. I would respect her wishes, for the moment. Lossie, I said, again, afore I left.

As I passed from her room to the kitchen, she spoke. It is too lonesome a world to go without it, she said.

WINTER, 1841

COLD MOON

On the fifth day of the new year, my son arrived. A son! My son.

My woman named him Alger.

The preacher threw us a grand fete, and to my astonishment Emmaline joined us. She crammed into the kitchen eyeing the child with such yearning I almost allowed her to hold him. She'd been forlorn, I could not help but notice, ever since the daughter Katie had been promised to Thomas Darling, a cotton planter serving twenty-five years to her eighteen, who resided far south of Hopewell County.

Lossie handed my son to Enoch.

He got your eyes, he said to her.

What a wonder my boy was, the way he gurgled and shrieked at every newfound discovery: his fingers, his toes, his mother's voice, his wee staff, the thong binding my braid, the stubble that grizzled above my lip. One morning, however, rather than joy, he began to emit bloodcurdling screams, and I feared he was on the cusp of death, until Lossie alleviated his suffering with a mixture of ginger, dill, chamomile, and sodium bicarbonate.

Gas, she said.

The woman was a gifted healer. From elements as common as honey and soot she could resolve most everything that ailed him. When she could not, rarely, quietly, she would resort to a darker art, one that I did not dare question, for though it seemed akin to magic, it worked despite its appearance of tomfoolery: the chanting of spells and the laying of hands, the wearing of strange charms—eyeball in shape and with blue-tinged irises. Perhaps my son was simply mesmerized by the sway of her voice or the sensual movement of her body as she evoked her unseen forces. Either way, I knew not to challenge my giantess.

When I expressed interest in her craft, she would enlighten me, depending on her humor.

Arsenic? I said one morn, reading a florid label in her collection of remedies. I tapped at the glass and examined its contents, a collection of gray granules. What magic doth it work?

In Plattsburg, she said as she heated water for the preacher's tea, Mr. Solomon took Fowler's Solution.

What, pray, is that? I asked.

A concoction of arsenic and carbonate of potash, said Lossie.

The preacher, she said, credited the tincture with his triumphant recoveries. Now it seemed he'd developed the habit of consuming a dash of pure arsenic as part of his diet, claiming it stimulated his taste for life. It was odorless and tasteless but too much could kill a man.

How much would that be? I asked, squeezing the bottle's cork.

Why, Mr. Young? You planning on poisoning someone?

Nay. I am only expressing curiosity.

Curiosity has killed greater cats than you, she said, taking the bottle back.

Yet here I am, I said proudly.

The weight of a dried pea, said she.

By October, my son could say "Da," and repeatedly, as if stuck on the sound. He grew at an astonishing rate, a trait indisputably passed on to him by his mother. By December, the top of his head easily surpassed my knee, and I was convinced he'd reach heroic proportion, a thought that pleased me.

An unpleasant reality, however, unnamed to date, had long been tapping on my shoulder, and I was no longer able to ignore it.

MIDSUMMER, 1842

RIPE CORN MOON

At last I'd amassed a goodly sum, my wages from carpentry well saved.

Within my hollow I rehearsed my argument, suiting the action to the word, the word to the action.

I arrived at dusk in the valley, my Bible in hand.

'Twas an agreeable evening, the end of his Lord's day, and I sat with the preacher on his porch, he in a grand rocking chair, I on a log bench. The light was luminous, the air ambrosial. An intermittent wind fluttered the flag he rarely kept out past sunset, its twenty-six stars rippling and then puttering out. As the light dwindled, signifying the holy time had passed, I commenced with earnestness.

The preacher listened coolly and nodded. With folded hands upon the filigreed head of his walking stick, he leaned and said, It is with considerable regret, son, but I cannot accept.

He outright declined to sell my son to me.

It is best to be satisfied with the length of rope I've extended you and my housekeeper, he said and rose stiffly to full height. And prudent to mind the natural order of things, praise Jesus.

I pressed a hand against the front door, restricting his departure. I'd not be so easily dismissed, you see.

Listen to me, son, he said, a grimness spreading across his lips. You have interfered with another man's property, my property, and by law I have the right to prosecute you. I have been lenient. I have ignored your indiscretions. I have not charged you, nor shamed you, nor put you under scrutiny.

I could not comprehend, I said. If he did not condone our union, then why did he allow it?

(Sudden thoughts flashed across the landscape of my mind, dry lightning igniting a firestorm: Had I been tricked? And if so, by whom? Did Lossie couple with me willingly—by her own estimation the answer would be aye. I did not doubt her veracity. She loved me, if not at first, most truly now, and I most certainly she. But then, and here I recalled her assurances the night interrupted by the preacher's sudden need to ambulate: If he didn't want you doing what you're doing, he'd've never offered me to you in the first place. The words pealed in my head. Had the man intended for me to play the sire and increase his workforce naturally? Was this what Lossie'd meant? I thrust it off, this mantle of unwanted questions.)

He tucked his white-striped chin to his chest. You were lonely, son, were you not?

My answer caught in my throat.

Then take solace in what I have offered you, lest I withdraw the privilege. He sighed. We must all suffer the consequences of our ungodly choices.

I've not betrayed thy Lord or any other.

Fornication outside of marriage is immoral, said he simply.

Then free her, I said, and I will take her as my wife. Allow me to rectify my misdeed.

The preacher hooted. What you must understand, he intoned mildly, is that the negro is simpleminded. Slavery is their natural condition. They require judicious care and protection, not freedom. He struck the porch flooring with his walking stick to emphasize his point.

I cracked open my tome, eager to stiffen my argument. My finger slipped too easily over the linen leaves, and I realized with an aching heart that I held not the family Bible with verses well rehearsed, but a volume of William Shakespeare.

I did not despair.

I had my remembrances, you see.

I inhaled and closed my eyes and welcomed the gray-inked letters against the page, my mother's dark hair against my arm as she read the passage to me. I spoke: Doth Paul not say in the book of Acts that we are all made of one blood, all nations of men to dwell on all the face of the earth? Verily, do we not all share one ancestor? Are we not all sons and daughters of Adam? Is it not possible for love to exist despite the discomforts of race? Free them both and allow me to care for and protect my family.

Soft laughter rose from the depths of his gullet. He coughed. Now, son, he said in a rather grave way. One must begin by petitioning the state's approval before any slave is freed, and we must abide that process. Imagine if we all went about emancipating whomever we please. It would be absolute chaos.

Then just the boy. I beseech you. Allow me to purchase my son and free him so no man shall be his master.

He shook his head and said he was uninspired to separate his cook from her progeny, particularly not when the offspring was still a babe. He had borne witness to the ill effect this wrought upon a slave; he had no desire to bring her such grief. She was a valuable servant, and he cared not to be without her.

I have not had a single runaway since my arrival, he said. Keep their families together and one has slaves who stay.

I could not help but act derelict. The words jettisoned from my mouth: I demanded he pay me half my son's value. (If I'd served as stud, I reasoned, it was my fair recompense.)

He felt his way to the bench and sat. Son, you are an Indian. Cherokee would be my guess, he said in a tone that suggested secrecy. Of what measurement is of no consequence to me. That you escaped the removals is a miracle. The good Lord gave you a refuge on that mountaintop, and there you shall have stayed, no doubt, had I not passed through that day. What the Lord has drawn together let us not tear asunder. I've no need to alert authorities or make inquires regarding your homestead, but the fact remains: You are a man without country and you do not own anything.

My mouth grew dry. I found I had a contradictory wish: to be invited inside, to retire for the night in the comfort of a newly feathered bed, not as myself, Riddle Young, mountaineer, misfit, but someone else, even Samuel, to fall asleep to the eerie clicks of nighttime creatures in the sanctuary of my room, whilst my father Solomon tortured some other man.

I do not deny that I am a genuine son of this soil, I said. I am loyal to it, guided by it. I would take the earth as my mistress if I could.

You are a heathen, on this we agree, he said, heartily inverting my argument.

My mother was of this land; this is true. More than either you or me, I said, aware of a strong force building within my chest.

Do not misunderstand, son. I am fond of you and your sister. Your origins do not restrict my feelings with regard to your predicament. To interfere with a man's offspring or his paramour is not my aim. I do not envy your position. Though you may not believe me, I do understand it.

I turned to face him, in light of his strange pronouncement.

The preacher seemed to gaze into the heavens, which shone a spectacular shade of violet. His face, awash in the cool light, developed a sadness I'd not heretofore witnessed: His lips wilted, and his eyes, though clouded, were weighted with grief. I could not bear to look at him further, as it seemed a sorrow most private, and instead sought refuge in the night sky. A pity he cannot see it, I thought, marveling further that the man could retain his faith in God without such visual evidence. Or perhaps blindness was what enabled it.

A proposition, he said, absently twisting a garnet ring around his smallest finger. It would give me great solace to know this farm will continue, and continue well, after I have joined our Father in heaven. Whereas my charges are a small flock, and I have always managed them alone; in my final absence, and here I will not mince words, Samuel will not be a suitable replacement for the scope of the job. You have a favorable way with my bondmen. They respect you. What I am offering you is the opportunity to oversee them.

I do not wish—

He raised his hand. Samuel views you fraternally, and while at first he will be displeased, he will come to see the wisdom of my decision. You as overseer will leave him free to play master, to dabble in the hobbies that please him. It is his mind that I trust—his financial acumen, his comprehension of the law above all things—and his enjoyment for a certain quality of life will drive him to succeed. Without a doubt, this is a fine formula, one that champions longevity.

And why would such an offer interest me?

Within the house, the tapers had been lit, and they shone upon Solomon as he spoke, casting him in a sallow aurora. An excellent and natural question, said the preacher. Once your service has begun, you shall be indentured to my son for a period of seven years. Upon the completion you may purchase your offspring at fair market price. By then, the boy shall be an age appropriate to separation.

What alternative did I have to the preacher's shrewd offer? To steal my woman and my son? To raise him, wed her, as fugitives? My fingers numbed, as did my lips, as if the preacher were drawing out my vitality.

Son?

I sought a tourniquet. I accept, I said.

He took my hand. His grasp was robust, and I answered his strength with my own firm grip.

He said with a rueful expression, It is an awkward place, this world, for someone in your condition. We both stand to profit, I assure you.

I wished him long health, though I did not yet know if I fully meant it.

Thank you. I intend to have it, said he.

As I headed down the steps, I ventured one last inquiry: Emmaline was spending considerable time in the company of his family; what did he think of her comportment?

He said she was growing into a lovely child of God, a fair beauty, and that she had the demeanor of an angel. Why did I ask?

Might you know of a lad to serve as potential suitor? Though she is still quite immature (nigh twelve winters), I am concerned for her future.

He said yes, actually, there was one with whom she had developed a noticeable attachment. He suspected the feelings were mutual and thought they would be well matched. He would investigate and send the gentleman my way.

I thanked him again for his (dubious) kindness.

As I turned toward Lossie's quarters, I judged the pact not too grimly; quite rightly, within it I felt a seed of hope.

Son, I heard him say when I'd reached a distance of ten paces away.

He stood in the open doorway, the bright burn of the hallway behind him, rendering him naught but shadow and outline. It is not Adam of whom Paul speaks, he said, but God, God who made the world and things therein, God who is our common ancestor, who giveth to all life, and breath, to all things. We all are the offspring of Him. And it is through His Son, Jesus Christ, who suffered and died for us upon the Cross, who sacrificed His blood, that we have the capacity for redemption, to accept salvation, to allow Jesus into our hearts as the one true Savior—white, Jew, negro, Indian, sinners all. Although I applaud your inventive interpretation, do not take for granted the distinction between the races. It is not accidental but designed by the Lord.

I spent a restless night, waking my woman in hope of easing my state with an act of the physical. I ravaged her and she, sensing my needs, matched me. The second night, not wishing to deprive her of a goodly sleep, I took the matter into my own hands. What is man without his passion? By the third, my wits had taken leave, and I crept out of her bed nigh the break of dawn.

I took down the corked bottle tormenting me.

Had not the man lived a long life? What could he be—fifty-two? Three? Had he not lived exquisitely? He'd won the Battle of Consumption, of Catarrh, of Dropsy, of Worms, of Whooping Cough. Ague'd not taken him, nor melancholia, nor flux. His only artifacts of the pox were his marred face and sightlessness. My stomach turned knowing his will and capacity to live for eternity.

But still. Who was I to play the Almighty?

Better yet, who was he?

I rolled the smooth glass against my cheek. The gray granules shifted and whispered their strangely sounding name: arsenic.

A helpmate to time, to hurry it along, as it might be.

Though I could not, I longed to consult with my giantess with my plan of wrongfulness.

It would be a feat of magic to walk in the world of white men and survive unmarked, she'd once said when I'd expressed a dream of leaving our confines. On this homestead my keys unlock every door, and the preacher relies upon me more than his own wife. Who are you to rob me of that? And what of the others? I feed them, I heal them. They seek my advice. I'm not leaving.

My woman's hand upon my shoulder—I felt it now.

I slipped the glass bottle into my robe pocket.

She hung a kettle of water over the hearth fire.

You are a formidable woman, I said as she cracked the last of three eggs into a bowl.

She laughed and beat them until they surrendered.

With renewed interest I watched as my giantess prepared the preacher's breakfast: fresh waffles served with its usual complement, a black tea from China. He was a man of habit who relished every morning a cup of the bitter drink.

The next dawn, I saddled the mare John Joseph and set off for Screamer Hollow. As I ascended the deeply shaded path, I drew in every earthly odor, every familiar scent of dung, sawdust, sap, when I found myself overcome by one that seemed impossibly dominant.

I did not see the species within my sight. Still, it seemed the entire forest was assembled from it.

My mount came to a sudden halt. Her neck stiffened. A sensation took over me: the presence of another amid the closely packed trees.

What do you smell?

Pine, Mother. Pine, I said.

I inhaled deeply and filled the emptiness of my chest with the scent of the stars.

What have you done?

'Tis done and nothing can stop it.

Did she caress my cheek? Nay, it was only a longing for such a feeling, set off by the thick scent of remembrance.

Pull thyself together, man, I said and nudged John Joseph with my heels, speaking to her in a soothing voice. Come now, that's it, carry on, aye, there you go. Her ears swiveled as she listened, and she sallied on, abandoning the unseen pine grotto and its conjured ghost. She negotiated fallen rock and winding streams without my guidance as I ducked under tree limbs and squinted in the scant light dappling through the leaves, at last arriving, at last dismounting, and walking up the three flagstones into the peace of my cabin.

The following day the sky blackened. Storm clouds exploded with rain that lasted three days. I remained inside my homeplace, listening to the drops fall on the roof and slap against the windowpane, a mighty cascade, a fountain.

On the fourth day, the sun rose again.

I stood staring into the fleam. It was the hour of long shadows.

I summoned the girl's image as it once was: feral and devoted to me, and found I twinged with a sensation I could only describe as longing. I did not miss her antics or her wanderings, but she was, indeed, my only blood kin. She'd progressed under the family's tutelage, becoming a social creature with charm and poise. And now what life of solitude had I condemned her to? How was I to find her a mate if I'd silenced the matchmaker? Unless the man worked from the grave.

Brother.

Emmaline, I said, awakening from my trance. She stood afore me, her face mottled, her nose scarlet.

'Twas terrible, she said and broke into a sob. There were convulsions. He grew mad, raving. It went on for three days. Nothing could save him. It was . . . He is dead, brother. Reverend Solomon is dead.

She threw her arms around my neck with such need. I held her and rocked her and sang her name. She mistook my tears of joy for sadness.

It is naught, I said, breaking her hold. Naught at all. Ah, Emmaline. I wrapped the girl in my arms and held her again, and tightly. I kissed her cheek and took a draught of her sweet hair. She was diaphanous in a cream silk frock; her complexion had paled ever more with the freedom from working the land. We looked ever less like kin. Ah, but no mind. I was delirious, as though my life'd just begun and I'd discovered a well of eternal happiness. Steady, I told myself.

And when I turned, I felt quite foolish.

The girl'd been squired by Samuel. He stood above the bank on the swath of bluegrass, a mirror of my own discomfit.

I offered him my condolences. Your father was a good man, I said.

He nodded and said he was with his maker now. Surely in a better place.

I had to agree.

He said he'd been advised of a contract his father had with me, and given the preacher's untimely and sudden death, could I prepare to commence my duties the day following Father's funeral?

That evening I stacked the calendars and built a small fire and burned them all. The emblazoned woven sheets crackled and wheeled embers into the air like a murder of black crows. I invented a dance, inspired by this whirling sight, not too irreverent or too celebrant, as seven long years lay ahead of me. I delivered one whoop, one fist pump, and one, nay, two, thrusts of my pelvis.

I packed solely my clothing and shaving instruments. I left my compendious dictionary, my Bible, and my works of William Shakespeare. They seemed not to belong in my new world.

Shortly after I arose the next day, I began my descent from the hollow. The moon still shone, and when the sun at last erupted, the two warring lights illuminated the sky until the nightly orb at last surrendered. In no time, it seemed, I emerged from the thick of trees to cross the truss bridge over the Cuchulannahannachee. John Joseph's ears pricked and my heart leaped. The preacher stood waiting on the far side, leaning casually against the rail. He appeared quite alive.

His image did not waver. His eyes, no longer cloudy, bored into me.

Mr. Young, he said as I approached.

My guilt, again, nothing more.

It is oddly freeing, he said and lifted the brim of his black hat.

To be dead or to see? I asked, passing him.

Are they not the same?

A week later, the preacher's wife followed her betrothed into the ground.

Standing alongside her casket, I recalled upon her face the constant look of one impoverished.

She'd lived as if stricken with a secret suffering, and for years I'd presumed its nature epidemiological, given the family's biology. But when, only days afore, she'd leaned over the preacher's own humble casket and lowered her shriveled lips to his, her impoverished look had transformed into a portrait of mortal anguish.

I posited: Perhaps grief had undone Mrs. Solomon B. Bounds, and not a banal wasting illness.

Yet how is one to tell the difference?

I thought of my father. What is this tie that links one life to another? When it is severed, are we not freed? Or, by the very nature of the bond, doth the tie only grow tighter, a falling body against the noose knot.

What is guilt but an act unacted or one overplayed?

SUMMER'S FADE, 1842

NUT MOON

In two years she will be of marriageable age, he said when I did not respond.

I took a black walnut from its bowl upon the harvest table, cracked its shell, and popped its moist meat into my mouth.

I have been taken with her from the first time we met, he said.

I am aware, I said, brushing the shell into a bowl.

Then do we have your consent?

Samuel stood afore me in Lossie's kitchen, requesting my sister's hand. I'd've laughed aloud if I were not indentured to the man.

Forgive me, said I, placing another walnut into the nutcracker, squeezing the levers together. Ere his untimely death, your father intended to speak with a gentleman, of his congregation I believe, whom he considered an appropriate match to my sister.

Sam regarded me coolly. My father did as you requested.

Aye? I said, awash with relief. Pray tell, who is he? I munched the nutmeat heartily and tossed the shells into the bowl.

I am the man with whom my father spoke.

I swallowed dryly. (Surely he jested. Or was it sport of his dead father, a revenge exacted from the grave? To serve as lackey to the mistress, my own sister.)

As if on cue, Emmaline appeared in the door, breathless and filmy eyed, the preacher's garnet ring hanging from a golden chain around her neck.

Oh, brother, she said, say yes!

THIRTY-THIRD CONGRESS. SESSION II.

Speech of Hon. A. H. Stephens, of Georgia,
In the House of Representatives

December 14, 1854

In reply to the remarks of Mr. Mace, of Indiana, on giving notice of his intention to introduce a bill to restore the Missouri Compromise.

Mr. Stephens said: . . . The act of 1820, by which Missouri was to have come into the Union, but never did, prohibited the existence of slavery north of 36°30'; but it said nothing at all on the subject of south of that line. The South never asked such a guarantee. The guarantee which the South has asked, and which has been established in the passage of the Nebraska bill, and which the South will never yield, was simply that the people on every foot of American soil, north or south, east or west, shall, when they come to form their State constitution, do as they please upon the question of African slavery, and shall come into the Union either with or without it, as they shall then determine for themselves . . . And this is all the guarantee we secured; all that we then asked; all that we asked in 1850; all that we asked in the Nebraska bill, and what we will ever maintain is, that the people in every organized community, in every Territory, when they come to form their own intuitions, shall do as they please in that respect, and come into the Union either with or without slavery, as they wish. I say, sir, that is the southern doctrine; and I say, also, that is the American doctrine.

WILLIE MAE
COTTON

⟨⟨⟨⟨⟩⟩⟩⟩

B y three months, I knew everybody's name and they knew mine.
There was Colonel Bounds and Miss Emmaline and Miss Emmaline's brother, Marse Riddle, daddy to Alger, whose mother was
Lossie. There was Absalom the groom and his brother Ambrose the blacksmith, who was married to Zenas the weaver. Their two grown children
were Jaz and Ashby, and they worked the fields with Morris, Cheney, J.
Quincy Adams, Sorrel, and Lil Sis. Sorrel and Lil Sis had two tots, Lewis
and Clark. The three gal sisters were Anna, Cassia, and Galilee, and they
were twenty-one, -two, and -three. As for Miss Saucy with her double-
blinking eyes, nobody knew where she come from. They say she turned up
one day in a grass basket beneath a flowering dogwood outside the double
log fence. That she was so-and-so's newborn and her people were free—she
had papers to prove it—but nobody knew why they ran off and left their
baby. Zenas the weaver say Miss Emmaline named the baby *Désirée* and put
her in the quaint house with the three sisters, who say she didn't look like a
Désirée at all, she looked like a Mary-Mary.

"Who catches the babies?" I ask Zenas one day in the loom room, where
she was spinning wool. Took only one breath to fill myself up with the
stench of oily sheep, and just like that, my spirits would lift. Now I ain't saying every foul scent is a pleasure, but even a rotting corpse had more truth
to it than a bottle of Miss Emmaline's *l'eau du toilette*.

Zenas looked up from her thread and say it didn't pay to be strange on
this farm, so why was I asking. I tell her we had a whole gaggle of grannies
on my old place. She say, "Your old marse got himself a regular slave factory

from what I hear." She say Lossie do all the catching but she ain't caught nobody since Clark dropped. I ask her how she knew about Marse Tom.

"He used to visit regular, courting Miss Katie. Now, shoo! Miss Emmaline shouldn't be on her own for so long."

Zenas was right. That miss had needs. A steady pampering, from bathing her to setting her slippery yellow hair to the washing and ironing of her fussies: flounces and *chemisettes* and *engageantes* and *broderie anglaise,* pantalettes and petticoats, collars of tatting and *crochette.* Miss didn't need no servant as much as a nursing maid or, even better, a companion, seeing how Colonel was always avoiding her, quick-stepping out of a room when he saw her in one. She acted like she didn't notice his about-faces, but she did. Hard not to notice someone walking out on you right after he looked you in the face.

While the three sisters and Miss Saucy took orders from Lossie, working sun to sun, tending the hello-yellow and making soap, candles, preserves, and so forth, I took mine from Miss. I did my best yes-ma'am-ing for her, and Miss was pleased, and why not, seeing how I kept my serving face out for her and the face of my own self-respect to myself, til one day that December. I got bold.

We were having our regular tea party. I say that if she don't mind, I was old enough to feed myself. Miss clapped her hands together and say, "Why, truly you are. Just look how much you've grown!" Now, maybe I wasn't no twigs and bones no more. Maybe my hands had some meat on them, and it turned out my face had cheeks instead of hollows. And maybe my dress didn't hang off me now that Zenas the weaver showed me how to tack and sew. But there weren't no growing miracles here, no shooting up double overnight, just a body and a costume better fit. Still, only a fool begging for a flogging would argue with a mistress. It paid off, my playing mute to her flighty remark, cause from then on I got to hold my own spoon and fork.

Not long after that, I got bold again.

I was sitting in her bathing chamber in a horsehair chair right next to her tub. I had a nice oak fire going in the hearth while she made her chatty talk, mumbling to her water phantoms. I didn't hear nothing but soap bubbles crackling.

"Miss, who you talking to?" I judged if I got to take care of her, I ought to know.

First, she looked at me without a sound. She was measuring me up, I could tell from her eyes, seeing if she could trust me. "Look," she say, sticking a fingertip into the bathwater. "Can you see them?"

I peeped through the hole she made in the bubbles. "Yessum."

Truth is, I didn't see nobody. It sure did make her happy, though, which made me feel kind of large, til she began tearing up and mewing like a lost kitten.

"Now, Miss, don't you do that. Someone might hear you and want to know what's going on."

Miss sobered real fast when I say that, too glad to have someone who believed her.

She say sometimes they ain't such a nice bunch of folks, her water folks. Her little people, she called them. They would trick her into dunking her head in the water, where they pulled strong on her hair. "But such trifles are the cost of befriending them," she say, for if she ignored them, they wouldn't let her talk to her mother and daddy.

I rubbed the bar of soap along her arm. "How long your mother and daddy been living underwater?" I wasn't making chitchat; I truly wanted to know. I knew about haints, but little people were something new to me.

Miss say her folks ain't living, they dead.

"You talking to the dead?"

And Miss say, "Yes, of course."

"You taking precautions, Miss?"

"Whatever from?"

"I wouldn't want them little people hurting you." I wasn't no expert yet, just relying on my own good instinct.

"Oh, pish posh," she say. "They wouldn't. They only tease." She say I should never mention such a thought again, for they might hear me, and then she might never get to speak to her mother and daddy again.

"You lucky. Getting to talk to your kin."

Miss Emmaline's eyes widened. She say, "I shall ask the little people to find your mother."

"Thank you, Miss, but she ain't dead."

"Yes, yes she is," Miss say and lifted her arms so I could soap her armpits.

"She brought me my dolly," I say fore I could shut my teeth.

Miss gawped at me like I was the one who wasn't making sense.

"I gave you that doll," say Miss. "An old negro woman begged me to take it before we left. She said it was yours. I had Lossie put it in your quarters after you took so dreadful sick. I thought it might help revive you."

I quit washing on Miss's back and dropped the sponge into the bath. She sank into the water up to her neck and splashed at her face, keeping her thoughts to herself, and I was glad for that. I didn't want to believe her. I couldn't believe her. I poured more hot water from my cruets into her bath and sat back down in my chair, neither of us saying nothing.

Now, not every slave owner was a beast, or every man who didn't own folks a treat. Truth got more shades to it than devil and saint. Same goes for the bond between a miss and her servant, the scale always wavering like a two-pan balance stacking unequal with the weight of power and heart.

"Wilhelmina?"

I say nothing, judging she was talking to one of her no-see-ums.

"Wilhelmina! I am speaking to you," Miss say.

"Sorry, Miss, I thought you were talking to a Wilhelmina."

"I was. I've decided to rename you. I find the one you have a trifle coarse." She stroked my cheek with the back of her hand. "'Tis only meant as an endearment," she say. "My name alone to call you."

Nobody touched me tender since my mother, and I'd forgotten how a loving touch felt. And it was loving—no denying it. But it didn't make me feel no better, no sir. I was tired, my head hurting from what Miss say about Mother. No time for thinking, though, not with Miss Emmaline's teeth starting to chatter, wanting her warmed towel and her nine layers.

"Wilhelmina, Wilhelmina," she say. "Wake up from your reverie."

Back in my bunk that night, I took my doll baby from under my mattress and threw the blanket over us. My chest was caving in.

I knew Mother been in this room. I'd seen her sitting in that chair. Heard her voice burning in her throat.

"What are you doing under there?" Mary-Mary say, rapping on top of my noggin.

"Go back to bed and mind your own."

She say she was having a reckless dream.

"What you want me to do about it?" I say.

She tugged my blanket down. "Can I sleep with you?"

"There ain't room for two."

She gave me a face meant to make me feel bad. "Hmph," I say, faking a grumble and scooting over.

We didn't say no words, just stared into the timbers, til Mary-Mary heaved a sigh so loud like she was the sorriest person in the world, and I finally had to ask her what she was so sad about. And she say she don't memory nothing from her dream, just the feeling of happy, and it was alive and warm and safe and cram-jam full of bust-out-loud love.

"That make you sad?" I say.

"Yeah. I got to be asleep to feel so good."

My head tingled something powerful, and I scratched under my bed turban.

"I saw you by the pond," say Mary-Mary. "Washing your hair."

"Yeah, so."

"I saw it," she say.

"Saw what?" I say, doing my best to play dumb.

"You know," she say, and she made a hand motion like something was shooting out of her head.

"You seen my glow?" I say.

She nodded.

"Anyone else seen it?"

"No." She was smiling, proud of herself, tonguing the gap between her front teeth. "Only I got the gift for seeing. Like you."

"You know other folks who glow?"

"No," she say.

"How you so sure, then?"

"You're not taking my word?"

"Don't see no reason why I should," I say.

"I let you wear my madras hanky," she say.

"Maybe you don't like it no more," I say.

"Now, now," she say.

I rubbed at my head again. "Don't know why I got it."

"You can't question the divine," she say.

"What's the Lord got to do with my glowing?"

"Don't ask me. Ask Him," she say.

"Hoo! You a strange one."

She poked me in the side, so I poked her back.

"You pretty smart for such a youngster," I say.

"We're the same age."

"No we ain't. I'm ten and a half. You only nine," I say.

"So you're the older one. Fine by me."

"Don't you forget it," I say.

"I'll remind you to your dying day."

"Don't doubt it. You a pest," I say. "You like a fly around a horse's eye."

"And you're the one around his ass."

We cracked ourselves up, Mary-Mary and me.

"You two be quiet. Some of us are trying to sleep," say Galilee.

For the rest of the winter, I shared my bunk with this saucy gal who could dream up happy, her sour breath on my neck, her scrappy toenails clawing my leg, my arm draped over her skinny side, our bellies touching, both us saying it was warmer that way, but the truth is we were both doing the best we could to hold on to the love while we were awake.

Come August 1856, I was eleven. Alger was fifteen. Mary-Mary was ten. We didn't know when it happened and neither did she. Us three were fast friends, or more rightly, I was the friend in the middle.

Every third Sunday that summer, a shriveled white preacher would come and sermon us in Colonel's praise house, a little whitewashed cabin with a potbellied stove in the middle and benches on either side. Everyone but Marse Riddle would show. He stayed away from the hello-yellow, never stepping inside, as chill to Miss Emmaline as the colonel, who sat next to his wife only on this holy day. The three gal sisters, Anna, Cassia, and Galilee, sat on the opposite side of the aisle, the rest of us backing them up, with Mary-Mary next to me pressing her bony hip into my meaty one and Alger always somewhere in my vicinity, smelling of new leather.

At noon, the colonel and Miss Emmaline would leave for the town and Marse Riddle went fishing. "Gather round, you all," Colonel would say, fingering the ivory handle of this pistol he got holstered to his hip. "The missus and I are going into Persimmon, and I'm leaving Absalom in charge."

So it was August and I been on that farm a whole year, and I was walking from the praise house to the pond thinking this ain't such a bad place.

I grubbed good. I housed good. No one beat on each other. No one was missing forearms or fingertips. No one died of heat or exhaustion.

"Not that way, Willie Mae," I heard Alger say.

Both him and Mary-Mary were ambling toward the cornfields.

I liked to be on my own after the colonel and Miss left, admiring the sheep by the pond, but I walked with them this time, Alger in the lead, followed by Mary-Mary, the stalks whacking our arms and legs. We must of walked halfway into the field when I saw a circular clearing and a whole bunch of us folks.

Turned out Ambrose the blacksmith knew Bible.

He talked slow and even, punctuating his sermon with grunts, groans, and whoops til we were plum in the middle of a sing-songing praising of the Lord, folks swooning, Ambrose urging us to love each other and to respect ourselves and the work we did. There was a place in paradise what one day would be ours, and folks sang out, "Ain't it the truth!" and "That's right!" the spirit thrilling right through us.

Just as I thought that farm and me were on knowing terms, something like that would take me.

Afterward all us gathered on the west side of the hello-yellow to visit dead kinfolk buried under a giant chinquapin tree. I didn't want no haint for a friend, so I took care to call myself. Alger snorted and say, "Who taught you that?" and I tell them about this haint who haunted the gin. I tell them how on my old place granny-who-cut-my-birth-cord warned folks to stay away from it at night. "'If you don't,' say Granny, 'that haint gon take it as an invitation, and then you'll find yourself with the worst kind of friend walking by your side day and night, never leaving you in peace til he drives you to your death.' All us knew it was true, cause at night the gin whirred and moaned even though the mules were long barned up. But this one ginner, he didn't take Granny's words for true. He say, 'I'm a good Christian man, I don't abide such bunkum.' Now, Granny knew she had to get past this man's stubbornness, so she say, 'The Lord has sent word to me. He say to give you this sifter to hang over your doorway, for a haint got to count every hole fore it can come in.' But the ginner say, 'Don't need it. That whirring is the wind.' The next day, Granny say, 'Then take this sheet of newsprint and paste it to the wall, for a haint got to read all the writing fore he can come in.' But the ginner say he wasn't gon get caught with no contraband. He didn't mind Granny's cautions, and he didn't take none of her cures, and sure enough, he died fore the end of the cotton season. The gin didn't make no whirring noises at night after that, and Granny say, 'See, our haint got a new friend.'"

Mary-Mary looked at me like I was a wise old woman and called herself. Alger snorted.

"Don't come belly-paining when you got not-wanted company," I say.

"As long as it's you, I won't complain," he say.

Most of them dead folks didn't have no grave markers, just smallish piles of stones, but most everybody knew who this one was and who that one was. Only Absalom the groom, who been with Colonel even longer than Lossie, ever got into a row over who was buried where.

"Stephen is right here," he say every third Sunday that summer, standing over a patch of grass looking like every other.

Someone would always take him on, and they would battle it out til Absalom would rememory some feature of this man Stephen's funeral, and then, like a Cuban mastiff, he'd find the right spot.

After supper one of these Sundays, Alger and me were cooling our feet in the pond. I'd invited him to come and admire the sheep with me. He'd laughed. "Why not?" he say.

My ankles were ashy and my toes gnarled, but Alger say they were good feet, well proportioned, with an impressive arch. Made me feel bashful, so instead of telling him thank you, I say, "Why don't someone carve a marker for this Stephen so Absalom can have some peace?" And Alger say Colonel don't let Stephen have a marker. He say it was just as well cause all that quibbling kept the memory of Stephen alive. So I ask who this Stephen was, and Alger leaned back on his elbows and say I got to promise to keep my teeth tight, and I say won't crack them, and he say, "Okay, then, listen."

Alger say that Colonel's tobacco fetched the highest price ever. Thirty-five cents a pound. "So?" I say, and he say, "Willie Mae, let me tell you the story." He say it was a miracle it grew at all, for it got too winterish in the valley to put up more than a single good patch of the lowest-grading tobacco, never mind make such a handsome profit. That these poor white crackers come from all over Hopewell trying to figure what made it grow so sweet, some even thinking Colonel was in cahoots with the Devil, for all his crops, not just the tobacco, grew plentiful. They come watching in winter when Stephen, Morris, Cheney, and J. Quincy Adams burned the plant beds to kill off the weeds and insects. They stayed til Sorrel and Lil Sis sowed the tobacco seeds and plowed the fields with peg-toothed harrows. In spring, they come back again, measuring how tall them stalks grew fore Marse Riddle topped off the pink flowers. But their scrutinizing and theorizing always ended with them slumping away complaining, not finding nothing disordinary.

"So what's the secret?" I say.

"The seed we plant, Stephen invented it. The tobacco it yields is as sweet as toffee, and it can take the cold. Then we flue-cure it with a charcoal furnace, which makes the flavor even smoother. When I was about nine, one of those farmers broke into the curing barn after Stephen fell asleep, and soon after, folks all around began flue-curing. So Colonel shot Stephen in the head."

First I didn't say nothing cause there ain't nothing to say to something so evildoing.

"Why don't those crackers just steal the seeds?"

Alger looked up at the sky. "That's why he shot Stephen. So we knew what would happen to us if any of them did."

On Mondays, life with Miss Emmaline got going over again.

We spent most of the summer in her drawing room cause she loved reading aloud, *Hunchback*, *Frankenstein*, Ed Poe, *Beowulf*, *Wuthering Heights*, all them tragic stories. What a picture she made, acting out all the parts. When she was feeling crafty, she left a book open and turned her back on me. But I never looked at them pages, I never left my cushy armchair, no sir, I wasn't biting. Finally she tired of her game and called me wicked and say if I didn't learn to read she'd beat me. So I pulled my chair over so Miss could teach me what I already knew how to do. She opened a volume of *Monte Cristo*. She say a colored man wrote it, but I judged she was goading me again. I ciphered new words, and I come to appreciate how each word strung up to the next like a thread, knitting and purling. I had a slow time of it, but Miss was patient, both us low speaking and slapping the boards shut if we heard someone behind the door. The story was full of murders and all kinds of scandal, including a slave who stood up against a white man in court, and two women who loved each other, and it wasn't bad, neither, if you like mannish writing.

Even though the sun would do right for reading, Miss kept the blinds and curtains shut. The light of her Argand lamp was more to her liking. It was fancy-from-Paris, made of copper and tin, with a skinny pipe chimney smearing an oily light over the room's gloom—the green wove carpet, plush-proper sitting chairs, corner tables, and a dozen ferns thriving alive in bell-shaped pots and saucers of gravel and water. She had some dried-up-dead ones too, stamped flat and pressed into white linen and framed, ornamenting the walls like a memorial. Miss had a real penchant for them hairy plants. Made the room creep, them fronds brushing the air, hankering for a kiss.

Now Miss, she liked her drawing room just fine, taking pride in all its parts, specially the long rifle hanging from a wood-scrolled rack next to the mantelpiece. Miss say it was her family heirloom and that she was a fantastic shot. I didn't doubt it, for Colonel gave her the freedom to amuse herself any way she saw fit, whether reading seamy French novels or sharpshooting at glass-bottle targets. Yes, sir, Colonel indulged my miss beyond privilege of her gender, and you would think she was wanting for nothing, but there was one thing Miss was missing.

Fore I left her one night, she called me back to her four-poster.

"Stay, Wilhelmina. I'm feeling lonely tonight." She held out her hand with the garnet ring. "I will entertain you with a story." She took the ring off and held it to the candle sitting on her end table. "*C'est exquis, n'est pas?*"

"Yessum. A real beauty."

"It used to belong to a slave." She put her ring back on and rested her hand in my lap.

Miss say her father-in-law, Solomon B. Bounds, once loved a gal named Lora Lee. He loved her fore he met his wife and he loved her after he married, and he went on seeing her whenever he visited his daddy's plantation. She housed in a cabin on the furthest reach of the land with her three offspring, who the daddy thought were his own. "Can you imagine a son with his father's favorite slave for years and both of those men married?" say Miss.

It was only a matter of time fore the daddy walked into this cabin one day and found his son busy with Lora Lee. "Oh, Solomon knew he was in terrible trouble. His daddy didn't take kindly to having his own son fornicate with his favorite property. As it turned out, everybody knew except Solomon's daddy—even both the wives." Solomon did what was best for everyone, she say. He fled.

"Not long after Solomon settled here, a parcel arrived from his daddy. Inside was this ring, Solomon's love token to Lora Lee," she say.

I didn't want to know what come of Lora Lee, and Miss didn't offer.

"I wear it to remind Samuel of his father's *infidélité*," she say, dropping her hand in my lap. "Plainly, with Anna, Cassia, and Galilee, one would think he has a constant *pense-bête*. They are his *demi-sœurs*, you know."

"Miss?"

"They are his half sisters. Lora Lee was their mother," she say, flat faced. "Close your mouth, Wilhelmina, and I shall finish my tale."

She say that when she and Colonel first coupled, she was thinking she'd be a mama lickety-split, for her husband was all too eager to breed. But the union left her unfit to sit for near three weeks. When they married, her childhood wasn't much more than a yesterday, so never mind him being too large for her small, they carried on. Course, it didn't bring no baby. Took Lossie telling her a woman got to mulch fore she can be occupied. When her monthlies finally dropped, Miss whooped and cheered, running to her husband in the tobacco stalks, panting, Samuel, Samuel, my dam has burst, my lady days have begun! Colonel say her behavior was not fitting her position, not to mention it was humiliating, his negroes witnessing such a disgrace. Miss hid in her *chiffonier* for a week, straddling her bleeding rag and weeping, but, she say, it didn't take long fore Colonel recovered his dignity and tended his wife.

When still she didn't grow big, she sulked, til one day Colonel say he would rather mount one of his ewes than his own wife. They'd take less effort and were known to satisfy. After that she was so deep down in the doomfuls that she ran off the farm, gone missing for days. Marse Riddle found her roaming their old homeplace, dirt-filthy and with her mind in a mix-up. So instead of his great love, she become Colonel's terrible shame. Even the negroes talked behind her back, she was sure of it. Miss ask her little people for their help, and they tell her she was draining her husband of his clout. If she wanted a child so bad, she had to start acting like a woman instead of an *enfant terrible*. So she bathed and had her personal maid, Polly

Calloway, crimp her hair and yoke it in a *chignon*, and she goes to Colonel in her finest *boudoir* dress, soft talking and purring, putting on her best behavior. But Colonel say, Emmaline, you're not well; you know you're simply not, and refused to take her. He didn't have no interest in picking her peach no more. Miss begged him to help her find her health. The next day, Miss say, Colonel rode into Persimmon to ask the help of the famous doctor, Dr. Oliver Smalls. Dr. Smalls had himself a license from the Board of Physicians of the State of Georgia, and was the only white doctor in the county. Miss was fancified with his certifications and took this as a sign of Colonel's renewed devotion. She put the three sisters and Polly Calloway in a tizzy of preparation like she was expecting a visit from King *Louis-Philippe*. She sat gazing at the mountain covered in clusters of white, not from snow, she say, as this was July, but from the blooms of chestnut trees. In the privacy of her drawing room, her maid Polly in attendance, she received Dr. Smalls, a behemoth of a man, with a full mane of wavy, dark brown hair, his one commendable feature. Miss say he was toad faced and square headed, though not unappealing, in the way charisma can take the place of good looking. He struck up a polite interview about the weather, moving on to her pallor and her health in general and, gaining her trust, dove into the nature of her complaining. Was she ever irritable or nervous? Yes and yes. Was she ever dizzy or weak of heart? Yes, yes! From the way he kept peering at the ceiling, Miss Emmaline wasn't sure if he was considering her predicament or studying the cornices and molding.

Finally, he turned back his sleeves. Mrs. Bounds, he say, it is necessary for me to study you in further detail. With your permission I will perform an examination. Miss stuck out her tongue and he pressed on it with a flat wood stick. He took a silver tool and lifted up her nostrils. He squeezed her neck glands and her armpits. And just when she thought she could take no more of this indignity—she never met no licensed doctor in her life, but this couldn't be how they acted—he ask Miss to stand. He drew his chair to hers and fished under her overskirts and pressed on belly and her womb, saying, Please relax, Mrs. Bounds, please remain still. When he was done, he sat back and say, Do you regularly fulfill your marital duties?

Most certainly, I do, she say, flustered. And then Miss confessed. No, not most recently.

Precisely, say Dr. Smalls. Madam, your symptoms follow pathology idiomatic of a hysterical crisis, and it is completely episodic.

Pardon? say Miss Emmaline.

He say it was a common nervous condition of delicate women like herself, and she was lucky, for it was treatable. Firstly, you must refrain from novel reading, he say, for this pulled blood away from her baby-making parts. Then he presented a tincture, which he say would strengthen her heart, improve her circulation, prepare her womb, and temper her mind. If she followed his prescription and resumed her marital duties, well, he was sure she would see steady improvement in her condition. However, there was another treatment, if Miss was interested, that could relieve her symptoms much sooner. He warned her that the method of cure come from *Marseille*, it was considered sinful by many, and there was risk of it becoming a habit. It was used most on widows or women of religion and piety, but for Miss he say he would make the exception.

Most of what this doctor say irritated or confused her, but anything French was appealing, specially if it was wicked.

Dr. Smalls say it was costly, but he would, for her, provide it at a discount. He opened his doctoring bag and took out three vials. Oil of lilies, muskroot, and crocus, he say, dropping a drip of each in the well of his hand and mixing them with his forefinger. May I? he say, and again Miss let him dig under her skirts. At first he fumbled, and she squirmed, for she found his prodding disturbing. Soon, though, his fiddling found a rhythm and something gushed inside her. She moaned and shuddered and slumped over herself. When she come to, she was reclining on her favorite *canapé*, with Polly Calloway looking at her with a face full of horrify.

Miss filled with an urge unlike no other: to kick this Dr. Smalls, to kick him swift, and in his necessaries. She unsteadied to her feet. Dr. Smalls stood by her side, looking expectant, and smiled. Miss swung her leg, but she missed her target—she was feeling wobblish still—and struck Dr. Smalls on his shin. What on earth? he say. She kicked him again, and he took off, limping from the drawing room, calling for help, but the three sisters just watched, covering their mouths and tittering. Miss took after that doctor with a fat book of Charlie Dickens. She hurled it, and the corner smacked him in the back of his square head. He say in a heated tone that Miss was far more ill than he could of imagined, and that never in his life had anyone reacted so poor to the therapy. He say that she was impossible. Then he took off out the door.

Miss ran back to the drawing room and got her long rifle. By the time she loaded it, that Dr. Smalls was halfway down the dogwood drive. Standing on her porch, she fired off a single shot into his doctoring bag. With a second, nothing was left but the handle.

Le mot impossible n'est pas en mon dictionnaire, shouted Miss.

The word *impossible* ain't in my dictionary.

Oh, she cried. She wept til her lids puffed shut and her snot was clear as jelly. She told Miss Lossie to give her some negro medicine, but Lossie say she didn't want to get involved with Miss Emmaline's bedroom business. Miss began throwing everything—pokers, bellows, fern plants, candle-holders, and lawn chairs—for all she wanted was the hurting inside her soul to stop. When Miss lifted her Argand lamp with its glooming light and headed for the curtains, Lossie changed her answer. First she told Miss to eat only cold foods and then to eat only hot. Miss rubbed lotions and swallowed tonics, but this one made her piss her underclothes and that one made her fart, this one gave her old-woman breath and that one made her sweat a swamp. And it sure didn't draw her husband into her *chambre*. Miss Lossie say she needed more patience, that the Bible say the agony of waiting brings the joy of fulfillment. But Miss Emmaline was defeated. She cried and say she wasn't sure no more that conclusion was worth waiting for. Lossie say, You can't give up, Miss. Sarah was ninety years old when she finally gave birth to Isaac. This only made Miss cry harder.

"Before I had you, Wilhelmina, I was terribly alone," she say to me, taking her hand off my lap. Her husband neglected her, her brother shunned her, and her only living friend lived a county away. All she had for company was her maiding girl Polly Calloway. "I was barely older than you when I wed, nigh fourteen. Samuel was as many years my senior, but I adored him." Miss say Polly was her first Christmas present from Colonel. She come with a husband, Edgar, and Miss Emmaline was touched he'd kept them together. Now Miss never had no maid-in-waiting fore this and no idea what to do with one, but this woman servant come trained, for Polly and Edgar been sold off as part of a dead man's estate.

Nine long years after Dr. Smalls, after enduring Lossie's cures, after hoping Colonel would ever tend her in the way a man do his wife, Miss walked into her chamber and found Polly Calloway's heel cupped in Colonel's palm and him sucking on each of her toes. They'd been carrying on for almost as long as Miss and him were married.

Miss Emmaline had Polly thrashed and then she had her sold. Everybody's trust be violated then, from Miss Emmaline's to the girl's man, Edgar, who ran off.

"Samuel must fight his *compulsions désagréables*," say Miss, tucking her hand under her pillow. "Unfortunately, they're in his blood. I've done my best to forgive him, to satisfy him, and if it does not bring forth a child, then *c'est pas grave*. Perhaps I am too old."

"Miss, you only twenty-five."

She shook her head. "I've made my peace with it," she say through teeth tired of clamping.

In the heat of August 1857, Alger rapped on the back door of the hello-yellow and stuck his head in, calling out my name. I was twelve. He was sixteen. His face was shiny with sweat. I met him at the bottom of the steps.

It was Alger who sewed me a pair of red cowhide shoes.

Under the shade of a walnut tree he say, "I staked the leather to make it pliable before I cut the pieces for the uppers. This way you can break the shoes in instead of them breaking you. I'll wager you don't get any blisters."

"You made these for me?"

"I did."

I say nothing when I slipped the first one on and it didn't fit.

"No, Willie Mae," he say, "You have it on the wrong foot. They're molded on curved lasts. There's a left shoe and a right shoe, see?

I took the shoe off and he lined each one up to its mate. "Now try," he say.

I put my feet in them and just stared. They were so damn nice and shiny I was afraid to walk.

"Go ahead," Alger say, like he was bucking up a toddler instead of a grown twelve-year-old. "Take a step."

"I know how to walk," I say. "You making me buggy. Just you back up."

I tested the fit, rocking my feet side to side. And then I took a step. And then another, and not too long I was strutting about, amazed that walking shoes should feel so light. Oh, I bawled like a real ninny, and I didn't even mind. I'd plain old forgotten what the devil joy felt like. Alger got alarmed and kept trying to peace me down, but I wanted to cry, and he let me have it out.

"They real comfortable, Alger, real first-rate," I say, once I got my blubbering under control. I was real impressed. "You talented. Thank you."

"You're welcome," he say with a sudden shy face.

"I don't like them," Mary-Mary say the next day. We were in the yard hanging laundry from hickory to hickory.

"I didn't ask you," I say.

Both us were ornery from the heat.

"You want me to give them back?" I say.

"Yes."

"You gon grudge me a fine pair of walking shoes."

"They're too loud," she say, tugging at my clothesline.

"Look what you done." A lacy dress lay dead in the dirt.

"I'll wash it," she say.

"No you won't." I took that dress from the ground and brushed it off fore I tossed it over my shoulder. "You know she don't like nobody touching her pretties but me."

"I'll make it up to you."

"So how you gon do that?"

Mary-Mary tongued the gap between her front teeth and then she flew right at me. Fore I knew it the girl was kissing me so firm and hard on the lips I near found myself knocked to the ground.

When she pulled off me, I looked around. "'Sorry' would of done."

"That's all you got to say?"

I sucked in my lips. "You taste like strawberries."

"Can't walk in a pair of kisses," she say with a face full of triumph. "Can't cuddle with them, either."

"You scram," I say. "I don't got to listen to your list of what I can and cannot do with my shoes. If I want to kiss them, I will, and if I want to cuddle them, I will. They can even sit next to me while I eat. Lord Jesus knows they won't trouble me the way you do."

Mary-Mary looked at me like I done something to hurt her.

"They a pair of shoes," I say. I grabbed clothespins from my bucket and started hanging Miss Emmaline's petticoats. "You special to me, I never once say you ain't. If you was a man, I'd marry you," I say.

"Now now, why do I have to be a man?"

"Don't be dim. Gals don't marry."

"It doesn't mean we can't," she say.

"You asking Colonel's permission? I don't want to be there for that."

"Marry me, Willie Mae."

"Fine, I marry you. Now go away."

And she did. She took off with a kick in her hips like this was her happiest day and she didn't never need no more dreaming.

I was walking from the hickory posts to the hello-yellow with a wicker on top of my head some time later, when Alger say he had to talk to me. "Alger, you gon knock me down and I ain't fixing to wash these linens over again. Between you and Mary-Mary, I got twice the laundry. Whatever you got to say can just wait," I say, and he say he'll do just that. He walked down the drive where this fellow was hanging on the fence. Sometimes a new-freed someone come up the wagon road and Alger would go greet them, wanting to know what was going on beyond the farm. They'd walk into the courtyard or lean on the fence like this fellow was doing and say: You seen so-and-so? They called Silas, Tennessee, Elijah, Millie, Julia, William, Boaz, Hercules, Alice, Luscious, Durango, Dee. They live here?

They were looking for family.

Done with my ironing, I headed out to Alger's shack. All his knives, punches, jiggers, hammers, and awls hung on the wall over his workbench, all them tools in size order. Hobnails, iron fillings, vinegar, ink, thread—whatever he needed he kept in plain view, nothing stacked, everything straightforward. And the scents—new leather, beeswax, gum water, oil of turpentine—all that was Alger.

I left the door to the shack open, but he come up behind me and closed it.

"Gon get clammy in here," I say.

He pulled out a four-legged stool. "Have a seat," he say.

I'd seen Alger's eyes go from serious to double-up laughing. I'd seen a whole range of emotions since we friended. I knew them eyes, and they always betrayed him, and at this moment they had a gritty-firm look to them.

"I used to imagine escaping. Like Henry Brown. I'd fit inside one of the hogsheads, and I'd break out when Colonel got to the warehouse," he say. "I'm running north, Willie Mae, and I want you to come with me."

I say, "Scuse me?" and sat down hard on a stool.

"You heard me right."

"Where's this North? How we getting there? We walking? Cause if you think them shoes you made me gon last, you got another thing coming." I winked to show I was joking.

"I'm being serious. I'll *buy* you shoes where we're going. I'll buy you a whole shop of shoes."

"What do you care about running north when your daddy's buying you freedom?"

Alger turned sour. He say his mother was holding everything up, been doing it for the longest time. Say he was too young to be free. And Alger say sixteen is a man, he's ready to be on his own. He say his mother only knows how to guide by fear, she only brave on her own turf. She don't know what lies beyond, and she too scared to find out. She tell Alger to be practical. She tell him why every dream he have never gon work out. He say he don't want practical, he wants a world larger than this farm, and he's willing to risk it. Alger say his daddy wanted to buy both their freedom, but his ma wouldn't hear of it. She say the evil we know better than the evil we don't, so his daddy don't buy nobody.

"How you like that," I say. "A man doing what a woman want."

"Yeah," he say. It was the first time I ever heard Alger sound snide. He say his daddy was always saying soon, soon, but Alger say he wasn't waiting for no more years to pass. He been saving his shoemaking money—Colonel been paying him a nickel a pair since he was a boy, and he could buy his own damn self, but he didn't have enough to buy me too. It would take him another good five years, and he wasn't fixing to wait.

"You out of your mind, Alger. You even got a plan? How about a map?"

Alger say he do.

"I can't go with you."

He looked hurt. "Why not?"

"I just can't. Ain't that enough?"

"No, Willie Mae, it isn't."

"There's loads of reasons. Like Lossie say, it's dangerous."

"I know that. What else?"

What else, he ask me. What else. So I spat it firm and final like it was the Lord's truth, like it made sense. "I ain't leaving without my mother. She gon come looking for me, like them free folks do."

Alger eyed me like he was trying to decide if I was grim serious or if I was making a bad joke. Then he say in this not-sure-he-should-be-saying-what-he-was-about-to-say voice, "Your mother isn't coming for you." He say it so concerned it made me mad.

"I got to get back to work," I say.

"She passed away," he say. He took my hand and held it. "You wouldn't let her go. You had a grip so tight Miss Emmaline insisted they let you sleep with your ma one last night, but she was already gone. You've got to know that somewhere inside you."

"Stop. What you doing ain't right." I was drowning in a barrel of a truth that I knew in my head but never took to my heart: When I last saw my mother, she was trablin from this side to the Lord.

"I don't mean to contradict you, and I sure don't mean to cause you any pain, Willie Mae," he say so soft I could hardly hear him.

"I sure would miss you," I say and pulled my hand from him.

But Alger Young did not steal away.

Not cause his daddy wasn't strong enough to defy the strong woman who was strong in all ways but one, her weakness her child, and who don't understand that? She thought she could protect him as long as he was under her thumb, figuring that peculiar institution was a safer place than the unknown world. But this ain't why Alger stayed. He was in love.

I'd seen a heart carving in the magnolia tree. Small enough not to be noticed. Unless you were A.Y. or W.M.

When he finally made his intentions known, it was October of 1858. I was thirteen. A woman.

Now, in October the nights were brutal cold, but I was having the best sleep of my life in a trundle bed with a horsehair mattress, under not one quilt but three. Miss Emmaline was suffering a toothache, preferring my company to Colonel's, who stayed in the chamber across the hall. I was sorry she had the pain, but I sure was enjoying the comforts of my new nighttime lodgings. So I was mighty put off when this splattering rain woke me. It was odd, the way it hit and quit, and I turned to see if Miss heard it too, but she was snoring away in her four-poster.

When that sound come again, I dragged myself from my snug and turned back the curtains, and who did I see about to heave a black walnut at me? Alger Young.

He waved me down, and I shook my head. He made like he was gon fling another walnut, so I grabbed my wrapper and met him in the back of the hello-yellow.

He was looking sharp in a felt hat and a long sheepskin coat, right down to his thick trousers and calfskinned boots.

"Evening," he say.

"Evening yourself. What if you woke Miss?"

"You're worth the risk," he say with a grin.

A chill went through me.

"Take my coat," he say and draped it over my shoulders.

"You be cold," I say.

"I'll be fine," he say.

A single cricket chirped.

He pointed toward the moon. "See those ridges and lines? Those are mountains."

"The moon got mountains?"

"It does."

"Next thing you tell me it got rivers and trees."

He laughed soft. "No, it doesn't have either of those."

I hugged his coat round me. "You haul me down in the middle of the night to tell me about the moon?"

"No."

He held out his arm and I took it.

"Where we going?" I say.

"Have some patience, woman."

We were walking toward the curing barn.

Once inside, Alger lit a lantern and sealed us in. It was empty—the leaves been moved to the packhouse a month ago—but cozy too, smaller than it looked from the outside. Tiers of hewn logs ran overhead in the vaulted roof, where shifts of tobacco litter hung limp as tired ghosts, giving the place a dressed-up, spooky feeling. It reeked of smoke, but I didn't mind it.

"You know, I've never seen your hair. You've always got a cap or that kerchief on," say Alger, leading me from the door to the middle of the room.

"And it's gon stay that way."

"I'd really like to."

"It ain't gon happen, Alger," I say, warning.

He stepped closer, and I backed up. "I'm not trying to grab it," he say.

"Good."

He fingered a small square of white under his chin. Had a dot of blood in the middle. Nighttime was an odd time to be shaving.

"You want to tell me why we in this barn at half past midnight?"

He coughed and say, "I got feelings for you. Don't you know that by now?" Never did a man sound more awkward.

I thought of telling him I cared for him, but not the way he was meaning. That I had those kinds of feelings, but for another. And she was runty and saucy and tasted of strawberries.

"I got to get back fore Miss wakes," I say instead.

The barn went dark.

"You can blow that lantern out, but that ain't gon keep me from finding the door," I say, backing up. I heard him stepping across the floor, and then I felt him standing near. "That you?" I say.

He took my hand and pulled me to him.

"Hoo, you fresh," I say.

And he laughed his soft laugh.

The top of my head fit right under his chin. I let him kiss me.

It wasn't so bad.

Then he kissed my neck.

"You giving me shivers," I say.

"I intend to," he say.

All toggered up, we jumped the broom the following June. We leaped high as crickets. I wore a veil made of window curtain, and Alger his only bow tie.

After his trying to make me his woman for months, I had finally let him.

He was a good man, a good friend, and he could crack my sides with laughter. I knew I done the right thing.

Mary-Mary quit talking to me except for no-word answers.

"I still love you best," I say the day of my celebration. I was pulling stockings from my chest drawer and piling them with the rest of my clothes on my mattress.

Mary-Mary was overhead on Anna's bunk.

"You supposed to be helping," I say.

She crossed her leg, near missing my nose. She was humming to herself, but I knew she heard me.

"You ain't being fair," I say.

The leg crossed the other way, near smacking my face.

"You can keep dolly," I say.

The legs didn't move. "I don't want dolly," she say. "I want you."

"You got me."

"No. He got you. What if he runs off?"

Sometimes I shared Alger's intimacies with Mary-Mary and often I regretted it. "He won't. And even if he did, I ain't going nowhere without you," I say. "You think I would give you dolly if I thought I was leaving? I ain't that generous."

"No, you ain't."

Fore the ceremony, Miss Lossie come in and tell Mary-Mary and the three sisters—who were making me pretty—to get out.

Lossie say, "Be respectful of each other. Take joy when there's joy to be had, know how to find joy." She looked like she knew she was supposed to make a speech, but she didn't know exactly what to say, and so it come stumbling out. "My son has a good heart, so don't you break it. He's headstrong, he's got big ideas, but I expect you know that." She wiped her hands on her apron and frowned. "Don't ever let a man run you over. Now get that dress on."

I'd made my dress from a set of old linens Miss gave me, and I got to say it was fine. Even Colonel say how nice I looked. He seemed light of heart, Colonel did, inviting his closest neighbors, Matterson and his missus, and their hands. I'd never seen a single one of them fore this, but strangers were friends that day. The party for the white folks was inside the hello-yellow and the one for us was in front of it.

When Matterson come, he bulged up the porch like a bulldog, snorting and coughing, stopping to spit enough tobacco juice to drown a dog, but we didn't let nobody spoil nothing that day.

Once everybody was in his seat, Colonel called Alger and me up the porch. It was the right kind of day for a wedding: the sun bright, the air free of soot, not one cloud of tobacco hanging over the farm like a suck-sapping stinkbug. Colonel wore a preacher's black hat and opened his Bible. After Alger vowed to do right by me, with a big smile and a loud "I sure will," Colonel turned to me and say, "Willie Mae, will you honor and love Alger? Will you forsake others until death do you part?" And I go, "I will, Colonel, I will honor and love Alger, I will forsake all others, I will care for him in the sickness and health, don't matter how poor we are, til death. I sure will." I got carried away in the moment and everyone chuckled.

The one person missing from my day was Mary-Mary. Colonel say if she wasn't gon come to the party, then she had to work in the hello-yellow, one less house gal to rent for the day. So everybody got what they wanted or the closest to it.

I started looking for her skimming past the parlor window—it was open and long white curtains were blowing through it—but I didn't want to pain Alger, who say he didn't need me paying any mind to Mary-Mary on this of all days, so I quit that and instead looked up at Colonel, who was looking up at the sky. A flock of mourning doves was diving down, a curve of gray more like one huge big blur of bird than thirty or forty smaller ones.

Fore folks could run from their seats, them birds landed two by two, filling the giant chinquapin, and started up a chorus.

Alger cleared his throat and Colonel say, "Yes, yes, by all means," and then he read, his finger tracing the verse as he go, *Every good gift and every perfect gift is from above, and cometh down from the Father of lights, with whom is no variableness, neither shadow of turning*. "Congratulations. I pronounce you man and wife."

And just as quick as our witnesses stormed in, they wheeled into flight, wings whistling.

Colonel took me aside and say, "I wish you happiness."

I say, "Thank you, Marse Colonel. I wish you the same."

That night we danced, everyone in high spirits, even Marse Riddle, wearing his best straw top hat, and Lossie, both them singing and stomping to a jubilee of spoons, washboards, and empty vinegar kegs. Alger had a funky way of keeping time, cradling between the beats, with the music but against it. We danced so much it felt like we were living and dying in each other's arms. To cool off, we drank drams of dewberry and persimmon wine. And when our feet grew fat from all that dancing, we sat in the yard at two long tables. We ate turnip greens and dumplings, cowpeas in hog meat, souse, collards, pigs' feet with plenty of vinegar and hot pepper, and biscuits to mop it all up. We had Lossie to thank for the good grub.

After, we ducked into his shack, and Alger and me pondered them mourning doves.

"They got such an awful sound," I say. "Like someone died. And so many of them, how is that natural?"

Alger say he didn't know, but the mourning dove was a faithful bird— it mated for life—and it was the daddy bird who found the best twigs for the nest, just as Alger would build us a quality home, and so he took it for a good omen.

He lit a glass lamp and set it on the workbench. Inside that globe was a piece of red flannel, and when the oil caught, the room flushed with loving light.

"You think of that yourself?" I say.

Alger pecked at my wrist. "Quiet, Willie Mae, I'm romancing you."

I let him fumble with the hooks up the back of my dress, but after a long while, he was still fighting for victory. His commitment was so deep I had to hide a smile. I thought of helping, but you got to be delicate with manliness. Then Alger got wise. He say my costume would lift up a whole lot easier than it would come down, so we hopped onto his cot and began kissing. His eyes were closed, and then he opened them, but I never closed mine in the first place, so we were both staring too close at each other, and I began to hoot, and Alger go, "What now?" losing his humor.

I say, "Alger Young, you have far surpassed my expectation on romance, that's for true." Next I knew, he was laughing too and both us fell off the cot, joyous at our own funny show. Then I saw the room wasn't red no more. It was silver.

My wedding veil was on the floor.

Alger didn't jump or yell. He didn't say, "What in the devil, woman?" or run out the door. No, my man didn't. "You okay?" he say, cupping me in his arms. We climbed back onto the cot and he spooned me. "I'm fine, Alger, just fine," I say. I stretched an arm long under my head and watched my light filling the shack, feeling a bucket of sad knowing he couldn't see it.

Love dropped March of 1860. I was near fifteen.

Zenas the weaver made Love a cotton slip and a dress of knit worsted, and when she gave it to me I choked up. Alger had to tell her thank you for me. She took my hand in hers, like we had some kind of secret, and I knew she had to be rememoring the time I asked her who caught the babies on this place, never thinking I might one day be making something that needed catching myself, and then I'd find out just what kind of talent Lossie truly was. Lossie who brought me back to life and brought Love into it.

Everyone say Love looked like a tiny Alger, born to charm. She had his dimples, his smile, and she measured real long.

Mary-Mary say she favored me in temperament.

"Oh yeah, what's that?" I say.

"Cranky," she say.

Now, Miss Emmaline, she let me alone for an entire week. I knew she was being bighearted, specially given her state. When I finally come back to the hello-yellow, I found her in the four-poster, propped up on her goose-feather pillows, eager to show me a baby gown from Paris made of the finest muslin cambric with tucks, pleats, eyelets, and a whole mess of scallops. "Don't you adore it, Wilhelmina?" she say, holding it to her chest. "It has a cap to match."

Everybody got his own taste. "It's real nice, Miss."

"Is that all?" say Miss, looking disappointed.

"Thank you?"

"Oh no, it's not for Lovelady Belle," she say, using the name she chose for my daughter. She laid the baby gown over her belly. "*C'est pour le bébé.*"

"Course, Miss. Don't know what I was thinking."

Miss Emmaline was seven months heavy. Her peach had finally ripened. Not long after me and Alger jumped the broom, Miss confided that my wedding celebration must of inspired Colonel, for since that day he been sowing his seeds with regularity. She had beamed when she told me and showed me her hand. There wasn't no garnet ring on it, only her wedding band.

"I gave it to Galilee," she say.

Alone in the hello-yellow. Everyone else discharged. Crickets fast fiddling. Nighttime. Miss upstairs, confined to her four-poster. April. Downstairs in the parlor two men were talking.

They were talking state rights and property value.

They were talking party of Lincoln and shallow pretenses.

They were talking treachery.

They didn't stop, neither, when I set down the snifters and carafe of bourbon. No sir, I was as invisible as the air they breathed and just as necessary.

Marse Tom Darling sat next to Colonel, looking nothing like I rememoried. Any part of him that stuck out of his clothes was piss yellow—his skin, his eyes, his fingernails, his gums and teeth, even the few strands of hair pasted over the top of his head. It was almost five years, but nothing in his face say he recognized me. He been with Colonel and Miss for two days, and each two of those days I had to wait on him.

Since he sold me off, his cotton burned down—a fire, according to Miss Emmaline, caused by a horrific and epic slave revolt—and Miss Katie, her dear friend, had died of consumption. For reasons my miss didn't share with me, Marse Tom sold off all his folks. In other words, the ones who wouldn't or couldn't run away, the ones who didn't die in the rebellion, and the ones the sheriff's posse caught and brought back. When Miss tell me, I thought of granny-who-cut-my-birth-cord and old Enoch, and Miss say, Get yourself a glass of water, Wilhelmina, you look ill. But I couldn't move. Miss say, For mercy sake, what is wrong with you? and I say, I got folks, I got folks, and Miss say, What folks? Start making sense. I tell her about granny and Enoch, and she say whatever happened to them, they weren't alone, and I say, How do you know, Miss? and Miss say that dying alone or living alone without someone loving you seemed the cruelest thing, and she wouldn't let that happen to nobody who was my kin. I knew she was lying. It was Miss's way of being kind.

Miss finally ask Colonel and found out that old Enoch had passed away fore the rebellion. Even she looked a little sad. She say he used to be her friend when she was a little girl. But no one knew nothing of granny, and when Miss pressed Colonel on it, he say Marse Tom insisted he never had no birthing woman matching the description Colonel gave him. Made me feel like I made that granny up, him denying what I knew to be the truth. But I wasn't gon let Marse Tom take my rememories from me too.

Miss say Marse Tom lost most of what he made from selling his field hands and servants, giving in to what she called those dreadful evils, cards and drink. His son, Tom Jr., he'd put in the care of Darling kin. I judged Miss didn't think much of Marse Tom, else she wouldn't be telling me all this.

Now he come to Colonel as a man putting his affairs in order.

I poured the bourbon into their snifters, gripping the bottle tight, and then Colonel dismissed me. I sat in the scullery on an upended crate til I heard them leaving the parlor and went to tidy it.

Colonel was waiting at the bottom of the staircase, holding Marse Tom's frock coat over his arm.

"We seem to have had a mishap," he say.

"Yes, Colonel."

Now, I knew about forgiveness. Ambrose preached it, warning what bitter could do inside you, how it could rot you out, but I wasn't feeling holy that night. I spread that coat on the counter and found a stream of bourbon down the front. I worked that stain like it was the man himself, hating it out with my slip of soap and split flour sack, and when I was done, I hung it on a garment peg, glad to get it off me.

"Girl," Marse Tom say from the front porch. He was sitting in a rocking chair, gazing out into the night. I stared hard into that darkness. I considered it a powerful and silent friend, for it was reliable, come every night, and didn't let me down. It was the same darkness God created, the same Mother's ancestors saw.

"My frock coat. Bring it."

"It's still damp, Marse."

"No mind."

I was trying to read him like I did Colonel and Miss, but I could get more off a dead man than I could off of him. I say nothing to his nothing. He took his coat and put it on with no help from me. I didn't offer. He didn't order. He didn't dismiss me, neither, so I kept on standing there.

We must of been like that for ten long minutes fore I broke.

"I was one of yours. Born on your farm," I say.

Marse kept staring into the dark.

"My mother was yours too."

He looked up at these brown-winged flyers banging at the porch lantern. By daylight dawn they'd be stunned dead from striking the cage so many times, drawn to a fire that would have killed them anyway. I near laughed, I was feeling so sorry for them.

"Too early for miller moths," he say.

"You called her Easter."

"I had several Easters. Had a Christmas too."

"This Easter dead."

"That so."

"She died on your farm," I say.

"It's been known to happen."

"Your overseer beat her to death," I say. Just then I felt someone at my elbow.

"Willie Mae," Colonel say, quiet, "let Mr. Darling alone."

I had no idea how long he been there.

"Your mistress is feeling delicate and would like you to prepare a hot water bottle. When you are done, you will meet me out back."

I broke in a sweat. I never been asked to meet the colonel nowhere.

I took a last look at Marse Tom, who was still staring at his nothing, wearing the face of someone living a life he regretted.

My eyes watered with each smear of ointment Lossie laid on me.

"Quit pacing, Alger, you making me wiggy," I say.

But Alger didn't quit. He was pacing to the door of our cabin to the table to the bed and back again.

Love began crying.

Milk was leaking down my stomach.

"You learn your lesson?" say Lossie.

"Mama!" say Alger. He was fuming like he wanted to brutal someone.

"Girl never been cowhided. Now she knows. Now she'll think before she speaks," say Lossie in her usual blunt.

"One more word, Mama, and I'll ask you to leave."

"Alger, hush and bring me Love and the nursing cloth," I say.

Love opened her mouth wide, the way newborns do, like a hungry chick, but I was slow moving, and she gummed hard on my nipple and not the tit. I winced.

Nothing worth having don't bring some pain, someone once say to me.

It was May, it was morning, and Miss was growing fretful. She was nine months and five days, weary for the waiting. She filled her time with eating. Never seen nobody put away so much grub. From the way she was eyeing me I was grateful I wasn't made of cake.

"Go tell Lossie I want another *chocolate marquise*," she say, nursing each fingertip. She sank back into her *chaise longue*.

"Yes, Miss," I say, footing to the door.

"No," she say.

"Miss?"

"Something's wrong," she say.

"You having a birthing pain?"

"I'm not certain," she say with a belch.

"Where you feeling it?"

"In my back." Then she gasped. "Don't go."

"I'm right here."

"I have to pass wind," she say, looking panicked.

"Then you go on and pass it."

"Oh, Wil," she say, tooting her bugle.

"That better?"

She smiled and then she cried out again.

"You got more wind in you?"

Miss shook her head. "Feel," she say, holding her belly.

It was hard and tight. Another pain took her, and soon they were coming mild but regular enough. Miss say I had to stay, and then there was no leaving her, not even to feed my child. At midday, the front of my dress bloomed, and Miss let Lossie bring Love to me. I heard my child fore I saw her, bawling the way little ones do when they got the milk hunger. As soon as I got Love latched on, she hushed.

"Sit beside me," say Miss, pointing at the ottoman.

I looked up, making sure I heard her right.

"I want to see," she say.

I didn't feel shy about nursing, certainly not in front of Mary-Mary or Lossie or my own husband, and I wouldn't of felt odd about it in front of Zenas the weaver—maybe the three sisters, but that was only cause we weren't close. If it was Sunday and I was eating in the yard with Absalom the groom and his brother Ambrose the blacksmith, with Morris and Cheney and J. Quincy Adams, with Sorrel and Lil Sis and Lewis and Clark, I would of found it natural to open my dress to feed my child. But none of them had the right to watch.

I sat next to her.

"Closer," she say.

I leaned over, worried she was gon ask me for a tit.

She say, "Does it hurt?"

"At first. Then you both learn."

She smiled a little, watching Love's ears wiggle as she fed. "What a blessing," she say.

"Yes, Miss."

Miss's smile shook. "I never knew my own mother, at least not in the flesh." I didn't know that about her, and it softened me some.

Love was squirming, and I had to shift to keep her in a good position. Miss watched our every move, gripped. When Love's hands dropped loose, and she began looking around this new-to-her pink room, I wedged my little finger in her mouth and broke the suction. Love let go and made that face she always did when her belly was full, dazed drunk.

"Is she done?" ask Miss.

"Yessum."

"Close your bodice."

"Yes, Miss."

"And give her to me."

"Miss?"

"I shall burp Lovelady Belle while you dress."

A day later, Miss wasn't making much progress. She was testy, bellowing orders from her four-poster. I had a good mind to tell her she ain't sick, she ain't the first one to be with child, and she perfectly fit to get up and walk round, it would do her good, make them pains come harder and faster and get that baby out, but she was too content to rant and fit. I imagined shoving her out the window, but I knew that was my lack of sleep talking.

"*Je ne peux pas accepter une plus de minute!*" she say with a flip of her legs over the side of the four-poster. "I must stand. Take my hands. Pull harder!"

I got her to her feet. Lucky she didn't topple me flat.

"Help me into my birthing gown," she say, wobbling to her *chaise longue*.

I took it from her *chiffonier*, but when I turned, Miss Emmaline's face was looking even paler than usual. "I need to lie back down," she say, stumbling a little. Then she howled.

"What is it, Miss, what are you feeling?"

"He's coming, Wil. My child is starting his journey." She grimaced and squeezed my hand.

"Miss Emmaline?" say Lossie from the other side of the chamber door.

"Send her away," say Miss, panting. "Go!" She waved me off.

I moved quick, opening the door.

"It's her time?" say Lossie.

"She starting, but she say to go away."

"Get me my birthing gown!" say my gasping miss, holding on to a bedpost. "Now!"

"Lossie wants to come in."

"I don't want Lossie. I want you. You shall help me do this. You know me. You know me, Wil." Her eyes were tearing.

I shut the door on Lossie, neither one of us liking Miss Emmaline's plan.

I helped Miss into her gown and heaved her back into her four-poster. "I got to go get clean linens and hot water," I say.

She gave me a weak smile fore her head sank into her pillow.

In the hall, Colonel was talking with Lossie. He ask me about Miss's health and constitution. He ask Lossie if I was competent. Lossie say I gave birth only three months ago and might of learned something. I appreciated Lossie's confidence and hoped she was right. For both Miss's and my sake.

Colonel say Lossie was to sit outside the door, and I was to keep it ajar, and at the first sign of any trouble, he didn't care what his wife wanted.

After seven hours of standing sitting walking pacing rocking kneeling crawling, all the while grinding her teeth against the pain, Miss was spent. She was lying in her four-poster, pushing and snarling and cussing, grabbing the sheets, shitting and pissing them. There ain't no place for modesty when you giving birth.

As Lossie and me put fresh linens under her, she sobbed, "I cannot do this. I cannot do this anymore."

Lossie say it sometimes takes three days to birth a child, so Miss was doing fine.

Miss sobbed even harder.

Another wave hit her, and she pushed. Out come a flood of pink—birthing blood, womb snot, child water, and, at long last, her baby.

"Lossie!" I say.

"I see it," she say, not the head but the toes, a breech, and the two of us hoisted Miss out of her four-poster, Miss looking at me with pitiful agony, and we made her stand, legs spreading, hands bearing down on her mattress. Lossie say, "Quit pushing, Miss! You need to wait for the next urge, so you don't hurt your baby. Willie Mae, get down there and hold up his legs."

The next pain seized Miss, and she screamed.

"You doing it, Miss," I say, reaching beneath the miss, holding the child steady.

"Close your hand around the cord," say Lossie. "You feel a heart beating?"

"I do, real strong," I say. Lossie showed me how to swivel the babe and sweep out his arms. She say take care with his head.

"Don't wait for another pain, you push now, you push your baby out," Lossie say to Miss. She groaned and pushed the rest of that child out in a gush. It was a girl.

"You did it!" I say.

Lossie held Miss under the arms as she squatted over a bowl to deliver the birth sac, while I sucked the water out of the babe's mouth with a bulb syringe. She began breathing right off, good strong breaths. When the cord quit pulsing, Lossie told me how to clamp and cut it. It was like cutting meat gristle, and it took Lossie reminding me that neither mother nor baby could feel it fore I could hold the scissors steady.

Lossie cleaned and stitched Miss and sat her in her lounging chair while I got busy washing the child. When Miss took the swaddled babe in her arms, her face flushed with fresh tears. She peeled the spun cloth away from the child's face and squeezed her tit, and the child took right to it.

"Look, Wil, look!" she say, her face a shining sun.

I smiled back at my miss, proud of myself and, I ain't ashamed to admit, happy for her.

The horses Manasseh and Ephraim heard it first.

Ephraim shuddered, while Manasseh stepped erratic and whinnied, his flanks and withers quivering. Ephraim was the first to crack. He broke into full gallop, careening toward the far end of the paddock, his ears pinned back, his eyes pulling so wide they were rimming with white. Manasseh catapulted after him, his nostrils flaring, his head tossing up and down like he didn't want to be left alone with the thing terrifying them. Absalom the groom sprinted over to the paddock but then the wind, at least what we thought was the wind, blew him flat down into the muck.

A storm was brewing, and it was coming from inside the hello-yellow.

We all heard it now, the wail of Miss Emmaline's grief echoing through the mountains surrounding the Fertile Valley.

With another gust of sorrow, the shingles rippled. They spun clean off the roof. An agony of open sores. The shutters slapped violence against the sides of the hello-yellow and the potted daffodils flew off the railing, near missing Colonel's head as he went running up the porch. Morning glories shut petal tight—they were gripping the trellis—and moonflowers squeezed the columns. Then the sky turned green and purple, and the wail grew into a howl.

From the fields, Marse Riddle come running, along with Morris, Cheney, and Lil Sis. They joined the others rushing livestock into barns, packing harrows, hoes, rakes, anything with tines or tongs into sheds, dropping iron locks in place, heading for safety inside their houses. Up on the hill, the sheep huddled.

I clung to the laundry post, the linens furling and unwhirling around the line, my hands tremblish, the post shaking furious despite its deep root, as if it was trying to cast me off. Alger was calling me, and I shouted back, but I couldn't tell where he was, so blinding was the rain falling. When the post whipped out of the ground, I was left freestanding. How I dug my heels into the ground, with nothing but my baby girl on my mind. How I leaned into the blast, taking it on, its ferocity inspiring my strength. Passing the trees bend-bowing, near breaking in two, the giant chinquapin, the oaks, the walnut trees, them magnolia huddling to protect their smaller kin. I leaned harder into the gale, dodging earthly debris, keeping my sight on the kitchen house til I stumbled to the ground over a dervish of arms and legs and skirt billowing: Mary-Mary, scrambling yet unable to rise, the wind's bite sharp and venomous. Now we were both in danger of being carried off. We braced against each other, the fury dragging us across the yard. Arms locked, we bucked on the storm's back until we were far flung. We crawled on our bellies to Lossie's door.

It was sealed.

The door was sealed.

We pounded and we shouted. Our voices drowned in the lash of rain. We crouched against the door, burying heads, clutching each other, praying, until the door gave and two strong hands heaved us inside. Marse Riddle.

"Where's Love?" I say.

"This way," he say, and we followed him into the bedroom. She was in a sling tied round Lossie's chest. Safe.

Lossie was bending over a body. Alger.

"He alive?" I say, my head spinning light.

"Aye," Marse Riddle say. "But he's hurt."

He had a cut sewn up along his temple. Lossie's skilled work.

"Sorry, Wil," he say.

"You got nothing to be sorry for."

"I didn't save you."

"I don't need saving," I say.

The storm wailed all through the night. We woke the next morning to a sound most unnatural. Silence. The birds of dawn were gone. Our doors opened to a stump-gouged wasteland of misery. Not a tree left save a lone peach. What remained of the land was pitted, pocked, and shocked. The tobacco and corn were ravaged, and several sheep and calves were dead. Mama cows roamed the pasture looking for their young, bawling a most sorryful tune, grief curdling their milk.

It was Miss Emmaline who had discovered her babe dead in the bassinet, and Colonel himself who dug her grave. No one tolled the chapel bell, seeing how she'd had no years, only a week, and the silence hurt all our ears. J. Quincy Adams built a right pretty box from heartwood pine and padded it with cotton and lined it with white satin. To see such a bitty small casket made the child's dying seem even more wrongful. I tended to her body, washing her careful behind her ears and between her toes. It was those tiny toenails made me hurt the most. I dressed her in the scalloped gown no one got to appreciate. Not one of us could get Miss to let go of the matching cap, so I lay her in her box bald-headed. The following night, we all sat with her in the praise house to show our respect. Later that night, Colonel joined us, bringing that shriveled white preacher. Miss never showed. The baby was buried in a plot next to the chapel, beside Granddaddy Solomon and his wife, Gay. A week later the engraver come with the child's stone.

Our Daughter. Budded on earth to bloom in heaven, it say.

Two weeks later Miss let us back into the hello-yellow. I took this for a good sign. I was wrong. Miss was a wreck. She wouldn't let me clean her up. When she ate, she didn't want me with her. She gave her dirties to Galilee. Anna tended her chamber, while Cassia and Mary-Mary took care of the house.

Miss had a new game for me. Find the dead baby's cap. "I don't know where I've left it," she would weep. At first, I thought she truly forgot what she done with it. I'd find it under a chair cushion, behind a green curtain, pressed in a book, or under her four-poster. One day, I found it on top of her *chiffonier*. Miss couldn't reach the top of it without a stepping stool.

She was disappointed when I gave it back to her.

"Where did you find it?" she say, dull.

"Top of the *chiffonier*," I say, keeping the irritation off my face.

"How do you suppose it arrived there?"

"Don't know, Miss."

"What were you doing at the top of the *chiffonier*, Wilhelmina?"

"Dusting."

"And is that one of your duties?"

"No, Miss."

"So I shall ask you again. What were you doing at the top of the *chiffonier*?"

"Looking for the baby cap, Miss."

"And what would make you think of searching there?"

I knew what Miss was pushing for. I'd seen her looking for the perfect spot. I'd seen her hide it there.

"I don't know, Miss."

"I see," she say. "Fetch me a fresh hickory switch."

From that day, she made me strip to the waist and beat me whether I found it or not.

So what if my skin bled and Miss Emmaline would never be satisfied?

So what if that wound-inflicted woman inflicted so many wounds there were now two women wounded in want of desperate relief?

Miss was inconsolable.

Til Colonel placed a newborn in her arms. Mine. A balm of Gilead to ease her paining heart.

Love refused her milk. Like a lamb she knew her own mother.

Wet nurse to my own daughter.

I thought, I will, I will, I will not die. In Alger's arms I rocked. "We'll get her back, I know we will," he say.

My spirit was dying. Mary-Mary say, "Don't you give up, Willie Mae, no, don't you do that, girl, you are alive."

It was Alger who could take it no more, who grabbed the hickory switch right out of Miss's hands and bust it over his knee. "Don't you beat my wife," he say.

It was Miss Emmaline who screamed like the broken switch was her own spine.

It was Marse Riddle who stormed into the drawing room.

Miss was a hellion, clawing wild, hurling porcelain plates, a poker, her Argand lamp, yanking down the curtains. The sunset burned as bright as a bloody egg, scorching her drawing room. Miss wasn't no bitty Miss no more—she was fearsome, filled with rage, and rage can make even the weakest person a reckoning force. Everybody ran for cover then. Marse Riddle out the front door. Alger in the hallway. I ran upstairs. I found Love in the dead baby's bassinet. Love in my arms.

I could hear Miss sniveling downstairs. When she went mum, I looked over the balustrade. Alger was pinning to the wall right outside her drawing room. He put a single finger to his mouth. *Hush.*

When Miss come out, she was holding her long rifle under her arm. Alger grabbed her and she butted him right under his sternum. Left him gasping on the floor.

She walked out onto her porch, raised her rifle, fired, and flushed her own brother out of the dead rose garden, sending him hopping across the treeless yard.

Miss burst into a fit of laughter.

It was Alger who got to his feet and charged her.

It was Marse Riddle who rushed up the stairs and wrestled the long rifle from her.

It was Colonel on Manasseh galloping right up to the steps.

"You will whip him," say Colonel; right after he tied Miss to her four-poster and locked her in with only Miss Lossie brave enough to stay. "I will not have him interfering with my wife."

"Nay," say Marse Riddle, his face stricken.

"It was not a request."

"I will not beat my son."

"If you do not, I will." Colonel pushed Alger out the front door and marched us all to the barn. Everyone who was mending a fence, a shed, a roof, the gate—wounds left from the storm—quit their work to watch our parade of grim.

Colonel was gon beat the chosen one.

Inside the barn, Marse Riddle say, "Solomon, please, don't. I cannot bear it."

All us looked at him, puzzled. Colonel's daddy been buried in that chapel plot for almost eighteen years, plenty dead.

"Sam," he say, correcting his slip. "We are as close as brothers, are we not?"

"Then don't beg, brother," say Colonel. His large head didn't look large no more. It was small and shrunk. "Remove your shirt," he say to my man.

Alger's back was a smooth of muscle.

"Take hold of the stall," say Colonel.

"What do you think you're doing to my child?" say Lossie from the barn door, only yards away, but her voice even larger than her tree-tall size. No one had heard her coming, for the keys that were always bouncing on her leg weren't on her belt no more.

Hanging from her hand was a carving knife.

Mary-Mary stood behind her. And Absalom the groom. His brother Ambrose the blacksmith and Zenas the weaver. Jaz and Ashby. Morris and Cheney and J. Quincy Adams. Sorrel and Lil Sis and Lewis and Clark.

They come with whatever tool they been using, a hammer, a wrench, an ax, a turning gouge, a chisel.

"Grab her," Colonel say, still thinking he was in command.

But no one budged.

Colonel looked at all the faces sizing him down. He told them to go back to the quarters and stay there. We were deep in the shade of that barn, but I could see the thoughts riffing from Morris to Cheney to J. Quincy Adams, like they were gauging how fast they could charge. Colonel must of seen it too, for he took out his pistol and cocked the hammer. He aimed at Lossie's chest. "It won't be on my conscience," he say. Love started crying.

Marse Riddle put his hands in the air like a convict and hobbled over to Lossie, right in front of her.

"I don't want to shoot you, brother," say Colonel.

"Perhaps you should," say Marse Riddle, making no sense.

Love cried louder. I cringed and looked over Colonel's shoulder at Alger.

"Colonel, sir," say Alger from behind him. "I'll take my beating. Here," he say, taking the cat of nine off the wall. But Colonel didn't turn.

Folks stood quiet as he took them in. And then he shot Absalom. Half the folks scattered. Colonel shot again. This time he hit Ambrose. Fore Cheney or Morris or J. Quincy Adams could get that pistol from him, he pressed the nose of that Colt right to Alger's temple. He say if Lossie didn't drop her knife he'd drop her son. That knife fell real quick, and then Colonel made J. Quincy Adams truss Lossie to the post.

Locked in the shoe shack, I sat on a chair rocking Love. Stripped of my man, I waited in the unknowing. Day become night and still I waited, my mind showing me all kinds of thoughts I didn't want to be thinking. The mind can warp on you, doing what you don't want, specially when you don't want it to. I knew what Tom Darling would of done in Colonel's place. He would of hung Lossie. He would of whipped Alger a hundred times and left him in the nigger box with no grub, or slit off his ear rims, his nose, or his manhood. He would of opened the Good Book and read some verse and sold my child off or given her to the coyotes, cause he could afford the waste. He would of put Lewis and Clark on the auction block to sell them away from Sorrel and Lil Sis. Zenas was too old to survive a beating. He would of put her in the stocks naked. He'd pray for rain. Morris, Cheney, and J. Quincy Adams were still young enough, so they could take it. He'd let his dogs skin them up. As for Jaz and Ashby, he'd shut them in with the three sisters in a pairing shack, don't matter they were his colored sisters, and beat Jaz and Ashby til the gals got big or he crippled the men, whichever come first. You have to make up your losses when you a marse. Lucky for you, you can breed them.

Only Mary-Mary he wouldn't touch. For that gal never was his slave, and even he had his own code of do-right. Found in a grass basket under the flowering dogwood outside his double log fence some fourteen years back with a note saying she was born free and papers to prove it.

Mary-Mary was always free. She stayed for me.

Next morning, Alger come with a hammer and pried off the four-by-fours Colonel nailed to the door. He say, "We're leaving."

Marse Riddle had bought his entire family.

"Mercy," I say, my eyes and nose stinging with confusion.

Alger say mercy had no hand in it. Colonel's tobacco crop was ruined, not a seedling left, and he needed the money. Alger say his mother alone cost more than double her cash worth. He and his daddy had to pool their savings and now not a cent of it was left.

"Listen to how you talk," I say, still unbelieving. "What about Miss? What about Love? Miss ain't keeping her?"

Alger held out a paper.

Fore he could speak, I cried out in shock. It was fancy, but I understood it:

Rec'd of Mr. Riddle Young three hundred and fifty dollars in full payment for a Negro girl named Lovelady Belle of a Mulatto Complexion aged two months. The above described I warrant sound in Body & Mind, a slave for life & free from all claims.

Hopewell County, GA. May 26th 1860

Col. Samuel Bounds

"Three hundred and fifty? Lord a mercy."

"I didn't know you could read," Alger say, like I done something personal to him. He leaned a hand on the workbench and coughed into his sleeve.

"Well, I can."

He coughed again. Blood showed through the back of his shirt. "He whipped you," I say.

"It's nothing, Wil. Just let it be."

"Let me see."

"Let it be," he say, strong.

"Ain't no shame," I say.

"I'm not ashamed."

"Right, then. Take off your shirt and let me tend you."

"Colonel said we best leave right now, before he changes his mind. Are you listening to me, Wil?" He took my hand in both of his. "Don't you open your mouth or give him cause, you hear?"

"I hear," I say. "What about Mary-Mary? We got to let her know."

He looked away.

"Alger?"

"We didn't have enough to pay for both you and Love. She gave Colonel her free papers."

"No, that ain't right. She can't do that," I say.

"She did."

"She freeborn."

"Not anymore," he say.

Almost all the hands were there to see us off, including Absalom and Ambrose, both alive but wrapped and hurting. Only Sorrel, Lil Sis, Morris, and Cheney were missing, charged with attacking Colonel and tie-beamed in what was left of the icehouse, say Alger. Galilee looked at me with her watchful eyes like she wanted to say something kind but didn't want to slow down our pace.

Upstairs, through the lace of the hallway window, I saw Mary-Mary, and then she pulled away.

"I got to talk to her," I say to Alger as we lugged Marse Riddle's belongings to his cart.

"No."

Alger dropped a crate and headed back for another. I hiked my skirts and chased him down.

"I ain't leaving without seeing her," I say.

"Take a gunnysack, it's lighter."

I followed him back to the cart. "If she comes out—"

"She's not," he say, final.

"Why?"

"Because I told her not to."

"Why would you do that?"

"I love you, Willie Mae, and I know you do your best to love me. I'm telling you she's not coming down, and you're not to speak to her. I'm not giving you a choice. You have to trust me. Now go and get my mother and Love."

I looked up at the hello-yellow, battered and beaten but still making its stand. I thought I saw the blink of her eyes, the slight of her hips. I could feel her reaching for me. I saw through the front door and up the staircase and down the sunlit hallway and I saw her turn. I tasted her strawberry breath. "Willie Mae, move," say Alger. "Don't test the colonel. For all our sake."

I hard-turned toward the kitchen house. When I come out with Love in a bundle on my chest and Lossie, who was looking so dead in the eye it scared me, Colonel himself was there on the front porch of his big house. So were three others—a Matterson and two Bloods—reinforcements, and they were wearing rifles.

Colonel didn't say a word as Marse Riddle harnessed his old mount, John Joseph, and he say nothing as Marse Riddle pulled the cart by its shafts up to the horse's shoulders, and nothing still while he looped the trace through the bellyband and tightened the girth. Not even as he fastened the crates and gunnysacks to the wagon bed did Colonel speak. He just watched from high up on his porch. Below him, them three gunslingers shifted their feet and rifles.

On the roof of the hello-yellow, a gray-chesty mourning dove was cooing.

At first I took Colonel for staring off into the forest as we pulled out, but the longer we rattled down that drive, the more it seemed his forlorn eyes were following the sleeping bundle in my arms. Soon, as we slow-rolled through the double gate and turned northeast, folks milled out of the front yard, leaving only Colonel. I held back, and then I raised my hand. To Colonel who was watching. To Miss who wasn't.

To Mary-Mary.

Then I faced the road, my heart battering in the hollow of empty.

I knew that tree aside the road. I knew its love-lettered carving. It cheered me to see it, like finding an old friend alive who you thought was dead. We passed the magnolia first.

Next come the giant chinquapin, with its crown-rounded top still raggedy, settled in a field among a group of saplings.

Up and down that public road I recognized them: the black walnuts and the dogwoods as we wove through the mountains, and they gave me courage.

Marse Riddle drove John Joseph at a steady clip, none of us speaking, everyone soaking up the spring music: leaves talking and mosquitoes droning, tree squirrels spit-calling or dancing for their mates. Nowhere no sounds of sowing or scything, nothing human at all, and I was glad for it. We weren't fugitive, yet we sure did feel it.

After a couple a miles Marse Riddle turned us onto a dirt road—a footpath, really, more than a wagon trail—in a lush green called Warwoman Hollow and into a forest so wet water was dropping off every branch. Switchback to ridge, dip to dip, stream after stream, rising and falling, everywhere a cataract, and so many tints dotting the mist, violet—hydrangea, say Marse Riddle—and pink—lady's slipper, he say—and ivory—mountain laurel. When we come to a creaky-looking bridge over a river the red-rust color of old blood, Marse Riddle say for all us to get out of the cart, that he was gon make sure it was safe to cross. He looked spooked, climbing down beneath to check the braces, like this bridge gave him a fright, but he wasn't gon admit it.

I never seen such a river. It was churning like a bad stomach over stumps and boulders.

"Your daddy know what he's doing?" I ask Alger.

Alger say he sure does, that his daddy built this bridge alongside his own father.

Marse Riddle rose from below, stepping ginger, knocking on the deck and the stringers, and testing each tie with his foot. When he quit his rapping and tapping, he held a single finger to his lips and all us listened. He seemed satisfied and say the bridge was fit for crossing. I stayed along his flank, carrying Love on my hip.

"All the rivers of the county feed it. 'Tis called the Cuchulannahan-nachee," he say, looking down at that red water.

I say that sure is a mouthful.

"'Tis a portmanteau of Cherokee and Scotch-Irish. 'Twas named for Cúchulainn, a hero of Celtic myth, a warrior who defended his home of Ulster fighting a great many battles."

"What's that reek? Skunk?"

He laughed. "Galax." He pointed at sprays of white flowers on the river's slopes. "My da thought the smell should've been enough to ward folks off."

This was the most I ever spoke with him, for I never much thought of him as a person til now. Fore that he was Alger's daddy or the overseer. Sometimes Miss Emmaline's brother, but rarely even that. He kept order, somewhat. He was mostly liked. He always seemed a bad fit to the place, surly, silent, unwilling, half dead. This man was something different. This man was alive. I saw it fore my own eyes, like cool shade and musky soil was what his blood needed, and this was his turf.

Soon we come to a place called Screamer Hollow, and there, on a plot gone wild, was a lump of green vines as big as a smallish cabin. Young trunks of sassafras and persimmon guarded like a circular fence. Rising sharp behind this wreck of land, old oaks and chestnuts marched up a blue black mountainside. There was majesty, but at the same time it was desolate.

With a hatchet and a briar scythe Alger and Marse Riddle hacked through the vines and freed Marse Riddle's old dwelling. The inside was a bitter-smelling stew of cooking grease, dried herbs, musty corncobs, old rainwater, dead mice, rat piss, and fouling underarms—wooo! Cobwebs yarned from an old rope bed to a heavy-looking table to a shelf of leather books and a stonewall hearth. It wasn't grand, but we didn't need grand. Freedom meant scratching for ourselves, and Marse Riddle's homeplace was a good place to start. He wiped the grit and sweat from his brow with the back of his forearm. "I fought many a battle here, but now I find the place a blessing. 'Tis funny the cycle of life," he say.

Later, when I pried open a corncrib, a blue so bright come sailing out the door and the slats—butterflies. One lit down on Love's head right above her eyes fore it quick took off, and I watched it til there was nothing more than the memory of color skipping like a rock on water over the valley.

"Summer azures and eastern tailed-blue," say Marse Riddle.

This was his gift to me, the proper naming of the world around us.

Took them a month, but in that time him and Alger mended the cabin and raised a second room. Next was a springhouse, an outhouse, and a barn for John Joseph. Marse and Lossie took the second room in the cabin for their sleeping, and me, Alger, and Love did ours in the chimney corner of the main, where we also took our meals and gathered for this new style of regular living.

I was unsure of the rules of this world, and my first weeks felt like forever falling. On this scratch of land, I could keep both my eyes on the same side of my head. It took some getting used to. Lossie was different too, shriveling like a tree in winter, her spunk gone. Marse Riddle kept saying, "Why not sit on the porch and take in this good air and rest?"—the last thing Lossie needed, but she would do just that and stare at her hands or put them into her pockets like she didn't know how to account for them. She say, "When you're not useful, you're good as dead," and he say, "No, my love, don't say that. We need you. This land needs you. Without you I'm lost." He smiled a private smile, and I had to look away. When Lossie finally slipped from her funk and began to learn the land, she found blueberries for preserves, persimmons for puddings, dandelion for wine, a whole mess of herbs and roots for doctoring. She wasn't her old self, but she found she had life in her yet, and she worked lively, cooking and brewing and drying and canning. As for Alger, well. He grew larger than the land; even more jaunty than the day I first met him. Marse Riddle bought him a map of the world, and then I was up late into the night, Alger talking latitudes and longitudes and meridians and navigations with a fervor. Had to make the man a no-qualms tea and threaten to kick him from our bed if he didn't let me sleep.

"Let me show you something before you turn in," he say.

"Only one?"

"Just one."

He showed me Africa. He ran his finger over the Lion Mountains.

I thought of my sisters and brother on this far-off continent who didn't know what come of their mother, who didn't know nothing of me, and I sat back down. I tell Alger of my mother for the very first time, and he listened, and for the first time since she died, I could feel the joy of her. You got to be careful with grief, that it don't shove all the other memories aside and one day you find yourself on this Mother Earth too far along and with a terrible fear: that you done lost the memories, they vanished like they ain't never happened, and you got to dig to uncover the dead, you got to pray they more than dust.

Come July, Marse Riddle penned a letter petitioning the government for Lossie and Alger's freedom. He say he didn't want to tempt the Fates, asking for the emancipation of us all at once. But he took me aside and made me a promise: I wouldn't be treated like a bondwoman, nor thought of as one neither. My life of servitude was ended.

Fore he left to post the letter, he let me read it:

I, Riddle Young, submit with Care and Industry that I have been able to purchase from Colonel Samuel Bounds a negro woman by the name of Lossie with whom by the consent of Colonel Bounds I have previous intermarried. Realizing that my child will be a Slave contrary to my wish without the interposition of the General Assembly, this petitioner is emboldened to ask that the State emancipate my said wife Lossie.

Hopewell County, GA. July 20th 1860

Riddle Young

As he did whenever he left Screamer Hollow, he warned us for our safety from wandering too far from the cabin without a pass. We were enjoying our life on the mountaintop too much to care about leaving it just yet, so we didn't ask for one, not even Alger. Still, we were relieved when Marse Riddle got back from town fore sunset.

The day following, after he returned from fishing, he banished us women from the kitchen, all hop in his lopsided step, and hoo! how he worked, banging around the hearth, refusing all help, igniting a fire that jumped too high and scorched up his apron. After he batted it out, he grinned, sheepish, and in good humor turned back to his frying pan.

When we sat down for our supper, I could only shake my head in disbelieving when Marse Riddle asked me to lead grace "for our family." I thanked the Lord for the fine meal before us, for Love and Alger, for Lossie and Marse Riddle, and then my voice stopped working from too much feeling, and I made quick with an *amen*. When they all say "Amen" back, I let free a smile that ran from cheek to cheek from how much pleasure it gave me.

"'Tis been some time, but I believe I still have the touch," say Marse Riddle, sitting tall in his swivel chair at the head of the table.

Lord, that trout was salty and the pone was as dry.

I mushed the pone down with water for Love. Alger slabbed his piece with a chunk of butter.

"Easy, son," Marse Riddle say, "we need to make it last."

Alger opened his mouth to speak, but something clogged his throat, and he hacked like a cat. I shouted, "Throw your arms up," and banged him on his back and out come a chunk of singed trout.

Marse Riddle say, "You alright?"

"I'm great, Da, just great," say Alger, wiping his mouth. "The trout is great. It's all . . . great." And he stretched his lips into a grin showing how good everything tasted, but I could read what his eyes were really saying: He rather be gnawing on a floorboard than anything on this table. I couldn't help from covering my mouth and laughing. Then Lossie caught the fever, and Alger too, and then even Marse Riddle chuckled and say, "Well, as I said, 'tis been awhile. Anyone for dessert?" All us groaned and Marse Riddle say, "Come, now!"

Marse Riddle was true to his word. We were familied.

Down in the valley, though, the family Miss Emmaline hoped to have never come to be. Colonel Bounds was a crippled man, and he had a crippled wife. He could not heal her. He could not mend her shattered heart. Miss had fallen into a living nightmare and refused to wake. Up the trail Jaz come to give us the news of Colonel hauling our sad, sorry Miss out of the pond, bloated and floating like a river-born rat. Poor Miss drowned herself, Jaz say. He brought a newspaper clipping from the *Persimmon Tribune*. He say it was from Colonel.

Marse Riddle spread it on the table, and I read over his shoulder. It was dated August 20, 1860.

Mrs. Samuel Bounds, living two miles from Persimmon on the once-renowned tobacco plantation of Colonel Samuel Bounds, committed suicide by drowning Saturday morning. She leaves no children.

Her remains were interred on family grounds.

Col. Bounds is among the most prominent men in this section of Georgia. Our sympathy goes out to the bereaved.

Alger's daddy spent the rest of the morning along the bank of the river cutting through his property. In the afternoon, Lossie sat with him, and later Alger.

"Go be with him, Wil," Alger say when he come back to the cabin, where I was laying the table for supper.

"Me? What am I gon say?"

"You spent the most time with her. You knew her best, in a way."

So I took up next to Marse.

He rubbed his hands in the river and wiped his face and ran his fingers through his hair. Gray the color of an old ax head made up most of his plait. He was forty-one or -two by my count. Lossie, around fifty-four. Old-timers. My old-timers. I thought to touch the man's shoulder, but I didn't know him well enough, so I pulled back.

"She brought Bounds down," he say, his voice both grateful and grieving. His gaze fell to the water. "She freed me."

Riding along the public road a month later with Marse Riddle—who say please don't call me that no more and agreed on "Mr. Riddle," even though he say it was fine to call him Da—we saw a tall, thin figure fitting a new fence rail. Jaz was looking more and more like his daddy, Ambrose, each time I saw him, withy but strong, with a quirky smile, a man.

Mr. Riddle slowed the cart, both us scanning for pattyrollers and pistols.

"How ya'll?" say Jaz.

"Couldn't be better," say Mr. Riddle. "And yourself?"

Galilee was in a delicate way, Jaz say.

"Congratulations," we say.

"Thankee," say Jaz, broad beaming.

"How's Colonel fare?" I say.

Jaz say Colonel was doing poorly. Been weak in body and spirit since Miss's passing. Jaz was headman now and Galilee the housekeeper.

We were jawing like old friends, so I ask Mr. Riddle to let me off. He say he didn't like the sound of that, and Jaz say Colonel hardly ever come out of the house, he didn't think I'd be in no danger, so Mr. Riddle wrote out a pass.

To the Sheriff of Persimmon and the Slave Patrol: The bearer, my negro woman Willie Mae, is hereby permitted to pass and repass without hindrance or molestation along the length of the Public Road to the trail in Warwoman Hollow to my homeplace in Screamer Hollow.

Given under my hand this 22d November 1860. Riddle Young

He say to stick to the road, to please don't stray. "I shall meet you back in the hollow," he say, and I waved him off.

"You looking plump," say Jaz with a smile.

"I'm happy," I say. "Where is everybody? This place looks bare." I didn't see no tobacco, only Indian corn and cattle, and I didn't see no one tending them.

He say his mother, Zenas, was dead. Died out natural a week after Miss Emmaline passed. His daddy, Ambrose, never got over the infection in his leg from the shot he took. Colonel brought in the colored doctor from town, but Ambrose's pride was even more wounded. He never did wrong by Colonel, not in any way long hurting—he hadn't even charged Colonel—and so he followed Zenas over the River Jordan, preferring the love of his faithful rather than the faith of the unlovable.

I say I was awful sad to hear that.

"Thankee," he say.

His uncle Absalom was mended.

"Glad to hear it."

Morris and Cheney survived their beating but run off fore the authorities come to take them to trial. Sorrel and Lil Sis were in jail.

"All this change," I say.

Jaz say more change was coming.

Leave predictions to grannies, I tell him. "What about Mary-Mary?" I ask. "How she?"

Jaz say she been hired out for the rest of the year. Colonel was hurting for hard cash.

"Where she at?"

"Strummers Knob," say Jaz.

"Matterson?"

"Yep."

My pass didn't cover the track to that bulldog's place. I took off the madras handkerchief.

"You grown your hair out," say Jaz.

"Alger likes it long."

"I bet he do," Jaz say with a wink.

I tell him to give Mary-Mary the handkerchief, to tell her to keep it for me, and he say he would do just that.

We heard him fore we saw him, shouting for us. The snow was hard falling, the flakes as large as chicken feathers. Third week of December. Mr. Riddle was riding back from town with a smile stretching from Alabama to South Carolina. He wasted no time watering John Joseph and running up the porch with a letter between his thick leather gloves. It read:

> Be it enacted by the Senate and House of Representatives of the State of Georgia in General Assembly met, That from and after the passage of this act, Lossie Young, who is, and has been for eighteen years, the wife of Riddle Young of the county of Hopewell, shall be, and she is hereby declared, to be free, and entitled to all the privileges and immunities appertaining to free persons of color generally in this State.
>
> And whereas the said Riddle Young since his intermarriage with his said wife Lossie has had a child, and whereas by the laws of this State the children follow the condition of their mother—
>
> Be it therefore enacted by the Senate and House of Representatives of the State of Georgia in General Assembly met, That the child heretofore born— to wit, Alger Young—by and in consequence of said intermarriage between the said Riddle Young and Lossie his wife, shall be, and is hereby declared to be free, and placed on the same footing that free persons of color are usually placed in this State, and entitled to inherit from the said Riddle, as his

father, any property which by the laws of this State would go to his child
should he die without a will.

Lossie and Alger were free people. Alger stubbed the snow with the toe
of his boot, embarrassed to be so happy. Mr. Riddle hugged his Lossie and
lifted the once-big-tall woman off her feet, and she let him fuss. It was the
first time I saw a man weep.

Next day, Mr. Riddle drafted my letter. He say he feared for his applica-
tion with the growing unrest between the states, afraid it would eclipse his
request, so he was gon dispatch as soon as the snow quit. Two days later he
left with it.

He come back that evening with my letter still in his satchel and a
Hopewell Weekly. South Carolina was no longer part of the United States.
Just two months later, Georgia, along with South Carolina, Mississippi,
Florida, Alabama, Louisiana, and Texas, were the Confederate States of
America. By April 1861 it was the War Between the States.

My freedom letter stayed on the mantel, never sent.

Not far from the homeplace, on the lee side of the hill, I was searching a
sandy patch for colicroot when I saw them, Mr. Riddle at the reins with
Alger joggling next to him, elbows on his knees, chin latched between his
thumbs and forefinger, looking thinkish. It always cheered me to see my
husband, even though I saw him every day. We'd been friended seven years,
married almost three. I was sixteen. Alger was twenty-one. Love was two.
Poor old John Joseph was nearing her final days. April 1862. Mr. Riddle
slowed the cart, and Alger jumped down.

Mr. Riddle had a line of dried blood beneath his eye. "See you home,"
he say.

"Why he cut?" I say to my husband. Spring was soft and hazy, and it
landed on Alger as he took off his green felt hat. He plucked a sheaf of long
grass and peeled the stem and plugged it in his mouth.

"So?" I say, digging at the herb I'd found in the soil.

He chewed on the blade and told me about the meeting.

His daddy had took on Matterson.

"Hoo! No."

"He did," Alger say with a wry smile.

"Lucky he didn't get killed. He too old to be fighting."

"He is," say Alger, "but he held his own. Matterson looked worse than Da by the time he finished with him."

He say he didn't think I'd have no more trouble with him, but I say don't be so sure. Matterson been deputized, and he liked to bulge his way up our dirt trail, bringing a Blood for his partner. A real skinny, this Blood was, feeble colored, like someone dipped him in chloride of lime and bleached him whiter than bone in the sun. Matterson always bullied me for a pass, don't matter how close I hugged the hollow, don't matter he knew exactly where I lived and who owned me. And even though neither Matterson nor that Blood could read, they hounded Alger for his free papers whenever they crossed him and made like they were gon tear them up—they signed their town motions with an *X*, Alger say.

He took the grass from his mouth. A conscription law been passed. All able-bodied men of Hopewell got to muster.

I frowned hard. "You too?"

"It's my duty," he say.

"You ain't answered the question."

Alger put that grass back in him. "It's my duty," he say again.

"I heard you the first time, able-bodied man," I say. I tossed my spade into my bucket and took off, fast-footing my way down the hill with Alger trailing after me.

I knew this war. I knew its skirmishes and bloodiness. I knew the horror of slave tortures. I knew Manassas, Oak Hills, Leesburg, Mill Springs, Elkhorn Tavern, and the one in Shiloh. When Mr. Riddle read his *Hopewell Weekly* aloud, I listened, and when he was done, he set them in a wood crate, where I sat reading the essays he didn't, and after, I glued them to the walls, not just to thicken them for winter but—and this I kept to myself, for Lossie didn't share my particular hoo-dooing ways—for protection.

I was moving so swift up the road to the homeplace that Alger was a steady six paces behind me. "What about Mr. Riddle?" I say back over my shoulder. "That gon kill your mother."

Alger say no, no, his father was too old. Only eighteen years to thirty-five got to go.

"Ain't that a mercy."

"I've got to do my part. Stop walking away from me."

I made an about-face. "Who else don't got to go?"

"How do you mean?" Alger say, suspicious.

"You know how I mean. Besides old men."

Alger looked at me the way he always did when he didn't want to tell me the truth but it wasn't in him to do it any other way. He square-eyed me and rattled off, "Overseers. Headmen. Unfit men. Slave owners with more than twenty slaves living within four miles of each other."

"What a bunch. Rich and sick. What about free colored?"

"Free colored don't figure either way, Willie Mae."

I didn't like hearing that. Meant nobody was making him go. Nobody was coming for him if he didn't. He could choose to stay if he wanted. "What about your daddy? You everything to him."

"He understands."

I held him, my head pressing against the breast of his butternut coat, both our hearts racing. Raging wasn't my nature, and I was scaring us both. I looked up and noticed a fine-line scar under his chin. "What's that from?" All sudden, I needed all the details that made Alger.

"That?" he say and huffed a laugh. "Shaving. It was one of the very first times I ever held a straight blade to my own throat. It was the night I took you to the curing barn. Remember?"

Something inside me was sliding off a shelf. "You told me the moon got mountains," I say. It was breaking, that something inside me. "I can't see you fighting alongside no driver. If you so compelled, go fight for the North."

Alger say a brawl broke out at the meeting between men for the war and those against it when one man made just that argument. He say some Hopewell whites trusted in Lincoln and were against the slave trade. "Though it isn't as simple as that, Wil," he say. He say he stood the same chance fighting alongside a driver in the North as in the South, for Yanks weren't no stand-up-do-rights; it wasn't so long since slaveholding was crying alive and healthy up there, and anyway, this war wasn't about folks fighting for our freedom, not in any personal way, like we were folks with rights and these rights were worth fighting for. It was about autonomy, economy, and the balance of power. He say Hopewell was divided, that most crackers around here were too poor, didn't need to own other folks, didn't want to send their sons off. He say only moneyed ones like Matterson and Colonel got slaves. The Bloods didn't own nobody, and neither did the

McGees, or the Crisps, or another white named Moore who took a liking to Alger. Never owned a slave in his life, this Moore, but he was doing his duty. This Moore was the one to encourage Alger, who say them Yanks got black men, slave *and* free, fighting for them, and Alger should have the same right to defend his homeland from the ruthless Yankee invaders.

"Your homeland?" I say.

"Yes," he say, strong.

My man wasn't winning me over with his noble talk, but I didn't blame him for his contradictions. I knew him well enough to know he was feeling conflicted. I listened to him make his case, for this what you do when you love someone so much they a part of you.

Alger say the brawl got real ugly, with a number of men getting bludgeoned, including Matterson, who was still roaring for a fight, even with both his eyes blackened by Mr. Riddle. "You've got to see, Wil, if I donned a Union suit, I'd be putting you all in real danger." Such a thing would be treason, and the penalty was death. He took my hand. He held it to his face and warmed his lips on mine. "I'll be back before you know it."

When he told Lossie, she surprised us with her triple calm.

In this new life where time was all her own, Lossie found she had a talent. First she say it was useless, for it served no one but herself. But soon she was knee deep in the pleasure of it and looking for subjects. Lossie could render a picture so vital it was right there, alive on the paper, so she drew her son fore he left her; she drew with her worst fear finally coming true— Alger leaving off, and to battle no less. She sat on the porch, a tan drawing leaf tacked to a lap easel, sketching her son as he stood in front of the tulip trees: Alger Young, in shades of charcoal, brown, and gold, his eyebrows, his dimples, his open-easy-loving face.

"I got to give you something to take with you," I say the next morning.

I knocked around inside, but there was no knickknack, nothing truly mine except my old dolly and my red shoes. I ran back out.

"I don't have nothing."

"I don't need anything to carry with me when I have you in my heart."

"I am glad I married you, Alger Young, even if you the most sappy-sentimental person I ever did meet."

"I know," he say and grinned. "I love you. I always did, and I always will."

The thing breaking inside bust into a hundred shards.

He kissed Love on her cheek, and one day I would tell her she got those indents by her daddy leaving his love impressed.

The war come and Alger left, my freeman, off to find his Orient.

We marked the time with letters.

When Mr. Riddle brought the first one home, it was March 1863.

Alger was still alive. Least he was three months ago, say the date on the letter.

He had no rifle musket, no sword, no pistol, no bowie knife—no weapon of any kind. The color of his skin fixed what he would carry. He was a body servant in a regiment of whites. He served a Captain Hailey in Company C of the Georgia 15th Infantry. He didn't sound bitter or angry. He say he missed us.

Mr. Riddle say the post wasn't making it through with any kind of speed, and let's do our best not to qualm.

In September we joyed again when the second letter come:

My Dear Family,

I think it ever more doubtful this letter will reach you. It has been a long time since I had the chance to write, and it is with love I let you know I am well. Our regiment camps in woods and builds shanties out of pine brush. We are getting fairly good rations now, bacon & hardtack, a little chicory coffee & sugar—just enough to make a good cup once a day. My blanket was stolen, but nothing else. You must not trouble yourselves about me. I am a contented man.

The Federals tried in vain to break our line but the Corps of the Enemy withdrew at last, and tomorrow we march.

I share with you some news that I suspect you will not receive otherwise: The Enemy President issued an order declaring freedom for all negro slave residents in any State of the Confederacy that did not return to the Union by the 1st of this year 1863. I do not know how such an order can be enforced at home, but I thought very much you would be pleased to know of it.

I have never wished to see you half as bad as in all my life. I think of you as I travel the lonesome roads.

A thousand kisses for Love from her daddy.
Have no Doubts.
As ever, your devoted & loving son & husband,

Alger Young
23 February 1863

We hugged each other, and I read the letter again for want of more personal words from Alger.

When I ask Mr. Riddle if I was free, he say this was the first he heard of it, and he didn't rightly know.

The third letter come in January 1864.

This letter say it was from a friend.

This friend say the last time he saw Alger Young was along the bank of Chickamauga Creek on September 20, 1863, where they were winning in battle, but he never seen so many dead. Over eighteen thousand, and that wasn't counting the enemy. He say Company C of the Georgia 15th lost 125, half their guns, that morning alone. They had since left the Chickamauga for Chattanooga, then Knoxville. He feared Alger been injured or left for dead, or worse, captured by the Unionists, along with their Captain Hailey. The friend say he wished he had more to offer. He say Alger was an honorable man. He carried wounded, mended sick, drove teams, carted guns, and cooked. He say he was a loyal man, a man of the South. He say they called him the dark-skinned Reb.

I took in the signature of Private Moore.

Mr. Riddle and Lossie broke down.

I held onto hope and the Lord.

Arm in a sling or a bandage round his head or leaning on a crutch, my Alger come up the hill every day, injured but living. He was alive, somewhere, wanting home, praying for it. I could feel it. Months went by, no word like always, and then something changed. It wasn't doubt that finally got me—I began horrible dreaming, every night, of mangled bodies, lying facedown on a battlefield of rolling hills. I spent my nights turning them over. None of them were Alger. Til one night the field was bare. The air stinking of powder. Smoldering farmhouses. There was a brown-leafed wood on all sides of this field and I ran into it, for I saw a man in a green felt hat and a butternut coat. "I been long looking for you," I say, hugging him.

"I'm right here, Wil."

I woke up sudden. I knew he was dead.

I held on to myself, the last warmth of him and his butternut wool arms still wrapped around me.

They come in May 1865. I was nineteen years old. Union soldiers crawling like army ants. They say we all were free. Then they drank and ate and set fire to everything from big houses to shacks.

From out of that smoke rose a bird, a gray-chesty dove, wearing a blue madras handkerchief. She flew up the mountain and into Screamer Hollow. Least that's how Mary-Mary tells it.

We measured the time in extraordinaries:

December 6, 1865. A date you never forget. The Thirteenth, the big men of the government called it. Freedom.

Next come the Codes. Any negro on the streets of Persimmon after nine o'clock in the evening must work seven days on the public streets or pay a five-dollar fine. No negro shall be allowed to come within the limits of Persimmon without special permission from his employers. Slaveholders knew what they done. They had enough fear to acid a hole right through the universe from North to South Poles. Making their Codes instead of forging more iron shackles. Us-them how everybody thinks. Never enough of nothing to go around. Fear be the pith of all evil.

In sixty-six, the big men wrote the Fourteenth, in 1868, they passed it: All us colored folks were citizens, guaranteed due process and equal protection under law. A freeborn from the North named Tunis Campbell become one of three blacks elected to the Georgia Senate. Alger Young would be the first to shout "Hallelujah" if he been there.

In sixty-nine the big men sent us their militia to keep the peace. Whites been building dens in Pulaski, and now they were spreading out and haunting the Georgia night, riding tall horses, calling themselves regulators, which just another way of saying pattyroller, stoking the hate, setting out to scare us, all to keep our men from the vote, to hold us back.

How I liked this word: *equality*. I taught it to Love.

She was nine and already reading better than I ever done, sucking the words right off the walls like she once done her mother's milk.

All the while, Lossie was fading, tangling our names, repeating what she just say five minutes ago. At first we tell her, "You just say that," but with Lossie looking confused and us feeling bad for showing her we noticed, we didn't call her attention to it no more. We acted like the mix-ups weren't there, for her sake, all the while not able to do nothing as her thoughts, her memories and rememories, they were leaking out like water from a wove basket. Mr. Riddle kept his pain in, but we could see it, a shake lip, a long stare at the floor. He didn't give up on her, no sir, he began telling her stories to keep her mind alive, tales about her own life, and she laughed or looked serious, caring for these characters, not knowing they were her and him and me and Alger and Love and Mary-Mary. He told her of a man named Enoch Golden who had a daughter he cherished. He held her hand and took her for long walks, ever so gentle with her when she refused to go, Lossie saying, "Who's this stranger, who are you?" til me or Mary-Mary tell her it was safe to trust this Mr. Riddle, he was a good man.

Lossie at the head of her seventh decade. Sunday. June. 1870. I rememory the return of summer azures and eastern tailed-blues. Mr. Riddle rounding fifty-two, sitting on the porch, rocking over the valley. The sun setting easy. Love pulling from my hand and running up and grabbing him a hug.

"Careful, girl, don't knock your granddaddy over," I say.

"I don't mind, I don't mind at all," he say, her arms a ring of golden brown around his old red neck, her head nuzzled to his chest, him stroking her. Just as fast as she was on him, she left, scrambling inside to set down her schoolbooks. Yes, sir. In a cove northwest of Persimmon there was a room of heart-pine lumber on a half-acre lot, raised by a freewoman and her husband for the learning of their five children and ours. Education. Alger would of fallen off his chair. We'd been making that long walk for two weeks, every day but Sunday, passing the plot where the hello-yellow once stood fore the federals burned it to the ground, when Jaz tell me the colonel done passed away. I didn't feel too much about it, other than to marvel on life and where it goes. Leaning over the fence, he tell me Galilee and her two sisters owned the farm now. If that didn't shock.

He say there been some big battle against it, the Matterson to the northwest of them, in Strummers Knob, and the son of Marse Tom—Colonel's nephew—himself come up from Collins County wanting that property, but neither of them won. As for Absalom, he rocked in a chair on the porch of the new clapboard raised in place of the hello-yellow, and he waved hale and hearty each time me and Love passed, as did Ashby and Anna, who were in love, and Cassia, who was not, and J. Quincy Adams, who was making wages working for the three sisters. Lewis and Clark been gone for years, gone in search of their folks Sorrel and Lil Sis, maybe still in jail, maybe dead. Since the war, the road was always filling with folks, and the whites took to complaining about it—we were wandering aimlessly, posing a threat. That's what they called us folks searching for kin with solemnity and hopeful heart.

I walked up the hill and onto the porch and sat in the chair next to Mr. Riddle, both us watching the sun sinking down.

"You shall find my will inside the book of sonnets, along with the deed. I've left everything to thee," he say. He traveled slow down the steps and the flagstones.

I say, "Why you talking like this? Mr. Riddle? You feeling okay?" and he say, "I believe I am."

He seemed fine; he did, standing there, until he fell, clutching his chest.

Mary-Mary and me didn't say nothing of it to Lossie til she asked for that fellow who liked to take her on walks.

We brought her to where we rest him, up the heap and next to his mother, and she laid a dried red trillium on his grave.

LOVE

⁂

1872

I am born of the Fertile Valley.

I am
Lovelady Belle Young.

A thrumming awakened me.

Not the rain of spring
nor a rousing thunderstorm.

Take all my loves, my love; yea, take them all.

The Devil was knocking on our door.

> Show me your deed.
> What's going on here, why you all dressed in masquerade?
> said Mama.

Shards of light shattered the eveglom.
A pine torch.
A Ghoul with a pale warble, his face burned black.
His Shadow on a tall horse under the tulip trees.

> Why don't you all, said Mama, wait right there.
> Don't you pull no tricks, the Devil said.
> Auntie whispered, What do they want?

Who's that? WHO'S THAT? said Big Mama, sitting up in our bed.
Everyone just hush, they drunk. Up-to-no-good-fools. I'm surprised
they don't ignite.

Mama kept the deed locked in a keepsake box.
Instead
she lifted a book from the cupboard and loosed a sheet from the weave.
A sonnet reborn.
All mine was thine before thou hadst this more
She paused at the fire shovel, the kitchen shears,
and the two-tine flesh fork before she opened the door.
The Devil passed the sonnet to the Ghoul, who walked into the Shadow.
Woe upon us. The Shadow could read.

Don't look like no deed to me, he said.
I told you not to pull no tricks, growled the Devil.

The Ghoul lowered his inferno.
The Devil fed the flame the words of love.

Tell me something, nigger, you sing? You jig? Play a mouth harp?
Why don't you sing us a tune. One of them nigger tunes about
salvation. Tell me, you still think you got the Lord on your side?

He reached down and grabbed Mama between the legs.
Her neck stiffened.
The Devil lowered his eyes.

I own this, he said.
Yes, marse, said Mama.
I don't like back talk, he said.
I ain't saying a word.
Sing us a tune! the Ghoul howled.

The Devil leaned against the rail.

I'm waiting, he said.

Mama's voice swelled out of her mouth, a beautiful sound.
Auntie reached a hand out and tipped the door closed.

Love, you got to go. Why? Your mama say so *Wade in the water* You got to run, Love, run to the river, and when you get there, you head for our bathing rock *Wade in the water children* It's shallow there, that's where you'll cross. Don't be scared *Wade in the water God's gon trouble the water* Once you get to the other side, you hide yourself in the woods, you hear me *Now if you should get there before I do tell all my friends that I'm coming too* You'll be safe in there. You'll be safe. The woods will harbor you.

Auntie steadied the chair, a swirl of fear upon her face.

Go! she rasped.

I swung a leg over the window ledge
and leaped.
The grass wet with dew.
The night dotted with stars.
I drummed up the hill and down the bank.
It was not hard to find our bathing spot.
I slid down the rock as flat as a gravestone.
The river parted
as I paddled across.
Into the wildwood, running.
A peep, a trill, high whistles, a grunt, and a squeak.
The forest sang.
Until,
A scream
Big Mama
A scream
Auntie
A scream
Mama

I from the forest, racing back.
I through the river, through the river run twice.
Up the bank across the rolling grass, the rabble rock.

No, Love, no!

Four women running, gasping for breath.

Three men thirsting for the women's death.
We leaped into the waters. The men on our backs.
The river moaned.
It quickened.
The banks pulled back, the riverbed strained.
An open wound. A swift sluice.
        Where's Love? a voice screamed.
I rememory
Mama lurching forward
and I falling back,
thrashing against water.
Mama screaming a grief to shatter all hearts.
We were
                Severed.

WILLIE MAE COTTON

WHERE I LIVE.

There ain't no way of living with your child's death. Every decision you made gets twisted when you look back.

We buried them three monsters where no one would find them. They drowned along with my Love.

From INSTRUCTIONS TO ENUMERATORS
U.S. CENSUS, 1920 QUESTIONNAIRE

Personal Description

120. Column 10. Color or race.—Write *"W"* for white; *"B"* for black; *"Mu"* for mulatto; *"In"* for Indian; *"Ch"* for Chinese; *"Jp"* for Japanese; *"Fil"* for Filipino; *"Hin"* for Hindu; *"Kor"* for Korean. For all persons not falling within one of these classes, write *"Ot"* (for other), and write on the left-hand margin of the schedule the race of the person so indicated.

121. For census purposes, the term "black" (B) includes all Negroes of full blood, while the term "mulatto" (Mu) includes Negroes having some proportion of white blood.

AMELIA J. McGEE

⸺⸻⸺

Fresh hay smells sweet, and our barn was replete with the scent, not just from the rack but also from the gutter, which ran behind the stalls and which I was expected to muck and line with fresh straw each Saturday at dawn. The hay, the animals, the manure, the well-worn and oiled tack—it all blended into a sultry smell that I could only describe as delectable. This was where I felt best, maybe because cleaning the barn was such a simple cycle of satisfaction: scoop out the manure, pour the waste into the spreader, wheel it out to the compost heap, and unload it by pitchfork. It would mature until we spread it out in spring, and from that fertilized soil more alfalfa and corn would grow.

But in the full week that had passed since my encounter with Biggie in front of Mr. Crisp's mercantile, I'd become utterly uncoordinated, as if my brain, so preoccupied with achieving his demise, had stopped communicating to my limbs. Nothing was simple anymore. I stumbled over a piglet and landed facedown in the slop; I spilled an entire bag of mash on the hens; I reeled out of our barn with a fresh load of milk, the entire bucket tipping over with a single misstep.

"But she ain't got no more," I moaned.

"We'll see about that," Momma said, breaking an egg single-handedly into a well of flour.

If my mother thought I could milk a dry cow, I sure wasn't going to argue.

In summertime, regular cows take to the pasture after being milked. But not our Peanut. There was nothing regular about her. For starters, rather than fresh grass Peanut loved hay. And sure enough, she was still dragging the fragrant fodder into her mouth with her big pink tongue, tugging it down from between the slats of the rack with zest and tossing her head back, savoring her meal, when I returned to the barn for the second time that morning.

I pulled out the stool and slid a metal bucket under Peanut's udder. She was an exceptional bovine, a Guernsey, not as large as Mister Bounds's Holsteins but a faithful provider. Even at the end of July, mountain mornings are dead-body cold, but the barn was warm with Peanut as its source of heat. She had a straight back with prominent hip bones and a glossy coat, and her ears were soft. Best of all, her milk was so rich in butterfat it was yellow. It was also Momma's secret ingredient.

When I tucked an ear into her smooth flank, she turned and looked at me as if to say, Again? I grabbed a teat and pulled. "Come on, girl, let your milk down. You can do it," I encouraged. In response, she swatted me with her tail.

"You could at least give it a try."

After a few feeble squirts I knew it was useless.

With the last of the long orange streaks melting from the eastern sky, I turned my hay-filled cow out to pasture and dawdled by the barn, knowing Momma would be as sour as a gooseberry gourd when I arrived empty-handed. Peanut, for her part, strolled cheerfully to the tonk of her cowbell, swishing her tail as she walked. I waved to Poppa and Buddy in the alfalfa fields, where they'd been since dawn, and watched Poppa as he guided the mules. Buddy walked a good clip ahead of them, shearing the purple-headed alfalfa with a scythe wherever it was too awkward to reach with the team.

I was hanging on our gate with my arms flopped over the top rail, lamenting my predicament, when I looked up and saw a figure turning off the Warwoman and tromping up our path. He wore a charcoal vest and a shirt the color of a tufted titmouse stuffed willy-nilly into baggy trousers. "What're you doing here, George Hailey?" I asked.

George looked like he had a chicken bone stuck in his throat. He squinted over at Poppa and Buddy. "This is for you," he said, shoving a cloth bundle at me.

I shrank back. "What is it?"

"A loaf of bread."

"For me?"

"For your momma."

I eyed it as if it were a snake of unknown origin. "Who made it?"

"My granny."

"Why don't you give it to her yourself?" I suggested, privately congratulating myself on my brilliant idea, offering George up as a distraction from my milkmaid failure.

He seemed unconvinced.

"Ain't you cold? It's nice and warm inside."

"I ain't."

"Well, you gotta be hungry."

He cocked his head and shrugged. "I ain't."

"What happened to your hand?" I asked, noticing the knuckles of his left one were raw and scabby brown.

"I cut it."

"Doing what?"

"Hittin' something."

"You ought not do that. Could get infected." I turned to go inside. "You coming?"

"I'd druther not," he mumbled.

I stomped my foot. "George Hailey, act like you're somebody an' look up when you speak an' open your mouth."

He raised his head, and I thought I saw a hint of a smile. "You sure are bossy," he said.

"I got a right. I'm standin' on my own property, ain't I?"

"I ain't here to argue with you," he said, amusement in his eyes.

"Good."

A crash of pans followed by a mild oath sounded from inside the kitchen, and I cringed. Though she had never taken the Lord's name in vain, Momma did resort to condemning inanimate objects—uncooperative oven doors, stubborn mason jars, the ice cream scooper—as if they were her intimate adversaries. I glanced at George, who looked even more leery at the idea of joining me, but together we mounted the steps.

"Wipe your feet on the mat," I ordered. "And tuck in your shirt."

I needn't have been concerned about George's presentation. It was Momma who was unkempt, as mad as a March hare, wild-eyed and flushed, her nose twitching as she remarked to herself, "My!" and "Goodness!"

Rebellious dark frizzles fought to be free of her kerchief, pieces jutted out from above and below its hem, and a corkscrew of black hair hung down from the back of her neck. She hustled from stovetop to tabletop and back again, snapping up three golden brown doughnuts with tongs, setting them to drain over the linens lining the tabletop, the oil sizzling as she slid three more into the fryer. After piping fresh raspberry preserves into a hole poked in the side, she finished each one off with a flourish of confectioners' sugar. They were totems of sweet perfection, and I could taste them without taking a bite.

I made a quick study of the kitchen: There was a Jeff Davis pie cooling on a rack and under a cake pedestal a pyramid of caramel clusters. Then I saw what I had been dreading: rows of small glass bowls of fresh-ground cinnamon and nutmeg, thinly sliced almonds, black raisins, and separated eggs; measuring cups of sugar and dried figs; a jar of sourwood honey; a sack of flour; butter—*all* the fixings for hallelujah pie *except* Peanut's buttermilk.

If George hadn't coughed, I don't know if Momma would have noticed us, so focused was her concentration, but he did. At first blank, her face filled with expectation and hope. Her eyes searched my person.

"Sorry, Momma," I stammered.

Her expression deflated like a soufflé.

"There ain't no milk, I swear it."

"*Any*, Mia. There *wasn't any* milk."

"Yes ma'am; no milk."

"What on earth am I going to do with you?" She wiped her hands on the dishrag hanging over her shoulder and pinched the bridge of her long nose. She stared out the double window above the sink, where Poppa and Buddy looked like two miniature figures entering a gingham-framed painting.

"Momma, the stove!" I said as fingers of smoke rose out of the bubbling oil.

"Heavens," she said, lifting the fryer off the burner. She took in a slow breath. "Forgive me, George, where are my manners? Good morning."

"Ma'am," he said, suddenly remembering his cap, which he swiped from his head. His pale hair stood at attention, electrified by static.

Momma quickly interpreted his expression, which must have matched my own. "Why don't you both pull up a seat and have a jelly-filled dough-nut," she said.

"George here brought a loaf a bread. Old Mai—Mrs. Hailey baked it," I said, thrusting forth his gift. "We was just talkin' about how we could go down to the Boundses' and fetch you some fresh milk." I hoped I looked penitent.

George glanced up from his jelly-covered mitts and balked.

"Ain't that right, George?" I said.

Momma shook her head. "No, no, you'll do no such thing. That won't do at all. I'll simply have to reorganize. Now, don't you forget to milk her tonight."

I had been forgiven. "No'm. I won't," I said between grateful bites. The jelly oozed out both ends as I sank my teeth into the middle of the doughnut.

When Momma suggested we lend our help to Poppa and Buddy, George's skin actually brightened. He was already at the kitchen door with his cap on when he stopped short and spoke clearly and loudly: "Thanks, ma'am. That was the best durn sweet I ever did set my teeth into."

"Why, thank you, George, anytime, and thank your granny for the bread," Momma said, unwrapping the bundle and appraising the dark loaf.

I didn't think it was possible, but George's face grew even redder as he pushed open the swing door.

We made our way into the field, where Poppa and Buddy were flipping the swaths cut the day before, allowing the sun to dry the other side. When Poppa gave George a clap on the back, George, being slight of body, nearly fell over. Buddy looked at me quizzically and sucked the side of his cheek, as if to say, What in Jove's name is he doing here? And I shot him a look that said, I dunno, why don't you ask *him*?

But then George surprised us: Old Maid Hailey didn't have much in the way of a farm—only her old nag and a simple garden—but he worked with expert speed and care, and by the afternoon we were ready to hoist hay into the barn.

Standing in the loader, Buddy showed George how to pry the grab fork open, fill the mouth with hay, and secure the tines. I never fought Buddy for the job. The tines were as sharp as a cat's claws and the grip as strong as a vise, and though I prided myself on a certain amount of fearlessness, I treasured my fingers more. A trip rope ran from the fork through four pulleys in the hayloft and out the opposite side of the barn, where it was hitched to Irish Bill and Harry's rig. That was my domain. After Buddy yelled "ready," Poppa, who stood above in the hayloft, would relay the command down to me, and with a loud "yhaaaa!" I'd set the team in motion, pulling on their leads. As they walked, the grab fork would rise, carrying the hay load up and into the loft, at which point I would ease the two mules to a stop and Poppa would position the load and spring the fork open. Not as fancy as the tractor Mr. Matterson used to pull their trip rope, but it got the job done just fine—and before the previous week's events, it hadn't rattled me one bit that Biggie was always going on about how he was allowed to drive his daddy's flashy machine.

But now he was popping into my mind without even being there to provoke me. And each time he did, my desire to squash him grew larger. Which only made me think about him more. It was a terrible cycle that left me anxious in the long pauses while George loaded the grab fork. I sought a distraction and found one in a line of brown ants marching over the soil to their hill, which I toppled with a quick swipe of my hand. Normally, I enjoyed watching them scatter in a frenzy, always hoping one would take the lead and start digging its friends out, though none ever did. But this time I felt bad about what I had done and tried to uncover the hole myself, only making it worse, and I was about to give up when I heard a familiar giggle. Even though the sound came from right beside me, I knew better than to turn toward it, and sure as sunrise I saw the bright blue of her ribbons up ahead, at the top of the butterweed hill. It was as if I'd summoned her.

"Lovelady," I said in a loud whisper, not entirely sure I was happy to see her.

Ever since we'd hatched our idea of revenge, I'd been expecting some guidance, or at least a miracle, not of Old Testament proportions, or even New. But instead, I'd been having nightmares, the kind that sent me paddling down into Momma and Poppa's room and crawling into their bed for comfort. For the past week I'd had the same one almost every night of three men drowning. They were dressed for a Halloween party, except the masks they wore weren't like the ones we made—out of paper plates or bags— they were made of human skin, and one of them looked like Biggie's porcine mug. I always woke up gasping, as if I were the one who had died, buried on a mountaintop covered with purple hydrangeas, three faceless women tamping dirt down over my grave. It was so vivid, and despite Momma's reassurances it wasn't real, I didn't feel any better.

Now Lovelady was blowing me a kiss, and so I blew one back, and we both covered our mouths. I was trying to figure out how I could go to her, knowing well that I couldn't, when I heard Poppa shouting at me. He was waving his arms and pointing at the mules. They were trembling and wrenching against their harness straps, pulling the trip line taut. "Whoa, whhhhooa!" I hollered.

"Back them up!" Poppa yelled.

Grabbing the reins, I tucked a foot into Harry's side strap and threw myself onto his back. If I could walk him backward, Irish Bill would stay in step; the eveners would keep them together. My father urged me on, and then suddenly the tension on the rope went slack.

I looked into the hayloft. Poppa was gone.

I sprinted to the front yard just in time to see George jumping down from the hay loader to where Buddy sat rubbing his elbow. Momma was running back into the house.

Poppa knelt next to Buddy, whose face was ashen.

"What happened?" I asked.

George answered. "The load started movin' before we were ready. Buddy got caught in the trip line and jerked right off his feet, grab fork and everythin', and he was swingin' upside down about to get his skull cracked open." He pointed to the hayloft. Overhead, the trip line dangled like a headless viper. "When you backed the team up, I sawed the rope real quick til it split," he said, patting the stag handle of his knife. He sounded more astounded than proud. "Sure glad that fork was closed. It woulda made mincemeat out of your brother."

"I'm right sorry, Bud," I said.

"S'all right," he said. "Wasn't much of a fall. I'm none worse for the wear, right, Pa?"

"You were lucky." Poppa extended his hand to George. "Thank you," he said.

I thought George would burst—he looked that happy. "Glad to be of use," he said, ducking his head.

"Yeah, thanks," Buddy added.

Poppa studied me. "What happened?"

"I dunno, sir. I only took my eye off them for a second. Somethin' musta spooked them."

He lifted my chin. "You feeling okay, Maggie Mae?"

"Yes, sir," I lied.

He gazed at me a second longer. He didn't seemed convinced, but he didn't know what to do about it, either. Counseling girlfolk wasn't Poppa's strong suit. He decided I should sweep the yard while George brushed down Irish Bill and Harry.

Buddy shuffled inside, where Momma had most certainly transformed the house into a hospital, while Poppa tended to the hay loader.

When I finished, my curiosity got the better of me, and I nonchalantly moseyed over to our new champion George, who had tied Harry to the fence post alongside the barn. "Thanks for saving my brother," I said.

"Just did what needed doin'." He ran the currycomb from the top of Harry's neck down his chest and over his shoulder, working in slow, firm circles, pulling the dirt and dislodging the scurf from his coat. George's forehead glistened with sweat and his cheeks were the healthy-looking red of a fellow enjoying his work.

"You want to use the dandy brush on his sides and stomach; he's sensitive and he don't like the comb there," I said.

George nodded. He swept the comb over Harry's rump and then pulled the brush from the tack box and attended to the mule's sides, stopping every few strokes to pull the hair out of the brush with the currycomb. When Harry's coat was clean, he moved on to his head, wiping the mule's face with a damp sponge, tenderly cleaning the inside of each nostril. As a finishing touch, he buffed Harry all over with a clean towel until the mule shone.

"He looks real swell," I said.

"Thanks," he answered, already running his hand down Irish Bill's foreleg to find the fetlock. Bill lifted his foot, and George caught it easily. With the aid of a pick, he dislodged the dirt and pebbles from the mule's hoof. As he bent over to tend to Bill's other foreleg, a dog-eared card fell from his vest pocket.

"Wow," I said, wiping dirt from the surface. "You got a Ty Cobb."

George looked up at me for the first time since I approached him. "Yeah," he said with a shy smile.

What little I knew of baseball I had picked up from Buddy, who was a keen follower of the sport. Ty Cobb was, according to Buddy, a brilliant batter, a tenacious competitor, and an amazing fielder, among other qualifiers that seemed to indicate he was top-notch.

"The Georgia Peach," I said smartly.

"Yup. From Royston. He's one of us."

"Sure is."

I was enjoying our conversation, even if it was mostly one-sided. I was discovering George was, in a word, likable.

"You want it?" he asked.

"Your Ty Cobb? I can't take your Ty Cobb."

"It's a candy card. From a stick of caramel. There's a team roster on the back. I got two more at home, tobacco cards. One's a color portrait and the other one he's stealing third base. The one stealing third's the best." He pointed to the card in my hand. "But it ain't like that one ain't special or nothing. I just like to carry it around."

"Like for good luck?"

"Yeah."

I nodded my understanding.

"His maw kilt his paw with a double-barreled shotgun," he added.

"How awful." Buddy had never mentioned that.

"Didn't stop him from becoming a winner," said George. "You got any cards?"

"Nawp. I collect teeth."

"You gonna be a dentist?" he asked.

"I ain't decided."

"I'm gonna be a baseball player."

"You are?" I handed the card back to George.

"Yeah," he said proudly.

"Who you gonna play for?"

"Prolly the Tigers, like Cobb. He's fierce. Plays ball like he's at war." He tucked the card back into his vest pocket. "He don't back down, neither, no matter what they say about him or what they do to him. I don't ever trade my Ty Cobbs," he said with a pat to his pocket.

I felt my face grow hot and worked a piece of mica schist from the ground with the toe of my boot. "But you were gonna give it to me."

"Yeah," he said, "that's different." George smiled to himself as he groomed Irish Bill, who looked deliriously content.

"You know, I got your red bandanna upstairs. I can go an' get it," I said, even more shy.

"S'all right, I ain't in no rush."

"Naw, you should have it back." I was halfway across the yard when I heard him call.

"What?" I said.

He set down the grooming tools and walked toward me. As he lifted his head, the sun cut under his twill cap, and I could see that his eyes were not gray at all but hazel.

"I thought you oughta know," he began. "I'm awful sorry. About, y'know."

"About what?"

"Y'know."

"Nawp, don't," I said.

"Sure you do," he said.

"No, I don't."

"That day. With Biggie."

I felt a switch go on inside me. "Quit mumbling, George Hailey."

He said in a clear voice, "I'm just saying that if you ever need—"

Anger flew through me, and I sought a target, no matter how misplaced. "Quit it," I said.

He looked perplexed.

"Quit looking like you got feelings."

"Whatever," he said, his eyes turning black and empty as if bored into by an auger.

But I was unsatisfied. "Well, get goin'. Get outta here. Shoo!" I shouted. "Go find your own family. This one's mine."

George stood as rigid as a corpse. I imagined whatever I hurled, he would not crumble, he would not crack.

"No wonder you don't got no friends but them niggers," he said with disdain.

I stood my ground as I watched him walk back to the barn, the grace in his step gone. He petted both mules on the head and stroked Irish Bill's cream-colored nose and Harry's gray muzzle, and he left our place with his back hunched, his arms ramrod straight, his hands thrust into his pockets, his face no longer gray or pink cheeked but livid.

That night, long after milking Peanut and just before I set off for bed, I sought the comfort of Buddy's company and found him on our front porch watching the sunset. The heat was heavy and the evening quiet.

I took the chair next to him, but he didn't seem to notice me. "Bud?"

He sat barefoot and shirtless, wearing only a bandage around his right forearm to cover the damage of the day, a cut Momma had sewn up with three cross-stitches. The soles of his feet pushed against the railing each time he teetered back in his chair, the front legs lifting as he rocked.

"Buddy!" I said, tired and feeling even more lonely than usual.

"Hmm? What is it?"

"Whatcha thinkin'?" I asked.

"Nothing."

I slumped in my seat and lolled my head to the side. "Don't look like nothing."

"I was thinking about Uncle Lorrie," he said without looking at me.

Uncle Lorrie was our mother's dead brother. At least that's how I always thought of him.

"What about him?"

"I found an old postal card from him in my dresser. He was only nineteen when he died. That was all he got."

I scrunched my face as I tried to recall our uncle. "He have a beard?"

"No."

"Really? I thought for sure he had a beard like Poppa. How'd he go?" I asked.

"Kilt in the war."

"The Great War?" I said cautiously, recalling my blunder with the Bartlebys the week before. Until they'd landed in the Boundses' field, I had thought the War Between the States was our most recent war. Though the Great War had occurred within my lifetime, I retained no memory of it. It was something my family never brought up—like the loss of Uncle Lorrie, as if in this way we would never feel the pain of his absence.

"That's right. In battle. Near a place called Saint-Mihiel."

"Ohhhhhh," I intoned, as if I had been there many times before. I picked some lint from between my toes. "Where's that?"

"France."

"Where's *that*?"

"In Europe, across the Atlantic, which is a large body of water, not to be confused with the Pacific, which is double the size an' the world's largest ocean. You oughta know, Miss Encyclopedia," he said.

I ignored his jab, as I was a naturalist, not a cartographer. "What was he doin' there?" I asked.

Buddy looked at me to determine if I was being sincere. Deeming me so, he spoke with eagerness: "Saint-Mihiel was the greatest air battle of the war. They fought for four straight days in the worst of weather. September twelfth to sixteen, nineteen eighteen." Buddy sketched a map in the air. "Saint-Mihiel was this wedge, right here, a *V* in the German front, really big, maybe thirty miles wide at the base and fifteen at the top, that cut into French territory. The bad guys, the Germans, they captured it from the French four years before and spent the whole time buildin' it up. Behind it was this Hindenburg line, a trench system with concrete bunkers and tunnels and barbed wire and machine guns and stuff. It was supposed to be invincible, but we sure proved them wrong. And it's a durn good thing too, 'cause if we hadn't, we wouldn't be Americans no more and we'd all have to speak German."

"Really?"

"Really."

"Who told you all that?" I asked.

"Nobody told me. They're facts. You ain't the only one who can read, you know."

I was impressed and crunched on the dirt under my pinkie nail. It was gritty and tasted metallic. "So, what *did* Uncle Lorrie look like?" I asked.

He scratched around the bandage. "He kinda looked like you sorta, only taller, naturally, and with real long hair. He was nice. And funny. He was always doin' flapjacks and handstands. You liked that. You'd laugh real hard."

"You miss him."

"Yeah."

"I miss Granny," I confessed.

"Yeah. One minute you're alive and then the next . . ." He snapped his fingers.

I wasn't used to this far-off Buddy, the one contemplating his mortality. I wanted to bring him back to me, to bridge a gap that I sensed even then growing between the two of us. "Can I tell you something?" I said.

He shrugged. "You don't see me stoppin' you."

I told Buddy about Lovelady. I told him how I met a ghost and she was my best friend. I told him about her visit to heaven, and how she slept through the winter like a bear, and she was never hungry, and I even told him about our swim. I told him how spirits can take your soul and that I wanted them to take Biggie's.

I didn't want to be alone with my secrets anymore.

When I finished, the sun had set and glow flies were floating through the dark. I felt such a relief, as if my head had been underwater and now I could finally breathe.

First Buddy looked disturbed, and then he broke out in a grin. "That's a right good story. Worthy of the Bartholomew McGee stamp of approval for excellence in story tellin'."

"It ain't a whopper," I said.

"Mia," Buddy said.

I didn't like his parental tone. I was miffed. "What?"

"It's good for added effect, insisting it bein' true and all, but don't go over the top. You'll ruin it."

"It ain't no story. I met a ghost. We're friends."

"Come on," he protested.

"No, Bud, I swan, it's one hundred percent true." I didn't know what else I could say to convince him.

A long silence passed between us, and I didn't dare look at him.

"I think Lovelady musta spooked the mules," I confessed.

Buddy gave me a look that I had never seen before. He was furious. "It ain't your fault. Accidents happen. You don't got to make stuff up, not for me," he said. "You tell anyone else that story?"

"No," I said, wishing I hadn't told him any of it.

"Good. Don't. No one'd believe you. They'd come for you with the crazy wagon and lock you up."

"Don't say that, Bud," I said, alarmed. "Preacher Reverend would believe me."

Buddy spat through his teeth over the railing. "Miracles happen in the Bible, not in the Warwoman. And I sure wouldn't go tellin' Preacher Reverend. There ain't room on the pulpit for more than one headliner, and you can be sure he ain't sharin' the bill. You'll find out what it really means to not have a friend in the world—folks won't take kindly you going around claiming you're some kinda visionary.

"A what?" The word sounded familiar, but I didn't know what it meant.

"A visionary. Someone who can see what ain't visible to the naked eye. Folks don't take to them, they lock them up."

"How you know that?" I asked, disturbed by the force of his argument.

"The pulps," he said. He was referring to his Eldritch Grimoire collection. They were dime novels, and Buddy was a devotee. Not that our parents knew. As with his bathing-lady card, they would never have approved of such a magazine, with its nightmarish covers of dark-winged devils, red-robed ghouls, brutes with the bodies of animals and the heads of horned men.

He rubbed his eyes and yawned.

"But the stuff in there ain't true," I said.

"'Xactly. Just like your ghost. They're right good stories."

I felt as if I'd been stung by a hornet.

"I'm goin' to bed. It's a scorcher tonight. You coming?" he said.

I watched a glow fly land on the railing. I put my hand up to the edge and let the bug crawl into my palm. Then I clasped my hands together. I could feel his gaze on me. "No," I said.

"'Kay. G'night."

The screen door banged against the frame.

I opened my hands and let the glow fly go.

An hour later, I drifted to sleep, only to find Lovelady lurking in my dreams.

"Look," she said, pointing to a curtain of honeysuckle dangling at the end of my room, a writhing veil of green and yellow tendrils. She drew it back with a flourish. We stood along a narrow river. The sun was piercing, and I saw a woman basking—no, bathing. It was Momma, this woman, and I shivered even though I wasn't cold. There was a man too: Preacher Reverend, his pince-nez perched on his nose, his flaxen hair center parted and gummed back. He walked down the bank, holding a drape of white cloth over his arms, and unlike Momma he was fully clothed. He wore a three-piece suit with a sprig of lavender in his lapel. I was horrified and turned to Lovelady, but she was gone. Preacher Reverend wound my mother tightly in the gauze like a spider its prey, binding her arms to her sides, and Momma did not struggle. As she sank into the waters, they reddened.

I lurched awake, gasping for breath. I did not run to my parents' bed. Instead, I tugged the sheets over my head and hid, afraid to fall back asleep. When at last I did, it seemed as if I managed to eke no more than an hour's rest. I woke the following morning exhausted. To make matters worse, Buddy was dragging his finger under my nose. It was the lightest of touches, a ploy we used to awaken Poppa. It made my father smile when he woke up. It irritated me.

"Wake up, sleepyhead," said Buddy.

"Mmmssmfff," I said, rubbing my face. "Go away."

Buddy commenced a reveille, his voice mimicking a trumpet to grating perfection, and I heard him marching around the room, his steps filled with pomp and circumstance.

"I mean it. I'm tired." I flopped onto my stomach and buried my face into my pillow, which was damp with sweat.

Buddy grabbed my heels and shook them. "Time to rise and shine. Prayer services ain't but an hour away."

"I swan, Bud, quit it." Hoping to stifle his babble, I pulled the pillow over my head.

"I know something to cheer you up."

"You do?"

"Yep," he said. "I milked Peanut for you."

"Thanks," I grumped.

"And," he said, yanking the pillow from my head, "Mr. Matterson came by early this mornin'. Seems he convinced those flying folks to give us a show, and they're coming this afternoon."

"Really?" I felt light again, and I gave my brother a big hug.

"No need to go all soft," he said.

I shrugged. "Can't a person hug her brother?"

"I s'pose." He straightened his collar and tucked his shirttails back into his overalls. "But don't you go making a habit of it. I got a reputation, you know."

"You mean with Cal-e-don-i-a?" I sassed, employing an exaggerated drawl, spicing each syllable with twang, and discovering I rather liked the flavor of her name drawn out.

Buddy gave me a double look. "Who told you that?"

I punched him playfully.

"Why, get back here!" he sputtered.

But it was too late for reprisals. I was revitalized, already sprinting down the stairs.

Almost everybody who could afford the quarter dollar was there, as well as many folks who couldn't. It seemed as if the entire county had come to see the barnstormers fly.

At church that morning there had been a jittery energy in the air. I hadn't heard a single word of Preacher Reverend's sermon as I fiddled endlessly with the hem of the yellow horror until Momma pursed her lips so tight they disappeared. Every Sunday, I fell in love with my mother again, and I did not like to displease her. With her black hair finger-curled, she sat straight in the pew with a regal air, and the slope of her nose and her high cheekbones set her apart from the other mothers; it made her distinctive. I knew Preacher Reverend too fancied Momma the prettiest woman in the sanctuary, from the way he always held her hand in the meet-and-greet line a trifle longer than the others. Momma didn't seem to mind, not even with Poppa standing behind her, pretending he didn't notice.

But my dream the night before had left me with a feeling I couldn't quite name, a mixture of uneasiness and mistrust. I *did* mind how he held Momma's hand, even if it wasn't my place to say it. And I had made a point that morning of *not* smiling at Preacher Reverend when he smiled at me, even with all the jumpy excitement about the aerial show mounting as we left the worship hall.

The day had begun with a gentle breeze, but now, as the Bartlebys prepared their flying machine, the wind keened and the air turned to broiling, hotter than a pot of collards. Jar flies bored into the bark of trees, beating their timbals so loud it seemed as if their spirited singing surrounded the entire pasture.

The Blood family had lent their land to the Bartlebys; it sat to the south of both Mr. Matterson's and the Boundses'. Men with dark rings under their shirt arms and women with ironed hankies pressed to their temples lined the area cordoned off between the road and the craggy field. Some folks sat on the fence running along the road, while children threaded themselves throughout the lower rungs, and the boughs of trees hung heavily with young men. Old-timers crammed into the tree shade, but I knew it wouldn't be much cooler, not on a day like today.

The heat didn't bother *me* a stitch. I was about to see the greatest show of my life, and I was one of the children jumping up and down with endless vigor, jockeying for a better view.

Buddy had taken leave shortly after we arrived—gone off, no doubt, in search of his Caledonia.

As I looked around the crowd, Mr. Crisp caught my eye, pointed at my new boots, and winked. I pointed at his, the yellow and black snakeskin lace-ups with brass toe caps and winked back, and he guffawed heartily. He stood with Preacher Reverend, who stared down at me through his pince-nez, while Dr. Cornelius Taylor accompanied his wife, who held a newborn against her chest. A plump of ladies congregated around her, admiring the baby. Doc Taylor looked formidable in a three-piece linen suit and dress shoes of gunmetal gray. He raised his binoculars and scanned the sky.

Overhead, large islands of clouds stretched across the bright blue, casting fast-moving shadows that brought not a stitch of relief from the sun. Old Maid Hailey had brought a collapsible stool and sat upon it with dignity; she wore a poplin dress and held a silk-lined lace parasol with an ivory handle in one hand and a fan in the other. I didn't see George and hoped I wouldn't. I did see his compatriot along the road; Biggie Matterson stood next to his father's black-chassised Model T Ford, its brass radiator and horn gleaming. He looked well groomed, for once, in a blazer and trousers held up by braces. Luther and Simon could be seen strutting about the crowd with fat chests of pride, buttons near popping off their matching short-sleeve shirts and knee-length knickers. Having been put in charge of collecting the fare for the day's event, they held their flour sacks of cash like two giddy looters after a victorious heist. Personally, I wouldn't have trusted them in matters pecuniary, but then, no one asked me. Only Miss Ida Crump stood alone, under a big black umbrella, which I figured was the Yankee version of a parasol.

Poppa hoisted me to his shoulders, and I laughed when I saw Turner sitting similarly upon Capable Means. They were with the folks from Washaway, behind a long, twisted rope to my left. I gave him a big wave. On either side of Capable were Missus Linden Bounds and Obidiah. I caught Obidiah's eye. He nodded and I beamed. I mouthed, "I like you," and immediately regretted it and clamped my hand over my mouth. Obidiah mouthed something back. "What?" I mouthed. He mouthed again.

I thought he said, "I like you too."

"Really?" I mouthed. I hoped he wasn't teasing me.

"What?" he mouthed.

"Do you really like me?" I shaped.

He shook his head as if to say he didn't understand.

Just then, Turner pointed with sharp jabs toward the field. The show was about to begin! I was torn between Obidiah and *The Phoenix*, but when I looked back at him, he too was looking at the field, and I vowed to find him later and learn his true intentions. It was the longest conversation I'd ever had with him.

My good spirits soared as Mr. Bartleby jumped off the lower wing, the gilded buttons of his boots shining. He tossed his duster around his neck and climbed into the rear cockpit, where he adjusted his cap and lowered his goggles, while his sister stood afore the aircraft and tightened her snazzy plum-colored hood. With an approving nod from her brother, Miss Bartleby gripped the propeller and called out, "Contact." Mr. Bartleby reached forward and flipped a switch. "Contact!" he responded. Miss Bartleby wrenched the propeller down. As it caught, the wooden paddles turned sluggishly, and then they whipped into a blur. With a thumbs-up salute, Mr. Bartleby signaled his sister, who kicked the blocks from the biplane's wheels and leaped into the front cockpit.

At first, *The Phoenix* coughed and sputtered like a rickety old man. We waited, holding our breath. Next came a loud clicking followed by a smooth whir, and the craft rolled forward. It bounced as it gathered speed, and then the tail lifted, the nose pointed toward the sky, and the wheels cleared the ground. *The Phoenix* had lifted off. Thick blue smoke poured out of the engine. It burned our noses and made our eyes teary, but we loved it, and we all cheered.

As the Bartlebys gained height over the trees, we squinted, using our hands as visors. The showy bird faded, the purple and gold body an indistinct blob until all that was left was the tiny dot of its fiery red tail that vanished as if into the air.

We waited.

"There it is," someone shouted.

My pulse quickened. From the south, rising from below the tree line, *The Phoenix* appeared as if by magic. As it grew larger, the colors revived. We applauded and then we frowned when the tail lifted toward us and the nose dipped as though the craft might somersault, the wings teetering left, then right, and then it recovered, leveling out, only to stagger wildly up and down. We took cautious steps backward.

Before panic could grip us, *The Phoenix* pitched toward the sky, curving up and over our heads. Someone giggled nervously. Once, twice it loop-de-looped, and on the third pass the engine lulled and *The Phoenix* hung motionless at the apex; the Bartlebys were suspended upside down.

"Ahhhhh!" breathed the crowd. "Extraordinary," exclaimed Mr. Crisp. Men patted one another on the back. Women fanned themselves faster. Turner's mouth was agape and Obidiah's eyes were wide with fascination.

Someone shot his finger toward the craft. It was Buddy, standing next to Caledonia and her red-tart lips. But there was no time to throw scorn or scowl at the real, live manifestation of my brother's secret love. *The Phoenix* was nose-diving toward the ground.

"Oooooh!" crooned the crowd.

Doc Taylor pressed his eyes to his binoculars, and Mr. Crisp ran his fingers up and down his suspender straps. Mouths hung open; we were all agog. A woman fainted. I looked down at my mother, who wore a hypnotized stare.

Suddenly, the biplane pulled back and soared away, billowing white smoke in its wake.

We exhaled. Relieved laughter peppered our applause.

"Where did they go?" someone asked.

"Yonder," another answered.

As *The Phoenix* rounded to the south again and began turning north, we could just make out the figure of Miss Bartleby climbing out of the front cockpit onto the upper wing and slowly rising to full height. She held her arms out and teetered, as if balancing on a tightrope and bracing herself against a terrible blast. She leaned forward, her knees buckling and straightening as though she were a coil.

We sucked in a collective gulp.

Next, she slid onto the lower wing, grabbing the bracing wires. When she reached the wing tip, she held on to a strut and swung around, leaned out, and waved. Her arm whipped backward.

"Hot-toe-mitty," said Poppa. "There must be a fierce wind up there." His neck had grown sweaty. "Loosen up, Maggie Mae, you're a-strangling Poppa."

"Holy Jove!" I heard my brother shout.

"Thaddeus, my God!" Momma said, taking the Lord's name in vain.

All around, we wore the same expression: utter astonishment.

Miss Bartleby was hanging upside down, a single leg hooked into a curved bar on the underside of the lower wing tip, holding on by the back of her knee, her arms spread gracefully to each side, her back arched. I thought I could see her smiling.

We erupted in applause.

Miss Bartleby made her way back to the front cockpit, and with that, *The Phoenix* came floating down.

"That was something else," my father exclaimed. He sounded exhausted, as if he had been piloting the aircraft himself. My mother slid her arm around his broad waist, and for a moment I was utterly content simply to be in their presence.

"Ladies and gentlemen, boys and girls! The show ain't over yet!" shouted Mr. Matterson through a megaphone. He was perched on the running board of his tin lizzie, holding on to the frame of the open window. We turned our attention back to *The Phoenix*, where Miss Bartleby stood holding a large dome-shaped cage, from which she removed a lavender guinea fowl. It was a stately bird with a wide, light blue, polka-dotted body and long, slender neck. It clucked softly as she tucked it under her arm and lowered herself once more into the front seat of the craft. Mr. Matterson announced: The guinea fowl would be released once the Bartlebys were aloft again; whoever caught the bird unharmed would get a free ride in the flying machine.

Everybody gasped.

"To be fair, ladies and gents, let's leave the chase to the children."

A cheer arose from youthful voices as a mild grumble of dismay deflated the older spectators.

"Pa! Oh, Pa! Let me down!" I was already scrambling to the earth.

"Easy does it, now," said my father, laughing.

To my surprise, Momma's face was radiant. "You catch that bird. Go on, now, Mia, GO!" She prodded me toward the clearing.

Forgoing pleasantries or apologies, I bumped into grown-up elbows and hips, forcing my way to the front. My progress was slow, so I fell to my hands and knees and crawled, my yellow horror bunching and tearing at the waist, but I didn't let that stop me. Soon a herd of crawling children joined me, and together we converged toward the open field. I heard *The Phoenix* drone as it soared overhead.

"Here it comes," a man yelled.

I broke out of the crowd and ran.

High in the sky, as *The Phoenix* flew steadily north, Miss Bartleby held the guinea fowl over the side of the craft in her two gloved hands. She tossed it up and the bird was driven backward as if carried on a slipstream, and then it spread its broad wings. It didn't fly so much as glide on the current. It was breathtaking.

I saw Buddy race by and I charged after him, pummeling the grass with my new boots. They were stiff and rubbed against my ankles, but I wouldn't be stopped.

"Not bad for a girl!" he said with a proud grin when I caught up to him.

I pushed hard to keep up with him, the guinea fowl soaring just ahead of us. The field jutted right, and we followed the sharp curve. The farther we ran, the fainter the crowd's encouragement sounded, until all we could hear was the pounding of our feet against the yellow grass.

As soon as we were out of sight of the adults, the game got dirty. Someone stepped on my heel and I stumbled forward. I looked over my right shoulder. George!

"You!" I said, regaining my balance.

"Was . . . an . . . accident . . ." he said, breathless, at my side.

Again someone troubled me, and this time I took a jab to my back.

"Ugh!" I cried, searching for the culprit, but all eyes were focused ahead.

With legs pumping like steam-engine cranks, I kept my sight overhead on the guinea fowl, and just as I was settling into a speedy rhythm, Buddy took off ahead of me again, cutting snappy lefts and rights. The other children shouted threats as they were forced off course. All but George. He began to mirror Buddy, the two of them scissoring back and forth, and then

I realized: *We* were playing dirty. I felt a surge of strength and shot forward, running the path Buddy and George were clearing for me.

"Run, Mia, run!" Buddy cheered as he and George blocked my competition.

I battle-cried and slipped easily by. The guinea fowl was in my sight, and I was the front-runner.

It had landed only yards ahead of me and stood in the grass, preening its feathers, apparently oblivious to the impending onslaught of children.

I belly flopped and grabbed for the bird, but the guinea fowl would have no part of it. With an alarmed squawk it bolted upright and fled on legs far too short for its unwieldy body. I gained on it, but it was as slippery as a buttered pig, and each time I clutched for it, I came up with an armful of air. Behind me, the contenders were rapidly gaining.

"Dadgummit!" I cried.

Suddenly, a little boy appeared aside the raspberry thickets growing along the edge of the field. It was Turner, and much like the guinea fowl, he was moving as fast as his legs could propel him, his mouth open in an expression of utter alarm. I pounced at the guinea fowl again and inadvertently rushed it directly into his arms.

He held the startled critter, nearly half his size, hugging it protectively, his eyes screaming his own fright. Without a doubt, Turner thought the bird's life was in peril and he was here to save it.

I searched for Obidiah and Capable, but it seemed as if Turner was the lone representative from his side of the rope. A wide circle of furious children began to close around us. Their white faces were boiling pink.

"Who do you think you are?" one snarled at me.

"What's *he* doin' here?"

"No niggers allowed!"

Several feet away, Turner sat cross-legged. He hunched down and buried his head in the feathers of the guinea fowl. It vented a hoarse cry.

I scanned the children's faces for Buddy, needing him more than ever. The number of faces sneering at me like I was a Salem witch was frightening. I didn't see him, and I couldn't help but think of all the times I told him I could take care of myself, and I hoped this wasn't his way of proving me wrong.

As I got to my knees, a pair of hands shoved me back down.

"Lay off me!" I growled.

The owner of the hands laughed and wheezed. I recognized that sound, and I turned around. Biggie Matterson was glaring down at me, the bruise around his eye a putrid green yellow.

"Shut up, half-breed," he sniped.

"Yeah, yeah!" came the rabble of voices.

Biggie lumbered over to Turner and toed his thigh. I cringed, knowing how much Turner hated to be touched.

"Let him alone, Biggie," I said.

"Let him alone," he taunted. He planted a leg on either side of Turner and unbuttoned his fly.

Turner's entire body shook as he shielded the bird against the yellow stream trickling down his head and neck.

I stood by, helpless.

"Look at him, he don't even say nothing when you whiz on him. You stupid mute," Biggie said, hitching his trousers.

"Nasty!" someone said.

"Good job, Matterson, now you done it. Who's gonna get the free ride now?" someone whined.

Biggie laughed and tried to wrench the bird away.

"Let it go, Turner, he won't hurt you if you let it go," I begged.

The bird screamed and pecked at Turner's arms, and still he held tight.

"Don't be dumb, do it!" I said, wincing at my own words.

He lifted his head, his face stained with tears.

"Please. It'll be okay. Ain't nobody gonna harm it, I promise."

He looked at me, and I nodded. He opened his arms, and the guinea fowl went scuttling through the children's legs. No one paid it any attention.

Biggie crouched and shoved his face into Turner's. "Don't you stare at me, nigger boy," he said.

Turner's eyes glazed over when Biggie poked him in the forehead.

"He let go of the bird," I said. "You can have it."

But Biggie stood over Turner's huddled shape. "It's time you learned a lesson."

"No!"

"Shut up, Injun girl," said a boy who had never uttered a mean word in the past.

"Let's string him up!" said another.

"And give him a whupping!"

"Yeah," the children howled.

"Who's wearing a belt?" Biggie called out.

"I got one," a familiar voice said.

The children searched for the volunteer. It was George, pushing his way through the pack. He skimmed a look at Biggie, who was twisting Turner's arms behind his back, and then at me. He walked over to Biggie and shoved him in the back of his head. "Let him go," he said flatly.

Biggie turned. "You hadn't ought've done that," he said when his eyes fell on George.

"I said let him go."

"Or what? You'll punch me in the other eye?" Biggie made a face like a frightened woman.

George had blackened Biggie's eye, not me?

"Or I'll split your fat gut from side to side."

Biggie released Turner and walked up to George. "I dare you," he sneered, popping his cap from his head.

The circle widened, and I crawled to Turner, dragging him into my arms. The reek of Biggie's urine made me gag.

"You ain't gonna like this, but I gotta get you outta here," I whispered against his face. I threw his arm over my shoulder and rose, hoisting him onto my side.

As we pulled away from the ring, a cluck rose out of the raspberry thickets.

"Looky there, Turner. It's your bird, see? Come on, wake up." I shook him but he didn't respond. His eyes were closed, his chin touched his chest, and he was heavy in my arms. As I dragged him, I heard grunts and the sickening sounds of flesh hitting flesh. Over my shoulder I saw a glimpse of a metal blade, and George cock-stepping forward and jabbing. I prayed none of the children would peel off after us.

The guinea fowl clucked again.

"Go away," I said, lugging Turner back toward the adults, his feet scuffing the grass. My heart bucked as I heard a cheer rise from the crowd of children.

The bird tracked us, keeping the thickets between us. When we reached a spot where raspberries no longer grew and a small gully began, the guinea fowl squawked again.

"What?" I said, annoyed. I caught a glint of light. Below was a narrow stream.

I pulled Turner down the slope, laid him by the edge, and knelt. I scooped my hands into the cool water and patted his face and forehead.

Turner opened his eyes.

"Gee, Turner, I'm sure glad you ain't dead," I said, my lips quivering into a smile for him.

From above the gully, I heard confused voices and someone shout, "There they are," and a horde of adults rushed past us toward the melee.

Meanwhile, the guinea fowl found a dusty spot and tossed the grit over its body. Once it was clean, it sat contentedly in the grass and pecked the ground.

Turner and I climbed back up the slope. At the top, we found ourselves in Momma's arms.

Doc Taylor's office in Persimmon smelled of rubbing alcohol, and the rattan seat had made painful waffles out of the back of my legs in the minutes since Momma and I had arrived. She pushed open the curtains, but it didn't make a difference. We baked while the overhead fan rattled.

She dropped back down in the seat next to me and smoothed my hair away from my face. "When we get home, I'm going to give you a nice bath. And don't you fret about your dress; I can fix that, that I can fix."

When Buddy and Poppa finally came out of the examining room, I rushed to my brother's side. He hobbled on one foot and leaned on a cane. His face was pale. "My ankle's twisted," he said.

I didn't have to ask if it hurt. It was swollen to the size of an acorn squash, if the enormity of the bandage was any indication.

He had stepped in a gopher hole during our chase, he explained, and heard a loud pop. He was glad, actually. He thought he'd broken a bone, but it was only a sprain.

"You'll need to stay off that foot for a good couple of weeks," said the doctor. His shoes made sharp clicks worthy of their gunmetal hue as he walked over to our parents.

While they consulted, Buddy and I stepped outside to wait on the brick pavement, hoping the shade of the awning would be cooler than Doc

Taylor's office. But as soon as I began to recount what had happened to Turner and me, I was interrupted by the shriek of a car horn. Mr. Matterson's Model T Ford was barreling down Main Street, followed at a fair distance by a drove of folks in wagons.

Biggie's chest racked and heaved as Mr. Matterson and Preacher Reverend hauled him off the seat. His mouth opened and closed with each thick, asthmatic gasp, his eyes desperate.

I turned away from the spectacle until I heard the examining room door slam shut behind Buddy and me, then looked out again at the crowd converged in front of Doc Taylor's office, the children clambering around, fighting to be heard, each parent asking the same question.

". . . Biggie grabbed George's wrist"

". . . and made George drop his knife"

". . . Biggie bent for it"

". . . but then George sprang onto his back"

". . . and Biggie spun around, clawing at George"

". . . but George was holding on strong"

". . . and they fell backward"

". . . and they wrestled"

". . . and then Biggie pinned George to the ground"

". . . but then Biggie started to wheeze"

". . . and gasp"

". . . he turned blue!"

". . . he moaned like he was hurting"

". . . and groaned"

". . . and foamed at the mouth"

". . . and flapped like a fish"

"—a whale!" a child laughed, and his face was promptly smacked.

But all agreed: When they had huddled around him, thinking to see the steel and silver blade of George's stag-handle hunting knife lodged in Biggie's flabby gut, they hadn't seen a single scratch.

Momma clutched my hand and led me to our wagon, her distress escalating as she told our father about what had set the fight off between Biggie and George: Before Capable could stop him, Turner had shot off and disappeared into the crowd. Capable and Obidiah had chased after him, shouting his name, searching in every direction, worried he had run for the guinea fowl. When they'd approached the entrance for whites, Simon and Luther Blood had barred them and demanded to know their business. When they'd explained that their little brother was lost and asked if anyone had seen him, Simon and Luther hadn't let them pass and instead had called over their daddy. After the news made its way through the crowd to Momma, she'd sought Missus Bounds, whom she'd found pleading with the Washaway crowd to help her find her son. Not too good for us now, eh, Linden? Momma had heard someone say to her.

Poppa was helping Buddy into our cart when a horrible sound came from Doc Taylor's examining room. "No! No!" Mr. Matterson was moaning. Another clamor flew out the window, a horrible wail of disbelief and horror. "My boy! Oh God!"

Poppa glanced at Momma, who said in a shaky voice, "Let's go, Thaddeus; take us home, please."

"Find him!" said Mr. Matterson in a hoarse growl. "I want you all to find that boy."

"Mia!" Momma called after me.

I ran without a plan, with only the need to escape. My legs carried me down Main Street and up the rocky hill to the Dividings. And then, impulsively, I turned left. I ran up the switchback, up Whispering Pines Road. For a while I was alone—only the beating sun, cornfields, rolling hills, cows sleeping in pastures, and the rough road accompanied me. And then I was headed toward a tunnel of interweaving trees, a bowing arbor. Once through that oasis of shade, I turned onto a road of small houses and swept yards with chicken coops and dogs roaming free. A meandering creek trickled alongside.

In front of one house stood a strange tree, leafless and without a sign of life but decorated with long-necked blue and green glass bottles stuck on the ends of the branches. Through the window I could see two old women taking Sunday supper. In front of another home, a family sat on their porch in swings and rockers and chairs. I heard laughter. A group of children was playing a game of tag, and several girls were jumping rope.

I was in Washaway.

The scrape of the rocking chairs, the clatter of plates, the children's shouts of glee—all came to a stop. Even the trees seemed to stand still and the wind seized. I could feel their stares and hear their whispers as a man finally approached me.

"Scuse me, miss, but you lost?" He was tall and thin, his chest sunken in. He wore a brimmed straw hat and his face was dark brown with freckles and kind. He held the hand of a little girl who looked at me with an unsettling fear in her eyes, as if I were a raider on the shore of her land, rather than a child in distress.

I opened my mouth to speak, but nothing came out. I turned around and ran back down the hill, and I prayed. I prayed for God to give Biggie back his life. Make him my Lazarus, I begged. I didn't mean to wish him dead.

"There she is!" I heard my brother shout. I could barely breathe, and my face burned with tears. They were riding up Whispering Pines Road, and I ran toward our wagon, for the first time scared of my father, who was angrier than I'd ever seen him.

"Get yourself back in this wagon, for the love of God, and stay put," he said. It was the sound of fear mixed with love, but to my nine-year-old ears, it was rage. "Now," he said, and I got in.

Momma sat with her hands folded in her lap, her face drained of blood.

Late that night, even though I was plain wrung out, I couldn't fall asleep, and so I headed down to the second-floor landing and listened to our visitor through the balustrades.

"I'm sorry, Dorothea, I wish I had something stronger to offer than coffee," Momma said.

"Coffee is just fine, thank you," said Old Maid Hailey. "I didn't know what else to do. The way they pounded on the door I was certain they meant to break in." She told Momma how Sheriff Fairstone had come to her house, just as evening fell. George wasn't there, she'd told him, insisting she didn't know where he was.

The sheriff was awful polite about it, she said.

Please, Mrs. Hailey, he said. I've got to do my job.

As Mrs. Hailey relayed it, she'd allowed him in and even encouraged him to poke through all the nooks of the house. She had nothing to hide, she told him, and she hadn't seen her boy since the afternoon. When Sheriff Fairstone stepped outside again, he announced to his deputy, He ain't here. To Old Maid Hailey he said, I don't suppose it would do me much good to tell you to bring him in when he comes home, but you might want to consider it, ma'am—make everyone's life a bit easier.

Old Maid Hailey's coffee cup clattered against the saucer as she continued, and I pulled myself even closer to the balustrades, pressing into them like a jailed prisoner.

About an hour later, George finally came home from wherever he'd been hiding, and shortly after sunset, Old Maid Hailey recounted, they saw four shining globes snaking up the craggy hill, four ghostly figures holding lanterns.

Standing in her doorway, hoping her heart would soon stop racing, she said to them: I'll tell you as I told Sheriff Fairstone, my grandson's not here. I don't know where he is. They were grown fool men, Old Maid Hailey said, dressed in bedsheets and pillowcases over their heads with cutout eye slits, nothing showing but the tips of their shoes. And as long as she lived she'd never forget them: yellow and black snakeskin, a dress set of metal gray, and a pair of boots with gold buttons. No ordinary brogans, like the fourth one. The men warned her, she said, to do what was right, and turn her grandson in.

She said she knew those boots and the dress shoes, even the brogans, a curse of having a keen memory, and she addressed each of them by name:

Mr. Crisp, she said to the snakeskin, perhaps you gentlemen would care to come in for a glass of sweet tea? It's awfully hot tonight. Or you, Doc Taylor, she said to the metal gray, I know how you enjoy butter cookies; I have a fresh dozen waiting in the larder. Turning to the boots with the gold buttons: And you, Mr. Bartleby, you must have had a long day showing us all your tricks, surely you would like to cool off with a beverage? As for the set of brogans, she said, Always a pleasure to see you, Reverend Elias.

Preacher Reverend? And Mr. Crisp, Mr. Bartleby, and Doc Taylor? I was shaking, and I didn't know why.

They declined the tea, naturally, said Mrs. Hailey, and then she confessed to Momma: The entire time she was conversing with the hooded visitors, George had been behind the front door with his slingshot, and she had been ready with her shotgun hidden in the folds of her gathered skirt. "The Lord must have been watching over us," she said. "Those fellows couldn't have beat a faster path down the hill once I named them. Oh, George," she said with a gasp and blew her nose.

"Where is he now?" Poppa asked.

"I don't know," said Dorothea Hailey. "He's run off again."

I heard Buddy stirring in his bedroom and ran up the stairs to my loft, too exhausted to take in any more.

But I woke in the middle of the night. Someone was sitting on the end of my bed. She was smiling.

"Hello, friend," she said.

"Are you a dream?"

"I am." She pulled back my sheet. "Come," she said.

"Where?"

"Follow."

"No. Not no more."

"Too late," she said.

"Why?"

"I have your soul." She cracked a grin.

My scalp leaped. "You can't have my soul. I ain't dead."

She laughed. "You don't need to be."

"But how?"

"You never called yourself."

"I did," I said.

"From the spirits under the hydrangea bush," she said.

"Exactly," I said.

"But you never called yourself from me," she giggled. "Not once."

"Don't matter," I said. "I'm making a stand. You don't get my soul. It ain't yours to take, and it ain't yours to share."

My ghost looked sad. "I thought you wanted a friend," she said.

"I did."

She smiled.

"But not no more. I killed someone," I said.

She smiled wider. "I know."

And then I awoke, frozen with fright. When my limbs thawed, I realized it was raining outside, a hard storm pelting drops against the roof and the window. I was in my room. I was safe. It was just a dream. I thought I heard my name, but I knew it was only the wind through the floorboards making that sad sound, a low moaning, like a hurt dog. But the longer I listened, the more I thought I could be wrong. I pulled myself out of bed and crept to the window, afraid of who might be waiting for me in the backyard.

Below stood George.

I had never felt more relieved.

I lifted the window and climbed down the oak.

"What're you doin' here, George Hailey?"

The rain dripped off his gray twill cap.

"I'm takin' off," he said.

"To where?"

"Dunno. Milledgeville, maybe."

"What's down there?" I asked.

"Dunno."

"You can't just go." I wiped the rain from my face.

"Sure I can. Ain't got nothin' here."

I huddled closer to the oak. "What about your granny?"

"She'll be okay."

"She really loves you. You shouldn't waste a granny."

"You're getting soaked," he said.

"Don't mind it."

He kicked a root. "Come with me," he mumbled. And then he lifted his head. "Come with me."

"I can't," I stammered.

"Why not?"

"'Cause that's crazy," I said.

"Yeah." He nodded. His eyes were rimmed with pink as if he'd been crying.

"He's gonna be buried tomorrow," I blurted.

"I know. I seen them . . ." His voice trailed off.

"Seen who?" I asked, not certain I wanted to know.

"Mr. Wilkins and Biggie. In the morgue. Figured it'd be the last place folks'd think of lookin' for me."

"That was right smart."

"Didn't count on seeing what I saw," he said.

I let him tell me even though my stomach was jumping.

"He was draining Biggie's blood," George said, his voice almost soundless, "and his guts, and filling him up with some stuff from a tank. God, it stank, the whole room just stank."

"Formaldehyde," I offered. "Keeps him from going bad."

"Too late for that," he said.

Neither of us laughed.

"I'm goin' to hell for sure," he said grimly.

"Naw, you ain't."

"Sure I am. I kilt a man."

"You didn't kill him," I said.

"He wouldn'ta had that attack."

"You didn't kill him," I said again. "I did."

"I ain't gonna fight you for braggin' rights," he said.

"I wished he was dead," I confessed.

"Don't mean you did it."

"Think God will care for the difference?" I asked.

"I think God can figure it out."

"I hope so," I said.

The rain began to let up.

"I better go," he said.

I pushed off the tree trunk and closer to him. I drew in his smell, which was still warm and wet as a sweaty horse and just as nice. "You ain't half bad, George Hailey."

"You neither, Amelia McGee."

Before he rounded the corner of the house, he turned. "I'll write."

I was only nine, but I had enough sense to know he wouldn't.

WILLIE MAE COTTON

⚬⚬⚬

The day after they buried the Matterson boy, a man sat alone on his porch. The grandson of Galilee and Jaz. Nathaniel Bounds. And what he was holding was a long rifle. I knew that rifle. It was the one Miss Emmaline used the day her world turned upside down. It was angled toward the sky, a grand blue sky, the kind the Lord creates to remind you of His perfection. The color of hope and good things coming our way.

"Good day," say Nathaniel Bounds. "What can I do you gentlemen for?"

"I think you know, Nate," one of the men say.

Ten become twenty. Twenty become thirty. They weren't wearing no masks this time. No hoods, neither.

"He's a child. What do you want with a child?" say Nathaniel Bounds.

"He broke the law. We got a dead boy on our hands," say their doctor.

"My son ran after a bird, and there's no harm in that. You've given up on the Hailey boy and now you're looking for someone to blame."

"You're smart for a nigger, ain't you?" a woman shout, and she flung a stone.

"I got history to this property, you all know that. I got rights," say Nathaniel Bounds on his feet now.

"Not no more you don't."

The news of it lashed up Whispering Pines Road to the heart of Washaway.

I rememory the day I almost broke.

In the bleak of the following morn, a group of our men footed to the valley to cut Nathaniel Bounds down.

A crowd of sightseers, gawking still and thrilling, jeered at them, and when a stump broke off, intending to menace, another one of their faction, a preacher man, stuck his arm out. "Let them pass," he say. "They're doing us a favor."

We took Nathaniel home. We brought him to his wife.

My chest cracks with the picture of that.

We buried him on his grounds, in the Land of Galilee.

I do my best to keep the hope.

I try not to lose the faith.

I got no intention of getting lost.

One day that sun gon rise again and give birth to whole new kind of blue, and that new blue gon deliver on its promise. I got time. I'm still waiting. And I don't aim to give up.

We had spent a good many years in Washaway, but short after we laid Nathaniel Bounds to rest, me and Mary-Mary headed back to our nest in Screamer Hollow. We were ready for whatever mercy that mountain had left to offer.

AMELIA J. McGEE

———⦿———

Turner's coonhounds bit Nathaniel Bounds's attackers, and so they shot his beloved dogs, the redbone, the bluetick, and the black and tan. The mob stormed the porch and tore at Mister Bounds's clothes. They grabbed the hatchet from Obidiah and hacked at his father's genitals. Then they shot Capable Means for felonious assault, meaning he tried to save his father. They would have torched the Land of Galilee, but that would have defeated their purpose.

Someone would photograph Mister Bounds dangling from the giant chinquapin, a bloody shirt tied around his waist, the remains of his face smashed in, his body charred, the garnet ring he wore around his pinkie finger gone. It would be printed as the first in a set of color-tinted lynching cards marked *The End of Nathaniel Bounds, Hung by a Mob in the Fertile Valley* and sold at Mr. Crisp's general store for two cents, like a postal card to mail to a nephew, a bathing beauty found under a brother's mattress, or a baseball card to give a friend.

Obidiah, my Obidiah.

A month later, on another Sunday, Mr. Matterson, Mr. Crisp, Doc Taylor, and Mr. Blood, faces I recognized as those of the fathers, husbands, and brothers from Warwoman Hollow, from the Fertile Valley, from Persimmon proper—when these ordinary citizens marched down the center of Main Street in their first parade, waving flags and holding banners, led by Preacher Reverend, we all listened.

"One God, one language, one flag!"

"One hundred percent American!"

"What does it mean?" I asked Momma.

She waited until we got home and we were alone, and what she told me scared me, especially when she said I must never repeat her words to anyone.

"Those banners are an atrocity," she said. Momma spoke with bare-faced frankness, and I sensed it was important that I try to understand.

She said it began after the War Between the States with a secret society determined to keep colored folks in their place. Whites were afraid now that the slaves were free. Afraid of revenge, of being outnumbered, of a tilt in power, these vigilantes tortured and killed colored folks, as well as anyone who sympathized with them. They spread their dens across countryside and city alike, but they eventually died out. Now they had risen again, expanding their roster of hate to include not only colored folks but also anyone who wasn't born in the United States, anyone who didn't worship the way they did. She said it was not only our county—it was nationwide. It was a secret that wasn't. It was family men. It was police officers, teachers, barbers, factory workers, mechanics, electricians, and grocers. Judges, mayors, governors, and senators. It was over two million members strong. It was the presidential campaign. It was the silence of Calvin Coolidge. She said she was telling me because I had to be careful, more careful than I had ever been, in what I said and did. And then she took a breath, realizing she was upsetting us both.

"But why was Preacher Reverend at the front of the procession?" I asked, my stomach shaking.

"You must always be polite to him and treat him with respect," she said with odd vagueness. She hugged me, something Momma rarely did, frightening me even more. "He's a man of great influence," she said. "Do you understand?"

In September a pair of mourning doves built a nest in our ancient oak. I watched them from Buddy's bedroom window every day, staying, as my mother wished, close to our homeplace and out of the Takatoka and away from Lovelady. Only long after I'd left Hopewell did I realize Biggie didn't die by anyone's hand—not mine or Lovelady's, not even his own.

As I sat in Buddy's bedroom, I watched the female sit on her chosen branch, the blue-headed male bringing her straw for the nest. After she laid two eggs, the two doves took turns sitting on them, with one flying away, eventually returning so the partner could leave to eat. They did this for four days. And then it began to rain, all day and into the night. I noticed, after the second day of the rain, that the male had not come back. I wondered if he was dead—maybe shot by a local boy, or perhaps he had become a meal for a cat. It was a terrible rain, and the female bird became soaked, drenched to the bone, until her colors were muddied and her feathers stuck out in clumps. I wondered if she would die of a chill. She sat with her eyes closed as the rain pelted her back, only once or twice opening them when she sensed me watching. She must be hungry, I thought. She hasn't eaten for days.

I knew better than to feed her. It would disrupt the order of nature; Momma had taught me that. But I couldn't resist. I climbed out onto the roof with a handful of sunflower seeds. The bird hunkered down. She cocked her head to the side and stared at me and blinked.

"I ain't here to hurt you," I said. "I'm here to help. You got to be starved."

I crab-walked farther down the slope as rain drenched my face. Again, I offered. But the bird only glared. Holding on to the roof with one hand, the seeds in the other, I reached out as far as I possibly could, and then I lost my balance. I grabbed the branch. It swayed, but the nest, closer to the trunk, did not fall, and the dove and the eggs were not upset.

I said a short prayer of thanks and crawled back to my room.

The bird kept her eye on me as she sat in the rain, protecting her eggs.

From SURVEY AND RECOMMENDATIONS CONCERNING THE INTEGRATION OF THE NEGRO SOLDIER INTO THE ARMY

Submitted by William H. Hastie, Civilian Aide to the Secretary of War, September 22, 1941

A job is never done until it is done right. I pointed out the fundamental error in the Air Corps training program for Negroes before it was inaugurated. I have continued to do so as the results of that error have become more apparent. It is inexcusable that the Army invests in national advertising for aviation cadets, organizes units in college communities to stimulate recruiting, plans for noncommissioned pilots, all to meet the increasing need for Army flyers, and at the same time requires a Negro to wait three years to begin pilot training. There is no satisfactory solution to this dilemma short of admission of Negroes to various existing schools for flying cadet training, rather than directing them through the bottleneck of the separate Negro project at Tuskegee.

AMELIA J. McGEE

⚬⚬⚬

D.C., Manassas, Harrisonburg, Roanoke, Pulaski, Marion, Kingsport, Johnson City, Erwin, Asheville, Franklin, Dry Creek, Unicoi Route 101, Blood Mountain Road. Home. I knew the bus route, the highway signs; I'd traveled it enough times, never staying too long, never needing more than a few nights' change of clothes.

"Not a trace," Buddy said when I arrived that evening at his homeplace in the Fertile Valley. A fire sparked in the hearth, and he stared into the golden light. The bags under his eyes were dark enough to match my own. Under any other circumstance, I would have found comfort in the persistent beat of rain against the roof and the applewood scent of his home, Cal's favorite to burn in the fall.

I couldn't help but look up at the calendar on the wall next to the doorway.

October 30, 1941.

Ella had been missing an entire day.

"The driver swears he left her in front of Wilkins's," Buddy said, scratching his beard, reminding me unsettlingly of Poppa. For all his bulk and grand stature, however, our father had been a mild man, as if he knew his own strength and also knew better than to use it. Buddy had turned into a man far more fierce. And dogged. After speaking with the dispatcher in D.C., he'd spent the previous night pounding on doors—had anyone seen her, did anyone know of her whereabouts? He drove up and down the Unicoi, never mind the deluge of rain, searching cornfield by cornfield and outbuilding by outbuilding, overturning every hollow log.

My lungs expanded enough to take a decent breath. Ella had grown up under Momma's roof, meaning she possessed the good sense to be polite but not engage with outsiders. She would never get into a car with a stranger. It would have been natural for her to look for shelter in such a heavy storm. But where?

Cal set a cup of coffee in front of me before pouring one of her own. I warmed my fingers over the steam, droplets of moisture collecting on my palms. "You couldn't have known the local would break down. Or that Walter wouldn't be home," she said. Eight months pregnant and looking the rebel even in her velveteen housecoat taut over her belly, she was still cordial and caring, her compassion toward me almost unbearable in the midst of my anxiety.

"Please, Cal. Don't."

"Do you think someone followed her from D.C.?" Buddy asked.

"No, no," I said. "No." The thought of it horrified me. As far as I knew, no one in D.C. knew my hometown. I'd never spoken of it, at least not by proper name. Over the years, I'd grown accustomed to keeping certain fragments of my past to myself. "What do we do? What do we do?" I wasn't in the habit of asking Buddy for counsel anymore, but my mind was spent, flitting from thought to thought, but not stopping long enough to gather any pollen of meaningful consequence.

Buddy pulled his cable-knit sweater over his head and wrapped it around Cal's shoulders. "Call the picket off," he said to me.

"What?"

"Do it, Mia."

"I don't have that kind of say, Bud. It's bigger than me."

"She's missing, for the love of Jove. Call the owner. Tell him you're calling the thing off. See what he says."

I dialed the operator. Got his number. Woke up his wife. Who? You. Have you lost your mind? It's that woman.

He was downright civil. I barely shook. Called me a few select words, said I was the criminal, and it's a wonder someone hadn't already locked me up, but hell no, he hadn't laid a hand on her. I could hear him grinning through the phone, pleased that I thought he would. I said I would call off the picket if he would just tell me where she was. He hissed at me and said he was going back to sleep, didn't I think I'd already made his life a living hell, and then he hung up.

"You think he's telling the truth?" Buddy asked.

"I don't know. I think so. I want to," I said. My throat felt constricted. "What if something awful has happened to her?"

Cal rested a hand on my shoulder, and I squeezed it.

"We're gonna find her, we will," my brother said.

And I believed him. I had to. We shut our minds to the alternative, and I was grateful to Buddy in a way I hadn't been since our childhood.

I awake in the dark. The mist gives away the time the way it glides around the grain silo and whirls across the field and suddenly is gone. Dawn. My bones ache as if they soaked up all the rain overnight and have no outlet to drain. I don't feel like a twenty-six-year-old.

By the time I've thrown on my blouse and trousers, Buddy has already dressed and eaten a bowl of grits, ready to resume the search for my girl.

It is October 31. Halloween. I have long lost my love of masks and phantoms.

Buddy gives little Thaddeus a squeeze and kisses Cal before he leaves. I ache for Obidiah and turn away, knowing better than to let my emotions show. Buddy never asks after him, and I know it's not out of spite but discomfort, and I decide to accept that. He's heading out to Persimmon to check in with the new sheriff, and to post lost-child notices in the places that have sprung up since I left home: Hopewell County Savings and Loan, the two five-and-tens with their lunch counters that forced Mr. Crisp out of business—as well as every church, including our own. Our congregation finally has its own pastor, a fellow I would not love, says Buddy, given my shaky faith and suspicion of men of the cloth, but I would not loathe.

As soon as Buddy's pickup has left the yard, I set out on foot, despite Cal's offer to borrow her motorcycle, needing to feel the ground under my own soles.

The rain has finally let up and the air is ripe with the sour ferment of foliage, a stench that is natural and wholesome to me. I button Obidiah's overcoat and shove my fingers into the pockets, now empty of change. I feel something else cold and pull it out.

His garnet ring. Once his only link to his father, now my only link to him as he waits in D.C., in jail, for his trial. I know he is doing what is important to him.

The sun is rising and shining on trees long denuded of their leaves. The branches drip from their undersides. Ella loves this tapping sound the drops make when they land on the sodden ground.

Give her back to me, I say, I pray, though I don't know if God or Nature is listening to me anymore.

She's nearsighted but oddly insightful.

She's drawn to all things that glitter. Shooting stars. The angel on top of a Christmas tree.

She doesn't like strawberries but loves blueberries and takes such pleasure in showing me, every time as if for the first, that her tongue is purple.

She sleeps in pajamas with feet. She likes the sandpaper sound they make on the floor.

She was born at 1:33 in the morning. Momma put her on my chest.

I stared at her. I made you, I said, disbelieving.

She was so tiny.

She had a full head of hair.

It was jet black, just like mine, and I was glad when it stayed that way.

Her baby toe curls under the fourth toe on each foot. A trait inherited from Obidiah.

When she was three months old, she started looking at me, really seeing. When I walked into the room, she would smile with a big open mouth and wiggle as if I were the source of all joy. She did that for no one else but me.

She can see what others cannot.

I do not regret who I am.

The man whom I love.

The girl I begat.

I walk up Blood Mountain Road.

Unlike Buddy, I don't have an organized plan. I only know that I woke with the urge to head to Warwoman Hollow. To our old homeplace.

When I pass the field where the giant chinquapin stands, I do not look back. I know what happened there.

Shortly after Mister Bounds's murder, Missus Bounds, Obidiah, and Turner moved to Washaway. For years, the Land of Galilee lay fallow. Missus Bounds refused to sell it to anyone from Hopewell; folks from Washaway wouldn't touch it. Finally she sold it to an outsider: Mr. Walter Wilkins. But the land was dead; even the peach tree had shriveled up. After Obidiah left for college—we had kept our love a secret from our families and neither of us knew I was pregnant—Missus Bounds took Turner to Harlem City and never came back.

Last year, Mr. Wilkins donated the land to the U.S. Forest Service, and slowly, life has returned to the Land of Galilee. It's called the Fertile Valley Dell now, part of the Anighilahian National Forest.

As cars pass me, folks wave and I nod, though I don't know who the passengers are, nor they me.

My home is both familiar and foreign to me now.

I open our old screen door and turn the lock.

The embroidered family tree still hangs over my bed in the sleeping loft. Dust clings to the frame and cloth.

I lie down and hug myself, imagining my father standing over me to tuck me in, the scent of cherry twist, the way he cupped his pipe. But when I take in a deep breath, all I smell is must.

Not long after I finally told my parents about Obidiah and me—Poppa dipped his head and Momma paled, distraught over the risks we had taken more than my condition—I gave birth. Then something inside me changed: I became anxious and unsettled, an insomniac, immune to every home remedy Momma brewed. They called it bad nerves back then. When I broke down after three long years and told my mother that I had to get out of Hopewell and I didn't dare take Ella with me, and that I was ashamed, Momma told me a story.

She told me about the Preacher Reverend.

She told me it was he who had brought the fraternity of Americanism and lily white to Hopewell County, quietly enrolling men over the course of four years, pushing its revitalized ideals of Protestantism, patriotism, politics, picnics, and parades until it became as natural as belonging to the Persimmon Lodge or the PTA. Almost the entire white population of Hopewell had been inveigled or charmed.

After services, when the men and women split into groups for Bible study, that was when Preacher Reverend would descend, telling the men it was a matter of morals and it was their duty. In 1924, Mr. Matterson had been our county's leader, and with the Knights of Hopewell so christened, so began the pressure to *purify* the valley. When Mr. Matterson invited Poppa to join the Knights, Poppa had declined, saying he couldn't afford the dues. When Mr. Matterson offered to sponsor him, my father again turned it down.

How come no one ever came knocking on our door, insisting? Why were we never terrorized? How had we been spared? I asked.

Momma told me of the pact she'd made with the preacher.

It was stolen glances and lowered lashes, she said. It was perspiration under her arms when Elias called her back to the pulpit after everyone else had filed out. Azaria, he'd say, I think you forgot your Bible. And Poppa looking so handsome with his hair combed back, in a clean pressed shirt under his double-front apron, waiting in the aisle.

My mother's Cherokee blood didn't bother Preacher Reverend. What's more American, he'd say to Momma, than being Indian? I traded my friendship to keep my family safe, she told me.

Shocked, I asked if Poppa knew.

And she said if he did, he would never tell her.

I cry remembering my parents. Their imperfections. Their love. Of each other. Of me.

As I head downstairs and out to the backyard, an anguish of love and loss takes hold of my chest.

I sprint up the butterweed hill.

I find the cairn that marks the old Indian trail.

At a pace that is as hard as my lungs will allow me, I follow the trail to the rim of the gorge.

My own name echoes when I call it out. I keep shouting until my name doubles back on itself, over and over again until all there is is Amelia J. McGee.

I am my own soul.

What I would give to change the past.

What I will give to have Ella back.

I sob and shout, "Give her back to me."

E. F. McGEE

Rise up, my love, my fair one, and come away.
For, lo, the winter is past, the rain is over and gone;
The flowers appear on the earth;
The time of the singing of birds is come,
And the voice of the turtle is heard in
our land.

—Song of Solomon 2:10–12

And then the sun nudges me. She dapples my eyelids. She stretches from the sky. The morning star. She shines through the drips that drop down the windowpane. It is dew, not rain.

"Where are you, boy?" I call out.

Brando's nails click as he scrambles to his feet. He wags his tail. He pants. He pushes his wet snout into my neck. "Cut that out, you're tickling me," I laugh and squish my head to my bad shoulder that is no longer bad 'cause it does not ache.

I tell my dog to find Willie Mae, and he trots to the front door, sniffing underneath it. He plops down on his haunches and wags his tail.

There is a note on the door. *Open me*.

It is autumn in the garden of Willie Mae. In every direction lushlush-lush. Honeysuckle and trumpet vines and umbrella leaf. Reds and yellows and browns and oranges. We walk across three flagstones to a tree. It has no leaves. Its branches are short and craggy. Blue and green bottles plug the end of every stump, and the sun makes colored shadows. The two ladies argue under it.

"I *am* combing kindly," Willie Mae says.

"If you're kind, then why am I so tender headed?" Mary-Mary says as she shifts in her seat and grumps and rubs her scalp. Her hair is wild. It is a flock of muddy goats flowing down a mountainside. She says, "Next time you need a night herbal, I propose you go and fetch them yourself. I didn't ask for the gift. When the Almighty was handing it out, I don't have any recollection standing in that line saying, 'Give me the gift of spotting hard-to-find herbs so I can be forever linked to your bossy side.'" She jumps and yelps, "You just keep at it and I'll be bald. Where's the hair you just ripped from my head?"

"I'm gon leave it out for a jaybird if you don't settle. Maybe next time you look where you going, specially when it's pouring rain. And you take a damn lantern." Willie Mae looks up from her work. "Hoo, mind my language, child. Glad to see you awake. Good to see you too Mr. Brando."

"Morning, ma'ams," I say.

"Morning," Mary-Mary says glumly.

I stare up at the tree of bottles.

"It clears the yard of animosities," Willie Mae says. And then she reaches into her pocket and takes out a handful of chopped corn. She rubs it into Mary-Mary's scalp and soothes her with mumblings, and now she ladles water from a tin bucket over her head until the water runs clear. Mary-Mary lifts her face to the sun, and Willie Mae towels her hair and parts it with a comb and braids it and threads blue and green beads like a string of jewels through each one.

When she is done, Mary-Mary looks like a bottle tree herself.

"Now, ain't you a beauty," Willie Mae says and gives Mary-Mary a squeeze. A flush grows in Mary-Mary's cheeks. "Thank you," she murmurs.

Willie Mae's smile is easy. "You looking revived," she says to me. "How you feeling?"

"Much better, ma'am," I say.

"You looking more than better. You looking ready to travel." She raises her hand to her forehead and looks down the mountain. There are no clouds, only sun shining. I can see the town in the valley below. It is my town.

Inside the cabin, my blue suitcase is open on the high-up bed. Willie Mae takes out a stack from her wardrobe. My coat! My squirrel hat! My muffler!

My Good Book and my Alice! The pages are thick and rippled and fan open, flipflipflip. I hug my books. I do not smell Momma.

"Willie Mae?"

"Yes, child?"

"Where did Momma go?"

"How do you mean?"

"I don't hear her no more."

"Well," Willie Mae says and rubs the sides of her mouth. "When a spirit moves on to where it's supposed to go, it's a far long distance to communicate. It's like they in another country, and we don't got the means to reach them. Understand?"

I do not.

"Don't you qualm, child. If you don't hear her, then she must have moved on, for this here cabin is one strong antenna."

"But what about the scary lady?"

"You worried your momma turned into someone like her?" Willie Mae crosses her arms. "I can't make you no promises, child, but you got to ask yourself: Was she the kind of folk that holds on to the past?"

"Momma was sad after Poppa died."

Willie Mae wags a finger. "That ain't the same thing. Love and loss is part of living. You got to dig down into the roots of you, get quiet inside, and ask: Do *you* think she's moved on, do you think she's gone home? Joined her ancestors, her family? Or do you think she's turned sour, maybe lost her courage on her journey? Too afraid to take a leap of faith and let go? Only you can answer that."

I stand real still. I bow my head and squeeze my eyes closed. I listen hard. I send my ears out, beyond the treetops, into the sky, to the moon and the sun and the stars. I follow my ears and fly to the ends of the universe.

"Momma's gone home," I announce.

Willie Mae nods. "Good, child, that real good. Nothing can replace the trust you have in your instinct, the trust you have in yourself."

She strokes Brando's head. "You a fine dog. I see you know that. Don't you let it go to your head." Brando leans his long body against Willie Mae's legs. "You're welcome," she says and she grins.

I look at Willie Mae. I put a memory in my mind. Of the lines in her face. Her silvery glow. The yellow that petals around each pupil like a sunflower. Her eyes are wet and she turns away. Mary-Mary puts her arm around Willie Mae's waist. "Now cut that out," Willie Mae says.

She squats down and holds my hands, and I give her a big hug. She holds me and I remember that too. In the arms of Willie Mae where there is so much love. Her glow changes from silvery to smoky orange. She is a setting sun. Then she stands. She clears her throat. "You get your coat and meet me back outside."

She goes.

I put on my coat and my squirrel hat. I wrap my muffler around my throat. I close my suitcase. Brando stands tall. He yawns and his ears flip backward. He slobbers my hand with his wet pink tongue, and this makes me happy. I gaze into his eyes, so brown and bright. I stroke his head and rub his ears. This makes him happy. The sun shines into the room and plots a crisscross pattern across the floor. We pad into the other room to the little window next to the door, and now I stand on my toes and see the colorful leaves shimmy as they welcome a speckled light. The speckles look friendly, and I open the door. We walk outside. The ground is solid. The garden is real. Willie Mae and Mary-Mary pull a canvas off an old car. They bicker over the best route to the Fertile Valley and Buddy's homeplace. I wave my hand through the light. The speckles waltz around me as if they are alive. I hold my hands over my head and stand in the shower of light. I know these speckles. I have seen them before. They grow brighter and brighter, and we can feel them tingling inside like flighty sonnets dazzling their spines. We feel filled with joy. Brando woofs, and I crouch and hug him. I bury my face in his fur.

I say, "Hold on, Brando, don't let go. Hold on tight. We're going home."

AUTHOR'S NOTE

I would like to offer my thanks to the following people, organizations, and sources:

Jane Ratcliffe, friend and mentor, godmother of *Glow*, who believed from the first word.

Patrick Gabridge; from the chrysalis of MIT we grew into artists. For his encouragement, guidance, and unique understanding.

Kim Gilbertson, for a wealth of love and support.

Darice Moyer, my childhood twin, for always listening to my stories.

The Community of Writers at Squaw Valley faculty, especially Michelle Latiolais, and my fellow alumni, for kinship and inspiration.

Readers **Michelle Adelman**, **Ed Porter**, **Aimee Whitenack**, **Tim Dyke**, **Gail Seneca**, and **Neila Wyman**, for their wisdom and insight.

Rose Gilbertson and the late **John Gilbertson**, for their recollections of farm life.

Julie Gold and **Laura Pearson**, for a room of my own.

Jennifer Sokoloski, for her enthusiasm and support.

Cinnamon Salvador, for her forensics expertise.

Jennifer Lund, for my country getaway, a restorative place to write.

"The Rev" of St. Helena Island, South Carolina, for showing me how to protect my soul.

The late **Robert Murray**, master storyteller, gifted educator, and former curator of the Foxfire Museum & Heritage Center, for his vast knowledge of Southern

Appalachian mountain traditions, as well as his patience, wit, charm, and big heart.

Mary Mance, for her trust and her memories of a Georgia childhood.

Andy Allen and **Caroline Crittenden** of the Bean Creek Alliance, inspirations both.

Rabun County Historical Society, for unlimited time with their formidable genealogy collection.

The Sautee Nacoochee Center of White County, Georgia, for its photographic retrospective, *Reflections from Bean Creek*, an unexpected trove along my travels.

Pilot **Duke Morasco** of the Rhinebeck Aerodrome. My research would not have been complete without soaring into the sky in a biplane. Special thanks for the safe landing.

Pilots **John Walsh**, **Bill King**, and the late **Charles Gablehouse**, for invaluable details and anecdotes.

Historian Rebecca S. Kraus of the U.S. Census Bureau, for her resolve and time.

The tomes *Voices from Slavery*, edited by **Norman R. Yetman**; *History, Myths, and Sacred Formulas of the Cherokees* by **James Mooney**; *Foxfire 11*, edited by **Kaye Carver Collins** and **Lacy Hunter**; *Foxfire 12*, edited by **Kaye Carver Collins** and **Angie Cheek**; *Sketches of Rabun County History 1819-1948* by **Andrew Jackson Ritchie**; as well as the audio series *Remembering Jim Crow, African Americans Tell About Life in the Segregated South*, produced by **Stephen Smith** of American RadioWorks® in collaboration with the **Behind the Veil Project**.

Liz Van Hoose, for her zest and editorial insights.

Lisa Bankoff, for making this book happen.

Mom, you endowed me with a passion for the written word, and **Daddy** the spoken. Without a doubt, I have inherited a double dose of curiosity. For these gifts, as well as for your love, encouragement, and succor, I am grateful.

And, everlasting, to my beloved **Joel Henry**, soul mate on this glorious adventure, and whose mind and heart nurtured *Glow* from the start.